About a boy...

Alex couldn't resist trying out her disguise. "Not so pretty now, am I?" she said with a grin.

"You've lost your mind!" Victoria had a death grip on the knob of the rickety, iron bedpost. She was trembling so hard the whole bed was shaking, its springs squeaking in protest. Alex wouldn't be surprised if the racket could be heard throughout the hotel.

She ignored her overwrought sister, knotting the straps of Adam's worn denim overalls. Her brother was a good half a foot taller than her, so if she used the buckles, the bib would drop down to her waist, revealing the curve of her breasts under the shirt. Once she'd tied the straps, it worked fine, the bib sitting high front and back, hiding any trace of her shape. She rolled up the cuffs and examined her boots. They were old and battered, but still clearly feminine. She kicked them off and put on Adam's big clomping boots instead. Her feet slid around when she walked, but they were far more convincing.

"We'll have to buy me some new boots tomorrow."

"You can't seriously be thinking about going out in public like that!"

"Of course not."

Victoria sagged with relief.

"You'll have to cut my hair first."

Victoria looked like she was going to throw something. Or faint. "What would Ma and Pa say?"

"Ma and Pa would say, 'Hurry up and get out of here before the Gradys catch up to you.'" Alex dug the scissors out of their bundle and snipped them in the air.

BOUND
for EDEN

———◆———

Tess LeSue

JOVE
New York

A JOVE BOOK
Published by Berkley
An imprint of Penguin Random House LLC
375 Hudson Street, New York, New York 10014

Copyright © 2018 by Tess LeSue
Excerpt from *Bound for Sin* copyright © 2018 by Tess LeSue
Penguin Random House supports copyright. Copyright fuels creativity, encourages
diverse voices, promotes free speech, and creates a vibrant culture. Thank you for buying
an authorized edition of this book and for complying with copyright laws by not
reproducing, scanning, or distributing any part of it in any form without permission.
You are supporting writers and allowing Penguin Random House to continue to
publish books for every reader.

A JOVE BOOK and BERKLEY are registered trademarks and the B colophon
is a trademark of Penguin Random House LLC.

ISBN: 9780451492579

PUBLISHING HISTORY
HarperCollins Australia MIRA edition / June 2016
Berkley Jove mass-market edition / May 2018

Printed in the United States of America
1   3   5   7   9   10   8   6   4   2

Cover design by Alana Colucci
Cowboy © Claudio Marinesco/Ninestock

For Jonny.

Still.

ACKNOWLEDGMENTS

Thank you to all the people who travel along with me. Big love to my parents, Barry and Su, and my brother Gerald; to Dean and Dot, Nick, Anna and Sam and their lovely girls; to Chelsea, Dan and Clare; and to Lucy the cat.

Thank you to my magnificent children Kirby and Isla for being patient with me when I'm lost in other worlds.

And to Jonny for being a solid five (idiot).

To Lynn: because beaches are weird. And to the exceptional women of SARA and the Romance Writers of Australia, with especial love to Victoria Purman, Trish Morey and Bronwyn Stuart.

Thanks also to Writers SA and to Flinders University for their support.

Enormous shout out to Kristine Swartz, for loving the books and letting them fly. And to Clare Forster, for believing in me for many long years. Many thanks too to Jo Mackay, Annabel Blay, Jessica Dettman and Stephanie Smith for working with me on the previous draft of this book.

Last of all: thank you! Readers are the best people on earth.

❧ 1 ❧

Grady's Point, Mississippi, 1843

ALEXANDRA BARRATT WASN'T a violent woman. Most times she couldn't even crush a house spider. But Silas Grady was no spider. Silas Grady was a blackhearted, lily-livered, weak-kneed swamp rat. If anything, death was too good for him.

She couldn't believe the nerve of him, knocking on her door like nothing had happened. He was swaying on his feet and there was still dried blood stuck to his neck.

"It's your only hope," he said thickly. "Marry me, Alex."

If Sheriff Deveraux hadn't been standing right there she might have forgotten she wasn't a violent woman and reached for the ax. But Sheriff Deveraux *was* standing right there.

"Marry me, Alex. I can keep you safe."

"Safe!" White fury licked at her. He was mighty lucky that ax was out of arm's reach. "And who will keep me safe from *you*?"

"Alex—"

"It's *Miss Barratt* to you, and how *dare* you come here after what you did today?"

"What I did . . .?" He swayed, confused.

Alex said a silent prayer. With any luck she could carry this off and get out of here before Gideon showed up. Silas was a lecherous, scheming idiot, but his brother was something much, much worse. "You arrest him," Alex demanded, turning to the sheriff.

The fat old man looked startled. He made a gruff *har-rumphing* noise and hiked his pants up. "Now, Miss Barratt, you know I can't do that."

"I know no such thing. Every week since Ma and Pa died I've come to you with a complaint about this man." She pointed a fierce finger at Silas's face. "He and his brothers have terrorized us. They've tried to starve us out. And you've done nothing!"

The sheriff grew red-faced, but didn't manage more than a mutter. It was all Alex expected from him, bloated excuse for a lawman that he was. "If you won't do anything I'll send for a federal marshal."

"Now, really, Miss Barratt, this isn't the frontier."

"It might as well be, for all the law there is around here." She lifted her nose in the air and tried to look imperious, which wasn't easy considering her rising panic. She had to get out of here before Gideon came. He'd probably made it home by now and found the mess she'd left . . . Oh glory, the thought was almost her undoing. Gideon was a maniac. Who knew what he'd do to her if he caught her?

"If you aren't going to arrest him, I don't see what choice you leave me." She kept brazening her way through it. Thank the Lord Silas was still concussed from that blow to the head. If he had half a brain he'd be demanding that the sheriff arrest *her*. He had fair cause: over the course of the afternoon she'd knocked him out cold, stolen his brother's property and assaulted his evil witch of a mother.

And it was entirely his own fault, she thought, fixing him with a black glare. He flinched and fingered the wound on the back of his head.

"I've told you at least twenty times in no uncertain terms that I won't marry you," she snapped at him. "But you won't take no for an answer, will you? Well, I didn't say yes when you starved us, and I won't say yes now. So get off my property! It *is* still my property, you know." She turned her black glare on the sheriff, who at least had the good grace to look shamefaced. "If you won't arrest him, you could at the very least escort him off my land! Trespassing *is* still illegal, isn't it?"

"Come on, Grady," Sheriff Deveraux mumbled. "You'd best try your luck another day." He took Silas by the elbow.

"I'm your last hope," Silas said miserably. "He won't hurt you if you're my wife."

"Get out!" The edge of hysteria in her voice was quite

real. She slammed the door behind them and yanked up the trapdoor to the root cellar, where her foster siblings were hiding. "Up!" she ordered. "Quick!"

"Give the gold back," her foster sister moaned as she struggled up the ladder. "Now, while the sheriff is still here."

"Are you mad?" Alex raced through the small house, throwing what precious little they still had into a sheet and tying it into a bundle. She tossed it to her foster brother, who was sitting on the lip of the cellar, looking despondent. "Don't worry, Adam," she soothed, running her fingers through his tousled hair.

"*You're* the mad one!" Victoria snapped. "Gideon will kill you if you don't give that gold back."

"He'll kill me anyway," Alex said grimly.

They heard a shot and Victoria screamed. Alex ran for the front window.

It was too late. Gideon was here. Poor, fat Sheriff Deveraux lay on the squashed dogwood blossoms, slain by Gideon's shotgun. As Alex watched, Gideon took a swing at Silas with the still-smoking gun. Silas managed to duck, but slipped on the fleshy blossoms and fell on his behind. Gideon kicked him.

"This is your fault, Spineless," he snarled. "If you hadn't kept sniffing after that bitch, none of this would have happened." The look on his narrow, ferrety face made the hair rise on the back of Alex's neck. It wasn't the anger that was frightening, it was the glint of barely suppressed glee. Gideon wasn't just going to hurt her, he was going to *enjoy* hurting her.

He looked up and saw her standing in the window. "Evenin', Miss Barratt," he called. Like they were meeting down at the store, or at one of Dyson's dances. She'd be damned before she'd show him fear. Alex yanked the blind down. It was a relief not to look at him, but a little scrap of cloth wasn't going to protect her from him. She bolted the door.

"Well, that ain't a neighborly way to behave," he called. God help them, the bastard was enjoying himself already. "Ain't ya going to ask us in for tea?" He laughed and Victoria started to cry.

"What are we going to do?" Vicky whined. "We don't even have a gun."

No. And the ax was still buried in the block out on the porch. Alex grabbed a couple of kitchen knives. They looked puny in her hands. "Here." She gave one to each of her siblings. "We'll go out the bedroom window. Go!" She grabbed a fire iron for herself.

Victoria looked down at the knife in horror. "What do you expect me to do with this?"

"Be careful," Adam said. "Ma said to be careful with knives. They cut."

Alex closed her eyes. What was she thinking? What good would a knife do Adam? He couldn't hurt anyone. *You were touched by God,* Ma used to tell him when the town children had laughed at him and called him names. The Sparrows had taken him in when no one else would have him. *You're one of His special children.* He was eighteen now, the same age as Vicky, but he was still a child. He would always be a child, and she had no right asking him to wield a knife.

"Don't touch knives," he said firmly as he looked down at the blade in his hand. "Don't touch the stove, it burns; don't touch the fire, it burns."

There was a knock at the door. "Last chance to be neighborly, Miss Barratt!"

"Go to hell!"

"Alex!" Alex heard the raw terror in her sister's voice at the exact moment she smelled the smoke. Victoria had opened the bedroom door to reveal a slow rolling cloud of smoke and the lick of orange flames. The bastard had set fire to the house!

"Oh, little pigs!" Gideon called, his voice bright with laughter. "Open up or I'll huff and I'll puff and I'll blow your house in!"

"We're going to die!" The knife fell from Victoria's fingers and clattered to the floor.

"No, we're not." Alex shoved Victoria and Adam toward the ladder to the loft where Adam slept. "Climb," she snapped. The smoke was rising and they coughed as they scurried upward. As soon as they reached the narrow loft, Alex threw open the window. There was a big old black cherry tree growing close to the house.

"You can't expect us to climb down that!" Victoria gasped.

"Why not? We did it all the time when we were children. Out you go, Adam. Be careful. When you get to the bottom, run for cover in the woods. If we get separated, we'll meet at the old fishing spot." She turned back to Victoria as Adam disappeared down the tree. "Did you hear me?"

"The old fishing spot, I heard." Victoria coughed. "If I die climbing down that tree, I'll never forgive you."

"Fair enough."

"Alex?"

"What?"

"What if Bert and Travis are out there too? They might have circled the house."

It *had* occurred to Alex that there were still two Grady brothers unaccounted for. But what choice did they have? They could hardly stay here and burn, could they? And walking straight into Gideon's arms wasn't an option. "I saw them heading into town earlier. They'll be out drinking all night," she reassured Victoria, although she wasn't sure it was true. Gideon might have fetched them home after all the kerfuffle.

She heard the crackle of wood and winced. "Hurry, before the whole house goes up." The two of them scrambled into the tree. Alex heard Victoria's shallow breathing. "Don't look down," she counseled. By the time they reached the bottom the house was an orange blaze.

"Oh, little pigs!" Gideon was coming around the house, his mad voice high and clear, even over the crackling of the fire.

Alex grabbed Victoria and they went belting toward the woods. And ran smack bang into Silas. Victoria screamed.

"Shut up," he growled, covering her mouth with his hand.

"You let her go!" Alex shrieked, clawing at him.

"Shut up the both of you, or he'll find us." Silas's eyes widened suddenly and he went very still.

"Adam!"

Her brother still had his knife, the tip of which was pricking Silas in the kidney. "Knives are sharp," he said, "knives cut."

"Spineless?" Gideon's voice was coming closer. "Have you caught a little pig?"

"Let her go," Alex hissed at Silas.

"Let me help you," he begged.

"You?" she scoffed. "I'd sooner trust an alligator than a Grady." Alex took the knife off Adam.

Silas regarded it with disdain. "That won't be any match for his shotgun."

"Run, Victoria. Take Adam and run."

"Where?" Victoria was wild-eyed with panic. "And what about you?"

"If we leave him, he'll only come after us. Get away. I'll meet you at that place I mentioned." She shooed them with her hand. "Go!"

She couldn't risk looking away from Silas. She was afraid he'd make a lunge for her. She could hear the crunch of bracken under her siblings' feet as they ran, and then they were gone and she was alone with Silas Grady.

"What are you going to do now?" He sounded smug. He had her. She couldn't run; he would throw her to the ground the minute she turned her back.

"I'll tell you where the gold is if you promise to let me go."

He shrugged. "Gideon will make you tell us where the gold is anyway."

"Spineless!"

She jumped. Gideon was so close.

"I can protect you, Alex," Silas whispered. "Your brother and sister are free. They can stay free. I can keep you safe."

Like hell. Alex's fingers tightened around both the knife and the fire iron. She would rather die than give herself to Silas Grady. But she couldn't die, she thought desperately. Victoria and Adam would never survive without her. They needed her.

"You promise you can keep me safe from Gideon?" She crept closer to him, playing for time. The longer she kept him occupied, the better the chance of Victoria and Adam getting away safe. The hilt of the knife was slippery in her sweaty palm. Did she have it in her to use it?

"I'd do anything for you," he said. It was hard to see his face in the falling darkness, and the glow from her burning home backlit him, rimming him with orange light. It was a mercy not to see his expression. She didn't want to see his stupid look of adoration, or the uncompromising lust in his eyes. She shuddered.

"Anything?" She crept closer, until they were almost touching. One thrust would send the knife sinking into his belly. Her fingers tightened around the hilt.

She broke out in a cold sweat and the knife trembled in her hand. She couldn't do it. She just didn't have it in her to murder a man. She pictured Vicky and Adam waiting for her at the fishing hole, huddling together in the darkness as the bullfrogs sang and the mosquitoes whined. If she didn't kill him now, she would have to sacrifice herself. She clenched her teeth. One thrust and it would be over . . .

No. She couldn't. The knife fell from her fingers and she tasted ash. "You win," she said softly.

"Oh, Alex." Silas's foul mouth crushed down on hers and his disgusting tongue jabbed at her lips. The minute she felt that thick, hot slug of a tongue she came to her senses. Revolted, she spun around and struck out. The fire iron whistled through the air and came down hard on the back of his head. Silas made a grunting sound and then slumped to the ground.

She heard Gideon closing in, still mocking her with a sound like a squealing pig. Panicked, she ran. Behind her, the black cherry tree had caught and blazed like a roman candle, and there was an almighty crunching noise as the house collapsed in on itself. Sparks flew skyward into the night. There went home.

Alex ran like the devil himself was after her. She had to find Adam and Victoria and get out of Grady's Point before Gideon caught up to them. She heard a gunshot echoing through the firelit woods. Never mind getting out of Grady's Point, they had to get out of the state, maybe even the South. She wouldn't rest safe until she'd put a thousand miles between herself and Gideon Grady.

❧ 2 ❧

Independence, Missouri

LUKE SLATER WAS mighty glad to see the dusty streets of Independence. It was a long trip down southeast, and he was ready for a drink and a bath and the soft warmth of a woman. He reckoned this would be his last time out this way. Once he'd picked up the prize stallion he'd come for, he could afford to stay put at home in Utopia. Then he could give Amelia Harding his full attention. It was high time she gave up her coy games and accepted his offer. The house was done now, after he'd worked all winter finishing the interior, and it was the finest house in the whole territory. He pictured her delight when he carried her over the threshold and she finally saw what he'd built for her. He'd even bought genuine lace curtains for the front room, just like the ones her mother had in their parlor. He'd worked his fingers to the bone over the last few years to pay for the best furniture money could buy. And he had every intention of making as much money as he could on this last run so he could hang up his traveling boots for good.

At the moment, saddlesore and weary, he couldn't imagine he'd miss the traveling in the slightest.

He sighed happily as his mare, Isis, threaded her way through the hardpacked-dirt streets. Luke liked the rawness of Independence: the bustle and noise and fuss, the new brick buildings and the mercantile stores bursting at the seams with everything a wagoner could ever need. He passed the courthouse and headed straight for Dolly's.

The cathouse was a blaze of light in the dusk. He could hear Dan Bannon banging away at the piano and Dolly herself singing lustily, if a little off-key. He hitched Isis and un-buckled his saddle and bags and hefted them over his shoulder. "Luke!" Dolly hollered the minute she saw him. She jiggled across the saloon and threw herself at him. He struggled to keep hold of his saddle.

"You said you wouldn't be back this way for another year," she said with a mock-scowl, fluttering her spidery lashes at him.

"I didn't think I would be," he replied, gently trying to extricate himself, "but I couldn't resist bidding on Jackson's stallion."

"How did you hear about that, way out there in the wilderness?"

"Jackson sent word."

"I wondered why he was taking so long to sell," Dolly said coyly, leading him to the bar, and gesturing at the barman to pour a whiskey. "Everyone knows he could have sold that stallion a dozen times over by now."

"If you don't mind, Doll, a bath would be mighty welcome. Have you got a room free?"

"Ah, pet, if I'd known you were coming I would have reserved the best. You know you're always welcome to stay. I'd let you bunk in with me," she said with a wink, "but even I'm booked tonight. There are two wagon trains leaving tomorrow, so there's a rush on. Why don't you sit and wet your whistle and I'll send my boy around the hotels and boarding houses to find you a room, eh?"

Luke let Dolly ease him into a chair and press a glass into his hand.

"I know there's a game on tonight, if you're interested? I'd be happy to put in a word and get you a seat at the table, then the minute I have a girl free I can let you know. Unless you'd like a tumble now?" She leaned forward suggestively, revealing the full swell of her impressive bosom. He could see where her powder had collected in the lines of her cleavage.

"As tempting an offer as that is," Luke said, taking her hand and pressing a kiss on it, "you know I like to bathe first. I'd hate to have you smelling of sweat and horse afterward."

Dolly snorted. "Sweat and horse is sweet compared to some we get around here." Her gaze flickered to a table in the corner, where two men sat hunched over a near-empty bottle of whiskey. They looked like mean drunks.

"There are two more of 'em, upstairs with Seline," Dolly told him in a low voice.

"You might want to check she's all right," Luke suggested dryly.

"I got the Mexican outside her door. He hears anything he'll be in there like a shot."

Luke raised his glass in salute and drained the fiery spirit.

Dolly had to leave him for a client, so he sat alone and drank until her boy came back with news of a room.

"There's only the common bunkhouse downstairs at Ralph Taylor's," the boy huffed, holding out his hands to help Luke with his saddlebags. Luke handed them over and the kid sank under the weight.

"A bed's a bed," Luke sighed, although he'd hoped for something more comfortable than Ralph's flea-ridden bunks.

"Mr. Taylor said if he'd a known you was coming he would have saved one of his suites for you."

"Suites? That what he calls them poky rooms upstairs?"

"Yes, sir. And he's doubled the price since last year."

Luke rolled his eyes.

"There's so many wagoners, he says, and so few beds. At a premium, Mr. Taylor says, sir." The boy paused. "What's premium mean?"

"It means people want it," Luke said, stopping by Isis. "You reckon Dolly would stable her for me tonight?"

"I reckon Dolly would do 'bout anything for you, Mr. Slater." The kid grinned. "She says if she weren't doing so well whoring she'd marry you in a second."

"Is that right?" Luke laughed. "Shame for me the whoring is so good, then."

The boy wrinkled his nose. "You can do better than her, Mr. Slater, she's mighty old."

Luke gave the boy a gentle kick in the seat of the pants. "Enough prattle, there's a bath waiting for me."

❧ 3 ❧

A LEX COULDN'T RESIST trying out her disguise. "Not so pretty now, am I?" she said with a grin.

"You've lost your mind!" Victoria had a death grip on the knob of the rickety iron bedpost. She was trembling so hard the whole bed was shaking, its springs squeaking in protest. Alex wouldn't be surprised if the racket could be heard throughout the hotel.

She ignored her overwrought sister, knotting the straps of Adam's worn denim overalls. Her brother was a good half a foot taller than her, so if she used the buckles the bib would drop down to her waist, revealing the curve of her breasts under the shirt. Once she'd tied the straps it worked fine, the bib sitting high front and back, hiding any trace of her shape. She rolled up the cuffs and examined her boots. They were old and battered, but still clearly feminine. She kicked them off and put on Adam's big clomping boots instead. Her feet slid around when she walked, but they were far more convincing.

"We'll have to buy me some new boots tomorrow."

"You can't seriously be thinking about going out in public like that!"

"Of course not."

Victoria sagged with relief.

"You'll have to cut my hair first."

Victoria looked like she was going to throw something. Or faint. "What would Ma and Pa say?"

"Ma and Pa would say, 'Hurry up and get out of here before the Gradys catch up to you.'" Alex dug the scissors out of their bundle and snipped them in the air.

"It's not right," Victoria said desperately, tears welling.

She'd been crying pretty much continuously since they'd left home.

"No, it's not," Alex agreed, pressing the scissors into Victoria's hand, "but you've seen the posters. That likeness is too close for comfort."

They'd first seen the poster in St. Louis. The Gradys were offering an impressive bounty for one Alexandra Sparrow. "But your name isn't Sparrow," Adam had said, bewildered, as Alex hurried them to the steamboat that would take them up the Missouri River. Upriver lay Independence, the gateway to the west, the first step on the Oregon Trail. At the end of the Oregon Trail was Stephen Sparrow, their foster brother, the only family they had left in the world. Stephen was Ma and Pa Sparrow's natural son, their only natural child. Alex, Victoria and Adam were foundlings. Alex had been orphaned when she was eleven, Victoria's mother had died when she was eight and her father had lit out, leaving her defenseless and alone, and Adam's family had abandoned him when he was near dead from the fever. The Sparrows had taken each and every one of them in, even though food was scarce and it put a burden on their own small family. Eventually they had adopted Victoria and Adam, but Alex hadn't wanted to be adopted. She remembered her own parents too well and with too much love to forsake their name.

Gideon knew she wouldn't be using the name Barratt. He assumed she'd use Sparrow but she wasn't stupid enough to use her foster family's name either, she thought contemptuously. It was a stab in the dark on his part, but the name hardly mattered when there was that likeness of her, and she'd had no doubt the posters would follow her into Missouri. Gideon was no fool. He would have guessed where they were headed. She'd barricaded them in their tiny cabin for the short journey and had their meals delivered to them, and they hadn't seen daylight again until they disembarked in Independence.

"Cut it, Vicky," she ordered softly, turning her back. She closed her eyes as the blades rasped through the thick, golden waves of her hair. It would grow back. And when it was gone she would no longer look like the woman on the posters.

Alex kept her hands clenched as her beautiful hair piled up around her feet. Finally, the last clump fell and Victoria put down the scissors. Alex examined the result in the fly-specked mirror. She felt a pang at the sight of her naked neck. Victoria had left a thick mop on top, which flopped over her eyes in messy curls, hiding a lot of her face. Her skin was still dirty from the dusty streets. At a glance she'd pass for a boy, wouldn't she? She took a deep breath. "I suppose we'd best test it."

"Test it?" Victoria's voice cracked. "You don't mean to go out like that?"

"That *was* the point of the exercise," Alex said dryly. "Don't fret, I won't leave the hotel. I'll just go down and ask where we go to buy a wagon."

"At least take Adam with you."

"No," Alex said firmly, stopping Victoria from waking Adam, who was snoring happily on the bunk in the corner of their "suite." "You can wake him if I'm not back in half an hour."

Alex closed the door on Victoria's hand-wringing and pulled Adam's saggy brown hat down over her freshly chopped hair. Struggling to walk in Adam's boots, she clomped down the stairs. She tripped over her feet on the final step and went flying into a youth who was standing by the front desk.

"About time," the boy snapped, shoving her back onto her feet. "Where's Mr. Taylor? Don't worry, Mr. Slater," he called across the entry hall, "this must be his new boy. Every week he's got a new one. No one wants to stay in this filth for long."

"Tell him to get me a bath ready."

"Yes, sir. You heard him." The boy gave Alex a shove toward the corridor. "Go heat some water."

Alex cleared her throat and tried to lower her voice. "I ain't Mr. Taylor's boy." Her voice came out husky and uncertain and, to Alex's ear at least, not at all boyish.

"You ain't?" The boy looked suspicious.

Alex shook her head. "I'm a guest." This time she thought she sounded more convincing.

The boy looked Alex up and down in disbelief, taking in the rumpled clothes and dirty face. Alex couldn't help tugging nervously at the overalls.

The man silhouetted by the open door sighed and reached into his pocket. "I don't care whose boy you are. I'm tired and I want a bath." He took a coin from his pocket and flipped it at Alex. She fumbled to catch it and it fell to the floor, where it circled lazily before dropping with a clatter by the scuffed toe of her brown boot.

She gaped down at Seated Liberty, glinting in the lamplight. A whole dollar? For drawing him a bath? The man must be a fool. Either that, or a very rich man indeed. Despite the bag of gold hidden in her luggage, Alex couldn't resist picking up the coin. She was done with being penniless. She tucked the coin into her pocket.

"Where's the washroom?" she asked.

The boy gave her a disgusted look and pointed. Alex headed off without looking back to see if either of them followed her.

"I'll go back and take care of your horse, Mr. Slater," she heard the boy say.

The washroom was outside, across the dirt courtyard. There was a stove burning in a corner of the room, but otherwise it was dark. Alex hurried to light the lamps and then she busied herself stoking the fire. There was a barrel of almond shells and pinecones and a stack of kindling, so it didn't take her long to have the stove glowing red.

As she worked the man came in and dropped his saddle and baggage on the dirt floor. He groaned as he sat down on the rough-hewn wooden bench. When she heard him take his boots off her stomach clenched. Good Lord, he wasn't going to undress *now*, was he? Her eyes widened in panic. She'd thought to fill the tub and leave before he disrobed.

"I'll just get the water," she mumbled, leaving without looking at him. She didn't want him to see her flaming face. She busied herself pumping water and setting it on the stove and never once looked his way.

"You're a wagoner?" he asked her as she watched the stove anxiously, waiting for signs of a bubble.

"A what?" She couldn't help it: she looked at him. And gaped.

There in front of her, half-naked, was the most incredible man she'd ever seen. She'd thought Silas Grady was big. But this man . . . he seemed immense in the small washroom. His shoulders stretched beyond the width of the doorframe and she couldn't look away from the expanse of his chest. Which wasn't surprising, she thought dumbly, as he wasn't wearing a shirt and she'd never seen so much naked flesh in her life.

His skin shone like oiled rosewood, a burnished warm brown, stretched taut over hard lengths of muscle. A faint black line of hair ran between his nipples and down his flat, firm stomach.

He cleared his throat and she was suddenly aware that she was staring. She tore her gaze from his body and made herself look at his face.

And, oh glory, that didn't help at all.

The man was simply perfect. His forehead was broad, his jaw square, his nose straight, and he had the most beautiful lips she'd ever seen. The blue-black shadow of stubble only served to emphasize the masculine strength of his beauty. He looked the way Lucifer must have looked, she thought witlessly: a dark angel. His hair was the rich, deep shade of damp Mississippi earth, and his eyes were black and liquid—not still, but turbulent, like a flooding river. She felt as though she might drown in them.

"I know you're not mute," he said, his voice low and rough.

Alex swallowed hard and tried to find her tongue, although she still couldn't look away from those intense black eyes.

"Sorry, what was your question?" Her voice came out at its natural pitch and she saw his eyebrows rise. Startled from her stupor she blushed and tore her gaze away from him, using all her willpower to keep her eyes trained on the tips of her boots.

"I asked whether you were a wagoner."

"A wagoner?" This time her voice cracked.

He sighed impatiently. "Are you heading west? With a wagon train?"

"Oh! Yes, sir . . . I mean, that is, we aim to . . ."

"The water's boiling," he said, nodding toward the vigorously bubbling pot and cutting off her babble.

Relieved, she took it from the stove and filled the tin tub. She was only too aware of his black gaze and almost tripped over her own feet in the process. Catching herself against the doorframe, she blushed furiously. In order to give herself a chance to regain her composure, she hurried out to the pump for a bucket of cold water to balance the temperature in the tub.

She was alarmed to find him unbuckling his belt when she returned. She dumped the last bucket of water in the tub as quickly as she could, sending splashes onto the dirt, and backed toward the door.

"Where do you think you're going?" he asked. "I didn't pay you a dollar so I could clean up after myself."

"You want me to wait?" Alex squeaked.

"I want you to heat some water for me to wash my hair, and strop my razor for me so I can shave. Then you can rustle me up a towel and clean up the bath when I'm done."

Alex was sorely tempted to throw the dollar back at him and run for her room. But his breeches fell to the floor and she couldn't breathe, let alone move. She'd had no idea . . .

"That water won't heat itself," he drawled as he lowered himself into the steaming tub.

Her hands trembling, Alex fetched more water. The cool night air hit her like a slap. She should keep walking, she thought numbly. Just leave the bucket by the pump and walk back upstairs to Adam and Victoria, bury herself under the covers and try to block out the image of him standing there naked in the washroom. All glowing brown skin and hard muscle.

Her limbs seemed to have grown loose and a strange pulsating heat was uncurling in her belly.

She could hear little splashes of water as he shifted in the tub. Her heart felt like it was fluttering up her chest and into her throat. She imagined what it would be like to touch him . . . would he feel as warm and velvety as he looked? Would he feel hard?

"Hurry up," he called from the steaming heat of the bath-house, "I need my back soaped."

Oh glory.

BY THE TIME she returned to the sultry confines of the small room, Alex's knees were practically knocking together. When she set the water on the stove her trembling sent drop-lets of water cascading to the burning iron hotplate, where they sizzled and spat.

"I must have brought half the prairie with me," the man behind her sighed. "Get that brush and scrub my back, would you?"

How she managed to cross the room and lift the brush from the shelf, Alex didn't know. She was painfully aware of her own body—she tried to walk more like a man, but only succeeded in feeling even more self-conscious.

She knelt behind him, safely out of his line of vision, and contemplated the wall of shining muscle before her. Tenta-tively she rubbed the brush over his shoulders.

"That's not going to shift anything," he told her, with no small measure of exasperation. "Put your back into it and use the soap."

Obediently, Alex scrubbed harder and the water darkened to a muddy brown. She could see the great fists of muscle in his back begin to loosen under her strokes.

"What's your name?"

Alex didn't have the wit to give her carefully chosen pseudonym. Distracted by that expanse of glowing wet skin, she slipped and almost told him her real name. "Al—Alexander."

"Al Alexander?"

"Uh . . . my first name's William," she invented swiftly, using her foster father's name, "William Alexander. But everyone calls me Al . . . or Alex."

"Alex." The sound of her name issuing from those sen-sual lips, in that deep voice, made her quiver.

She was surprised when he twisted around and offered her his hand. She stared at it dumbly for a minute before she real-ized that he meant for her to shake it. She clasped it and almost gasped at the white-hot bolt of sensation that ran up her arm. When he let go, her hand smarted, as though it had been burned.

"So you and your folks are taking the Oregon Trail?" he asked as he scrubbed his face.

She nodded and then blushed when she realized he couldn't see her. "Yes, sir."

"It's Luke."

"Luke." The name came from her breathlessly, like a sigh.

"I'm captaining a party headed for the Willamette Valley," he told her conversationally. "You mind getting me that razor now?"

Alex did mind. She was just beginning to relax enough to enjoy rubbing the brush in lazy circles over that strong back. But, remembering the coin in her pocket, she set the brush aside and went to his saddlebags.

"It's in the one on the left."

The leather was supple with age and wear. Alex couldn't believe everything he managed to fit inside the one saddlebag. She eventually found the razor inside a soft leather case. There was a strop hanging by the door, and she made fast work of sharpening the blade.

"You joined a party yet?"

Alex shook her head. "We only got into town today."

"Where are you from?"

That was one question Alex had no intention of answering. "You sure are nosey," she observed tartly, handing him the razor.

He laughed and, if it was even possible, the flash of his white teeth and the dent of a dimple in his cheek made him seem even more beautiful. She'd had no idea men like this existed. There certainly hadn't been any like him back home in Mississippi.

For a moment she wondered how it would have been if he'd met her as Alexandra, in her best pink-flower patterned Sunday dress, instead of as this scruffy boy. Would he have found her pretty? Would he have smiled at her, showing that heavenly dimple? The thought made her feel fluttery and light-headed.

What on earth was wrong with her? She'd never reacted like this to a man before.

"And you sure are close-mouthed," he observed. "Hold the mirror for me so I can shave, there's a boy." Alex took the small square of mirror from his shaving kit and held it before him. "Kneel down," he ordered, and Alex obeyed, kneeling beside him.

She was acutely aware of his proximity, of his wet flesh, and of what lay beneath the shivering surface of the murky bathwater.

"Have you outfitted yourselves with a wagon yet?" he asked as the razor rasped over his rough stubble.

"No, sir . . . I mean, Luke."

"I know an honest wagon maker who won't overcharge you."

"Maker?" Alex echoed, unable to disguise her dismay. She'd assumed they'd be able to buy one ready-made. "How long will it take to make one?"

Luke eyed her, the wicked blade pausing mid-stroke. "Why? I thought you weren't signed up with a party yet."

"I just . . . We thought . . . We're in a bit of a hurry," she admitted.

"You do realize it's a six-month trip?" he drawled, and once again the razor slid in a long, rasping arc over his lean cheek.

"I know," Alex said defensively, "we just want to leave as soon as we can."

"In a spot of trouble, are we?"

"No." But she knew he could tell by her face that they were.

"And when would you like to leave?"

She didn't care how beautiful he was, he was beginning to irritate her with his questions. "None of your business," she snapped.

One dense black eyebrow lifted and she thought she saw his lips twitch. "I'm only asking because we have room in our party. But you'd need a wagon."

Alex chewed her lip.

Luke finished shaving, without asking another question. In silence, she fetched the warm water and waited as he

soaped his thick, dark hair. When he closed his eyes and
tilted his head back she poured, watching the fall of water
shimmer pale gold in the lamplight as it rinsed the soap free
and left him clean and shining, like a newly carved marble
statue.

She spun on her heel when he began to rise from the tub,
and scrabbled for a towel. She thrust it at him and busied
herself dampening the stove.

"You know, you ought to have a bath too," he said speculatively, and she was conscious of his bulk blocking her exit.
"You're filthier than I was."

Alex felt a wave of horror splash over her like a bucket of
icy water. She shrank inside the baggy overalls and shook
her head vehemently.

"I can't see your skin for the muck," he continued.

Oh heavens, what had she got herself into?

❧ 4 ❧

FORTUNATELY FOR ALEX, they were interrupted by an outraged gasp.

There, in the doorway of the bathhouse, stood Victoria. Her brown eyes were huge as they took in the mostly naked man standing in front of her sister. Her cheeks flamed. "What is going on here?" she blustered, obviously half-scared to death, but trying for Alex's sake to be brave. "Adam!"

Alex could hear Adam shuffling across the courtyard and she shook her head frantically. Adam hadn't seen her dressed up like this yet, and she knew he'd give her away. "Go back to the room, Adam," she called quickly, glaring at Victoria. "We'll join you in a minute."

"Alex?" Adam's lazy voice drifted through the open door. "Vicky said you were gone."

"I'm not gone. Go back to the room now."

"I can see the moon."

"Really? You can tell me about it when I come up."

"Righto."

Alex heard him singing softly to himself as he went back inside. She darted a glance at Luke, and saw him watching them curiously, his towel loosely tied around his hips. Now that Victoria was here she felt ashamed of herself. Nice girls didn't do such things. Victoria would certainly never get herself in this position.

Alex cleared her throat guiltily. "Victoria, this is Mr. . . ." Alex paused, realizing that she didn't even know his last name.

"Slater."

"Mr. Slater. He's captain of a wagon train."

Victoria had turned to face the courtyard, her back to

Luke Slater's indecent state and her gaze firmly fixed on the water pump. Even from across the room Alex could see that she was as red as a beet. "I don't believe a reputable operator would do business in a bathhouse," she said primly.

"I paid your brother to help me with my bath," Luke said smoothly, thinking to placate her, but his words had the opposite effect.

Alex had rarely seen Victoria lose her temper, but she certainly lost it now. "You get upstairs this minute," she ordered shrilly, crossing the room and seizing Alex by the arm. "What are you thinking? Ma and Pa would be ashamed of you!"

Her words cut Alex to the bone. "I can explain—"

"And you will." Victoria almost dragged her sister from the steamy room, keeping well away from the indecent man in the towel.

Luke watched in bemusement as they disappeared into the darkness of the courtyard. He could hear the poor boy being chastised all the way across the dusty yard, through the corridor and into the depths of the hotel.

He looked back at the greasy bathwater and sighed. He'd have to clean it up himself, before he went back to Dolly's for a drink and a hand of cards.

"WOULD YOU LET go of me?" Alex complained, wrenching her arm away from Victoria as they climbed the stairs. "There's no need to get so upset."

"There's no need to . . .?" Victoria trailed off, too angry for words. "Forgive me if I'm mistaken, but wasn't that a naked man down there with you?"

"He thought I was a boy," Alex hissed, glancing around to make sure there was no one to overhear.

"Well, you're *not*," Victoria hissed back.

"He can introduce us to a wagon maker."

"I don't care if he can introduce us to President Tyler, you were out of your tiny mind getting yourself in that position." Victoria slammed the door behind them as they entered their room. "Get out of those clothes this minute. Your little plan has gone far enough."

Alex rolled her eyes and flopped down on the bed. A

cloud of dust puffed up from the saggy old mattress and she sneezed.

"Bless you," Adam said sleepily from where he lay on his bunk, staring out at the full moon. "I can see the man, Alex."

"What man?"

"Don't go changing the subject, I haven't said my piece yet." Victoria snatched the hat off Alex's head.

"The man in the moon."

"Yeah? What's he doing?"

Victoria sputtered and yanked at Alex's sleeve. Alex rolled out of her grasp.

"I think he's making cheese."

"Leave me be," Alex snapped when Victoria kept coming for her.

"I mean it, Alexandra Barratt, you get those clothes off this instant."

"We have to find a wagon and a group to join, you madwoman," Alex shrieked as Victoria pulled on the straps of her overalls. "You don't honestly think people are going to do business with two women?"

"We have Adam."

"The moon is made of cheese." Adam's dreamy voice stopped Victoria in her tracks. As Alex watched, the anger drained from her face and she slid to the bed, the battered hat dropping from her fingers.

"It's the only way, Vicky," Alex said carefully, bending to retrieve the hat. "The Gradys will be looking for a man and two women. We didn't use our names when we checked into the hotel, and I told that man down there that our name was Alexander. There's no reason they'll ever find us."

"What if they *see* us?"

"If they see you, just tell them you haven't seen me since the night of the fire. They'll think I ran off with the money."

"That doesn't explain why Adam and I are heading out west," Victoria said sourly.

"Sure it does. Our home is burned to the ground, you have very little money and you have a brother in Oregon. Where else would you go?"

"Oh, Alex, why is this happening to us?"

Alex's heart ached to see her sister's despair. If she had

those Gradys here, in front of her, she would kill them with her bare hands, just see if she wouldn't.

"Stop worrying and go to sleep," she soothed, even as she enjoyed her murderous fancies, "everything will seem better in the morning."

"You keep saying that," Victoria grumbled, "but it never does."

Alex heard the clang of tin in the courtyard and moved to the window. Below, in the silver moonlight, she could see Luke Slater emptying his bath. She couldn't believe he could lift it—filled with water it must weigh as much as he did.

Even fully dressed he looked magnificent.

"You're blocking the moon," Adam complained, and reluctantly she tore her gaze away and left the window.

He'd said there was room in his traveling party, she mused dreamily, indulging in fantasies of spending months at his side. Then she caught sight of her reflection in the mirror. Alex wasn't usually vain, but right then she wished with all her heart that she hadn't cut off her beautiful hair. She scowled at the scruffy boy in the mirror, and he scowled right back at her.

5

Luke was a reasonable man. He didn't pick fights. But neither did he back down from them.

"Who are you calling a cheat?" he asked calmly, holding the stranger's gaze.

The man and his brother had been losing steadily to Luke. The more they lost, the more they drank. The higher grew the neat stacks of bills and coins in front of Luke, the blacker their scowls became. Luke had guessed they'd be trouble almost from the moment he sat down. He kept trying to catch Dolly's eye, hoping one of her girls would be available and he'd have an excuse to fold the game, but she was rushed off her feet all night.

"No honest man wins eight games in a row."

"I believe Mr. O'Brien won the hand before last," Luke corrected, careful to keep his voice neutral.

Ned O'Brien, a bookish, buttoned-up easterner, shifted nervously in his seat.

"One hand," the man sneered, not sparing O'Brien a glance.

"Roll up your sleeves," his brother demanded, "so we can see what you've got stashed up there."

"Don't be a sore loser."

"Loser!"

Fortunately, Luke saw the punch coming and managed to dodge the man's meaty fist. The table went sprawling, sending cards and cash flying. The coins clattered across the bare floorboards and there was an instant rush as men grabbed for them. Luke swore. There went his winnings.

He heard a bellow and looked up to find both men charging at him like wild bulls. There was no way he could escape both of them, so he resigned himself to the pain, lowered his head, and charged them right back.

The collision rocked the room.

"What in all the seven hells is going on in here?" Dolly screamed from the staircase.

Luke didn't look up. One of the brothers was down and winded, but the other was still standing, his scowl blacker than ever.

"Cheat," the man hissed under his breath.

"Come closer and say it," Luke suggested.

"Cheat!" the man bellowed, rushing him again.

Luke landed a punch, but then strong arms seized him from behind, immobilizing him. He struggled, but the man's grip was as strong as iron. Don't tell me there's another brother, he thought wryly.

The man he'd punched laughed, rubbing his side, which still smarted from Luke's fist. "Thanks, Bert." He approached Luke slowly. "My brothers and I don't hold with cheats."

Behind him, the winded brother got to his feet. Luke figured he'd better act soon, or they'd be on top of him. Without warning, he threw his head back, smashing his captor full in the nose. He heard a grunt as he jerked free. Bert was bent double, clutching his broken nose, blood gushing over his hands. Luke planted his foot in the man's belly and shoved him to his knees. One well-aimed kick finished him off.

He spun on his heel and pounded the next one full in the face before the man had even registered that he was free of Bert. The man went down like a dead weight.

One left to go. This one was obviously having second thoughts though. He backed away slowly, holding both hands up, palms out.

Luke heard laughter and looked up. On the landing beside Dolly stood a runty-looking man, wearing nothing but a sheet. He was lean and ropy with muscle and his face was pointy and sharp. He reminded Luke of a weasel. As Luke watched, the weasel tucked the sheet around his waist and gave Luke a round of applause. "I ain't never seen a man take on my brothers and win," the weasel said. "Particularly Silas. He ain't just big and mean, he's crafty."

"Which one's Silas?" Luke asked dryly.

The weasel pointed to the body at Luke's feet.

"I'd like to know who's going to clean up the mess," Dolly sniped, pulling her wrapper tighter over her loose breasts.

"Not me, I want what I paid for," the weasel said, giving Luke a calculating look before shoving Dolly back toward the bedroom. Luke was glad to see the Mexican climb the stairs and position himself firmly outside Dolly's door, just in case she called for him. Luke didn't like the look of that weasel at all.

"I think I managed to get most of the bills," a voice said tentatively at Luke's elbow. He turned to see Ned O'Brien holding out a large portion of Luke's winnings.

"Thanks," Luke said, surprised. He honestly hadn't expected to recover any of it. He took the handful and peeled off a few bills for Mr. O'Brien.

"Oh no," the man demurred.

"Please. It's not often I get to meet an honest man." Luke pressed the money on him. "Let me buy you a drink too."

"What about them?" O'Brien asked nervously, glancing at the brothers. Travis was slapping Silas gingerly on the cheek, trying to rouse him, and Bert had his hands full trying to staunch his bleeding nose.

"I don't reckon they'll give us any more trouble tonight."

Luke was right. Eventually, once the blood had slowed to a trickle, Bert helped Travis carry Silas out of the cathouse. Neither of them so much as looked Luke's way.

"You handle yourself very well," Ned said, sipping his whiskey cautiously.

"I have brothers of my own. I've had practice."

"I do wonder how I'll manage to survive out west," the easterner sighed, examining his own slender hands.

Luke laughed. "Oh, it's not as rough as all that. Not if you're going to Oregon. We're mostly a farming people."

"You're a farmer?" Ned said dubiously.

"Horse breeder. Although if you talk to my brother Tom, he'll tell you we run cattle. And if you ask my brother Matthew, he'll say we're in the lumber business."

Ned looked confused.

"We can't rightly agree on what we should do with the land. We tried to vote on it, but what we got was one vote for horses, one vote for cattle and one vote for lumber."

"Sounds like you might have an empire on your hands."

"Either that or a damned failure." Luke drained his whiskey. "And what do you do, Mr. O'Brien?"

Ned cleared his throat nervously. "It's Dr. O'Brien actually."

"A doctor? And you're heading for Oregon? You know, we're in need of a doctor in Utopia. It's a great little place in the Willamette, green as Eden itself."

"I'm not sure if you're in need of a doctor like me."

"Why, what's wrong with you?"

"Oh, nothing's *wrong* with me. It's just that I'm not that kind of doctor."

"What kind are you? Like a dentist? We need a dentist too."

O'Brien laughed awkwardly. "I'm afraid I'm not as useful as a dentist. I'm a doctor of Philosophy."

"You're a philosopher?"

"English literature. I did my thesis on Milton."

"Milton?"

"*Paradise Lost.* 'Who would not, finding way, break loose from Hell . . . And boldly venture to whatever place Farthest from pain . . . ?'" he quoted, smiling wanly.

Luke grinned at him. "You're talking to an uneducated man, Doc."

Ned smiled back. "And you are talking to a man 'deep-versed in books and shallow in himself.'"

Luke gave him a puzzled look and watched as he swallowed the glassful in one gulp.

"So what does a doctor of Milton do?"

"I was teaching at the university back home."

"We need a teacher too."

"Is there anything you don't need?"

"A horse breeder, a cattle rancher and a logger."

Ned laughed.

"Whose party have you joined?" Luke refilled the doc's glass.

"None yet, although I was talking to a Mr. Hennick today."

"Abel? Ah, don't go joining up with him, his compass is off. Last year he ended up in California. I know another party you can join. It's a little more expensive but well worth the price."

"Who's the captain? Would I know of him?"

"Reckon so." Luke gave him a wink. "Charming man, and a damn fine horse breeder."

Ned looked startled. "You?"

"Ned O'Brien?" A sultry voice interrupted them and they turned to see a buxom brunette with brightly rouged lips. Her breasts spilled over the top of her corset.

Ned flushed scarlet. He cleared his throat again.

"My wife died last year," he said apologetically to Luke.

"You don't need to make excuses to him," the whore laughed. "Luke and I are old friends. Hopefully, he'll be coming up after you."

"I don't think so," another voice disagreed smoothly as a luscious redhead sashayed up to Luke and rested a possessive hand on his neck.

"Hey, Seline," Luke greeted her, hauling her onto his lap. "What took you so long?"

"Honey, if I'd a known you were here I would have been down hours ago."

Ned watched uncomfortably as the redhead kissed his companion full on the mouth, pressing her lush body hard against him.

Luke stood and swept the whore up into his arms. She squealed happily as he took the stairs two at a time, bearing her off to the closest bed.

☙ 6 ❧

"Y OU DON'T LOOK like you at all," Adam said.
        "I should hope not. You remember what we talked about?"

"You're a boy."

"That's right."

"Even though you're a girl."

"But no one, apart from you, me and Vicky, knows I'm a girl."

"I like you better as a girl."

"I'll be a girl again when we get to Oregon."

"Promise?"

"Promise. By then I'll be desperate for a bath," she said dryly, regarding her filthy skin. "But for now we need to get organized. I'll meet you both downstairs."

"Where are you going?" Victoria asked sharply.

"I'm going to get the name of that wagon maker off Mr. Slater." Victoria's lips thinned in disapproval, but Alex ignored her. "Don't forget to keep the gold with you," she told her sister. "Put it in your bodice, where it'll be safe." Alex had divided the gold into smaller bags. The bag with the most money went to Victoria, one was squirreled away in their bags and the other was hidden under a loose floorboard under the bed. Victoria wore a padded bodice (she didn't have much up top and was sensitive about it) and so the outline of the bag was well disguised. Alex didn't carry one herself. If the Gradys found her, she had to be ready to run, and she had no intention of taking the money away from Victoria and Adam. She jammed the hat on her head. But if she had her way that wouldn't happen. Not if Slater pointed her in the direction of a strong wagon and a competent captain.

Alex couldn't deny that she was excited at the thought of seeing Luke Slater again. Deep down, she knew she could find a wagon maker without his help; she was simply fabricating a reason to seek him out.

She all but skipped down the stairs to the front desk, where Ralph Taylor sat with a cup of burned-smelling coffee and a two-week-old paper that had just arrived on the riverboat. "I need to speak to Luke Slater," she announced in her best low-pitched boy voice. The hotelier didn't bother to look up from his paper.

"He didn't come back from Dolly's last night. I dare say you'll find him there."

"Dolly's?"

"At the end of the street turn left, go three blocks, make a right and you won't miss it."

"Thanks. Could you tell my sister where I've gone when she comes down?"

He grunted, which she took for an assent.

Outside, it was a spectacular spring morning of pale blue and yellow-green. Even the dusty street looked pretty in the fresh golden sunlight. Alex shoved her hands deep into her pockets. It was mighty odd being out in the world as a boy. At first she felt dreadfully self-conscious. It was like being out in public in her underwear. Except that the layer of filth made her feel safely anonymous, and after a block or so she found herself loosening up. Her gait changed, becoming less of a glide and more of a stride. She looked around and gained even more confidence when she realized that no one was taking any notice of her.

She liked not having to worry about keeping the hem of her skirt out of the muck and she liked the way she could take deep breaths without her stays. All in all, being a boy wasn't too bad.

She stopped dead when she rounded the corner and caught sight of Dolly's. It was impossible to miss the sprawling two-storied building that was more than a little crooked. There was an eye-catching sign out the front: "Dolly's—Girls! Girls! Girls!" If Alex hadn't already guessed that she was looking at a cathouse, she did the moment she saw the women sunning themselves on the porch.

They were in their underwear! Or less. There were bare shoulders and bosoms and legs wherever she looked. Beneath her mask of soot and dirt, she blushed with shame for them.

"Morning, lovey," one of the women called suggestively, catching sight of Alex standing in the street openmouthed, staring at them. "Fancy a tickle?"

There was a burst of laughter.

"Oh, Flora, he ain't old enough to know how to use it yet."

"Don't listen to her," Flora called down to Alex, winking. "You don't have to do anything—just let nature take its course."

"Which at your age won't take long at all!" another woman hooted, setting them all off squawking.

Alex was mortified.

"Leave him be," the oldest of them said, fanning herself lazily. "You looking for someone, honey? Your pa maybe?"

The thought of Pa Sparrow in a place like Dolly's made Alex blanch. He wouldn't have gone within a stone's throw of such an establishment, and he would have been scandalized to think that his foster daughter was talking to a whore. Imagining his disapproving scowl, she felt she should turn on her heel and leave. But, to her own astonishment, she didn't.

"I'm looking for Luke Slater." The words were out of her mouth before she knew what she was doing.

There seemed to be a collective sigh among the whores. Certainly there was a wave of white flesh rising and falling.

"Just go upstairs and wake him, honey. He's asleep in Seline's room."

Go upstairs? Into the house?

Alex's skin burned at the thought . . . at the same time she was deeply curious as to what the inside of a whorehouse looked like. For some reason she pictured thick carpets and chandeliers, velvet and satin and mirrors.

She was bitterly disappointed.

Dolly's was as raw as the rest of the town—new unpainted timber, where the nail heads glinted, still bright silver and new. And it was a pigsty. No one had bothered to clean up after the night's entertainment: the spittoons were full and there were empty glasses on every spare surface. The whole place smelled of stale sweat, cigar smoke and something else she couldn't name.

She picked her way through the scattered chairs and made her way up to the second floor, where she paused, nervous. The woman hadn't mentioned which room he was in. Seline's room. Which one was that? There were more than half a dozen doors along the landing and down the corridor.

Gathering her courage, she knocked on the first one. When there was no answer she poked her head in. It was empty. Even more nervous now, she tried the next.

"Let a girl get some sleep!" a woman moaned, pulling a pillow over her face. "Ain't it enough that you're at me all night, do you have to be at me all day too?"

"I'm just looking for Seline's room," Alex stammered.

"Two doors down."

"Thank you." Alex closed the door hurriedly.

When she reached Seline's door she paused. Her heart was thundering in her ears and her chest felt tight. It suddenly occurred to her that they might not be sleeping . . .

Before she could chicken out she knocked on the door. There was no answer. She knocked again. Silence. Should she look in or not? Did the silence mean that the room was empty, or that they were asleep, or something else altogether?

Swallowing hard, she eased the door open and peered through the crack.

He was in there, all right. She'd know that broad back anywhere.

Didn't the man ever wear clothes?

He was sprawled on his stomach, with his face buried in a pillow. Slowly Alex's gaze traced the contours of his body beneath the sheet.

There was a moan and Alex's heart stopped. A tangled mass of red hair rose from the other side of Luke.

"Whaddya want?" the whore complained, rubbing tiredly at her face. Her rouge was smudged and there were black rings around her eyes where the paint had run.

"Uh . . . him," Alex admitted, nodding at Luke and twisting the brim of her hat between her fingers.

The woman struggled to sit up and look Alex up and down. Alex was horrified when the sheet fell free, exposing the whore's large breasts. Her gaze flew down to her boots and she felt her face burn. She'd never blushed so much in her life as she had in the last twenty-four hours. Did no one in Missouri have a sense of common decency?

And if it was this rough here, what would it be like on the frontier?

Seline leaned over Luke, her breasts brushing his bare back as she ran her fingers through his thick black hair.

"Darlin'? You've got company."

"So I feel," he said sleepily.

Alex stole a peek and saw him roll over with a bleary but wolfish grin, his eyes lingering on Seline's exposed flesh.

"Not me," the whore teased, and Alex was sure she heard the hint of a giggle in her voice, "him."

Luke blinked and followed Seline's gaze to the door, where Alex shifted uncomfortably from foot to foot.

"Well, if it ain't Al Alexander. Aren't you a little young for a whorehouse? You don't look more'n twelve."

"Mr. Taylor said I could find you here."

"And you did." One of Luke's hands was rubbing lazy circles on Seline's back. Alex wished he'd stop. She couldn't help wondering how it would feel to have that large hand caressing her back instead . . . judging by Seline's expression it would feel pretty good indeed.

"You said you knew a wagon maker?"

"You sure are in an all-fire hurry, aren't you?"

"I just thought you might be able to point me in the right direction," Alex said lamely.

Luke gave her a good-natured grin. "Sure I will. But maybe a little later. I've got my hands full at the moment."

He certainly did.

Alex mumbled an apology. She felt absolutely ridiculous. What had she been thinking? The man was in a whorehouse, for heaven's sake. He was hardly going to be in the mood to talk wagons with a scruffy boy.

"I'll find you at Ralph's around noon," he called after her.

Alex could hear Seline giggle as the door clicked closed behind her.

❋ 7 ❋

LUKE WAS HALF expecting the tears. He seemed to have that kind of effect on women.

"I'm sorry," Seline sniffled, "I shouldn't have asked."

Luke sighed and stopped buttoning his shirt. He took the girl in his arms and gently stroked her back. Why did it always end this way? He thought the whole point of hiring a whore was that there were no strings attached, but here she was asking him to take her with him. "I'm so miserable here," she'd whispered, looking up at him with her big moist eyes.

Last time it had been Gracie weeping into his shirt. And the time before that Margaret had actually wrapped herself around him and begged him to marry her. Marry her! Much as he liked these girls, he wasn't looking to keep them.

"You're too much of a knight in shining armor," Dolly scolded him every time he left. "You need to treat it like a business transaction. And for pity's sake, stop spending the night!"

"I thought you liked my money."

"I do, but I'm not fond of the miserable whores you leave behind. They mope for days after you leave town."

He sighed again now, thinking of the look that would be on Dolly's face when she saw his wet shirt, with its telltale kohl stains.

He did his best, he really did. He never slept with the same one two nights in a row. He never sweet-talked them. Well, not intentionally. It wasn't his fault he was a friendly guy.

"You don't hate me, do you?" Seline asked in a small voice.

"Ah no, love." Damn. That right there was his problem. At the word "love" she gave a shivery sigh and burrowed into his chest. He wondered how he was going to get away.

"You don't want to come with me, lo—" He caught himself mid-word and cleared his throat. "A pretty town girl like you has got no place out there in the wild."

"I grew up on a farm," she told him, pulling back to look up at him with shining eyes.

Hell. He gave her an awkward pat and disentangled himself. "I have to go meet that little runt about a wagon."

"You'll be back tonight?"

"Haven't planned that far ahead, to tell you the truth. There's a lot to be done before we head out." He hated the way her face crumpled, but he resolutely pulled on his jacket and gave her a quick kiss on the forehead. "I'll see you soon."

He was mighty glad to get out of there. He headed for the back door, knowing most of the women would be hanging around the front porch—like a bunch of well-fed spiders, just waiting for a helpless man to blunder into their sticky webs. Why couldn't women just enjoy things as they were? Why did they always have to be wanting more than a man could give? Hell, if Amelia would just marry him he wouldn't be getting mixed up with these women in the first place.

He grabbed a biscuit from the kitchen on his way through and felt his spirits lift the minute he was out in the sunshine. He wasn't one for the indoors. Give him the wide-open sky and the endless plains and he was a happy man.

By the time he reached Taylor's he was whistling a merry tune and tipping his hat at every pretty girl he passed. The runt was waiting for him on the porch of the hotel, looking somewhat out of sorts. Sitting on the steps at his feet was a big lad, barrel-chested, and a bit simple-looking in the way he had his head tilted way back watching the clouds scud across the deep blue sky. Sitting in the rocker was the runt's sister, the one who'd thrown the hissy fit the night before. She wasn't bad-looking, Luke noticed now. She had a nice, fresh-faced wholesome look.

"Mornin'," Luke said amiably. "Sorry to keep you folks waiting."

"This is my brother, Adam, and my sister, Victoria," Alex volunteered stiffly.

"A pleasure to meet you. I don't often get to meet real ladies." Luke tipped his hat at the sister and flashed his dimple.

Victoria flushed and one hand rose to fiddle nervously with the ribbons of her bonnet. Alex scowled. "The wagon?" she reminded him shortly.

"Right this way. May I?" He offered Victoria his arm.

Alex watched in astonishment as Victoria smiled at him and descended the porch steps to accept his escort. What had happened to her snit about decency and morality?

"So you're heading out to Oregon?" she heard him remark smoothly as she and Adam fell in behind them.

"We have a brother out there," Victoria simpered. Alex glared at her back. Hypocrite. "He's a pastor in Amory. Do you know Amory, Mr. Slater?"

"There's a red horse, Alex," Adam said, pulling her arm to get her attention. She gave him an absent smile and tried to catch Luke's response.

"Can I get a red horse, Alex?"

"Maybe when we get to Oregon." Alex swore under her breath when Adam veered over toward the horse. She grabbed at his arm, but he was too strong for her.

"Hello, boy," Adam cooed, reaching out to rub the white star on the nose of the red-brown horse hitched in front of the bank. "Do you want to go Oregon with us?"

"Not that horse, Adam," Alex explained patiently. "That horse belongs to somebody. We'll have to find you a different red horse."

"But I like this one."

"Fond of horses, eh?"

Alex jumped; she hadn't realized Luke and Victoria had followed them.

"Fond of *this* horse," Alex sighed.

"He wants to come with us," Adam said stubbornly.

"Looks to me like you've got a 'she' there, not a 'he,'" Luke drawled. "Lovely little mare too."

"He's a girl?" Adam's brow furrowed and Alex's heart beat faster, afraid he'd let something slip.

"He's a girl," Luke confirmed. "I've got a horse just that color back home in Oregon, a young gelding. Very sweet natured, and as fast as all blazes."

"And that one's a boy?"

Luke paused, obviously restraining himself from making a smart remark about geldings. Instead he nodded, doing a bad job of suppressing a grin. "He's for sale too, if you're interested."

Adam looked questioningly at Alex.

"We'll see," she told him firmly. "I'm not saying yes, mind, just maybe. Say good-bye to the horse now, we have to see about the wagon." She took Adam by the elbow and steered him back out into the street.

"That was very good of you," she heard Victoria murmur to Luke.

By the time they reached the wagon maker's Victoria was rosy pink and flirting prettily and Alex had been subjected to a monologue from Adam about his red horse waiting in Oregon.

"Well, here we are," Luke declared, holding open the gate and ushering them through to a yard full of wagon skeletons. Some were bare timber structures, still without wheels, others had wheels but no canvas roof. None of them looked travel-ready.

The air was heavy with the fragrance of cut timber and linseed oil as they followed Luke toward a work shed at the rear of the dusty property.

"Archie?" Luke called.

There was a thump and the sound of a gruff voice swearing.

Alex blinked as they entered the shed, momentarily blinded after the brightness of the day outside.

"That you, Luke?"

By the time Alex's eyes had adjusted to the darkness, a small man with a shiny bald pate had jumped down from the wagon he was working on and was approaching them, wiping his hands on his pants. "What are you doing here? I thought you were staying put from now on?"

Luke shrugged. "This is my last trip."

"You say that every time."

"I mean it this time."

Archie snorted. "You mean it until the next time Jackson has a horse for sale."

Luke grinned. "If I get that stallion tomorrow, I won't need any more horses. I'll have all the studs I need."

"If you get him."

"I'll get him."

"Just don't let my Adele see you. Last time you left she cried for a week."

Luke held his hands up. "I never encouraged her, I swear."

"You don't need to," Archie grumbled. "If only that girl of yours would marry you and put the rest of them out of their misery."

Alex noticed a shadow pass over Luke's face. What girl of his?

"Arch, these are some new friends of mine. I told them you were the most honest wagon maker in town."

Archie snorted again. "He gets a commission if you buy from me," he told them, "and he needs the money to buy that stallion."

"What did I tell you?" Luke declared, grinning at them. "Honest to the bone."

Alex couldn't help but smile back. His grin was so wicked and his eyes so warm. The man certainly had a fatal charm.

"So you need a wagon." Archie pulled a notepad out of his pocket and licked his stub of a pencil. "When do you need it by?"

"The runt seems to think they're in a rush," Luke drawled.

"I can't do anything before the eighth."

"The eighth!" Alex and Victoria exclaimed, both looking appalled.

Archie blinked. "Whose party are you in?"

"We haven't signed up with one yet," Alex admitted.

"I said they could join mine," Luke said, as if to remind them.

"He's more expensive," Archie told them, leaning in and speaking as though in confidence, "but he's worth it."

"When do you leave?" Alex asked Luke, her heart skipping a beat at the thought of spending the next few months with him.

"Next week."

"Next week!" Alex felt sick to her stomach. She'd thought they would be out of Independence in a day or so at the most. She had a flashback of their house smoldering in the gully, and of Sheriff Deveraux's body lying in a heap at Gideon's feet.

"We need to leave as soon as we can," Victoria wailed.

"Can't do it much faster," Luke told them, bemused. "You'll need that time to get outfitted. Besides, you don't even have a wagon."

"And I can't do anything for you until the eighth," Archie said firmly.

Alex swallowed hard. That just wasn't good enough.

"Excuse us," she whispered weakly, taking Victoria's arm, "I need to discuss something with my sister." She led Victoria out of the shed and around the corner.

"Give me the gold," she whispered.

Victoria's eyes widened. "I can't. I did what you said: it's in my bodice."

"So get it out."

"I am not undressing in public," she hissed.

Impatient, Alex turned Victoria to face the corrugated iron wall of the shed. "I'll stand lookout. Unbutton and get that gold, or we're not going anywhere, unless it's with the Gradys."

AN HOUR LATER they found themselves the proud owners of a nearly finished wagon. It was one of the lighter, smaller ones.

"You won't need so many animals to pull this one," Archie said, indicating the still-uncovered wagon. It didn't look any different from a farm vehicle to Alex.

"It'll save you money," he continued, not meeting their eyes. The wagon was worth about four hundred dollars, but they'd paid almost twice that. "I'll have it ready for you in a couple of days."

Alex was aware of Luke eyeing the remaining gold as they left Archie's shed, and she was glad most of it was still safely tucked away in Victoria's bodice.

"Is there a party leaving earlier than yours?" she asked him.

"Probably," he said with a shrug, "but you won't find a captain as good as me."

"But you don't leave for a week."

"And I told you that you'll need that week to get provisions. As long as we leave by the end of the month we'll be fine. We'll be safe in Oregon well before the first snows."

Alex jingled the bag of gold at him. "I don't think so."

Luke eyed the runt speculatively, wondering about the shift in power between him and his sister. Last night the girl was tearing a strip off him, but today he seemed to be the one in charge. And he was the one that the brother—Adam—seemed to heed. Luke couldn't work it out.

"Where would we find out about other parties?" Alex demanded.

The runt certainly didn't act like a normal kid. What twelve-year-old spoke with such decisiveness and authority? He must be older than he looked.

"I reckon the town square would be the place to look," Luke told Alex slowly. "I was planning to head over myself, to drum up some business, if you want me to show you the way."

THE TOWN SQUARE was chaos. There were more wagoners than Luke had ever seen in one place, and he'd seen his share of wagoners departing Independence. The pull of the west was luring both easterners as well as migrants from the old world, who disembarked in New York and set out overland to find land and a new life. They had queer accents and even queerer ways. Luke had a feeling he was witnessing the beginning of a flood. He'd heard tell some of the captains were taking on double the clients this season, and from the crush in the square it looked like it was true. Damn fools. It was hard enough looking after a score of people, let alone two score. There must have been more than two dozen wagons crammed on the hardpacked dirt of the square. It was a warm late-spring day and a fine cloud of dust hung in the still air, kicked up by oxen and horses and a townful of boots. The white canvas arches shone in the sun like an armada of sails on a calm harbor. They wouldn't stay white. By the end of the voyage they'd be dusty and stained.

The noise in the square was incredible: a hundred voices speaking at once. Children darted in and out of the crowd, shrieking as they swerved through the melee. The laughter was raucous but Luke saw a fair share of pinched, frightened faces. They were right to be frightened. They had long months of hard travel ahead of them. They'd need to trust their captains to keep them close to water and not to stray away from fertile lands, where their animals would have feed. Some of them would sicken, some would starve, and some would die. Not a few because they'd trusted a guide who led them off track, or who was ill-provisioned, or slow, leaving them subject to the wicked bite of winter.

"You said we'd be able to find a wagon train to join here," the runt said, his eyes fixed on the chaos. "It'll be like looking for a needle in a haystack," the kid muttered under his breath.

"We'll wait until this lot have gone and then we'll see who's left. They'll be the ones looking for a party, or looking to lead one." Luke led them to the courthouse steps, and they jostled their way up to get a good view of the proceedings. Gradually the wagoners climbed into their wagons and the screaming children disappeared beneath the shining white hoops. At the far edge of the square a man climbed onto the seat of the lead wagon, gripping the hoop for support and waving his hat in the air. "Three cheers for Oregon," he shouted.

The wagoners cheered. Some idiot fired his gun in the air. And with creaks and chatter, cheers and whistles, the train rolled out. It took almost an hour for the square to clear and by then the dust had risen in a red fog. Victoria coughed delicately into a handkerchief while Adam covered his face and the runt sneezed.

"The first wagon will have crossed three counties before the last one gets out of Independence," the man next to Luke said, shaking his head.

"Who's captaining them?" Luke asked.

"No one," the man said in disgust. "They elected one of their own to lead them. Damn fools."

"So people go west without hiring a captain?" the kid asked him as they descended the steps into the thinning cloud of dust.

"Some do." Luke gave the boy a sharp look. "It's not something I'd recommend."

"No. You'd recommend I pay you to do it."

"I'd get you there alive." He headed for the shade of a sycamore. "There'll be captains lining the square," he said shortly. It was no skin off his nose if the boy wanted to sign up with another party. Luke would have no trouble making up a party without them. He never did.

"I don't see why we don't just go with Mr. Slater," Victoria complained as Alex dragged them around the square. It was hot and they were covered in dust.

"You weren't so keen on signing with him this morning."

"That was before we got to know him."

Alex rolled her eyes. Before he turned his charm on you, you mean, she thought sourly. But she wanted to go with Luke Slater too, especially after she met the other captains. They found grizzled old fur trappers, rumpled bleary-eyed drunks and mean-looking cowboys; there were surly men, and men who talked a mile a minute; men who claimed to have led the first expedition to Oregon City, and men who claimed to have never lost more than a quarter of their wagoners. A quarter! It made Alex feel sick to her stomach. Was she leading her family to their deaths?

She eyed Luke Slater from across the square. He was young and strong and sober. He didn't seem like a fool or a villain. He was expensive but she had more than enough Grady gold to pay for him . . .

But he wasn't leaving for an entire week. And there were the Gradys to think of. They'd be here soon, if they weren't here already. Alex scowled. Luke was the best choice, but she couldn't afford to wait a week. She turned back to regard the captains she'd just spoken to. She sighed. She'd just have to interview them again. At least one of them would have to make a better impression this time. They certainly couldn't make a worse one.

"Where are you going?" Victoria asked.

"I need to make a choice."

"Well, I'm tired," her sister snapped. "I'm going to sit down on that bench under that tree."

The tree by Luke Slater, Alex observed grumpily. She

could sit in the shade and moon over Luke while Alex baked in the heat and did all the work.

LUKE HAD JUST about made his quota when Victoria sank onto the bench behind him, fanning herself prettily with her handkerchief. "Who did you like the look of?" he asked cheerfully.

"None of them," Victoria said, wrinkling her nose.

He laughed. "And your brother?"

"He's just being stubborn," Victoria said firmly. She bit her lip and then straightened her shoulders and met Luke's eyes. She was blushing, he saw. "You'd best put us down for your party, Mr. Slater. I'd hate for you to be booked up by the time Alex realizes what a damn fool she . . . he . . . is."

And that was his quota. Luke grinned and turned back to the square. He could see Alex and Adam talking to Slumpback Joe. Even from here he could make out the cranky set of the runt's features as he argued with the old trapper.

"Well, look who we have here."

Luke sighed at the sound of the voice. He'd had a feeling he'd run into these idiots again. He turned to see Silas swaggering toward him. He supposed he should count himself lucky that the cretin hadn't brought his brothers with him.

"If it ain't the cardsharp," Silas said. Luke could see he was itching for a fight.

"Haven't you learned your lesson?" Luke asked.

"I ain't the one who needs to be learnin'."

"Let's not make a fuss in front of the lady," Luke suggested.

"What lady?" Silas followed Luke's gaze and spotted Victoria. His nostrils flared with shock, and once again he reminded Luke of a bull. "You!"

Victoria, never a brave soul, chose that moment to swoon. Luke caught her as she tumbled from the bench.

"Where's the other one?" Silas demanded.

"What other one?"

"Where is she?" Silas was turning scarlet with rage.

"Who?" Luke was genuinely clueless.

"The sister."

Luke looked down at the woman in his arms.

"The other one," Silas snapped.

"I haven't met any sister," Luke told him.

If possible, Silas's face turned even redder. "Why should I trust a cheat like you? I know your type. You think every beautiful woman should be yours."

"I didn't even know she had a sister," Luke insisted. "She's heading out to some brother in Oregon. She just joined my party."

"Gideon said they'd go to Stephen. Fools." Silas spat in the dirt. He sized Luke up through narrowed eyes. "She pay you in gold?"

"She ain't paid me at all yet. And she won't if you've frightened her to death."

"You swear you ain't seen her sister?"

"No," Luke snapped, reaching the end of his patience. "Now if you'll excuse me, the lady needs some attention."

"You might want to tell her to keep out of sight," Silas snarled at his back as he left. "My brother will do more'n scare her if he knows she's here."

BY THE TIME Luke reached Ralph Taylor's place the girl was coming to.

"Where's your room?" he asked gently. When she told him he took her straight upstairs and lowered her carefully to the bed.

"How are you feeling, Miss Alexander?"

Victoria thought she must be dreaming. Men didn't look at her that way. They looked at Alex like that all the time, all soft and tender on the surface, with something hungry underneath. But now here was this man—this chiseled, square-jawed Adonis—looking at *her,* plain old Victoria Sparrow, with such concern. He'd carried her in his arms as though she'd weighed as little as a feather. And now they were alone and she was helpless on the bed before him. Victoria felt her stomach clench, and not from fear.

"What's going on here?"

Never had her sister been less welcome.

Alex and Adam tumbled through the door. Alex looked suspicious as she took in Luke and Victoria's positions on the bed. Her expression blackened with rage. "You weren't at the square," she accused. "I was worried, so we came looking. And good thing we did, because look what we found."

"Nothing inappropriate," Luke said to soothe the runt. "She fainted and I thought the bed would be the best place for her. I don't have much experience with swooning ladies."

The runt snorted in disbelief and turned a dubious look on his sister. "You fainted?"

"It was the heat," Victoria lied. Luke gave her a startled look, but she ignored him.

"Why don't you run down and get some fresh water for your sister, runt?" Luke suggested. "She looks like she could use a cool cloth on her forehead."

"I can help," Adam said.

"Yes, you can," Luke agreed. "You can pump the water for Alex."

Alex didn't look like she was going to budge. Victoria made a slight whimpering noise and slumped back against the bed.

"Can't you see how pale she is?" Luke scolded. "Go get that water."

Alex felt well and truly dismissed. She snatched up the water pitcher and stomped downstairs. They were up to no good, she just knew it.

As soon as the door closed behind them, Victoria sat up, wringing her hands. "I only lied so I wouldn't worry them," she said nervously. "Did Silas see Alex? Were his brothers there?" She was as white as milk and shivering like a leaf in an autumn gale.

"He was asking about your sister," Luke told her gently. He pulled the blanket up to cover her, noticing how she flinched at the mention of her sister. "Don't fret. I told him the truth."

"The truth?" Her eyes were as big as saucers.

"That your sister ain't with you." He looked around the hotel room but there was no obvious sign of a hidden sister.

"No." Victoria's voice cracked. "My sister has gone east. We parted ways in St. Louis." She cleared her throat. "She abandoned us. She wasn't our blood sister anyway, just a stray Ma and Pa took in when her parents died."

"What did he want with her?"

"What did he want with *you*?"

"I ran into a spot of trouble with them over cards last night." Luke frowned. The poor girl was in serious distress at the thought of those vultures. "He said to keep you out of sight of his brother."

"Gideon." Victoria shuddered.

"Why is that?"

"He wants my sister," Victoria told him miserably. "He'd hurt us to get to her."

Luke fell silent. "Would it help if I get word to them that your sister left you?"

Victoria nodded. Then gave a despairing shrug. Then the tears began to fall.

Luke was a sucker for tears. "I'll see if we can leave a bit sooner than I'd planned," he said, rubbing her back.

"What about Alex . . ."

"Alex is a boy," Luke said firmly, "and I'm guessing you're his legal guardian. So, in my book, it's you that gets to decide which wagon train you join."

Looking up into his shining black eyes, Victoria knew exactly which wagon train they were joining. Luke Slater's. Even if he was headed to the ends of the earth.

❧ 8 ❧

ALEX DIDN'T RECOGNIZE her anymore. Her plain and mousy sister was blossoming into a pretty young woman. She walked around pink-cheeked and glowing, smiling witlessly at all and sundry. It was infuriating.

And it was that man's fault.

"What do you think you are doing?" she hissed at Victoria in Cavil's Mercantile, where Victoria was in the process of buying a length of lovely yellow calico.

"I'm going to make a new dress," Victoria said blithely. "Luke says there's a dance on Saturday night, to farewell the wagon trains leaving, which includes us."

"Oh, he does, now, does he? And how are you planning to pay for this new dress?"

There was a glint of gold in Victoria's gloved hand.

"That money is supposed to get us set up in Oregon!"

"One new dress won't hurt."

Alex sputtered helplessly as Victoria sailed up to the counter with the bolt of yellow cloth firmly in hand. She was outraged in so many ways. Firstly, because it really was a waste of money. When on earth would Victoria need a new yellow dress on the trip west? When she was fording rivers, or helping to dig out the wheels of their bogged wagon?

And secondly, Alex had to admit, she was outraged because she didn't see why Victoria should have a new dress when she was walking around in Adam's cast-offs, her face buried beneath a revolting mask of dust and dirt. It just wasn't fair.

Being a boy certainly wasn't all it was cracked up to be, she thought sulkily as they walked back to Taylor's. Here she was lugging sacks of grain, while Victoria sailed along with only the scrap of calico weighing her down. Then she had to head out into the blazing heat of the day to look over a bunch of smelly animals, while Victoria got to sit in the cool of the hotel sewing her pretty new dress.

"Come on, Adam," Alex snapped, "we'd best leave her to it. Try not to give yourself a callus while we're gone."

"I've never been to a dance," Adam said as they headed downstairs.

"Sure you have," Alex disagreed half-heartedly, still stewing. She was secretly picturing herself in the yellow calico.

"I don't think so." He frowned, straining to remember a dance.

"In old Dyson's barn, remember?"

"With the cows?" The memory dawned visibly on his face.

"They put the cows outside for the dance."

"But it smelled like cows."

"And chickens," Alex agreed. And there'd been no one to dance with but Pa, Adam and the old men. Except for the Gradys, of course, who always turned up half-drunk and belligerent. Silas would make a beeline for her, Alex remembered distastefully, recalling the way he'd slicked his hair back and worn his best suit (the one that was tight across the shoulders and shiny on the knees) in order to impress her. Why couldn't he ever take no for an answer?

He'd hover over her all night, until she gave in and danced one dance with him. And then he always held her too close and trod on her feet. More often than not the evening would end with him proposing to her—again—and getting red-faced and angry when she refused him. It got so that Alex stopped attending the dances in Dyson's barn, just to avoid the unpleasantness of it all.

"I don't like chickens," Adam said now, "they have nasty feet."

Alex laughed.

"I swear you seem a different age every time I see you," a voice drawled from behind them, and there he was again, the bane of her existence, the man who'd turned her sister into a spendthrift.

Luke was staring at her with a calculating look and Alex's heart stopped.

"Just how old are you anyway?"

"Old enough," she said shortly.

He snorted. "Yeah? Well, you laugh like a girl."

"Alex says I laugh like a donkey," Adam told him proudly.

"I can't say I've ever heard a donkey laugh," Luke replied.

"They sound like this." Adam demonstrated.

Alex caught Luke's eye and couldn't help but laugh. She caught herself and tried to turn her giggle into something more masculine, but all she managed to do was choke, and the next thing she knew he was pounding her on the back. And none too gently either.

"Where are you two going?" he asked as he pounded. Alex was sure she was going to have bruises by the time he was done.

"We're buying horses," Adam said excitedly.

"Not horses, mules," Alex corrected. "To pull the wagon."

"I wouldn't get mules if I were you," Luke cautioned. "They're more likely to be stolen. Ox is what you need. Cheaper, and useful for farming when you get to Oregon."

"And I suppose you know a man who can sell us an ox?" Alex said dryly.

"You'll need at least two." He grinned. "I can take you there after the auction."

"Auction?"

"I'm off to buy a horse."

"A horse?" Adam's ears pricked up and before Alex knew what was happening they were front and center at a horse auction.

"Slater!" A fat man with a sparkling white mustache bellowed, crossing the crowd to greet Luke. "I sure am glad you made it!"

"I just happened to be up this way and thought I'd stop by," Luke said coolly.

The fat man guffawed. "I just bet you did. I just bet you're only here for a look-see." He took out a cheroot, neatly snipped the end off and lit up. Billows of blue smoke puffed from beneath the pristine mustache. He looked a bit like a steam train, Alex thought.

Luke smiled implacably at Jackson. The old goat must

have invited every horse trader and breeder in the surrounding states to see the stallion. It wasn't often that such prime horseflesh was available in these parts.

"I'd hate to see you miss out after you've come all this way," Jackson said cheerily. "But you know, he's worth it. Don't let a few extra dollars put you off; that horse'll make you your money back, no doubt about it."

Luke kept his smile steady. He wasn't about to let Jackson know how much he wanted the stallion. That horse was going to be the making of him. With Jackson's stallion he could settle down for good, and win Amelia to boot.

"What's so special about this horse?" Alex asked as they watched Jackson steam away, heading off to whisper into the ear of another hopeful buyer.

"Wait till you see him. He's an Arab." Luke was stone-faced.

She realized with a shock that he must be nervous. She looked at him curiously, noting the tightness around his full lips and the way he was cracking his knuckles. As she watched she saw his eyes narrow.

He swore. "They're the last thing I need right now."

Alex followed his gaze and her heart stopped. Across the yard the Gradys were elbowing their way through the crowd. Silas, Travis and Bert were a walking wall of muscle, but it was their weedy little brother who made her break out in a cold sweat. She heard the phantom echo of his maniacal laughter as her home crackled and burned.

She suppressed an urge to run. If she ran, they'd notice her for sure. Instead she tugged her hat lower and slouched, trying to look as boyish and un-Alexandra-ish as possible. She shoved Adam behind Luke. When he protested she pinched him into submission. "The Gradys," she hissed at him. "Remember what we said about hiding?" There was such a crush of bodies around them that Adam was well hidden, even though he was in plain sight.

Luckily, they were all the way across the fenced yard, and Jackson chose that moment to call for the stallion. All eyes, including those of the Gradys, went to the magnificent gray being led into the yard.

The minute Alex saw him she knew what all the fuss was
about. He was young and glossy, with an elegantly arched
neck and a high tail. Alex had never seen an animal like him.
He was a prince: high-stepping and regal. She could feel
Luke tense beside her and she heard Adam take a breath.

"Ain't he a beauty?" Jackson declared proudly. "Pure-
bred, with the papers to prove it."

"Glory," Alex breathed, "a horse like that must cost a
fortune."

Luke gave her a swift dark look, but refused to comment.

Alex had never been to an auction before and was surprised by the terseness of it. No one smiled. Every bid was
made in a low, clipped voice or silently, with a wave of a finger. She couldn't make head or tail of who was bidding.
"Was that you?" she whispered to Luke. "Was that last bid
yours?" He ignored her and she swiveled her head, trying to
catch sight of wagging fingers. "Did he say one hundred dollars?" she gasped. "One hundred dollars!"

Luke's face was even stonier than before. He looked kind
of frightening, Alex had to admit. There wasn't a trace of
humor on the lean planes of his handsome face.

"One twenty to Slater," Jackson called, immediately following with "One twenty-five to Mr. Jessop."

Alex saw a muscle jump in Luke's jaw. By the time the
price had doubled his finger had stopped wagging and the muscle had stopped jumping. His jaw was set in a hard, angry line.

"Another five to the stranger," Jackson called with a nod.
Alex followed his gaze and gasped when she saw Gideon
Grady, grinning like a cat with the cream. Every time someone bid, Gideon upped them by five dollars. Where did he
get the money? she thought with dismay. For that matter,
where had he gotten the money she'd stolen from him? She
hadn't even taken all of it—she'd only managed to grab one
bag before Ma Grady came at her. It made no sense, swamp
trash like the Gradys having a stash of gold like that. Not to
mention the jewelry. And then there were the papers she'd
found secreted in the lining of the bag . . .

She shivered, remembering the look on Ma Grady's mean
old face. They were no good, the lot of them, and she couldn't
wait until she could forget about them and their gold.

"And another five!"

The sound of Jackson's voice startled Alex back to the present. Across the yard she could see Travis slapping his younger brother on the back and grinning.

"Aren't you going to bid again?" she hissed at Luke. She couldn't bear the thought of Gideon getting that magnificent animal. Gideon's animals had a habit of winding up lame, or blind, or just plain dead.

"Too rich for my blood," Luke said gruffly, and she could hear the disappointment heavy in his husky voice.

"Going once to the stranger," Jackson called, letting the silence hang, before he called out again.

Alex shifted restlessly, scanning the crowd to see if anyone would bid.

"Going twice to the stranger . . . ?"

Gideon spat a stream of tobacco juice through a self-satisfied smirk, and her stomach twisted. She'd be damned if she'd let that little weasel win the horse.

"Another ten," she called out, her voice clear and strong and, to her ears at least, entirely feminine.

Every head in the yard turned her way. She pulled her hat lower over her eyes.

"And five!" Gideon sounded a little sour.

Was he close to his limit? Alex wondered hopefully.

"Fifteen more!" she bid, deepening her voice, and tucking her chin under to ensure that her face was completely hidden by the brim of her hat.

"And five." Gideon sounded real surly now.

"Twenty!"

"What are you doing?" Luke's voice demanded, close to her ear. "You can't have that kind of money."

"And five."

She heard the cold rage in Gideon's voice and she knew she had him.

"Fifty!" she hollered, her voice breaking.

A hubbub broke out. The horse must have set some kind of record with a price like that!

"Going once to the lad by Slater . . ."

"This ain't a game," Luke warned her, taking her arm in his hard grip. She shook him off.

"Going twice . . . ?" Jackson looked inquiringly at Gideon.

Gideon narrowed his eyes as he stared across the yard. He spat a stream of tobacco juice and then sneered, turning to leave. His brothers trailed him. Alex took a deep shaky breath as they left the yard.

"Sold, to the lad!" Jackson mopped at his brow, feeling quite overwhelmed by the profit he'd just made.

"What are you, crazy?" Luke demanded.

"You said he was a good horse," Alex said weakly, suddenly feeling the enormity of what she'd done. Had she really just spent nearly all of their money on a *horse*?

"Is that our horse now, Alex?" Adam asked excitedly.

Alex couldn't bring herself to answer. "I think I need to sit down." She looked around for the nearest seat. There weren't any. Her knees were trembling and she was a little worried she might faint.

"My boy!" Jackson declared, approaching them with his arms wide, and his smile wider. "May I say you got quite a bargain today."

Luke snorted.

"That horse there is a one-in-a-million animal."

Alex looked over at the stallion, which was being led toward her. She swallowed hard. What on earth was she going to tell Victoria?

"I have the papers here, if you have the money . . . ?"

Alex fumbled for the bag of gold. Did she have enough with her? Victoria still had some of it. She opened the leather bag and peered in, but her vision was a little blurred and all she could see was the dull sheen of gold. Gold that was no longer hers.

"Would you mind—" Her voice was shaking, so she paused for a moment to clear her throat and collect herself. She held the bag out to Luke. "Would you mind counting out Mr. Jackson's money for me?" She pressed the bag into his palm and he looked at her curiously.

"I just need a moment . . ." Alex stumbled off, heading for a measure of privacy behind the stables. Once she was there she threw up.

"If I were your sister I'd tar the hide right off you."

She groaned. Why had he followed her? The last thing she needed right now was for the most beautiful man in the world to see her bent over the dirt and horse dung, emptying the contents of her stomach. "Go away. I thought I told you to pay Jackson."

"I did. He's busy chomping down on all your gold, checking if it's real or not."

"It's real." Although Alex felt a sudden shiver of terror. She *thought* it was real . . . but what if it wasn't? What if the Gradys had been counterfeiting? Oh, she felt sick again.

"Serves you right," Luke said, watching her clutch her stomach. "Wasting your money like that."

"Wasting! You wanted that horse too!"

"Not for that price, I didn't."

"I couldn't let Gideon get him," Alex said miserably. "You don't know Gideon. He would have mistreated him."

Luke shook his head, exasperated, but Alex noticed the admiration in his eyes when they returned to collect the stallion.

"What's his name?" Alex asked Jackson as she accepted the papers.

"Whatever you want it to be," Jackson laughed, lighting up another cheroot.

"I think we should call him Blackie," Adam suggested.

"But he ain't black," Luke said.

"Blackie was Adam's puppy," Alex told him. Poor Blackie had been an early victim of their altercations with the Gradys.

"This can be Blackie Junior," Adam said solemnly.

"He don't look like a Blackie Junior," Luke protested, as Adam took the rope from Jackson's stable boy. "It ain't manly."

Jackson laughed and bid them good day, his hand curled protectively around his bag of gold.

"Blackie Junior will do fine," Alex interrupted them, sensing Adam's dismay. She was rewarded with a glowing smile from her brother and a disgruntled look from Luke. "But what on earth are we going to do with him?"

"I know a place you can stable him, for a small fee."

"Of which you get a commission," Alex guessed sourly.

"As long as it's cheap—we're pretty broke now, and we still have to buy the oxen."

"But we've got Blackie Junior now," Adam protested.

"He's not for pulling the wagon."

"Is he for riding?"

"I guess." Alex was a mess of nerves as they walked through Independence. The Gradys were sure to see them. She chewed on her lip. She might have to keep them all locked in the hotel room, just as they'd stayed locked in their cabin on the steamboat. Only there were still oxen to buy, and supplies to lay in. She had too much to do to hide in the hotel.

Alex couldn't believe it when she realized where Luke was leading them. "You want to stable my horse with a bunch of whores?"

"Dolly's stable is cheap and the kid takes good care of the horses. My horse is here."

Alex was too tired to argue. She settled herself on a hay bale while Luke went inside to rustle up Dolly's boy. She listened to Adam murmuring to Blackie Junior and closed her eyes, leaning back against the stable wall.

"I just had to come and see the record-breaking horse for myself," a strident female voice announced.

Dolly stood silhouetted in the doorway, a crimson ostrich feather curling around her painted face.

Alex saw her kohl-lined eyes widen, and then the scarlet lips split into a smile.

"My dear," Dolly drawled, "that outfit does absolutely nothing for your figure. Why, one would hardly know you were a female."

❧ 9 ❧

A LEX GAPED.
    Dolly gave a playful laugh and strolled into the stable, cocking her head and sweeping Alex with an evaluating gaze. "Women are my business, darlin'. I can spot a pretty girl, even underneath an acre of filth."

Alex rose from the bale, sick with shock and dismay.

"Don't worry," Dolly assured her, "your secret is safe with me. For now." She strolled over to the stallion, giving Adam a seductive smile. "My, aren't you a big one."

"Leave him be." Alex hadn't meant to sound so sharp, but her nerves were shot after the events of the afternoon.

Adam was gaping too—at Dolly's exposed cleavage.

"I'm having a quiet day." Dolly pouted, running a finger up Adam's arm. "You'd be doing me a favor, keeping a lady company . . ."

"Please," Alex said helplessly, "he's . . . he's not right."

"I'm not one to judge."

"Please."

Dolly sighed and gave Adam a brisk pat, in the fashion of a mother rather than a whore. "Can't blame a girl for trying to rustle up a bit of business, can you?" She threw Alex a rueful grin. "Now, boyo," she said to Adam, "why don't you lead your priceless horse into that stall down the end, next to Luke's mare. You give him one of them blankets and some feed and water while I talk to your *brother*."

Still slightly bewildered, Adam did as she suggested, after looking over at Alex for her approval. She gave him a nod and watched as he and Blackie Junior disappeared into the depths of the stable.

Then she watched warily as the whore approached, crimson feather bobbing with every step. "There's no need to look so frightened," Dolly objected, "I don't bite. At least, not unless I'm paid to." She grinned and settled herself on the hay bale and patted the spot beside her. "Now, why don't you sit right here and tell me what you're doing in that getup."

Alex looked nervously over her shoulder.

"You worried about Luke?" Dolly guessed. "Don't tell me that lummox ain't figured it out yet? Men are about the dumbest creatures God put on this earth, I swear. Don't you worry your pretty head about Luke." She patted the hay bale again. "Seline caught him and, believe me, she won't be letting him get away in a hurry."

Dolly laughed when she saw the shadow pass over Alex's face. "Not you too? That man sure does leave a string of broken hearts behind him." She began to laugh harder. "And as far as he knows, you're a *boy,* so he ain't even turned the charm on you yet."

"He does seem a bit of a flirt," Alex said darkly, succumbing to Dolly's beckoning pats and joining her on the hay bale. She didn't want to admit it to herself, but she was hungry for details about Luke Slater.

"Oh now, he don't mean no harm. It's just how he is. Mix that gentleness and sweetness with those looks, and he don't even need to flirt."

"But he does."

"He sure does," Dolly agreed, "but there ain't a woman in the world who'd want him to stop."

"I heard mention about a girl back in Oregon?" Alex fiddled with a stalk poking up out of the bale.

Dolly's eyes narrowed. "You've got it worse than I thought."

Alex flushed and was glad for the layer of dirt to hide it.

"Whyn't you tell me why you're hiding behind that muck?"

There was so much concern in Dolly's voice that Alex found tears springing to her eyes. It seemed so long since anyone had asked after her. She'd spent every waking moment since her foster parents had died worrying about other people. She'd forgotten how nice it was to be the center of someone else's attention.

Dolly noticed the tears and removed a handkerchief from

her corset, pressing it into the girl's hand. She rubbed motherly circles on Alex's back and clucked softly.

Against her better judgment, Alex poured out the entire sorry tale. Except for the bit where she stole the gold. "Silas won't stop until he's got me in front of a preacher," Alex said despairingly.

"Oh, pet." Dolly drew Alex to her bosom and dropped a sympathetic kiss on her head. She knew how it felt to be responsible and alone.

"You sure don't waste any time," Luke drawled from the doorway.

Alex leaped free of Dolly's embrace. How much had he heard?

"I think he's a little young, Doll."

There was a woman hanging off him, Alex noticed. The same redhead she'd found him in bed with. She was out in broad daylight in her underclothes, with her corset laced so tight it pushed her large breasts almost all the way to her chin.

"Too young?" Dolly tossed her head, sending the crimson feather shivering and dancing. "Darlin', as long as the equipment's all there and operating, who cares how old it is?"

"I care," Luke said shortly. "The boy and his family are traveling with me and I promised his sister I'd watch out for him."

Alex's mouth popped open. What had Victoria said?

"She pretty, this sister?" Seline asked, narrowing her eyes.

Alex thought she saw a flash of impatience on Luke's face but it was gone almost before she could register it. He looked down at the redhead and grinned. "Now, don't be jealous. You know nobody can compare to you."

Dolly cleared her throat.

"Except for your employer, of course. She outshines the sun itself."

Dolly snorted. "Enough nonsense. I've talked to the boy about that overpriced gluepot. I'll keep him on one condition."

"What's that?" Luke and Alex asked simultaneously.

"The boy has to come up to the house and have a bath. He's a disgrace."

"I told him so the other night," Luke agreed, "but he wouldn't wash."

Alex was shaking her head vehemently. What was the crazy woman thinking?

"You take his brother back to his hotel," Dolly instructed Luke, "and I'll take care of the boy."

"No," Seline whined, wrapping herself around Luke. "He was going to come upstairs with me."

"He can go upstairs when he comes back."

"I have to buy some oxen first. Give me what's left in that bag"—Luke held his hand out to Alex—"and Adam and I will buy the animals."

"I think I'd better come," Alex said hurriedly, thinking of the Gradys.

"Nonsense," Dolly snapped. "I'll bet you know next to nothing about livestock. Let Luke go." She snatched the bag of gold off Alex and tossed it across to Luke.

"It'll be safe with me," Luke said softly, meeting her eye. And for some reason she believed him.

"Now, come on with you." Dolly grabbed Alex by the arm and marched her out of the stable, ignoring her protests.

"What are you doing?" Alex demanded, but Dolly refused to answer until she'd ordered a bath from the kitchen maid and sequestered them in a room upstairs.

"Here," Dolly said abruptly, removing a key from the bunch at her waist.

Alex looked at the key in bewilderment.

"This room is empty at the moment. Delia went and married one of those wagoners." She pressed the key into Alex's palm. "There's an outside staircase to the balcony and the door opens onto the landing right outside this door. You can come and go as you please."

"I don't understand."

Dolly rested one hand against Alex's grimy cheek. "You ain't got the slightest idea of the trip ahead of you, darlin'. It's going to be long and difficult, and you're going to be coated in that muck the entire way. Let me at least give you a place you can come to before you leave; a place where you can be a girl for a bit. You get in that bath when it comes and you enjoy it, you hear? You can dirty yourself up again right after, but at least while you're in here you can be fresh and pretty again for a while."

Alex could feel the tears welling again. "Why would you do this for me?" she whispered.

"Because I know what it's like to be a woman alone in this world, and it ain't easy."

"I'm not alone."

Dolly rolled her eyes. "You're worse than alone, pet. You're *responsible*."

The door creaked open and the kitchen maid appeared with a tin tub. Alex turned away to hide her tears.

"You ask a couple of them lazy whores to help you haul some water, Mary," Dolly told the maid sharply. "Don't let them get away with sitting on their fat behinds while you do all the work."

When they'd heard the maid's steps fade down the stairwell, Dolly's scarlet lips split into a terrific grin. "Now, let's see what I've got for you." She opened the wardrobe and began pulling out petticoats and gowns, feathers and ribbons and lace. "I want to see how pretty we can make you!"

She had no idea.

As Alex undressed, Dolly couldn't believe what she was seeing. Gone was the ragtag boy, with his beanpole figure and big childlike eyes. In his place was one of the most spectacular women Dolly had seen in her entire life. And she'd seen a few.

She wasn't supposed to be looking, but she couldn't resist—she peeked in the mirror as Alex undressed. And was so surprised she turned and stared openly.

She could make a fortune if she had this one on her books.

The girl had an almost perfect hourglass figure, with a dramatic waist and lusciously curving hips. Her breasts were full and firm, and her skin was creamy and unblemished, the shade of a ripening peach in its first sun-warmed blush.

Dolly had to force herself to turn away. She was having fantasies of taking the chit downstairs and auctioning her off, the way the stallion had been auctioned off earlier in the day. Dolly thought Alex would have a fair chance of fetching even more gold than the stallion had. "What did your people do?" she asked, trying to distract herself from thoughts of all that money . . .

"Pa Sparrow was a preacher," Alex sighed as she sank into the deliciously warm water.

Ah. Dolly's fantasies evaporated. She had no chance of turning a preacher's daughter into a whore. Resigning herself to simply being a Good Samaritan, Dolly moved to the tub and helped Alex wash her newly shortened hair. Alex scrubbed her face and slowly the mask of dirt dissolved. Dolly found herself once again astonished.

"How can anyone think you're a boy?" she exclaimed. The girl was simply beautiful—ripe lips, smoky-gray eyes, and a stubborn little chin with the hint of a cleft. There was nothing masculine about her whatsoever.

"They don't, unless I wear all the dirt," Alex admitted ruefully. "And those." She gestured a dripping hand toward the bandages lying discarded on the floor. She still had marks on her chest from where the bindings had bitten into her flesh.

"I can see why that Grady varmint ain't giving up without a fight!"

Alex pulled a face at her, and then sighed happily and reclined back in the tub. She hadn't felt so relaxed since . . . she didn't know when. She inhaled the scent of the soap, a pleasant musky rose, and wished she could stay right here forever—warm and clean and safe.

"You'll wrinkle up like a prune if you stay in much longer," Dolly clucked. She noticed the disappointment on the girl's lovely face and smiled. "I ain't kicking you out." She gathered up Adam's old clothes with a grimace. "I'm going to take these filthy things and get Mary to wash 'em for you. It's a warm enough day—they ought to dry on the line in no time. In the meantime, why don't you lie down and have a rest. I'll bring your clothes back when they're dry." She tossed some clean undergarments on the bed before she left, her crimson feather dancing merrily.

Alex looked at the brass bed. Its covers were turned down

invitingly and a couple of plump feather pillows beckoned. She supposed a little nap wouldn't hurt . . .

LUKE THOUGHT HE'D have to use every bit of his charm to get Dolly to stable the oxen. She didn't like livestock. She said they smelled. So he was astonished when she agreed at once.

"Tell my boy to make sure he feeds and waters them," she said, pouring them both a drink. Luke narrowed his eyes as he watched her toss back the whiskey.

"Oh, I get it," he said, as an idea dawned on him, "you got your hands on some of the lad's gold too." He sighed. "What did I tell you, Doll? I'm s'posed to be looking after him, not fixing him up with whores. The kid must be about twelve." Luke gave her a disgusted look.

"He's older than he looks," Dolly said dryly.

"What, thirteen?"

"Don't you go gettin' all high and mighty on me, Luke Slater. I bet you'd dipped your wick by his age."

"We ain't discussing my wick."

"Seline!" Dolly bellowed with a wicked grin, summoning the whore Luke was avoiding. Luke winced.

"That ain't fair," he muttered.

"You looked pretty friendly with her before—she seems to think you were coming back for a visit."

Luke grunted. He'd been perfectly happy to see Seline in the kitchen earlier, but then she'd gone and got all tense and jealous about Victoria. Now she'd probably be pouty with him, and want to be petted and reassured.

Dolly took pity on him. "Go hide upstairs. I'll send Ruth or Ellen up before Seline can find you."

"Maybe I'll just head back to Ralph Taylor's," he said glumly, remembering Ruth's face the last time he'd left her. Like he'd cut off her arm or something.

"I'll give you both of them for the price of one," Dolly offered quickly, worried she might be losing a sale. And not only today's sale—what if he stopped coming altogether? When he was in town, Luke was a good customer. She'd have to give the girls a stern talking-to.

They heard the faint sound of Seline's voice in the kitchen and Luke looked to the front door for an escape route. Through the frosted glass of the window he could see the silhouettes of a few of the girls sunning themselves on the porch. He was trapped.

He headed for the stairs.

"I'll send them up," Dolly called after him, happily draining Luke's untouched whiskey too.

"Not Ruth," he called back over his shoulder.

When he reached the upstairs corridor he paused. All of the doors were shut, and he had no idea which ones were occupied and which weren't. Margaret's room, Cora's room, Gracie's room . . . he didn't want to see any of them. He considered the doors indecisively.

"Delia," he announced to the empty corridor. Delia wasn't the prettiest woman in the world, or the cheeriest for that matter (she always wore a look like her dog had just died), but she wasn't prone to hysterics either. She'd never cried on him as far as he could remember, or begged him to take her with him when he left. The worst she ever did was look up at him with those mopey basset hound eyes.

"Was that Luke I heard?" Seline's voice carried through the cathouse, deciding Luke once and for all. He hightailed it down the corridor and into Delia's room at the far end. He closed the door as softly as he could, hoping Seline wouldn't hear it. Hoping none of them would hear it.

"Sorry, love," he apologized quietly, turning his warmest smile on mopey Delia. Only . . . mopey Delia wasn't there.

There was a woman in the bed, but it sure as hell wasn't Delia. His eyes traced the contours of her body through the thin sheet. This woman wasn't even the same species as Delia. This one was all lush curves and hollows . . . arcs of warm flesh that made a man's palms ache to touch them. Her face was buried in the pillow, hidden from him, but her neck was a graceful creamy arch where he could see the faint beat of her pulse and had an idle impulse to press his lips against it. The vision sighed in her sleep and shifted. The sheet fell, revealing a skimpy white linen chemise . . . and a bounty of divine ivory flesh.

Drawn irresistibly, Luke crept closer. Why hadn't Dolly

told him about this beauty? He sank onto the bed beside her. She was even more perfect close up. There wasn't a blemish on that smooth skin. And this close he could see the full out-line of her breasts through the whisper-thin material; they were full and round, and he could see the dark stain of her nipples though the linen.

He couldn't help himself. He traced a fingertip slowly around the shadow, watching as it hardened, reaching toward him in silent invitation. He saw the pulse leap in her neck and, acting on the impulse this time, he lowered his head to kiss the hollow where it throbbed. Her skin was hot and damp under his lips and she smelled of musk and roses.

She moaned ever so softly and turned, and Luke saw her face. Beautiful. He'd never seen a whore like her.

What must Dolly be charging? It didn't matter, Luke decided, this one was worth any price. Look at those lips—wide and full, and the color of ripe strawberries.

Damn the expense.

Luke leaned over her and pressed a featherlight kiss against the strawberry lips. She tasted like powdered sugar. He kissed her again, more firmly, and when she moaned he slid his tongue against the moist opening of her lips.

Alex was having strange dreams. She was back home, watching the house burn. And then the fire had moved to her belly and was licking through her like wildfire. Her breasts felt full and heavy, and she was arching . . .

She woke with a gasp.

Wouldn't you know it, Luke thought, looking into wide gray eyes the color of a rainstorm: beautiful.

"What are you doing?" The words escaped her breathlessly.

Even her voice was beautiful: low and husky, it was like warm fingers running down his spine.

Alex tried to gather her thoughts. It was Luke. Luke was sitting beside her on the bed, looking at her with a burning black gaze. She couldn't think, not while he was so close, not while he was looking at her like that. Why *was* he looking at her like that?

Alex remembered and gasped again, scrabbling for the sheet. Oh glory, she wasn't dressed! She wasn't wearing Adam's clothes, or the mud! He knew!

"Ah love, there's no need for that," he said warmly, taking the edge of the sheet in his long brown fingers and giving it a tug.

She held on to it with a death grip.

"It's all right," he coaxed, edging closer, and pulling insistently until the sheet came free, "money is no object."

Money? Alex frowned. Then she realized he was staring and followed his gaze to her breasts. Glory! The undergarments Dolly had left for her were indecent. She might as well be wearing nothing at all. And, Alex realized, mortified, her nipples were jutting through the thin fabric, dark and insistent.

She made to cover herself but Luke caught her wrists. "Don't," he said huskily, "you're beautiful."

He looked into her eyes and she couldn't breathe. So *this* was why Victoria was acting like such a ninny. The man had some kind of power . . . Alex could feel herself becoming liquid, melting like silver over a smithy fire, becoming malleable in his hands.

There was such tenderness in those hot black eyes. Tenderness and . . . something else, something wicked.

When he moved to kiss her she was too stunned to protest. His lips were firm, commanding. He pulled her toward him, until she was pressed against the hard length of him, and she could feel the cold edge of his belt buckle against her stomach. As his tongue traced the inside line of her lips, coaxing them open, his hands ran up her arms and over her shoulders, finally coming to rest cupping her face. His thumbs rubbed lazy circles beneath her earlobes.

Could you die from a kiss?

Oh, she was good, Luke thought as he broke the kiss and looked down into her eyes. They were smoky with desire. Eyes like that could drive a man wild.

And then there was the way she kept her lips slightly parted, as her breath came fast and shallow, causing her firm, round breasts to stretch the fine linen, until he thought the fragile fastening might break. All so seemingly artless . . .

He ran his finger down the long arch of her neck, lingering briefly on the leaping pulse, and she shivered. He followed the curve of her breast, into the dip of her cleavage, and came to rest on the small cloth-covered button that held the gaping chemise together.

Stop. The word rang in her head, but she couldn't make herself say it. She was mesmerized by the look of wonder in his eyes, by the way the trail of his finger left a blaze of heat in its wake. This is wrong, she thought witlessly, but for the life of her she couldn't gather her thoughts for long enough to think why.

For a long breathless moment they both watched his fingers fiddle with the tiny button, and then with a flick the button slid free of its fastening and the chemise fell open, sending her tumbling free.

Perfect. It was the only word to describe her. Desire surged through him like a flood.

Some small rational part of Alex's mind was screaming at her to say something, to run, to save her honor. But the rest of her wasn't listening.

She wanted him to touch her. She'd wanted it since the first moment she'd seen him in the bathhouse. And *she* wanted to touch *him* . . .

Why *didn't* he touch her? She was aching for it. There was a strange pulse inside of her, slow and tantalizing, causing her to arch toward him, ever so slightly. When he did reach out, his fingertips seared her, white-hot, and her eyelids fluttered closed. Oh glory, who knew? Who knew anything could feel this good . . . At the first moist flicker against her nipple her eyes flew open again. He was using his *mouth* . . .

Neither of them heard the click of the door opening. But they both heard the shriek. And a moment later mean hands were clawing at Alex's hair.

❦ 10 ❦

"HELL AND DAMNATION, Seline," Luke growled, pulling the whore bodily away from Alex.

"Let me go!" Seline spat, kicking and bucking like a wild animal.

Alex's scalp was stinging from the assault, but she had enough wits about her to cover herself with the sheet and brace herself in the corner of the room. Who knew if the crazy woman would get away from Luke and come after her again?

"I ain't running a boxing ring!" Dolly bellowed as she appeared in the doorway. She put her hands on her hips and surveyed the tableaux before her. Behind her, a dozen curious faces appeared.

Alex blushed, miserably aware of her state of undress and her kiss-swollen lips.

"Who the hell is she!" Seline shrieked.

Wild-eyed, Alex looked to Dolly for help.

The madam cleared her throat awkwardly, and fingered her paste necklace. "If you must know, this is my cousin . . . Beatrice. Just arrived into town this afternoon."

"I didn't see her arrive," Gracie said suspiciously.

"Don't see how you could have," Dolly sniffed, "as you ain't stirred from the porch all day. Lazy cow."

"Lazy!" Gracie scowled. "I make you more money than all the rest of them put together."

"Now, hang on a minute," a skinny brunette complained, "I make at least as much as you do!"

Alex pulled the sheet higher and wished they'd go argue somewhere else. She wanted to get dressed so she could scurry back to Adam and Victoria. She grimaced, imagining the lecture she'd get from Victoria if her sister ever found out about what had happened . . . Her gaze drifted to the bed.

"Oh, who cares about how much money you make," Seline shouted, drawing Alex's attention back to the chaos in the doorway. The redhead was still clamped between Luke's strong arms. Alex couldn't help noticing the hard play of muscles beneath the burnished skin of his forearms, the rich color of his skin contrasting so magnificently with the creamy white of his shirtsleeves, which were rolled up to the elbow. Her gaze followed the bulging line of his arm, across the enormous width of his shoulders, up to that lean face. Her breath caught in her throat when she realized that he was looking right at her. And had, in fact, noticed her perusal of him. As she watched he returned the favor, and the heat of his gaze as it traveled the length of her barely clad body was like a physical caress. She blushed.

"And who cares if she's your cousin," Seline was carping. "Luke was mine this afternoon!"

"Only because you didn't give him a choice," Gracie snapped. "He might have wanted to be with me."

"Or with me," the brunette chipped in.

Seline snorted. "You? He ain't been with you, Cora, since you tried to stow away in his wagon."

The brunette gave a squeal and launched herself across the room at Seline. Luke caught her with one hand, struggling to keep Seline contained with the other. "That's enough!" he hollered, his deep voice shaking the lamps. "Would you all get out of here. The lady and I were in the middle of something."

"No, we weren't!" Alex squeaked.

A dozen pairs of hateful eyes turned on her. She lifted her chin and glared right back at them.

"I beg to differ," Luke said, his voice growing lower and huskier.

The hateful eyes grew murderous. Glory, Alex thought, she'd be lucky to get out of this room alive.

"She ain't a whore, Luke," Dolly interrupted sternly.

Alex collapsed against the wall behind her in relief. Surely that would save her?

It didn't.

Seline gave a bloodcurdling scream and hurled herself toward Alex. Alex scampered over the bed and grabbed the brass spittoon by the wardrobe. She brandished it at the attacking whore like a weapon, only to find her already recaptured by Luke.

"Not a whore!" Seline was sputtering. "So she's *giving* it away! Why the hell would he come to any of us, when she's giving it away for free!"

"Don't tell me you've never given him a freebie," Dolly observed darkly.

"Ain't you even a little mad that you won't be getting any money from him because of her?" Seline goaded.

Dolly's eyes narrowed. She looked back and forth between Alex and Luke.

"It was a misunderstanding," Luke told her with a regretful sigh. He looked over at the beauty, who was still holding the spittoon like it was a battle-ax. She'd left the sheet in the corner of the room, and was magnificently displayed in the sheerest of linen. Legs as perfect as the rest of her. "I thought she was a new girl," he said.

"No," Dolly replied, also with a sigh of regret, as she too regarded the curves revealed by the skimpy underwear. The chemise was still gaping, revealing the ripe swell of Alex's cleavage. "I wish she were. But Beatrice here is a preacher's daughter. The working life ain't for her."

A preacher's daughter? Luke's eyebrows shot up in surprise. He hadn't thought a preacher's daughter could kiss like that. "You're related to a preacher?" he drawled, giving Dolly a dubious look.

She raised her nose in the air. "I'm a Christian woman," the whore said proudly, ignoring the titter from the girls behind her. "Now, you lot clear out so my cousin can make herself decent."

"I'm still free . . ." Seline said invitingly, tilting her head to look up at Luke. He dropped her in disgust.

"Sorry about the mix-up," Dolly apologized. "Any of the others will look after you."

"I've lost my appetite," Luke replied, his gaze lingering on Alex. Dolly sighed. That was the problem. You couldn't show a man a steak dinner and then serve him cabbage soup . . .

"It was a pleasure meeting you, Miss Beatrice," Luke said slowly, holding her gaze. "I'm sorry if I gave any offense." He noticed the way she was breathing quickly and a languid smile spread across his lips. "Hopefully I'll see you again before I leave."

He inclined his head politely and headed back downstairs to take care of the oxen. He whistled as he went. There'd been no mistaking the desire in those hazy gray eyes, or the earlier heat of her kiss. Luke had a feeling that if he got her alone again she'd forget all about being a preacher's daughter . . .

Alex turned scarlet under Dolly's amused and knowing stare. *"Beatrice?"* she asked, in an effort to distract the older woman. She wrinkled her nose at the name.

Dolly shrugged. "It was the best I could do off the top of my head. I do have a cousin Beatrice, only she ain't a preacher's daughter, and she's nowhere near as pretty as you. In fact, she ain't pretty at all."

"Are my clothes dry?"

Dolly lifted an eyebrow.

"I should be getting back now," Alex said evasively.

"Oh, I'll get them for you," Dolly told her, sinking down onto the mattress and leaning back on her arms. "As soon as you tell me what was happening in here to make Seline so jealous."

If it was possible, Alex turned an even more vivid shade of scarlet. "I was sleeping when he came in." Her voice was shaking, so she paused.

Dolly's eyes twinkled wickedly. "So our dashing Mr. Slater came in and found Sleeping Beauty. I can just imagine the look on his face—he must have thought he'd struck gold."

"When I woke up he was kissing me," Alex admitted.

Dolly grinned. "And you, being a good preacher's daughter, screamed and slapped him roundly across the face."

Alex regarded her feet miserably and Dolly collapsed, laughing. "Oh darlin'," she gasped, "there ain't nothing to be ashamed of. That man could have a nun flat on her back in a minute."

"I thought you were a Christian woman," Alex scolded, scandalized.

"So how did it feel?"

"What?" Alex snapped, being deliberately obtuse.

Dolly laughed again. "Fine. Keep it to yourself. I'll send Mary up with your clothes and a pot of muck."

"What is everyone going to think when 'Beatrice' disappears?" Alex asked her curiously.

Dolly gave a dismissive wave of her hand. "Oh, I'll just tell them you were disgusted by my profession and left to stay at a respectable hotel."

"Oh." Alex looked at the room key, still lying on the dresser where she'd left it.

"I've got no problem if you still want to use the room," Dolly assured her, "but I think you'd be taking a gamble. That Seline will be watching out for you, and she's mean when she gets riled."

"I noticed," Alex said, gingerly feeling her still-stinging scalp.

"Well, it's been a pleasure," Dolly said, giving her a quick kiss on the cheek. "Do come for a visit—as the boy—before you leave. I ain't been so entertained in years." She paused in the doorway. "Once you've mucked yourself up, head down the balcony stairs, and try to keep out of sight. There's been enough drama today."

Once Dolly had left, Alex moved to the window and peered through the lace curtain. She could see Luke below, drawing water from the well, and striding toward him, hips swinging, was mean old Seline. Alex ground her teeth. She wished Mary would hurry up with her clean clothes; she was itching to hear what the buxom redhead was saying to him.

❖ 11 ❖

LUKE DIDN'T MUCH care to hear what Seline had to say. He'd had it with the lot of them. Moping and weeping and pleading and scolding—like they had some kind of claim on him. "I ain't looking for a wife, you know," he grumbled, as he lugged water into the stable for the oxen. The fact that he was looking after livestock that didn't even belong to him made him feel blacker still. Where the hell was that runt?

"Don't be mad," Seline pouted, following him.

"What else am I s'posed to be? You barge in on me and act like some jealous shrew . . ." He trailed off in disgust and emptied the water into the trough. The two oxen immediately shoved their big slimy noses in and started slurping. He saw Seline eye them with distaste and couldn't resist a grin. "I ought to throw you in there with them."

"I think you're being awful unfair," Seline told him hotly. "You only come to town once a year. Why should I give up my few nights a year just because Dolly's got some cousin who is willing to give it away for free? You did promise you'd come back for a visit with me today."

Luke sighed. "I s'pose I did," he admitted. "And I was going to, but then you got unreasonable about Victoria."

"Victoria?" Seline's face darkened again.

"The runt's sister. And there you go again, looking like some kind of thundercloud."

Seline sashayed closer and rested her palm against his chest; she tilted her head and looked up at him through her lashes. "I'm sorry. You know I'm a passionate girl." Her hand trailed down his chest, to his stomach, and lower. "Ain't that why you like me?" She fitted her body to his and rose on tip-toe to kiss him, her tongue assaulting his mouth instantly.

ALEX COULDN'T BELIEVE it. Within half an hour of leaving her bed he was all over another woman. She grabbed a hay bale and tried to hurl it into the stall where the oxen were still snorting and slurping at the trough. The bale bounced off the rail and thudded into Luke, knocking him and his whore sideways.

"Watch what you're doing," Seline snarled.

"Sorry," Alex muttered, in a voice that implied she wasn't sorry at all.

"Where in the blazes have you been?" Luke said. "I've got better things to do than look after your animals."

I bet, Alex thought sourly, remembering the intense blackness of his gaze and the heat of his kisses. "Dolly tried to make me take a bath," she mumbled, inventing quickly.

"Don't look like she succeeded."

"I don't like baths," Alex said sullenly, even as she thought longingly of the hot water and the musky rose soap she'd enjoyed. What a waste. Now look at her, filthy again, and looking for all the world like a flat-chested, prepubescent boy.

"I'm amazed Dolly let you touch her, looking like that."

Alex blinked.

"Don't look all innocent at me," Luke accused. "She went and confessed everything. In my book you're far too young. Mark my words, you've time enough to waste your gold chasing after women."

"Hypocrite," Seline giggled. "Don't listen to him, you can come and waste your gold with me any day."

Alex gave her a black look.

"Here's your change." Luke tossed her the bag of gold. It was considerably lighter, and the few pieces left made a disconsolate clicking sound as she caught it. She glanced over at Blackie Junior, happily munching on his oats. What had she been thinking? What did she need with a horse?

It was all *his* fault; she wouldn't have even been at the auction if it hadn't been for him. He was nothing but trouble. Alex glared at him.

Luke didn't notice. He was too distracted by Seline's wandering hands. "I'll go for half-price," she was whispering in his ear, "and I'll make it *all* up to you."

Alex scowled. The man didn't care which woman he was with. She had to resist the urge to give him a kick.

"Make sure they're fed," Luke told Alex absently as he let Seline lead him from the stable.

ALEX HAD TO bite her tongue at dinner that night when Victoria was singing his praises. They were holed up in their room, eating picnic-style on the bed, hiding from the Gradys.

"Don't you think it's the sign of a true gentleman to look after us this way?" Victoria twittered.

"We're paying him," Alex grumbled.

"Speaking of money," her sister said, pausing and pursing her lips, "Luke told me what you did."

Alex's head snapped up and her cheeks flared scarlet. For an instant she could feel the brush of his fingers against her bare skin and that strange, insistent pulse deep inside . . .

"The horse?" Victoria prompted.

Of course. Blackie Junior. Alex pressed her cool palms to her cheeks, silently berating herself. Luke had no idea he'd kissed her today. In his mind, he'd kissed Dolly's cousin.

"You know we need that money," Victoria said primly, "but Luke said not to scold you. He said that you did it out of the goodness of your heart. That you knew he didn't have the money here in Missouri to pay for the horse. He told me about how when we get to Oregon he's going to buy the horse off us."

"He did, did he?" Alex said darkly. Why that mercenary . . .

"We're not selling Blackie Junior are we, Alex?" Adam asked in alarm, looking up from the mashed potato he'd been shoveling into his mouth.

"Don't talk with your mouth full," Victoria reprimanded him. "Where are your manners?"

Alex gave Adam's arm a squeeze and shook her head ever so slightly, and he returned to his potatoes happy. She'd be damned if she'd give that man the satisfaction.

"Luke's arranged a meeting of everyone in our party tomorrow at Mrs. Tilly's Tearooms," Victoria chattered happily. "So we can see who we're traveling with, and so he can give us some final instructions."

"When exactly did he tell you this?"

"When he brought Adam back. He showed me the oxen—they really are ugly, aren't they? I think I should have preferred mules. But I suppose Luke knows best."

Alex wondered when he'd become "Luke" instead of "Mr. Slater." He was a fast worker, that was for sure. She bit her lip as she regarded Victoria's dreamy expression. She sure would hate for her sister to get hurt.

She was mighty tempted to tell him so, the next day at the tearooms, when he greeted Victoria with an enormous smile. Victoria practically turned to liquid. Flirting with whores was one thing, but leading on an innocent like her sister . . .

"Now we're all here, I'm going to make a few announcements, and run through the equipment and supplies you should have, and then we'll just take the time to get to know one another," Luke declared after they had settled themselves in Mrs. Tilly's side room.

Mrs. Tilly was a widow in her fifties. She had rosy cheeks and sparkling blue eyes, and was clearly smitten with Luke.

"He always holds his meetings here," she had confided in Alex and Victoria when she led them through to the room. "Such a lovely man."

"Isn't he?" Victoria agreed with a sigh.

Alex had to restrain herself from snorting. Lovely man, my foot, she thought sullenly; he just knows how to wind every female of the species around his little finger. Just look at him now, up there at the front of the room, comfortable with every eye upon him, oozing charm, making sure to make eye contact with each and every one of them. She was gratified when he blinked, startled, as he met her evil stare. Not everyone is taken in by you, she snarled silently.

She was so busy with her evil thoughts that she didn't hear a word he said. She supposed it didn't matter, as Luke himself had helped to outfit them, but she found she couldn't join in any of the conversation afterward. Then again, no one really expected her to—they all thought she was just a child. She even found herself ushered over to the table set up in the corner for the children. All of them were between the ages of five and ten, except for fifteen-year-old Jane O'Brien, and they amused themselves by torturing one another and throwing food.

Alex didn't like the way Jane was looking at her. "How old are you?" the girl asked. She was one of three sisters and had big brown eyes and a spattering of freckles across her nose.

Alex cleared her throat; she was still uncomfortable with lying. She was almost twenty, but she forced herself to say, "Sixteen."

"You don't look sixteen."

"I'm taller than you."

Jane gave her a shy look through her eyelashes and Alex's heart sank. She knew that look. It was the look Victoria kept giving Luke. Fortunately, Mrs. Tilly chose that moment to deliver plates of sandwiches and pastries to their table. "I know you children aren't too fond of tea, so I've made a nice batch of lemonade. With extra sugar." She gave them a wink.

"Do you think I could have some tea, please?" Alex asked politely.

"Me too," Jane said quickly. "After all, we're really not children anymore."

"Of course not," Mrs. Tilly agreed, beaming at them and clucking like a mother hen. "I'll bring over a pot."

"Where are you from?" Jane asked, and Alex looked longingly at the other table, where the adults were getting to know one another. Victoria was sitting between Adam and a bookish-looking man, but she was desperately trying to catch Luke's eye.

Luke was too busy talking to a bunch of the men to notice.

"That's my father," Jane said, following Alex's gaze, and Alex realized she meant the bookish man next to her sister.

"I'm with Victoria and Adam. Next to him."

"You're family? You don't look like them."

Alex wondered how on earth she could tell, what with all the muck Alex had smothered on herself. "I'm adopted," she explained shortly.

After another few minutes at the children's table, fending off cucumber-sandwich missiles and Jane's attentions, Alex just wanted to leave. But she could tell by the stubborn look on Victoria's face that she was planning to stay to the bitter end, in the hopes of catching a moment alone with Luke.

"You're in a foul mood today," a voice drawled from above, and she looked up into those horribly familiar black eyes.

One of the boys chose that precise moment to hurl a strawberry tart at her; it landed with a wet squelch against her cheek and the table erupted into giggles. "I can't imagine why," Alex told him dryly, wiping strawberry jam from her face.

"I suppose now that you're . . . all grown up . . . you think you don't belong with the children." His eyes were twinkling and she knew by "all grown up" he was referring to the experience he assumed she'd had with Dolly.

"Oh, Mr. Slater," Jane exclaimed in her defense, "there's an awfully big difference between ten and sixteen."

"Sixteen?" His eyes narrowed dubiously as he considered Alex.

She set her jaw stubbornly and stared right back at him. "Nearly seventeen."

"That's practically a man," Jane said earnestly.

"Jane and Alex sitting in a tree," her younger sisters, Susan and Ellen, chorused in singsong voices. Jane picked up splattered strawberry tart and threw it at them.

Luke laughed at the long-suffering expression on Alex's face. "I came over to get you, runt. I want you to show the Watts brothers the way to our *friend's* place." He lowered his voice significantly and Alex realized he meant Dolly's cathouse.

"I wouldn't mind a walk . . ." Jane hinted.

Both Luke and Alex looked at her, horrified.

"Ah . . . I've got to feed our animals right after," Alex lied.

Jane's face fell. "But you'll be at the dance tomorrow night?"

"I guess so." Victoria had spent the last two days trying to convince Alex it was safe to go. *They think that you abandoned us and are heading east,* her sister had said as she happily sewed her new dress. *What's the bet they're on a steamboat this minute, heading back to St. Louis.* Alex wasn't convinced. But they were about to leave civilization for a good long while and she didn't have the heart to disappoint her sister. She could only hope that when Gideon found no trace of a blond woman spending his gold here in Independence he would follow the rumor east.

Jane gave Alex a shy smile as she rose from the table. "Maybe we could have a dance?"

"I don't dance."

Luke laughed and clapped her on the shoulder. "He's just being modest, Miss O'Brien. Alex is a great dancer—he'd love to dance with you."

Alex took care to tread on his foot as she passed him, and resolved to tell Seline that he wanted to see her tonight. And then she might tell Flora, Margaret and Gracie the same thing. They'd just see how he liked dealing with the four of them.

"Your sister ain't spoken for?" Henry Watts asked Alex curiously as she led them to Dolly's. Alex gave him a sour look. She didn't appreciate him asking after her sister when he was off to visit a whore. "She sure is pretty," he said.

"Sure is," his brother Joseph echoed. "And not in an obvious way. She looks like a real decent girl."

"She is," Alex said shortly.

She didn't go into Dolly's when they got there. She watched them mount the front steps and then turned and dragged her feet back to the hotel. Victoria and Adam weren't back yet. She lay on the bed and stared at the water stains on the ceiling. She felt tangled up and out of sorts, and for once it had nothing to do with the Gradys, or with finding enough food, or with getting them out to Oregon. All she could think about were the swirling currents of a wicked black gaze . . .

She turned her head and saw Victoria's new yellow dress hanging from the door. It was simple but very pretty, the cheery color of sunshine and buttercups. It would suit Victoria's coloring tremendously. Alex pictured her at the dance, a graceful sunbeam, pretty and feminine, twirling around the floor . . . led by strong muscular arms. Her chestnut hair would be pulled up into a loose cascade of curls—or maybe she'd even wear it down, the way Alex no longer could—and she would stare blissfully up into those tender, teasing, seductive eyes.

Alex's insides twisted with jealousy. If only she could dance with him. She closed her eyes. She could imagine the way his hands would feel on her body . . . Only she didn't need to imagine, she thought with a sigh. She knew how it felt.

It felt like heaven.

❖ 12 ❖

EVERYBODY IN INDEPENDENCE turned out for the Saturday night dances. Almost weekly there was a new batch of wagoners about to head out, feeling merry and ready to kick up their heels.

The town square was hung with paper lanterns and lined with stalls selling ale, lemonade, sandwiches, corn on the cob and cakes. Children ran squealing through the dusky lavender twilight as the band tuned up on the courthouse steps.

Victoria looked prettier than she ever had in her life. Her chestnut hair hung straight and glossy to her waist, adorned with a blue satin ribbon. The yellow dress fit her like a glove and made the most of her slender figure, and the color made her skin glow. Alex was green with envy. Not that anyone could tell—the green tinge to her skin was well camouflaged by the dirt.

The members of their party had claimed a trestle table under the large sycamore, and Alex watched them greet Victoria warmly. The single men snatched their hats off their heads and practically tripped over one another in an effort to offer Alex's sister a drink, a seat, a sweet or their hand for the first dance.

No one even noticed scruffy old Alex.

At least no one except Jane O'Brien. "Oh, you came," she exclaimed, blushing prettily. "I wasn't sure you would. You look . . . nice."

Alex looked down at herself and wondered if the girl was blind. Then she noticed the way Jane was plucking at her own blue dress and realized that she was expected to return the compliment. "You look nice too," she said glumly.

"Would you like to take a walk and get some lemonade?"

"Jane." Ned O'Brien was striding toward them, giving Alex a hard look.

Jane started guiltily. "Oh, Daddy. Alex and I were just going for a walk."

Ned shook his head. "I'd like to talk with young Mr. Alexander, if you don't mind."

"Oh, Daddy," she sighed, but she obeyed. Alex noticed she kept shooting wistful glances back over her shoulder as she went.

"Now," Ned said, looking deep into Alex's eyes, "I don't want you to get any ideas regarding my daughter."

Alex flushed, feeling inexplicably like a criminal.

"She's very young and she's led a sheltered life. She doesn't know how forward she can seem."

"No, sir," Alex mumbled.

Ned cleared his throat. "I saw you at," he lowered his voice, *"Dolly's* the other day."

Alex wished the ground would open and swallow her up.

"And I can't say that I approve," the easterner continued, "but I'm not your father. What I will say is that we have a long trip ahead of us, and I expect you to treat my daughters the way you would treat your own sister."

Alex felt as though the dirt had soaked through her skin. She'd never be able to clean it off. Not only did people look at her and see a scruffy boy, they saw a scruffy reprobate, the kind of person no decent parent would let their daughter associate with. How ashamed Ma and Pa Sparrow would be of her, let alone her own parents. All of them must be turning in their graves. Alex slunk to the table, feeling like the lowest of the low.

"Why, Miss Victoria," a smooth voice said, sliding through Alexandra's funk, "aren't you a sight for sore eyes."

Alex couldn't believe the change in him. She'd never seen Luke Slater dressed up before. The man looked wonderful in rumpled traveling clothes, incredible in his everyday wear, magnificent wearing nothing at all, but there just weren't words to describe him when he was dressed up in his best suit.

The cut of the jacket made his shoulders seem wider and

his body longer and leaner, and the brilliant white of his shirt made his skin look very dark. He'd had a haircut, Alex noticed, and a close shave. Somehow, he looked even more masculine now that the high cheekbones and strong jaw were smooth.

Alex was having trouble breathing. And so too, she realized, was Victoria.

Luke took her sister's hand and lifted it to his lips. Alex couldn't tear her gaze away. "You look pretty as a picture in yellow."

Alex wanted to scream. How could he look at her sister that way? After . . . after *what*, she thought scornfully. After he looked at you with those hot black eyes, when he thought you were a whore?

But she couldn't help the acid feeling in her stomach when she watched Luke lead Victoria onto the makeshift dance floor. She was mesmerized by the sight of his large brown hand on her sister's buttercup yellow back, and by the flirtatious smile he aimed down at her. What was he saying? What was he whispering in her ear? Oh, it wasn't fair. She just bet if she had come dressed in a yellow dress Luke wouldn't spare Victoria a second glance. It was a mean thought, but Alex couldn't shake it. Mentally, she ran through the dresses she owned—her old blue, the dove-gray, the muslin sprigged with bunches of pink roses—and imagined prettying herself up and coming down to the dance. What would he think? Would he ask her to dance? Would he want to kiss her again?

"What's got you smiling like a halfwit?" Luke asked her as he joined them at the table. Sebastian Doyle, the driver of the chuck wagon, had claimed Victoria for the next dance.

"Nothing." Alex tried to compose herself. She was dreadfully aware of Luke's thigh brushing against hers on the narrow bench.

"She's a mighty fine dancer, your sister."

Alex grunted.

"Your brother ain't bad either." Luke nodded to where Adam was enthusiastically squiring five-year-old Ellen O'Brien. "How come you're not out there? That Jane seemed pretty keen on you."

Alex gave him a dark look and he laughed. "I know it ain't because you're too young for girls," he teased.

Alex wanted to kick him.

"I'm going to get an ale. You coming? I'll buy you a lemonade."

She went, despite her violent feeling toward him. They joined the Watts brothers at the stall. "Our shout," Joseph insisted, already lugubrious with drink.

"He's a little young," Luke protested when Joseph handed Alex a glass too.

"I'm not that young," she said, irked. She was mighty sick of him treating her like a child. After all, he hadn't thought her childish when he'd come upon her half-naked at Dolly's. Oh no, he'd had no qualms about her age then. She took the ale defiantly.

Luke shrugged but still looked disapproving. "Don't come complaining to me when your head hurts tomorrow."

"One drink won't hurt the lad," Joseph laughed. "We all started sometime."

They stood by the side of the dance floor, drinking and watching the lively swirl.

"She's really not spoken for, your sister?" Henry asked in disbelief.

Alex shook her head and took a gulp of the bitter amber liquid. She had a feeling this was going to be a long journey if she had to watch these men mooning over her sister the whole way. She took a peek at Luke. He was watching Victoria too.

The gray, she decided: if she could, she would wear the dove-gray dress. It matched her eyes and made her skin look paler. She imagined it was *her* Luke was watching on the floor, being twirled about by some other man. Would he be jealous?

But she *couldn't*, she thought morosely, taking another long sip. She couldn't wash her face and dress up in her lovely gray dress. Because of the Gradys. She couldn't risk having them see her.

By the time she finished the ale, Alex was feeling warm and loose-limbed. Rebellious, she bought the next round, and made short work of another ale. Luke shook his head at her and left to dance with Victoria again. Alex couldn't watch any more. The whole night had taken on a nightmarish cast—the music seemed loud and discordant, the lanterns garish, and everywhere she looked she saw the gay flash of yellow skirts.

"I'm going to feed Junior," she told Adam abruptly, stalking up to where he was dancing.

Her brother looked back and forth between her and the dance floor, torn. He was having a fine old time, but the thought of missing out on seeing the horse was torture. "I'll come too," he decided, although he couldn't help looking back over his shoulder as they left. "Aren't we going to tell Victoria where we're going?"

"We'll be back before she misses us," Alex said shortly.

The town was silent and dark as they walked to Dolly's. Everybody was at the dance. Even the whorehouse was quiet when they got there. The piano was still, and there were just a bunch of bored whores sitting around the saloon with a few heavy drinkers.

As soon as they got there Alex had an impulse to find Dolly. She was the only one who'd understand the way Alex was feeling. "You feed the horse, all right, Adam? I'll be back in a minute."

Adam didn't mind. He was in his element in the stable, whispering to Junior and the oxen. "Can I give him a brush, Alex?"

"Sure," she said. "I reckon he'd like that."

When she left he was rummaging through the shelves, looking for the brushes. Alex made for the back door, and was halfway across the kitchen when Dolly came sailing in, resplendent in green satin. "Oh, I wouldn't go in there," she said, catching Alex by the arm and spinning her about.

"I was looking for you."

"Well, you don't want to go in there. Have a look." Dolly pulled the door open a crack and Alex peered through. All the Gradys were at a table in the corner, playing cards.

"Who's winning?" Alex asked dryly.

"The skinny one, who else? He's smarter than the rest of

them put together. All I can say is thank heavens they're big drinkers, because they sure aren't spending money on any of my girls."

"Why not?"

Dolly shrugged. "They'll be upstairs by the end of the night, but that runty one is worried they'll fall asleep and get charged for the whole night."

"Sounds like Gideon."

"What are you doing here?" Dolly demanded. "Why aren't you at that dance?" She pulled a bottle of whiskey and a couple of glasses down from the cupboard. Alex had never seen a woman drink whiskey before. But then, she remembered, she'd never seen a woman drink ale either and she'd had two tonight.

Even so, she refused the whiskey.

"I wish I could go to the dance," Dolly sighed. "All dressed up and flirting with those big handsome men. I saw Luke on his way there." She gave Alex a sly look. "He was looking pretty fine tonight, wasn't he?"

Alex's nod was sour.

"I'm sure Beatrice would love to be there with him," Dolly observed. "I bet he wouldn't be able to keep his hands off of her." Dolly laughed when she saw how close to the mark she'd hit.

"Don't tease," Alex said miserably.

"Aw, darlin', it's no fun being young and pretty and having to hide your light under a bushel. I don't see why you don't say to hell with it for tonight and just head out there as Beatrice."

"You know why I can't," Alex complained, jerking her chin toward the saloon door and the Gradys beyond.

"Oh, *them*." Dolly narrowed her eyes. "Well, I ain't much of a fairy godmother, but them I can do something about."

Alex was baffled when Dolly knocked back her whiskey and headed back to the bar. "Well, I ain't making a red cent tonight!" Alex heard her exclaim in disgust. She crept to the door and peered through. Dolly was posed in the middle of the room, sweeping everyone in it with a dark glare. "What kind of whorehouse is it when the whores are sitting around gossiping and not one of them is flat on their back?"

Alex watched as Dolly sashayed over to the Gradys' table. "You gentlemen feel like doing me a favor? I don't like my girls being idle—it makes 'em lazy. Since the dance has killed business for tonight, how about I offer you a deal? Two girls each for the price of one?"

Silas, Bert and Travis looked up eagerly, but Gideon didn't stir.

Dolly grunted. "You still worried I'll charge you if they fall asleep? How about a flat fee, then? The same price, whether they sleep all night or party all night? Once in a lifetime deal. Better take it before I come to my senses."

Gideon looked up at her with narrowed eyes. "Seems awfully generous."

Alex's heart sank. Whatever Dolly was up to wasn't going to work. She watched as Dolly gestured helplessly at the empty room. "It's either that or I make *no* money tonight."

Gideon grinned wolfishly. "Looks like it's our lucky night, boys." There was a clatter as they rose from their chairs. "I get first pick," Gideon said sharply.

"I'm the oldest," Silas objected.

"So you can go second. Don't forget who has the gold."

Alex watched as they chose their women and disappeared upstairs.

"Send up a bottle of whiskey to each room," Gideon called down.

"Mighty generous of you," Dolly said, and Alex could hear the irony in her voice. "They woulda drunk a bottle each tonight anyway," she told Alex when she returned to the kitchen. "What are you standing around for? Come on, upstairs with you."

Alex looked at her, puzzled.

Dolly rolled her eyes. "Your reason for staying in has been taken care of, Cinderella. Time to make yourself pretty and get on down to that dance, before it's all over."

"But my clothes are back at the hotel."

Dolly grabbed her and began shepherding her up the back stairs. "This is a house full of women. You think I don't have clothes?"

"But I don't want to look like . . ."

"A whore?"

Alex flushed, worried she'd given offense.

"I can do demure as well as the next girl," Dolly told her, completely unruffled, "I just choose not to."

Back in Delia's room, Dolly once again emptied out the wardrobe. Alex had never seen so many dresses in her life. "All of these were Delia's?"

"Heck, no. These are communal. Most of them are kept in my room, but with Delia gone I thought I'd store the overflow in here."

There were muslins and satins, velvets and silks, in every shade of the rainbow. Just about all of them were cut daringly low. Dolly caught Alex examining them dubiously. "Don't worry about that, it's nothing a bit of gauze or lace can't fix. There's water in the pitcher there, wash yourself up in the washbasin while I go through these. Do your hair too, we can't have you going out with half a ton of grease in it."

It seemed to take forever to get the dirt off. Alex scrubbed and scrubbed until her skin shone pink. And she had to wash her hair twice. By the time she was finished the water in the basin was black.

She stood wrapped in a towel, waiting for Dolly to finalize her choice.

"I think the satins and silks are a little much for a country dance," the whore mused aloud. "The peach is wrong for your coloring. Personally I like this pale green, but that might be because I'm wearing green today. Once I get a color on my mind I just can't see anything else."

Alex crept forward to look at the dress. It was the palest green, like young leaves, and it had an off-the-shoulder neckline, ruffled and trimmed with ivory lace.

"It's lovely," Alex said.

"It don't look at all like something a whore would wear, does it?" Dolly said with a grin. "Now and then I get a young one working for me, and some men like the virginal look." She tossed Alex some light and lacy undergarments, a pair of stockings and a whalebone corset. Alex hurried to dress, feeling a little bit like it was almost midnight and on the first stroke she would turn into a pumpkin.

Dolly laced the corset for her and lowered the dress over her head. Alex smoothed it over the bell of her petticoats as

Dolly did up the row of buttons at the back. When she looked in the mirror she gasped, horrified. "This is virginal?" she asked in a choked voice.

The corset plumped her breasts up until they strained at the low neckline of the gown. She looked like she would overflow at any minute.

Dolly ignored her and tried to yank the neckline up a little higher. "It looks demure on some girls," she muttered, "just not girls with your measurements."

They both regarded Alex in the mirror. All they could see was the generous swell of cleavage. Alex moaned. "I can't go out like this."

Dolly chewed her painted lip thoughtfully. Then she turned back to the riot of clothes on the bed and fussed about for a minute. "Aha!" she exclaimed, pulling a length of gauze from the tangle. Artfully, she draped it around Alex's bodice, securing it at the back with a knot.

"Respectable enough to be seen out in public," Dolly exclaimed triumphantly, "but not so respectable as to hide your God-given assets." It was true. Her breasts could still be seen, faintly, through the gauze, but without the sight of naked flesh, it didn't seem so scandalous. "Now we have to do something about your hair," Dolly clucked, eyeing the drying gold-streaked waves.

Alex couldn't see that there was much that could be done, but she'd forgotten that she was dealing with an expert. Dolly sat her down on the bed and poked her and stuck her with a fistful of hairpins, until Alex's hair no longer looked shorn. It looked like it had simply been pinned up.

"Of course, it still don't look like you've got much hair . . ." Dolly mused thoughtfully. Then, seized by another idea, she tore a cloth rose off an old velvet dress and pinned it in Alex's hair.

"It will be dark," she said, "maybe with that old thing distracting them no one will notice the hair."

Alex stood and moved to the mirror. There was nothing childish about the woman staring back at her. Her heart fluttered with excitement as she thought of the expression on Luke's face when he saw her.

❧ 13 ❧

LUKE WAS HAPPY with the party he'd put together. They were a decent bunch of people and they seemed to get along famously. Not like last year's bunch. That had been the worst trip of his career; too many bachelors and not enough women to keep them civilized. He'd sworn to give up the trail for good after that one, and he might have if he hadn't heard about Jackson's stallion.

The stallion. His gaze dwelled on Victoria, a swirl of yellow on the dance floor, and a satisfied smile played about his lips. Such a reasonable young lady. He was sure he'd have no trouble persuading her to sell the animal when they got to Oregon. He just needed to borrow a bit of cash from his brother Tom, and the horse was as good as his. His eyes sparkled as he thought of what he could do with the Arab. He had a lovely little filly, also a gray, that he would pair him with first. Their colts would fetch a pretty price. Hell, he might even take them down to California and put them up for auction.

A low whistle pulled him from his thoughts. "Would you look at that," Henry Watts said in a reverent voice. Luke followed his gaze. And there she was: beautiful Beatrice. She of the perfect legs, and face, and . . . everything else.

He grinned. He'd known she would turn up eventually. What else was there to do in Independence on a Saturday night? He ran a hand over his freshly cut hair and straightened his starched collar. He'd gone to the barber this afternoon, having a feeling that tonight would be the night he would see her again. He didn't usually care about his appearance, at least not unless Amelia Harding was around, but tonight he had wanted to look his best. He'd even bought

some cologne and splashed it on, and he wasn't the kind of
man who wore cologne. He'd never worn it for Amelia. He
paused, discomfited by the notion. Unsettled, he pushed
away thoughts of the pretty brown-eyed girl at home. She
was a thousand miles away and beautiful Beatrice was right
here.

OH GLORY, HE was heading straight for her. Even though it
was what she wanted, Alex felt nervous and uncertain. She
clasped her hands together in an attempt to hide the fact they
were trembling. He was looking at her *that* way again. Inti-
mately, as though he knew what she looked like without her
clothes. *He does, you ninny,* a little voice hissed in her head.
Alex was blushing by the time he reached her.

"Good evening, Miss . . ." Luke trailed off, and gave her
a slow smile. "Do you know I don't even know your name?"

Alex gulped. Her name? What was her name? She couldn't
give him her real name. She looked around the square, desperate for inspiration to strike. Nothing. And now he was giving her a very odd look indeed. Blushing brighter, she looked
down at her dress. "Green," she blurted, "my name is Green."

"Miss Green," he said smoothly, taking her hand. She
could tell by the sly narrowing of his eyes that he could feel
her trembling. "I can't begin to tell you what a pleasure it is
running into you again."

Oh, this was going to be easier than he'd thought. The
little lady couldn't keep her eyes off of him, and her skin was
moist with nerves. Not to mention the way she trembled like
a leaf in a strong breeze.

He was sure she was no virgin, parson's daughter or not.
Virgins didn't respond the way she had. They didn't kiss you
back with such heat, or arch against you when you caressed
them. At least, he didn't think they did. Amelia certainly
didn't. She set him firmly in his place and told him that he
was a scoundrel and a rogue and to get off her front porch
before she called for her father. And then, once he was off
the porch and safely back on his horse, she looked up at him
shyly through her eyelashes and told him he was welcome to
come back next Sunday afternoon to sit with her for a spell.
It was enough to make a man daft.

This one wasn't like that. She didn't look up at him through those thick curling dark lashes. She looked him full in the face, and her eyes were honest and clear. Like a mountain stream, he thought as he stared into them. Or shale, wet from a storm. They were a dozen shades of gray all blending together in patterns of light and shadow.

Luke blinked and recovered himself. A man could get lost in those smoky eyes. "Would you like to dance, Miss Green?"

Alex was still reeling from the intensity of his gaze. It was as though he'd looked right through to the core of her.

When she didn't respond Luke led her gently toward the dance floor. She was minutely aware of the feel of his palm cupping her bare elbow, and of the heat of his body so close to hers. "Are you always this quiet?" he whispered into her ear, before gliding away to take his position for the reel.

She was as rigid as a tent pole for the first dance; every muscle was tensed. She was painfully aware of his hands on her body, and of the distance between them when he moved away. The air between them thrummed with invisible energy, like the crackling of a summer lightning storm. Her nerve endings were zinging with anticipation, and she felt sure something wonderful was shimmering just out of sight. What was it about Luke Slater that turned her into such a wreck?

It was only after a couple of dances that Alex felt herself begin to relax. Oddly, it was the way his gaze fixed on her, unwavering, that calmed her. Tonight, she realized, he was hers completely. Before long, Alex found she was enjoying the dance immensely. The fiddles were lively, the night was balmy and scented with sugars and spices, and Luke Slater was a wonderful dancer. And why wouldn't he be, a little voice piped up in her head; the man seems to be wonderful at everything. She caught his black gaze and he gave her an insouciant wink. She giggled. She couldn't help it. She was helpless against the full force of his charm.

Luke couldn't remember the last time he'd enjoyed himself as much. When beautiful Beatrice smiled at him, he couldn't help but smile back. Even her smile was perfect, he realized, wide and enthusiastic—strawberry lips parting to reveal small, even white teeth.

At the end of a particularly lively reel, he spun her to the edge of the floor until she was laughing breathlessly. "Wait here a minute," he excused himself, and she watched curiously as he took the courthouse steps two at a time, heading for the band. He whispered something into the fiddler's ear and Alex noticed money change hands.

He ran back down to her, looking boyish and wicked, his cheeks still flushed from dancing, his dark hair flopping over his forehead with every step.

"What did you do?" she laughed.

He grinned and took her in his arms. One strong hand rested in the small of her back as he pulled her close against him, and the other claimed her hand and guided it to the nape of his neck. "I simply drew to their attention the fact that those reels were exhausting the ladies, and that it was time for a waltz. Or two. Or three."

Alex couldn't resist the twinkle in his eye. As the music swelled into a slow and lovely two-step, Luke guided her back onto the floor. With every step he seemed to draw her closer, until they were stomach to stomach and chest to chest. Alex was having trouble breathing again. He was so hard against her, and she could feel his legs brush hers through the weight of her skirts.

He captured her gaze and held it, as firmly as his arms were holding her body; his eyes were blacker than midnight, like the surface of a river on a moonless night, like the darkest shadows in the deepest woods. Alex thought she could lose herself completely in those eyes.

As the two-step melted into a waltz, his gaze grew warmer and more intimate and Alex felt herself melting into him. His hand was drifting slightly lower on her back, until his fingers were pressed against the curve of her bottom. Glory, it was fortunate they were in public, or who knew what she'd let him do.

Luke scowled when he felt a hand tapping him on the shoulder. He ignored it, but it grew more insistent, until it was almost thumping him in an effort to be acknowledged.

Not now, he wanted to snarl, not when she's all hazy and soft with desire. He knew that if he could have another dance, he'd be able to waltz her off the floor and under the sycamores, where he could steal a kiss. Or two. Or three. And after that . . .

But now here was damn Henry Watts, looking up at him like a hopeful puppy. And what had Henry done to his hair in the last hour or so? It was plastered flat to his head and still bore the imprint of a comb, like a neatly furrowed field.

"May I cut in?" Henry asked, darting a glance at the lovely girl in green.

"I won't mind," a shy voice suggested. To Alex's horror, Henry's partner stepped into view from behind Luke's back. It was Victoria.

Luckily, her attention was on Luke and she hadn't noticed Alex yet.

She couldn't, Alex thought wildly, suddenly feeling the full weight of her guilt. What was she doing? Spoiling Victoria's night, that was what she was doing. Out of pure jealousy. Because she couldn't bear Luke Slater thinking that Victoria was the pretty one. Feeling sick with shame, Alex spun on her heel and fled, shielding her face with her hands. Please let Victoria not recognize her!

"Hey," she heard Luke call after her. "Beatrice!"

Thank God for Dolly and her cousin Beatrice. Now Victoria would just think Luke's partner had been a crazy woman in a green dress. Not her own hateful sister, risking their very lives, just so she could dance with the man Victoria fancied herself in love with.

Alex tore through the empty streets, her breath rasping in her ears and her heart pounding. It wasn't until she'd run up the back stairs at Dolly's and shut herself in Delia's room that she let the tears spring to her eyes. What kind of monster was she?

"I GUESS SHE didn't want to dance with me," Henry said numbly, back at the dance. He fiddled self-consciously with his freshly combed hair.

Luke ignored him and started after Beatrice. Where the hell was she going?

Victoria gazed after him with a sinking heart. She should have known. Here she'd been feeling like the prettiest girl at the dance, enjoying more male attention than she'd ever had before in her life, but, of course, there was a prettier girl. There was always a prettier girl. It was usually her own sister, she thought glumly. And if Alex could have come in her dove-gray dress instead of in Adam's baggy old clothes, Luke would probably have been chasing after her instead of some girl in green. Victoria straightened her shoulders. At least it wasn't that, she thought, cheering up. At least she didn't have to watch him mooning over Alex. And it was she, Victoria Sparrow, who was about to spend several long months in the wilderness with him, not some woman in green. She barely made it halfway back to the table before she was intercepted by another dance partner, and Victoria found that her spirits were considerably improved.

Luke reached Dolly's in time to see Beatrice dart around the side of the building. He followed. He was only in town for another day or so, and he didn't intend to waste the advantage he'd gained tonight. What if he didn't see her again?

He was astonished when he rounded the house to find Adam in the dark and dusty yard between the building and the stable, walking the stallion in the moonlight.

From the corner of his eye he saw the swish of skirts and noticed Beatrice disappearing across the balcony and into the cathouse.

"Look, Luke, he likes me!" Adam called, his voice loud in the still night.

Luke forced a smile. All he wanted to do was fly up the stairs after her, but he genuinely liked Adam and couldn't bring himself to brush him off. "What are you doing, Adam? You're missing the dance."

A frown crossed Adam's face. "I know, that's what I told Alex."

"Alex is here again?" Luke said with a measure of exasperation. He really was going to have to give Dolly a piece of his mind. She was taking advantage of the boy's youth.

"Don't be mad at Alex. We'll go back before the dance is over."

"I'm not mad," Luke assured him.

"Blackie Junior needs the exercise anyway."

Luke looked at the stallion dubiously. He wasn't sure the stallion would regard being led slowly around the yard as exercise. "I'm still not sure about the name, Adam. How about something more dignified, like Apollo?"

Adam wrinkled his nose.

Luke glanced up at the window to Delia's old room, where a lamp was burning. "Not Apollo," he mused absently, already moving toward the stairs. "I'll think of something else."

"That's all right, I like Blackie."

"If I see Alex I'll send him down to take you back to the dance."

Adam brightened. "I liked the dancing," he said, but Luke was already out of earshot.

Luke tried to enter the house as stealthily as possible, worried he might run into one of the girls. When he opened the door he was greeted by muffled sounds of pleasure, both real and feigned, coming from some of the rooms. The sounds increased his sense of anticipation as he approached the door to Delia's room. Beatrice's room.

Alex almost leaped out of her skin when there was a soft knock at the door. She froze, unsure what to do. Before she could do anything the doorknob began to twist and her stomach turned over. She'd forgotten to lock the door behind her. Oh glory, and she was in a whorehouse! What if it was a customer looking for a whore? *Like Luke the other day,* the little voice whispered, and heat flooded her with the memory.

Luke eased the door open, careful to do it slowly, as most of the doors at Dolly's were still new and prone to squeaking. She was standing in the center of the room, as though she'd been waiting for him. Maybe she had, he thought, as he took in her flushed cheeks and naked shoulders. The demure gauze wrap she'd worn was balled up on the floor, and her dusty slippers were discarded nearby. Maybe her flight hadn't been a flight at all—perhaps it had been an invitation. She didn't tell him to leave, and that was certainly invitation enough for Luke. He eased into the room and closed the door behind him with a click.

Alex meant to order him out. She really did. The words were on the tip of her tongue. But the sight of him lounging against the door, large and intimidating, and yet with one boyish lock of hair curling over his forehead, making him so very approachable, dissolved the words in her mouth. She had a mad impulse to push the silky dark lock away from his eyes.

The way he was looking at her caused a loosening in her belly. He looked so very serious . . . no, not serious . . . intense. *It's desire,* the little voice sighed, and Alex shivered. She'd had men look at her with lust in their eyes, but never with desire like this. His slippery black gaze was full of silent promises.

If that wasn't an invitation in those smoky-gray eyes . . .

Desire flooded him and he knew from the charged air between them that she felt the same way. She was breathing fast and shallow again, causing her lush breasts to surge against the near-indecent depth of her neckline. It was the dress that cinched it. Without that scrap of gauze, she was no lady. It proved him right. No virgin kissed the way she did; no virgin looked at a man with such desire; and no virgin wore a dress like that.

Alex felt her knees turn to water as he moved toward her. He walked with a slow predatory grace and she felt like a helpless deer, preyed upon, frozen by the stare of a creature about to devour her. If she could have spoken, she would have broken the spell. But she couldn't speak. And even if she could have, she wasn't sure she wanted to.

He towered over her. She had to tilt her head back in order to meet his gaze. He stopped so close to her she could feel the heat radiating from his body, and feel his breath on her cheek. The moment stretched out for an eternity, until Alex's nerves were stretched to breaking point.

And then he lowered his head, and his mouth claimed hers in a searing kiss.

The only part of him to touch her were his lips, but she felt utterly possessed. His full, soft mouth moved over hers, so tender despite his hunger for her. Skillfully, he teased her lips apart and then his tongue was sliding into her, sending ripples of fire coursing through her.

She swayed, and reached for him in order to steady herself.

Luke felt her hands slide up his chest and over his shoulders. It was the final invitation. He moaned and crushed her against him, his strong hands finally seizing her.

She felt the kiss deepen and had to cling to him for dear life. She had no idea what was happening to her. She'd never felt such a storm of sensation. One of his hands gripped the back of her neck, while the other hand curved over her buttocks and pulled her hard against the heat of him.

Luke was growing wild, struggling to control his desire. No kiss had ever driven him to the edge like this. She kissed him with such passion, promising so much. He had to pull away. He wanted to savor the experience, not to have it over in one swift and glorious explosion.

"Slow down, sweetheart," he whispered against her lips. He tried to set her back from him, but she swayed on her feet and he couldn't help smiling. He didn't think she was aware of how her fingers were digging into the muscles of his back. He took her hands in his and lowered them to her sides.

Alex couldn't think. She could barely breathe.

She almost moaned when he stepped away from her. She didn't want him to stop. His kisses felt so wonderful; they sent a warm river cascading through her.

It didn't help, Luke realized. Standing back had only allowed him to see her swollen lips and the plea for him to continue in the swirling smoke of her eyes.

He was taut with wanting her.

Alex gasped when his fingers brushed against her mouth. His thumb rubbed over her swollen lips. Instinctively, she kissed it. He froze. Feeling an unexpected pulse of power, Alex shyly flicked her tongue against the pad of his thumb. She heard his swift intake of breath and smiled against the press of his skin.

What was she doing? Some fading, rational part of her mind was appalled when she licked circles against his paralyzed thumb. But she was tired of being rational. She wanted this wild moment when all thought was driven from her head. Right now she wasn't Alexandra Barratt; she wasn't responsible for the welfare of her family; she wasn't being pursued by one man who wanted to own her, and three more who wanted to kill her. Right now, in this moment, she was merely a physical being swamped by sensation. All that mattered was this moment, and this man, who wanted her.

Her tongue was driving him wild. He didn't understand it. He felt like a callow youth again, struggling to contain himself. She was disappointed when he pulled his hand away, he could tell by the look in her eyes. Well, he wouldn't let her be disappointed for long.

Alex melted into him when he kissed her again, and didn't notice his fingers on the buttons at her back. He had her half out of her dress before she realized what was happening. He felt her stiffen and deepened his kiss again. His fingertips traced the line of her spine and she felt shivers of delight follow in their wake.

Was it wrong to enjoy his touch? Was it wrong to want him to keep touching her . . . to touch her everywhere?

She was every bit as perfect as he remembered. His kisses trailed to her neck as he fumbled with the laces of her corset. He found her pulse and grazed it with his teeth; by the time he reached the hollow of her neck and lapped at it with a hot, demanding tongue, the corset had fallen to the floor. Now lush, soft curves were pressing against him. Sweat beaded on his brow and his hands grew rough as they tugged the chemise down over her shoulders. He wanted to see her.

She should feel ashamed, she thought dazedly, but she didn't. Strangely, as her clothes fell away, she felt freer, and more confident. Maybe it was because of the awe in his face and the hunger in his eyes.

When she was naked, except for the sheer stockings tied with satin ribbons at her thighs, he pulled back again, in order to look at the length of her. She was magnificent. Her skin was rosy and dewy with perspiration, her breasts were full and heavy, the nipples dark and thrusting with desire, and the rest of her was one delicious curve after another.

She noticed the tremor when he reached to touch her and felt her confidence grow. She arched toward him as his hands slid over her, following every dip and crescent. The deep languorous pulse was back, thrumming through her. She had never felt so alive. She wanted . . . *something* . . . so badly.

She tensed when he sank to his knees in front of her. His fingers pulled at the satin ribbons and then his hands were running over her legs as he eased the stockings over her calves. As he went he trailed kisses over her abdomen, pausing to look up at her wickedly when he reached the dark shadow at the juncture of her thighs.

Alex flushed.

When he stood again she was suddenly aware of the fact that he was still fully dressed. "I don't think that's fair," she breathed.

"What?" he asked as he reached for her.

She eluded him, retreating until the back of her thighs hit the bed. "I want to see you too."

Her words were almost his undoing. He swallowed hard when she slid onto the bed, her arm draping over the brass post and her eyes all but devouring him.

A dark light ignited in his eyes and he gave her a slow wolfish grin. Alex felt a fluttering in her belly as he removed his jacket and let it fall to the floor. He had no idea that she'd seen it all before . . . and the fact that she'd seen every last naked inch of him only seemed to heighten her anticipation now.

The white shirt fell, revealing the familiar expanse of burnished rosewood flesh and the dark line of hair curling down in a V to the waistband of his trousers.

He could feel the intensity of her gaze focused squarely on his fingers as he undid his buttons. His pulse was racing.

As he was revealed to her she unconsciously pressed against the brass of the bed, and the cold metal felt delicious against her overheated flesh. This time she didn't look away. She drank in every detail.

He couldn't take much more. Or so he thought. But then she rose and came toward him. He tensed, expecting her hand to sweep across him as his had caressed her. Instead she paused, within arm's reach, and tilted her face up to him.

"Kiss me," she whispered.

It unleashed him. He swept her into his arms as his mouth came crushing down on hers, and he carried her to the bed. He was frantic with wanting her; his hands were everywhere at once as his tongue explored her, and his knee parted her thighs.

The river coursing through her became a flood, and she

was helpless, borne along by its power. The pressure of his knee against her drove her wild. She was moaning into his kisses and he could take no more.

The first touch of his heat was marvelous. But then, with an awful, shocking thrust came pain.

Alex went rigid and instantaneously her head cleared. What was she *doing*?

Through the mad red haze of desire Luke felt the resistance, and then felt her sudden stillness, but he was beyond thought. That one thrust was enough to send him spinning over the edge into ecstasy.

Alex clenched her teeth against the unbelievable pain. Tears stung her eyes. Dear God, what was she doing?

As Luke swam back to consciousness the realization assailed him. She was a virgin. How could that be? He raised himself up on his elbows and looked down at her. Her face was turned to the side. Her eyes were scrunched closed and there was the slick sparkle of tears on her cheeks. "Beatrice," he sighed, and she winced.

Before he could say more they were aware of a commotion in the yard outside. An orange glare lit the window and they could hear raised voices and feet pounding down the corridor outside the door.

Luke rolled away from her and went to the window. He swore. "The stable. It's on fire."

Numbly, she watched as he struggled into his clothes. Then she heard a scream and her eyes flew wide. Adam. That was Adam screaming.

❧ 14 ❧

A LEX TUMBLED OUT onto the balcony and stopped dead as she was slammed by a wall of heat. She clutched the bed sheet closer. Gideon, she thought desperately. This was Gideon's work. The stable was an inferno. The flames licked at the stars, flaring white-orange like giant pointed tongues, and the roof of the stable cracked alarmingly. She couldn't see Adam anywhere.

"Damnation!" Dolly yelled, flying from the house, feathers streaming. "Somebody run, fetch the sheriff before it spreads to the house! Cora, Gracie, get to the water pump—the rest of you fetch all the buckets and pails you can lay your hands on!"

"Get dressed," Luke said tightly from the bedroom doorway. He was pulling his boots on. "The house is liable to go up too." As soon as his boots were on he was off down the stairs to help Dolly.

Alex struggled to breathe. The night air was acrid with rolling black smoke. She scoured the yard below, looking for Adam. Through a swirl of sparks, flying like fireflies, she spotted him. He was lying facedown by the water trough.

"Adam!" Alex's voice cracked. She pelted down the stairs and across the yard, feeling the sparks burn as they touched her. The sheet she'd carelessly thrown around herself was in danger of catching fire. "Adam!" There was blood all down his face. So much blood.

Collapsing beside him, she pushed the hair off his face. He had a gash across his forehead and his left eye was swollen closed. But he was breathing.

It was her fault. She was responsible for him and she'd left him at the mercy of the Gradys while she . . . while she . . .

She'd *known* the Gradys were in the house. What had she been *thinking*?

Were they still here? Terrified, Alex clutched the sheet to her naked body and looked around the yard, which was hellish in the light from the fire. She had to get Adam out of here. But he was so big, how could she ever lift him? Madly she scooped water from the trough and flung it at her brother's face. "Wake up, Adam."

There was an almighty crack. Alex turned to see the stable collapsing, sending a volcanic burst of sparks and debris skyward. Timber from the roof of the stable landed on the cathouse, setting off a dozen more fires. Was Gideon watching his handiwork? Was he waiting in the shadows for her?

Adam moaned. Alex rubbed her wet hand through his hair and bent to kiss him. She felt like bursting into tears when she saw him open his eyes. "We need to go," she urged him. Could he stand? "Please, Adam. We need to get out of here before the Gradys find us."

"The Gradys," he moaned.

Somehow she managed to get him to his feet, although she bore most of his weight. They took a few staggering steps. The town fire bell was ringing and people were flocking to the fire, some to help, some to gawk. Alex led Adam behind the burning cathouse, into the darkness. Once they got away from the cathouse the streets were near deserted. Everyone was at the fire. Thank the Lord, Alex thought, groaning under Adam's weight. She made a less than convincing boy dressed only in a sheet.

They snuck in the back door of Ralph Taylor's hotel. He and his boy were on the porch, watching the flames leap above the rooftops. "Whole town might go up if they don't put it out soon," Taylor was saying as Alex and Adam disappeared up the stairs.

Alex's knees gave out as they reached their room and both of them went tumbling onto the brass bed, which rocked and screeched under their combined weight. Alex regained her breath and then settled Adam. She yanked his overalls off, so she'd have something to wear, and covered him with the blankets. He was clammy and his eyes were glassy. "Hold on," she huffed. "Let me just get dressed and I'll fetch the doctor." She clambered into his shirt and overalls. There was no hat. Hers was still at Dolly's and Adam's was lost to the fire. She glanced in the mirror. She was covered with soot. The Gradys wouldn't know her if they saw her. She hoped. Her boots were back at the cathouse, so she had no choice but to go back out barefoot.

"Alex?" Adam's voice was weak and he sounded tearful.

"Don't fret," she soothed, bending to kiss him again. "I'll get you a drink of water before I go for the doctor."

"It was Gideon, Alex."

"I figured as much," she said.

"He hurt me." His hand went up to his swollen eye and she winced. He could have been killed because of her. Never again, she swore. Adam and Victoria came first.

She had no idea where Victoria was, she suddenly thought in shock. Dear God, Gideon could have her.

"He took Blackie, Alex!" Adam called after her as she bolted for the door. Damn the horse, she thought. She had to find her sister.

She locked the door as she left, to keep him safe. *It's a bit late for that, ain't it?* She could hear Gideon's voice in her head, mocking her. She tried to ignore it.

She pelted through the empty streets to the town square. The colored lanterns still swung in the breeze, the tables were still laden with food, but there were hardly any people left. "Have you seen my sister?" Alex asked the fiddler, who was packing away his fiddle. "She's got brown hair, and she's in a yellow dress."

"Everyone's gone to the fire, lad," he said. Alex was gone before he finished snapping his case closed.

"I AIN'T LEAVING my house to burn!" Dolly railed at Luke. She had her sleeves rolled up and was trying to send the girls into the house with pails of water.

"It won't do any good," he snapped, snatching a pail from Seline's grasp and pushing her toward the street. She didn't need much encouragement. By the time she'd reached the gate the others were following, darting terrified glances back over their shoulders at the inferno.

Luke caught Dolly's glare and held it. "Be sensible," he coaxed.

She swallowed hard and looked up at her house. It was all she owned in the world. Luke followed her gaze in time to see an upper-story window blow out, sending glass spraying into the yard below. With a stab of horror, he remembered Beatrice. He hadn't seen her since he'd left the bedroom. His gut twisted. Oh hell, she was still inside.

He was up the stairs and into the house before Dolly knew what was happening. Luckily the fire hadn't spread to the back of the house yet. But he could hear the roof burning and knew that he didn't have much time. The house was already filling with poisonous smoke.

"Beatrice!" He burst into the room, only to find it empty. Her clothes were still strewn on the floor. Damn. She definitely hadn't been out in the yard. She must be here somewhere. He looked in the cupboard and under the bed. Maybe she was scared and hiding. But there were only clothes in the cupboard, and all that was under the bed was a thin film of dust. As he got to his feet he noticed the telltale bloodstains on the bed and blanched. A wilted cloth rose lay in the tangle of sheets . . . she'd been wearing it in her hair, he remembered numbly.

The ceiling above him groaned alarmingly and he snatched up the cloth rose and left the room. He tore along the corridor, calling her name as he threw open every door. No sign of her. Downstairs there was no sign either. Although he did find Mary, cowering in the kitchen. "Come on," he ordered hoarsely, grabbing her arm. "Out, before the whole place goes up! Have you seen Dolly's cousin? Have you see Beatrice?"

Mary shook her head, her eyes huge with fear.

Luke swore. He hoped to God she was outside with the rest of them, but when he emerged, coughing, she was still nowhere to be seen. He deposited Mary with the cluster of frightened whores and headed for Dolly, who was railing at the sheriff.

"I'm losing my livelihood and you're just *standing there*!" she bellowed at him, her singed feather trembling in sympathy.

"I can't find Beatrice," Luke said tightly, interrupting her.

Angrily, she shook him off. "Bugger Beatrice! Look at my *place*."

"She's your kin!"

"Beatrice is fine," she snapped. "I saw her leaving the yard before. If you want to go chasing after her, be my guest. Personally, I'd have thought you'd be a little more concerned about your damn horse." She turned back to the sheriff. "Why the hell aren't you saddling up and going after the bastards? You heard my boy, they lit it on purpose!"

"My horse?" Luke echoed. "Isis will turn up," he said. She wouldn't have run too far. Then an awful thought occurred to him. "Your boy did let the animals out, didn't he? When he first saw the fire?"

"They took your horse."

"Who took my horse?"

"Those Gradys," Dolly snarled. "They beat up that poor simple lad and took your horse and the stallion. And then they set fire to my place." She yanked her stable boy forward. "Ain't that right?"

"Yes, ma'am." The boy nodded frantically. "They was all laying into the feeb and asking him about his sister. I *told 'em* the sister was at the dance and they lit out, but not before they knocked him out cold."

Luke's stomach sank all the way to his knees. "Where is he now?"

"The feeb?"

"Don't call him that," Luke snapped.

"He was facedown in the yard by the water trough."

"Well, he ain't there now," Dolly said. And then she began lambasting the sheriff all over again.

Luke swore as he regarded the burning house and collapsed stable. Beatrice would have to wait. He had to find out if the Alexanders were safe first.

"LET ME GO!" Victoria squealed, trying to free herself from the cruel grip that threatened to snap her wrist.

"You keep squirming like that and I'll tar the hide right off of you, just see if'n I don't."

Victoria gasped, outraged.

Alex ignored her, dragging her along the dusty street. She'd found her sister out front of Mrs. Tilly's Tearooms, watching the fire and flirting prettily with a small knot of admirers. Her rage was born of relief, but Victoria wasn't to know that. "Standing there unchaperoned with those men," she muttered under her breath.

Victoria snorted. "Look who's talking. You took Adam to a whorehouse."

"To the stables!" Alex disagreed, glad it was too dark for Victoria to see her blush.

"And what about the night I found you in the bathhouse with Luke!"

Alex blanched. Her sister was right. She was a filthy hypocrite. And Victoria didn't even know the worst of it. She dropped her grip of her sister. "Come on," she said glumly, "we need to find a doctor."

"I was just *talking* to a doctor," Victoria said haughtily. "Dr. Flint. He was the tall one with the mustache. The one who said I looked like a daisy." She giggled. Then she frowned. "Why do we need a doctor?"

Alex told her. And next thing she knew she was the one being marched down the street, her wrist threatening to snap in her sister's iron grip.

❧ 15 ❧

"**B**E SENSIBLE!" DOLLY implored him, as they watched Luke slide the last bullet into the barrel of his six-shooter.

Luke ignored her. Victoria, still in her pretty yellow calico, burst into fresh tears. The sound was getting on Alex's nerves.

They were in Taylor's small dining room. The doctor had been and gone and Adam was sleeping upstairs. The whores had taken over the downstairs bunkhouse, and could still be heard chattering behind the closed door. Victoria had only just recovered from the shock of Adam's injury when they all tramped in, half-naked and sooty. Alex wasn't sure her sister would ever recover from the sight of so many whores. Every time Victoria looked at Dolly she hiccupped and started crying again. When Luke announced he was leaving she fell apart completely.

"Why don't you let the sheriff handle it?" Alex said quietly, unable to look away from the cold iron of his weapon. He gave the barrel a flick and it spun, and then he snapped it closed with an ominous click. He didn't say a word. Alex found his silence terrifying.

"You'll get yourself killed," Dolly said waspishly. "And for what? A damn animal."

"You ask these people if it's just a damn animal," Luke replied coldly, gesturing at Alex and Victoria. They were a sorry-looking pair: Victoria was red-eyed and wilted and Alex was black with soot. "The kid spent their fortune on that animal."

Dolly threw up her hands. "It's only money! It ain't worth dying over."

"You were willing to risk yourself for the house."

Dolly clenched her jaw, but didn't answer. Alex thought she suddenly looked older; the lines bracketing her mouth seemed deeper, more pronounced. But when Luke picked up his saddlebags all thoughts of Dolly's age fled. "You promised to take us to Oregon," Alex said, a little wildly. "We paid you!"

"Sebastian will captain you until I catch up." Luke pulled his dusty hat over his black hair. He looked deep into Alex's eyes. "I *will* catch up, runt."

Alex swallowed hard. She wanted to throw herself at him, to hold him back with every last ounce of strength she had. Luke might be a big man, but no one man was a match for all four Gradys. "Take care of your family," he told her as he took his leave.

"But you don't even have a horse! You can't go."

"I'll buy one off Jackson." Alex jerked when he laid a hand on her shoulder. "You're all set to go, runt. Ralph said that he'll sell you his mules. Just load up the wagon and meet Sebastian in the square." He lowered his head and dropped his voice, so that only she could hear him. "Go to Cavil's in the morning and buy yourself a gun. Sebastian will teach you how to use it."

Alex swallowed hard. She wished she could turn her head and press her lips to the dark hand resting on her shoulder.

He saw the tears filling Alex's eyes and squeezed the small shoulder. Poor kid. He had to shoulder a grown man's burden at an awfully young age.

Luke didn't say anything to Victoria. He simply offered her his clean bandanna so she could mop her tears. If anything, Luke's gesture only seemed to make her cry harder. Impulsively, she threw herself at him and sobbed into his shirt.

Alex scowled as she watched Luke's big hand rub Victoria's yellow back. She couldn't help noticing his ease with weeping women. He smoothly disentangled himself and suddenly Alex was the one being drowned in Victoria's tears. Victoria's arms closed around her neck, almost strangling her.

She watched over her sister's head as Luke said good-bye

to Dolly. Even though he lowered his voice, Alex heard every word he said. "Tell Beatrice I'll be back," he told Dolly, "and . . . tell her I didn't know . . . I didn't realize . . . She'll know what I mean."

Dolly caught Alex's eye and Alex blushed. The whore didn't waste a minute cornering her after he'd left. "I need water for my girls to bathe," Dolly announced in her most imperious voice. "You, boy, I'll pay you to lug buckets for us."

Alex followed Dolly outside, wishing she could join Adam in the big bed instead. She was exhausted by the events of the day.

"I'd give you Luke's message, but I know you were eaves-dropping."

Alex gave her a sour look.

"No need to glare at me. I'm not one to judge." The whore sank down onto a bench in the washroom with a sigh. She sat considering something for a moment and then, as though she had made a decision, she reached into her cleavage and pulled out a small square of folded brown paper. "I planned to give you this anyway." She held it out.

Alex took it warily. "What is it?"

"Drink it like tea. Steep it in boiling water for a few min-utes and then drain the lot."

Alex frowned.

"You have enough responsibility without adding another mouth to feed."

The penny dropped and Alex gasped. It had never oc-curred to her . . . she flushed, feeling incredibly stupid. She'd grown up around animals, she wasn't ignorant of the way these things worked. How could she not have even thought of it?

"The girls and I use it. It works most of the time," Dolly told her.

Alex was still staring, dumbfounded, at the brown pack-age. Her heart was thundering in her ears. Dolly was right, the last thing she needed right now was *more* responsibility. But Alex couldn't help imagining what Luke's baby might look like . . . *her* baby. Her very own flesh and blood. She hadn't had real flesh-and-blood kin since her parents had died when she was eleven. Ma and Pa Sparrow had kindly taken her in, just as they'd taken Victoria in a couple of years before; Alex loved her foster family, but deep down she longed to look into someone else's face and see herself.

She'd never told anyone, not even Victoria when they lay awake at night and whispered secrets, but her dearest wish was for a family of her own. She pictured herself at a dinner table, surrounded by children, a whole swarm of them chattering and laughing, and opposite her, at the head of the table, would be her husband. Alex didn't know what he looked like, but she knew he would love her and he would take care of her. Her problems would be his problems, and they would face them together.

Alex sighed now as she looked down at the square of brown paper. She certainly hadn't pictured it this way. Alone. Hunted. Facing an uncertain future.

She couldn't think about it now. She was so tired. Her eyes were still stinging from the smoke, her throat was raw from yelling, and her head ached. Alex tucked the package away and resolved to think about it some other time, when she wasn't so overwrought.

She heard a moan and looked around to see Dolly staring miserably at her own feet. "Would you look at that?" The older woman gestured at her ruined satin slippers. One was missing its pretty buckle. "Those came all the way from St. Louis. I had another pair just like them in red." She moaned again. "Not anymore."

"What are you going to do?" Alex asked her.

"Start again, I suppose. It's the only life I know."

"You could come with us."

Dolly hooted. "Me? On the frontier? I'd certainly never replace my slippers there! Ah, honey, this place ain't exactly civilized, but it's good enough for me. Besides, there's a fortune to be made here, the way you wagoners keep coming through. Although, where I'm going to find the money to start up another cathouse . . . Well, I might have to bring in an investor." She pulled a face. "It don't seem fair to siphon off the profits to some lazy bastard when I'm the one doing the hard work."

Alex chewed on her lip. Dolly had been awfully good to her . . . Knowing it was foolhardy, she decided to trust the whore. "Can you keep a secret?" she asked quietly, inching closer.

Dolly looked at her curiously.

Alex fumbled under her shirt until she found the leather bag. Her fingers trembled as she opened it. At the bottom of the bag the few remaining coins winked at her in the dim light. She ignored them and felt for the tear in the lining. There was the soft rustle of paper. Nervously, Alex eased one of the bills free of the others and withdrew it. "I want to thank you for the way you've looked after me," she whispered, holding the bill out to Dolly.

The whore took it as warily as Alex had taken the brown package earlier. Alex watched as she examined it. Dolly's eyes flew wide and her jaw dropped. There, in Dolly's hand, was a government bond worth one thousand dollars.

"Where did you get this?"

Alex swallowed hard. What she was about to tell Dolly, she'd never told anyone.

"SILAS TRIED TO starve us," she said slowly, the memories rising to the surface. "He figured eventually I'd give in and marry him. But I never did . . ."

By the time winter thawed and spring was frothing the pantry and the root cellar were just about empty and they'd all grown thin and irritable. Silas took to visiting every other day, always coming just before dinnertime, when they were at their hungriest. He'd slouch his way over the fallen dogwood blossoms and come to rest under the big old hickory tree by the front porch. He'd just stand there, shoulder to the rough bark, and watch the house with a smirk hovering around his mouth.

At first they tried to ignore him. If they were outside they retreated into the house, but none of them could resist peeking through the window.

The day they finished the last jar of preserves, Alex couldn't take it anymore. She stalked outside, hands on her hips, only wishing she had a gun to brandish at him. "Get out of here," she ordered tersely. "You're trespassing."

"Now, don't be so ornery," he said, straightening and

holding his hands out. He smiled. She thought he was doing his best to be charming. The problem was, Silas Grady didn't have an ounce of natural charm in him. His smile looked like a leer. "It's just a neighborly visit."

Alex glared at him.

"Me and my brothers cain't help but notice that you seem to be fallen on hard times, Alex."

"It's Miss Barratt to you."

Silas narrowed his eyes. "There's no need to be so prickly, *Miss Barratt*. It's just one neighbor looking out for another."

Alex snorted.

Silas began approaching, cautiously, the browning blossoms squelching under his boots. "I just came to find out what we can do for you."

"You can give us back our damn cow, and all those chickens you stole."

"I don't think I like what you're insinuating."

He kept on coming and Alex felt a thrill of fear. Why, oh why didn't she own a gun?

Silas reached the porch steps and paused. One meaty hand rested on the graying wooden rail. Alex flinched when his boot hit the first stair. He noticed and grinned. She had to fight the urge to run. She might be many things, but she hoped a coward wasn't one of them.

She was still standing there, rigid as a tent pole, when he settled in front of her. She tilted her head back to meet his eye. One of his dirty fingers stroked her cheek. She tried not to jump, but she couldn't help it. "You've got so thin," he said softly. "One word, Alex. You just need to say one word and it will all be over. Just say yes. I'll make sure you won't go hungry again."

The finger reached her lips and she batted it away. She didn't bother to disguise her revulsion. "I wouldn't marry you if I were on death's door!"

"What if it were them?" he asked, nodding to the house.

Alex turned and saw Victoria and Adam through the warped glass window of the house.

"That sister of yours is nothing more'n a bag of bones. You might get through the summer but what about when winter comes? What then? All you need do is say yes. This is a grand piece of land. I'll build you a new house, one with a pump right in the kitchen if you want."

The minute Alex turned back from the window he crushed her against him and his foul tongue was probing her mouth. Furious, Alex threw her weight against him. Fortunately for her, Silas was balanced precariously on the edge of the top step. In his shock he went tumbling. Alex grabbed for the porch post so he couldn't take her with him. She heard the heavy thud of his body hitting the ground.

For a moment she felt triumphant. But then she realized he wasn't moving.

"Oh Lord, you've killed him!" Victoria wailed, bursting from the house. "You've killed him! They'll come for us for sure."

Alex ignored her and flew down the stairs. She nudged Silas with her boot and his head lolled sideways. There, where his head had been, was a jagged rock, now specked with blood. Cold terror flooded her. Glory, she *had* killed him.

"We'll all be murdered!" Victoria was wailing.

Alex knelt and reached trembling fingers toward Silas's throat. "He's not dead," she said with relief when she found a pulse.

"It hardly matters," Victoria howled, growing truly hysterical, "look at the blood! Imagine what they'll do to us when he goes home like that!"

"Hush," Alex snapped. She couldn't think with all the noise. She chewed on her lip. She should just roll him into the swamp and let him drown. That would solve their problems. One day, he'd just float by and no one would know who had done it. Who'd suspect the Sparrows, those half-starved children of the poor old pastor? And without Silas, the other Gradys would forget about them. It was only because Silas was so set on Alex that they even bothered to harass them.

But as she looked at the unconscious man, Alex knew she couldn't do it. It would be murder, pure and simple, and she wasn't a murderer. He might be one of the nastiest creatures God put on this earth, but he was still one of God's creatures. Alex sighed and sat back on her heels. "Come on, Adam!

We'll drag him back to their property, and leave him where they'll find him."

"Are you mad?" Victoria was practically pulling her hair out. "Go to their property? With their *brother* practically beaten to death? Do you know what they'll do to you if they see you?"

"They won't see us," Alex said firmly. "And don't be so dramatic. He's hardly beaten to death—it was an accident. It's nothing but a small knock to the head."

"What if they come for me while you're gone?"

"Lock yourself in the root cellar," Alex said, exasperated.

"You know I hate the dark!"

"More than you hate the Gradys?"

Alex and Adam hefted the man and set off through the thicket of cherry birch and dogwoods, toward the Grady place. Halfway there, Alex was exhausted and had to pause for a rest.

"He sure is heavy," Adam observed, also huffing. They were both worn out from hunger.

Alex tensed when they heard voices. She was glad they were screened from the path by the undergrowth. As an extra precaution, she pulled Adam flat to the ground and held her finger to her lips.

"Where the hell is he anyway?" Bert's voice boomed through the thicket.

"Where do you think? He's always off sniffing around that Barratt bitch."

Alex stiffened and reached out to take Adam's arm in a warning grip.

"She sure is pretty."

"That don't mean he has to marry her."

Their guffaws faded as they headed in the direction of town. Well, at least that was Bert and Travis accounted for. Now there was just Gideon and their witch of a mother to worry about. When she was sure they were gone she pulled Adam to his feet. "We'd best hurry." This time they each took him by an armpit and dragged, letting his boots bounce over the rough ground. By the time they reached the Grady house they were hot and breathless.

"We'll leave him by the well," Alex rasped. "They're bound to find him there."

The Grady house was a dump. Alex didn't know how they survived—their vegetable patch was overgrown with weeds and their chicken coop was broken; the hens just ran wild in the garden, vulnerable to predators, laying their eggs willynilly. Alex had never seen any of the Grady boys do a lick of work. They seemed to thrive nevertheless.

After they dropped Silas by the old well, Adam dashed back to the cover of the woods, but Alex paused. There, just out of arm's reach, was a fat orange hen. It tilted its head, looked at her with one beady eye and clucked. Alex felt her mouth water.

She looked cautiously at the house. It was silent. There wasn't even a thread of smoke coming from the chimney. Her grumbling stomach decided her. She inched toward the chicken. It gave another cluck. "There, there," Alex soothed, "come to Alex now." She took another step and the hen shifted nervously to the side. Taking a deep breath, Alex lunged.

With a squawk, the bird went skittering across the weedy yard, wings flapping furiously and feathers flying. Alex was too hungry to think. She tore after it, even though it was heading toward the house. She could just about taste roast chicken. She chased it around the side of the house, tripping over the thick vines and weeds. With a scream, she fell through the half-open door of the root cellar and tumbled down the stairs.

She lay on the cold hardpacked dirt floor, breathing heavily. Had she broken something?

She heard a whimper and her blood froze.

She scanned the room as she scrambled to her feet, but her eyes hadn't quite adjusted to the darkness after the late-afternoon sunshine outside, and all she could see were silhouettes.

She heard the whimper again.

"Who's there?" Alex started backing up the stairs. She should never have chased that damn chicken. At that moment, as she gave up on the idea of roast chicken for dinner, she should have run, but the whimpering kept her rooted to the spot.

As her vision adjusted she saw the gleam of eyes in the far corner of the room.

"Who's there?" she repeated, hearing a tremulous note creep into her voice.

"Please, Miss," a terrified voice moaned from the dim corner. "Oh, please help us."

That sure wasn't Gideon's voice. It was deeper. And Alex couldn't imagine Gideon would ever sound so scared. Fear wasn't an emotion Gideon Grady felt—it was an emotion he caused.

Against her better judgment, Alex crept forward.

And was horrified.

THERE WERE PEOPLE chained to the wall.

The man was badly beaten, one of his eyes was swollen closed and there was blood crusted on his face. An older woman was chained to his right; she too was bruised and swollen. To the man's left was a younger woman—she was the one whimpering. She had an iron collar around her neck and attached to the collar were two short chains, leading to two more collars . . . collars that were clamped around the necks of two small children. The youngest one couldn't have been more than five.

All of them, including the children, had pale pink scars on their shining black skin.

She'd had no idea the Gradys owned slaves.

"Please, Miss, you've got to help us." The man's chain rattled as he started away from the wall. Alex's nerves were so shot she jumped, and she saw the man wince.

Alex looked around wildly. How on earth was she supposed to help them?

The man gestured to a cupboard in the corner. "His ax."

Alex could hear the blood roaring in her ears as she hurried to the cupboard. There was a heavy chain and padlock. She looked back at the slaves helplessly. The children had such huge dark eyes. She would remember the way they looked at her for the rest of her life.

Suddenly, she remembered the jangle of keys on Silas's belt as she and Adam dragged him through the birch thicket. Before she could have second thoughts, she darted for the stairs. She heard the younger woman wail and knew they thought she'd given up.

At any moment she expected to hear a shout as someone spotted her. But all she could hear was the buzz of bees among the last of the blossoms, and the lazy clucking of the chickens. "Don't wake up, don't wake up," she chanted under her breath as she reached for the bunch of keys at Silas's waist. She almost died when he took a hitching breath, but he didn't stir.

She was shaking so hard as she returned to the cellar that the keys clattered and chimed. She almost fell down the stairs again because she didn't allow time for her eyes to adjust to the darkness.

"Praise the Lord," she heard the older woman moan.

Alex had trouble fitting the first key into the lock because of her trembling. She had to steady her wrist with her other hand. Her hair was standing on end as key after key failed to fit. What if Silas didn't have a key to the cupboard? Oh glory, she'd die of terror if Gideon were to show up and find her down here trying to free his slaves.

Finally, a key slid home and the padlock opened with a click.

And there was the ax. It was so heavy she could barely heft it.

"Step away," the man ordered the women and children. "Aim for the fastening, Miss." He gestured to the iron spike driven between the stones of the cellar wall. "I'll do the rest."

Alex tried her best, but the ax was heavy and her aim was bad. It took her several goes to even hit the spike. She would have given up in tears if it weren't for the calm voice of the man and the big desperate eyes of the children.

She yelped when the ax head finally struck the spike forcefully enough to loosen it. She felt tears well when the man tugged the spike from the wall. He took the ax from her and expertly struck at the chain loops until each of them were free to move. Then he turned back to Alex. "Now you need to do mine."

She looked in horror at his chain. Glory, with her aim, she would decapitate him!

"Quickly," he urged. "Do it lower down if you're scared."

He held the chain against the dirt floor. She struck. It took four swings, but eventually the loop broke.

They all ran for the stairs, the man holding the length of chain hanging from his collar so that it wouldn't hit anyone or make a racket.

"Hell and damnation, who left the door to the root cellar open again!" Gideon's voice rang across the yard, and they all froze. Without looking down, Gideon kicked the door closed, and they were plunged into darkness. "Ma! Where are those lazy bastards!" they heard him holler. "They've been down at my moonshine again!"

Above they heard the shuffle of feet and the slamming of the porch door as his mother came out to see him. "How should I know?" the old woman said waspishly, her voice thin and mean. "Silas has been gone most of the afternoon and the others just left."

"I know damn well where they are," Gideon snapped. "They're off selling my liquor to those Pascalls. They'll only charge half what it's worth, and drink the profits on the way home."

"If you knew, why'd you ask?"

They could hear Gideon spit. "I'll give them what for," he grumbled, his voice fading.

Alex heard a creak and then a rhythmic noise as Ma Grady settled into her porch rocker. "We can't go out this way," she hissed, "the cellar comes out right by the porch. We'll have to go through the house and out the other door."

They fumbled in the dark until they found the rickety stairs leading up to the kitchen. "I'll go first," the man told Alex, stepping in front of her and hefting the ax.

She felt only marginally comforted.

When they reached the door at the top of the stairs she had a sudden fear that it might be locked, but it wasn't. It squealed softly as the man eased it open, and Alex's heart stopped again. They tried to move as silently as possible as they crossed the old floorboards. Alex realized with horror that there was no exit from the kitchen. One door led to a main room; through the window they could see Ma Grady rocking in her chair.

They turned the other way, toward a bedroom. Alex's pulse leaped every time one of the old floorboards creaked.

The rocking stopped and there was a grunt as Ma Grady rose.

"Hurry," the man hissed, ushering them into the room and silently closing the door. He held a finger to his lips and they stood as still and silent as statues.

Beside Alex was a bureau. It was loaded with a pile of drawstring bags, shaving gear and an oil lamp; one of the drawers was open and she could see the glint of a blade amid the mess of papers and junk inside. A cutthroat razor. Slowly, she reached for it. She'd feel much safer holding a weapon.

As her hand closed around the hilt she could hear Ma Grady bustling about the kitchen. She turned to grin in triumph at the man beside her as she withdrew the razor from the drawer. His eyes widened and to her horror she felt her hand knock the bureau. With a crash the oil lamp tumbled to the floor, smashing at their feet and showering them with glass and oil. All noise in the kitchen ceased.

"Out the window!" she hissed, her heart in her throat. The razor clattered back into the drawer. "You go first and help them out," she told the man forcefully, feeling the weight of her guilt hit her.

The older woman had already thrown the sash up and in a heartbeat the man was through the window and was lifting the children out. Alex struggled to shift the bureau in front of the door. As she did, it tipped; the bags went cascading to the floor, the drawers slid out and there was a shower of gold coins. Alex gaped at them. Gold? She scooped up a leather bag and felt its weight. There must be a fortune in those bags!

There was a deafening roar and the door exploded inwards. Alex gaped. Thank God she'd moved the bureau; it absorbed most of the buckshot. All she could hear was a strange muffled ringing, but she could see clear enough that Ma Grady was reloading her shotgun.

Alex didn't pause to think. She threw the heavy bag of gold at the old woman. It hit her full in the face and Alex could hear the crack of her nose snapping. The old woman stumbled back, struck her head on the wall behind and fell like a sack of potatoes.

Oh glory, she was taking the Gradys out one by one today.

She shrieked when someone grabbed her arm. She hadn't heard Adam calling, or heard him come through the window. Her ears were still full of that odd ringing.

"Let's go!" she said, not knowing if she was whispering or shouting.

On her way out, she couldn't resist grabbing more leather bags. She figured the Gradys owed her.

"WHAT HAPPENED TO those poor people?" Dolly asked from her position on the washroom bench, her eyes huge.

"I don't know," Alex admitted helplessly. It was a question that kept her awake at night. "They were gone by the time Adam and I ran. We headed straight home and gathered our things." Alex paused. She was too tired to recount the rest of the tale: the way Silas had turned up on her doorstep with the sheriff, Gideon's mad glee, the murder of Sheriff Deveraux, and the way Ma and Pa's house had burned to the ground, the black cherry tree flaming like a roman candle. She wanted to forget it all, not relive it.

"I can't keep this," Dolly said ruefully, holding the bond out.

"Why not?"

"You think word won't get to them that some old whore was suddenly cashing in a one-thousand-dollar bond? I don't want those boys coming to my door." Dolly shivered.

"What will you do?"

Dolly grinned. "This old cat still has a few lives left. I'll be fine. Worst comes to worst, I'll give Ralph Taylor a lifetime of free tumbles to let us use this place until I can get enough scratch together to rebuild my own."

Reluctantly, Alex took back the crumpled bond.

"Take my advice, darlin'. You burn those bonds, you hear? What you've got there is a date with the wrong end of a rope. Theft of that scale is a hanging offense."

"They can't have got it legitimately," Alex defended herself, pushing aside the memory of Sheriff Deveraux at her door.

Dolly shrugged. "Don't mean much. You can't spend that kind of money. People will notice."

Alex stared miserably at the bond, then she straightened her shoulders and made for the stove.

"Aw hell, not here!" Dolly squawked. "You don't want to leave the slightest trace! You wait until you're out on the trail, and don't burn them all at once. You do a few now and then, so you can make sure every last bit of them burns. And you make sure you're the one to douse the fire the next morning. Check for anything left unburned. Bury it deep, you hear."

The gravity in Dolly's voice resurrected Alex's terror.

Dolly looked at the girl's pinched face, still covered in soot, and sighed. The poor love. "You get to bed, darlin'. Everything will seem better in the morning."

"I always say that to Vicky, but it never does."

❧ 16 ❧

Luke couldn't believe it when the trail doubled back to Independence. He'd been tracking them for a couple of days, sure they were headed for St. Louis, but then they suddenly turned right around.

There'd been some kind of dispute. He found signs of it at their campsite. There was a big mess of footprints, where they'd struggled, and the imprint of a man's back in the dirt. But why would they go back?

To get what they'd come for in the first place, Luke supposed.

But they'd be damn fools to go back to town. Not when the sheriff was looking to question them about the fire at Dolly's—not to mention the theft of prime horseflesh.

Even though his new mount, a pacy little sable mare, was tiring, he urged her on. He kept picturing the way Victoria had fainted dead away at the sight of Silas. They were looking for a sister . . . *She abandoned us,* Victoria had said. Well, it didn't look like the Gradys were convinced.

When he caught up with the wagon train, Luke resolved to get some answers out of the Alexanders about this mysterious sister of theirs.

The trail went cold just outside Independence. Luke got down off the mare, but he could see no sign of them. Why would they wise up now and disguise their trail? He scowled and circled the outskirts of the town, determined to find something. But there wasn't so much as a single print.

"I think they're back in town," he told Sheriff Keeley, when he finally found the man at Gibson's Saloon.

Keeley was a genial pot-bellied man, with a steel-gray walrus mustache and a big grin. "That can't be. Someone would have spotted that horse. Since the auction, it's the most famous horse in the county."

"The trail leads back here."

"Right into town?"

Luke frowned. "It stops just outside."

"Just stops?"

Luke nodded abruptly.

"So you don't know for sure that they actually came into town?"

"Where else would they go?" Luke snapped in frustration.

Sheriff Keeley shrugged. "Who knows? Maybe they're waiting on someone."

"Have you got the 'Wanted' posters done yet?"

"I tell you what . . . I'll get a few of my boys on the street, send word around that the horse thieves might be back. At least we can get everyone looking out for that horse."

Luke rubbed his face tiredly as he watched the sheriff amble off. He hadn't slept for the last couple of days. He'd been so focused on finding the Gradys, he hadn't realized how worn out he really was. He was in no shape to continue the search. He supposed it would do no harm to clean himself up. Get a decent night's sleep and let the mare recover. And it would give him a chance to look Beatrice up. He hadn't managed to see her before he'd left, although Dolly swore to him that she was safe and sound. They had a bit of unfinished business to resolve.

DOLLY KNEW HE'D had no luck finding the Gradys the minute he walked into Ralph Taylor's.

"Luke!" Gracie and Seline cried simultaneously, both throwing themselves at him.

"Get off him, girls, can't you see the man's worn out? You can harass him after he's had a nice bath and a lie-down."

"I'll get your bath," Seline volunteered.

"No, you won't," Dolly disagreed. "If I know you, girlie, you'll be climbing in there with him. There's time enough for that later. I'll run the bath myself. Come on, Slater, leave your saddlebags here."

Dolly ushered him through to the washhouse and fussed

about, heating water. They didn't speak until he was submerged in the tub. Dolly had settled herself to beating the dust out of his clothes, but even she couldn't resist the odd peek at the exposed skin gleaming in the late-afternoon sunlight. "So," she said slyly, "I hear you and my cousin got better acquainted the other night." She watched his shoulders stiffen. Lord, the man was all muscle; just look at the way he rippled when he moved.

"What did she say?" Luke demanded.

Dolly's eyes narrowed. She'd never seen Luke concerned with a woman's opinion before. He usually took it for granted that he gave satisfaction. "Nothing much," Dolly said vaguely.

"But she said something."

"She saw you at the dance, obviously. And then you came back to the house . . ." Dolly let the sentence hang. She didn't want him to realize that she was fishing for details.

Luke stared down at the surface of the water, although not seeing his reflection; instead he saw a pair of smoky eyes and felt the heat of a firm, arching body. "I had no idea she was an innocent," he admitted. "I would have left her alone if I'd known."

"Would you?" Dolly said dubiously.

"I would have tried."

She snorted.

"Is she upset?" Luke asked, remembering the way she'd stiffened under him, and the tears on her cheeks.

Dolly grimaced, thinking of Alex, covered in soot and her brother's blood. Somehow Dolly thought the loss of her virginity had paled in comparison to the rest of the night.

"She is, isn't she?" Luke drew his own conclusions from Dolly's silence. "I'll talk to her." He made to rise from the tub, but Dolly stopped him with a gasp.

"No! Don't be ridiculous. You might as well finish your bath." She racked her brains helplessly, trying to think of an excuse for Beatrice's absence. Out of the corner of her eye she caught sight of Seline and the girls loitering outside in the yard, waiting to pounce the minute Luke emerged. Hell, she thought, it wouldn't hurt the man to learn a little humility when it came to women. "Besides," she said slowly, still looking at the girls, "there's no point, she's not here."

"What do you mean?"

Dolly examined him. Did he sound a little anxious, or was she imagining it? "I hate to tell you, Luke, but she left."

"Left?" He was disappointed. She could tell by the way his face fell. Dolly was flabbergasted. Luke Slater was disappointed. Over a woman. When there was a whole flock of them waiting for him just outside.

"She's headed for home," Dolly told him. "She left on yesterday's coach."

"Where's home?"

His question took her completely by surprise. Was he thinking of going after her? Hell. "Back east," Dolly said, watching him curiously.

"She didn't sound like an easterner. She sounded southern."

"She was originally," Dolly invented swiftly, "but the family moved to Philadelphia."

"Philadelphia," he said glumly.

Dolly had to pinch herself to see if she was actually awake and not dreaming the whole thing. Luke Slater was glum over a woman! "You seem quite taken with her," she said cautiously.

Luke blinked, and then frowned. "I just didn't want to see her hurt."

"Uh-huh," she said skeptically.

"Her being a virgin and all."

"I'm sure she'll be fine," Dolly assured him, feeling a pang of pity. She didn't think Luke had the slightest idea what was happening to him. She thought of Alex, all dirtied and dressed like a boy, right under his nose. She grinned as she wondered how long it would take him to figure it out.

"Next time you write to Beatrice," Luke said, clearing his throat awkwardly, "maybe you could mention how I asked after her."

"I will." Dolly rose to stoke the stove so she could heat him a little more water. "Now, are you going to tell me what happened with those Gradys?" she asked as the almond shells crackled in the fire and released their fragrant smoke.

"Lost their trail." Luke slumped back in the tub. He hadn't realized how much he'd been looking forward to seeing Beatrice. Philadelphia! Hell, that was halfway across the country. In the opposite direction to where he was headed.

He tried to push away any thoughts of her, relaxing back and closing his eyes. He swore. The minute he closed his eyes all he could see was her: the way she'd looked that night, walking toward him, naked and lush, her lips moist, tilting her head back and whispering, *Kiss me*.

"How far out did you lose their trail?"

He wasn't sure whether to be grateful for Dolly's interruption. Part of him wanted to banish Beatrice from his mind to keep from torturing himself with visions of what he couldn't have, but another part of him wanted to lose himself in the memory, to relive every moment: touching her, tasting her, feeling the pull of her fingers through his hair and the touch of her tongue against his lips.

He flushed when he realized Dolly was waiting for an answer. "Just outside town."

Dolly frowned, not understanding.

"I mean, they headed southeast for a day, and then turned around and came back."

"They came back?" Dolly felt a thrill of fear.

"Yeah," Luke said thoughtfully. "I can't for the life of me figure out why they'd come back."

"Maybe they're looking for somebody," Dolly suggested, swallowing hard, and remembering the feel of the thousand-dollar bond between her fingers.

"Silas said they were looking for a sister."

Dolly's knees gave out and she sank onto the bench. Her head spun as she listened to him recount everything Victoria had told him. Dolly found she was holding her breath and let it out slowly. "I never heard tell of a sister," she said shakily. She had to get word to Alex. The girl had to burn those bonds as soon as she could. Although, Dolly thought a little wildly, maybe she'd be better off just giving them back. If she burned them the Gradys would just keep coming after her, never believing the money was gone. Oh, what a mess.

"Maybe they'll follow the Alexanders until this sister shows up."

"Out," Dolly ordered sharply.

"What?"

"Get out. Get out of the bath. You have to leave now."

Luke was looking at her as though she'd lost her mind.

"You have to go," Dolly insisted. "You need to find the wagon train before they do."

"There's no rush," Luke told her. "I know exactly where it will be."

When he didn't move, Dolly grabbed his wet hand and tugged. "What if they aren't looking to *follow* the Alexanders?" she cried. "What if they decide to hurt them? You saw what that weasel did to Adam."

"That was because Adam tried to stop him taking the horse." Luke pulled his hand away. He took in Dolly's flushed face and the wild look in her eyes. What on earth had gotten into her?

"What if they hurt them to get information out of them? To find out the sister's whereabouts?"

"Victoria said she abandoned them. They don't have a clue where she's gone."

"But the Gradys don't know that!"

"Well, we'll just have to see that they find out, won't we?" he said thoughtfully. He shook his head. "What kind of heartless woman would leave three kids like those to wander out into the wilderness?"

Dolly glared at him. "Everything she does is for them!"

Luke was bewildered. "How do you know?"

"I don't," Dolly lied helplessly, "but I know how a woman's mind works. I'm sure she's just trying to protect them."

"You're not making any sense."

"Forget making sense. Just get out of that damn bath and go after them!"

Luke let her pull him from the bath and within the hour he was back on the mare, still tired and hungry, and completely baffled by the whore's behavior. She'd really developed some feelings for that runt of a boy. Luke couldn't see what appeal a skinny boy would hold for a woman like Dolly. As long as he lived he would never understand women.

✦ 17 ✦

IT WAS DIFFICULT to stay awake.

She'd been driving that horrid wagon for more than ten hours, and then she'd had to help Victoria cook dinner and wash the dishes. All she wanted to do was crawl into the back of the wagon, wrap herself in the itchy old blanket and sleep. But no, she had to sit up until everyone had gone to bed, just so she could burn those damn bonds.

Alex yawned and wished everyone else was as tired as she was.

There was one communal cooking fire in the center of the circled wagons. The warm days gave way to crisp spring nights, so clear the crackle of the fire traveled clearly from one side of the camp to the other. The night sky was a vast sprawl of stars and the moon rose and set low over the plains, like a great white pearl. The livestock were tethered between the fire and the wagons; the area acted as a makeshift corral, stopping the animals from wandering, and protecting them from theft. While the O'Briens and the Crawfords retired early every night, yawning and rubbing their sore backs, and the newly wed Ulrichs rarely stirred from their wagon after dark, the more experienced travelers tended to sit up late around the campfire, chatting and sipping from Sebastian's store of liquor. "Not too much now," he'd warn, pouring them each a stingy mouthful, "we've got to make it last."

The Watts brothers always moaned and kicked up a fuss. "Damn, Doyle, that ain't enough to even wet my tongue."

"Not the way you drink it," Sebastian said. "You boys wouldn't know the difference between whiskey and moonshine."

"Nothin' wrong with a bit of moonshine now and then."

"So, pick yourself up a batch when we get to Fort Kearney, and leave my whiskey the hell alone."

Alex wondered if men were always so coarse when women weren't around.

"Alex," Adam whispered, trying to get her attention from the darkness outside the flickering ring of light.

"What is it?" Alex asked, waving her hand to beckon him closer. When he stepped into the light the mules came too. They followed Adam everywhere. "You've got to stop feeding them sugar," Alex told him, exasperated, "or they'll never leave you alone."

"I don't mind," he said, pulling one of Cranky Bob's long furry ears through his fingers. He'd named them all, like they were pets, and, in a fit of pique after being bitten for the umpteenth time, Alex had renamed them. Now they were called Cranky Bob, Surly Sue, Ornery Frank, and Crusty Bill. Alex hated those mules. They kicked, they bit and they gave her the evil eye whenever she went anywhere near them. She wished she could have the stolid old oxen back. That was one more thing to hold against the Gradys. They'd taken her oxen and stuck her with these evil animals.

"What do you want?" Alex sighed, watching Cranky Bob nuzzle her brother affectionately.

"I need to . . . you know what."

"So go," Alex said, even as she clambered to her feet, knowing what the reply would be.

"I'm scared of the dark."

"Come on." Alex tried to keep well out of Bob's way, but the beast still tried to take a bite out of her. She hissed at him. It took Adam forever to step outside the circle of the wagons. Crusty Bill had hold of his jacket and wouldn't let him go.

"Can't they come with us?" Adam pleaded, as he tried to extricate the jacket from Bill's huge teeth. "They won't run off or anything."

"No." She swore the *heehaw* that followed was Bob's way of cursing her.

Once she'd managed to get Adam away from his admirers, Alex led him to the hole they'd dug downwind. There was a new moon, so the darkness was almost total. Alex turned away to give her brother some privacy. She tilted her head back to look at the dense spray of stars above. The sky seemed bigger out here, the stars close enough to touch. She almost reached out her hand. She was sure the stars would feel rough, like grains of sand.

She near leaped out of her skin when she heard hoof-beats. Who would be riding in this black night?

What if it was Indians?

"Adam," she hissed, "hurry up!" She hoped the others could hear it too, but she doubted it. Their voices were louder than the sound of hooves, even out here beyond the wagons. She had to get back and warn them.

When Adam didn't answer she went to find him. She couldn't leave him alone out here. He'd die of fright.

But he wasn't at the hole.

Her heart stopped. "Adam!" she hissed again.

The hoofbeats were getting louder. She scanned the area around her, but it was so dark she couldn't make out much more than a few shapes in the blackness. None of them were moving, so she assumed they were shrubs.

"Adam," she called again, her voice louder and more desperate. He wouldn't have wandered off, not in the darkness; he was so scared of the dark. And then, to her shock, the hoofbeats came to an abrupt stop and her brother's voice rang through the clear night air. "What's the name of that horse?"

Alex couldn't stop the squeal of fright that escaped her. She ran toward the sound of his voice, but she stumbled over the rough ground and went flying, skidding her face against the dirt and coming to rest practically underneath the dark horse. The horse was startled and reared, hooves pawing at the air. Alex heard a sharp curse as she rolled out of the way.

Now flat on her back and panting with fear, she looked up into the annoyed face of Luke Slater. "What in hell do you think you're doing?" he snapped.

Alex couldn't answer. Until that moment, she'd had no idea how scared for him she'd been. She closed her eyes and said a quick prayer of thanks. She must have imagined the Gradys killing him in a hundred different ways.

She heard the creak of his saddle as he swung down.

"She's a lovely horse, Luke," Adam said admiringly.

"Yes, she is," Luke agreed, handing him the reins. "Her name's Delilah."

"Like from the Bible."

"That's right." Luke held out his hand to help Alex up.

"Samson should never have trusted her," Adam said as he stroked Delilah's nose.

"Never trust a woman, Adam," Luke said, sounding amused.

"Not any woman?"

"Stop filling his head with nonsense." Alex scowled at Luke, ignored his hand and clambered to her feet.

"It's something you should learn too, runt."

"Don't be ridiculous. Women are every bit as trustworthy as men." She couldn't believe they were having this ridiculous conversation, as though he hadn't been away for a week, as though he hadn't been out to commit murder. *As though she'd never kissed him and felt his hands on her body.* The wayward thought shocked her and she tried to push it away. But it had unlocked other thoughts, and she couldn't help but trace the lines of his long body with her gaze. She'd forgotten how magnificent he was. His broad shoulders strained at the dusty cotton of his shirt, his strong jaw was rough with stubble, and his beautiful, full lips . . . she mentally shook herself. What was wrong with her?

"That just shows how young you are, runt. Once you've had a bit more experience with women you'll realize how duplicitous they are. They'll swear till they're blue in the face that they don't want anything from you, and the next minute they're crying because you won't marry them."

Alex's eyes narrowed. Who was begging him to marry them? Those whores at Dolly's? That mystery girl back in Oregon?

Luke took the reins from Adam and started toward the wagons. "Is there any food left? I'm starving."

Alex sputtered for a moment and then started after him. "Aren't you going to tell us what happened?"

"Nothing happened. I lost them."

"You lost them? Lost them *where*?"

"Does Delilah want a drink, Luke?" Adam asked, following on his heels like an overexcited puppy. "There's water over here for the mules. She could share that."

Alex was so distracted by thoughts of the Gradys, imagining them looming out of every dark shadow, that she didn't notice Crusty Bill sneaking up on her. When his teeth sank into her rear she screeched.

Luke's gun was out of its holster in a second. Alex gasped when she found herself looking straight down its barrel. She glared at him and pushed it aside. "Would you mind not pointing that thing at me? It was just that damn animal." Alex rubbed her sore behind and resisted the urge to kick the mule. It would only upset Adam. And who knew if the ornery beast wouldn't come after her in a fury?

"Tarnation, runt, you scream like a woman."

Alex scowled.

Luke laughed. The kid was a mess. His clothes were so huge he looked like a scarecrow, he was filthy, and he was holding onto his rear end like it would fall off if he let go.

"You didn't find my horse, then?" she needled him.

"Or your horse?" Adam chimed in sympathetically. "She was a nice horse too."

"The hunt ain't over yet," Luke told them cryptically. He didn't want to worry them. In truth, he'd found a partial trail. Just a few prints that disappeared into a stream, but it was enough. The Gradys were following the water, knowing that the wagon train wouldn't stray too far from it.

Luke overtook them easily. He knew the trail like the back of his hand, whereas they were in unfamiliar territory. He considered lying in wait and facing them head-on, but the fact was, he was exhausted. He hadn't slept for more than a couple of hours at a time since the night before the fire, and even then it had been sleep snatched in the saddle. He needed his wits about him to face those brutes.

He lit out after the wagons, putting a comfortable distance between himself and the Gradys. He planned to catch up to the group, rest a little, and let them come to him. All he'd have to do is ride scout every day, and eventually they'd turn up. When they did they'd learn what happened to horse thieves in the territories. And it wasn't pleasant.

Alex eyed him suspiciously. The hunt wasn't over? She

didn't like the sound of that. What was he doing here if the hunt wasn't over? Where the hell were the Gradys?

"Rustle me up some food while I settle Delilah, would you, runt?"

"Can I help you, Luke?" Adam asked.

"Sure thing. You ever brushed a horse before?"

Alex could hear them chattering as she headed for the campfire. Rustle him up some food. What was she? Some kind of servant?

"Luke's here," she told Sebastian and the Watts brothers.

"Thought we heard a woman scream?" Henry said curiously.

"Nice of you to get off your backside and see if she needed help," Alex muttered under her breath.

Joseph slapped his knee and hooted. "The boy's sassing you, Henry."

"I notice you didn't get up either," Henry snapped.

"Luke wants food," Alex told Sebastian, ignoring them. "Can I get something out of the chuck wagon?"

"Help yourself."

She threaded her way between the oxen, mules and horses, muttering under her breath. She wasn't sure why she felt so irritable. Shouldn't she be thrilled he was back safe? Maybe she would be if he weren't always ordering her about. Or laughing when she was assaulted by demon animals.

She paused over a bag of beans and sighed. That wasn't it. Not really. If she was honest with herself she was irritated because he looked right at her and didn't *see* her. How could he look into her eyes and not know who she was? After he'd touched her . . . tasted her . . . *possessed* her.

She had a sudden desire to walk out there and show him just who it was he was ordering about. She could see it clear as day in her head. She would stalk out there, through the dancing firelight, walk right up to him, and kiss him. At the first press of her lips he would know. His eyes would burn, the way they had that night at Dolly's, and he would look at her and *see*.

Wouldn't he?

❧ 18 ❧

THE ONLY THING Alex kissed that night was her pillow. And it wasn't even a real pillow. It was just a sack of flour. It was hard, uncomfortable and it didn't kiss her back.

She buried her face in it, scrunched her eyes closed and tried to block out the sound of male voices drifting over from the campfire.

She'd been so tired before Luke showed up. She had longed to go to bed. Now here she was, stretched out under her itchy blanket, as wide-awake as it was possible to be. She'd made Luke his dinner, washed the frypan and sat down to wait them out. She'd been able to feel the leather bag full of bonds pressing against her belly. She had to burn the wretched things. She stared into the flickering flames and listened to the men talk; most of it was boring talk of farming and politics and she found herself starting to doze.

She started awake when Luke's hand settled on her shoulder and gave it a squeeze. "Get to bed, runt."

"Don't call me that."

"You're falling asleep," he said patiently. "Get to bed, Alex."

She winced. That was infinitely worse than "runt." To hear her name said in that low, rough voice was torture. Worst of all was the note of tenderness she detected. She didn't want that kind of tenderness from him. Not the tenderness of a big brother; not when she'd known the tenderness of a lover.

He took her hand and tugged her to her feet. "Off with you." He gave her a gentle shove toward her wagon.

She paused before she climbed the wooden step and watched as he laid out his bedroll. He left his boots on, she noticed. He settled himself close enough to the fire for warmth, and dropped his hat over his face.

"Night, Luke," Adam called sleepily from his position under the wagon.

"Night."

Now here she was with her face buried in a bag of flour, straining to hear his breathing. It was ridiculous. And yet, she swore that she could make it out, beneath the rise and fall of voices, beneath the soft whicker of horses and the rumble of Adam's snoring. That steady susurrus was him, she was sure of it.

He was out there; only the waterproofed canvas separated them . . .

Alex pressed her face into the flour bag. She was never going to be able to sleep.

YET SOMEHOW SHE did. She woke early, before anyone was stirring. Alex figured she could burn the bonds before people started rising at dawn for their morning coffee. She tried to be as silent as possible as she crawled from the wagon. She was awfully stiff from sleeping on those hard boards. She poked her head from beneath the canvas flap and almost screamed to find herself face-to-face with Cranky Bob. And right behind him were the rest of them. Their eyes shone black as oil in the watery predawn light.

"Get," she hissed. "Go on, get out of here."

Bob simply snorted at her, and the rest of them didn't so much as move a muscle. Alex frowned. She wriggled back through the canvas flap and fussed through the supplies, muttering to herself. Victoria moaned and rolled over, pulling the blanket up over her head. "Just another few minutes," she mumbled.

Poor Victoria. She wasn't coping too well with the traveling. She was bruised and sore from the jolting of the wagon and always close to tears at the lack of even the most basic amenities. Out of consideration, Alex stopped muttering as she looked for the right sack. The sugar was coarse and brown and full of lumps. She picked out some of the larger lumps and crawled back to the flap. Cautiously sticking her head out, she glared at the mules.

"Is this what you want?" she hissed, showing them the sugar. Cranky Bob bared his teeth. "Fine. Go and get it." She tossed it away from the wagon. They turned to go after it, but she was certain that Bob gave her a backward look, as though warning her that he couldn't be bought quite so easily. Lord, how she hated those mules.

She climbed down and crept to the campfire. She could hear Adam snoring, and Luke was still stretched out in his bedroll, although he'd turned on his side and his hat now lay in the dirt. Alex picked it up and placed it gently beside his saddlebags, then headed for the opposite side of the fire so she could check he didn't wake while she went about her business. She stoked the fire until it was burning neatly, and quickly withdrew a few bonds. One by one she fed them into the flames, watching as they ignited, blackened and curled. After she'd burned a handful, she stopped, remembering Dolly's caution. She raked the coals, searching for unburned fragments. She couldn't see any, but she'd be sure she was the one to douse the fire later, so she could check the cold remains. Then she'd follow the whore's advice to the letter, as she had every morning, and bury what was left.

As she worked soft apricot light stained the eastern sky. Alex had never seen sunrises and sunsets like the ones out here on the plains. Some mornings the sun rose soft like this, apricot shading to warm golds; other mornings it blazed pink and orange; while on others the light was garishly red, brassy as a whore. Today streamers of low clouds caught the rising sun, buttery in the apricot wash. On mornings like these, hope stole over Alex with the warm kiss of the sun. Maybe they'd make it all the way to Oregon without ever seeing the Gradys again.

After she'd set a pot of coffee to boil, Alex sat back on her heels and finally allowed herself to examine Luke as he slept. Her heart constricted at the sight of him. He looked younger. The hardness of his jaw had softened in sleep and he didn't look quite so intimidating. His eyelashes were dark fans on his cheeks, and those incredibly full and enticing lips were slightly parted. The man was too beautiful to be true.

"Good morning." The whispered greeting just about made Alex jump out of her skin. She'd been so focused on Luke she hadn't heard footsteps approaching. It was Jane O'Brien. The one person Alex had been desperately avoiding.

Her father watched Alex like a hawk, which was mortifying, but the fact that Ned disapproved only seemed to make Jane like Alex more. She took every opportunity to seek Alex out, and Alex took every opportunity to flee.

"Couldn't you sleep either?" Jane whispered as she sank down beside Alex. Alex made to rise, but Jane laid a restraining hand on her arm. "Don't go. We haven't had a chance to talk since the dance."

"I think my sister's calling me."

"I don't hear anything." Jane cocked her head and gave Alex a flirtatious smile.

Alex cleared her throat nervously.

"You don't need to be shy around me, Alex."

"I'm not—" Alex was cut off mid-sentence as Jane lunged forward and kissed her. It was an inexpert kiss, close-mouthed and clumsy, but full of enthusiasm. Alex was too shocked to move.

"I hope I'm not interrupting anything," a lazy voice drawled.

Alex looked over to find Luke propped up on one elbow, regarding them with an amused grin. She shoved the girl away from her and wiped her mouth.

"You won't tell Daddy, will you, Mr. Slater?" Jane asked desperately.

"That all depends," Luke mused, and Alex could see the twinkle in his eye, "on whether Mr. Alexander here has been taking liberties with you."

"Oh no, *I* kissed *him*!"

"Well, in that case, no."

Oh, how Alex wanted to slap the stupid smile off his face. She glowered at him, but he wouldn't stop grinning at her.

"Just mind you don't go getting ideas, you hear, Alex? Miss O'Brien is a lady, after all." Lady, my rear end, Alex thought sourly. The girl was shameless.

"Jane?" Ned O'Brien's voice drifted through the morning air and Alex jumped. Jane squealed, leaped to her feet and dashed back to her wagon.

"You don't waste any time, do you, runt?"

"I told you not to call me that."

Luke laughed and stretched. "Is that coffee I smell? Get me a cup, would you?"

There he went, ordering her around again. She almost dropped the pot when he stood and began unbuttoning his shirt. In the apricot light his skin glowed. Her memory hadn't done him justice at all. Her hand trembled as she poured the coffee and it splattered against the rim of the mug. Button by button, inch by inch, more of that smooth, hard body was revealed. She couldn't look away.

He balled up the shirt and bent over his saddlebags. And there was a view . . . a wide range of taut and tensed muscle. Alex had to set the coffee cup down; she was splashing the stuff over her boots. This couldn't be natural, the way she was feeling. Could it?

"Oh, Mr. Slater!" The feminine squeal startled them both. Victoria was standing there, hands bashfully held over her face, ostensibly shocked by his state of undress.

"Beg your pardon, Miss Alexander, I didn't think you'd be up so early." Luke rose in one smooth movement and pulled a fresh shirt on. Alex noticed he didn't seem to be in any hurry about it. She also noticed the way Victoria was peering through her splayed fingers.

"Coffee's ready."

They both turned to look at Alex, as though they'd forgotten she was there, she thought crankily. Invisible Alex, everyone's servant boy.

"I didn't know you were back," Victoria said breathlessly to Luke, lowering her hands as he fastened the final button. Alex didn't miss the way Victoria ran her hands over her plain dress, surreptitiously neatening the folds of her skirt.

"Only just," Luke told her, taking the coffee mug from Alex and passing it to Victoria. "I got into camp late last night."

"I'm surprised I didn't hear you."

"I'm not, the way you snore," Alex couldn't stop herself from saying.

"I don't snore," Victoria said primly. "You must be thinking of Adam."

"I certainly heard *him*." Luke grinned. "He always so loud?"

"Always," Victoria said, and she actually giggled. Alex turned away, disgusted.

"You forgot my coffee, runt."

"No, I didn't," she objected, "you gave it to Vicky." But she still filled another mug for him.

"I'm sorry about his manners," she heard Victoria apologize in a low voice. "I'm afraid he's had no guiding hand since Ma and Pa passed."

Alex glared at her. No guiding hand, indeed.

"A boy needs a man around," Luke remarked. "I sure had my work cut out for me with my brothers after our parents died."

"I bet they were glad to have you," Victoria said dreamily as she sank down on the blanket Luke had folded for her to sit on.

Alex gathered her sister wasn't planning on helping with breakfast. She couldn't resist kicking dust on her as she walked past on the way to the wagon. Victoria didn't even notice, which made Alex feel even crankier.

Adam was up when she emerged from behind the canvas flap with a hunk of bread and a pan of bacon. He was trying to elbow the mules away from the pail of water so that Delilah could get to it. "Come on, now, Sue, be nice," he was saying patiently, "and boys, you know the rule: ladies first."

"Breakfast, Adam."

He gave her an absent wave, but didn't look up from the animals. Alex sighed. She'd have to make up a bacon sandwich for him to eat later. When she got back to the fire Sebastian was up and whisking a pan of eggs. "Want some?" he asked, as he yawned and scratched his stubble. "It's the last of the eggs, at least until Kearney."

"Sure. You want some bacon?"

"Sure."

They stood companionably by the crackling fire as the bacon spat and sizzled and the bread fried in the melting fat, and watched Victoria falling over herself to keep Luke's attention.

"Don't your sister cook?" Sebastian asked.

"She cooks."

Sebastian looked pointedly at the spatula in Alex's hand and she flushed.

"You give them an inch and they'll take a mile," Sebastian warned.

"I'll keep that in mind."

One by one the others crawled from their wagons and took their places at the campfire. After they'd finished eating, Alex dumped the dirty dishes unceremoniously in front of Victoria. "I'm going to hitch the mules to the wagon. Unless you'd rather?" She didn't wait for an answer.

"Hold up, runt."

Alex couldn't believe it when Luke tossed one of his saddlebags over her shoulder. Her knees almost buckled under the weight. "I'm not a packhorse," she snapped.

"You sure woke up on the wrong side of the bed," he remarked as they headed for the animals.

"I don't *have* a bed," she said sourly. "I have a flour sack and a horse blanket."

He laughed. "Don't tell me, with all your gold, that you didn't think to buy bedding?"

"We bought bedding," Alex said stiffly. "Adam's got his own and I'm supposed to share with Victoria."

"Supposed to?"

"She hogs the quilt."

Luke laughed again.

"You're awfully happy, considering you came back empty-handed." She was gratified to see a shadow momentarily darken his face, but then he was grinning again, and that awfully alluring dimple flashed at her.

"Give me time, runt." He whistled and Delilah gave a whicker and trotted over to him. Adam followed. And the mules followed him.

Here came one of the most hated parts of her day. Alex dropped the saddlebag with a thump and regarded the mules balefully. She'd found it was best to deal with the ringleaders first, and that meant Cranky Bob and Crusty Bill.

"Right," she said, addressing them directly, and placing her hands on her hips, "what's it going to be today? Are we going to do it the hard way or the easy way?"

The mules eyed her. Then Bob tossed his head and gave a honking *heehaw.*

"That's what I thought," Alex said grimly, rolling her sleeves up.

"Let me just give them the sugar, Alex," Adam pleaded.

"No way." Alex shook her head vehemently. "We did that yesterday and that son of a one-legged goat kicked me. I told you"—she shook her fist at Bob—"I *told* you there'd be no sweet-talking you anymore. You let me harness you or . . . or . . ." Alex fished around for a suitable threat. "Or I'll take a switch to you."

"Alex, you wouldn't."

"I warned them, Adam."

"They'll be good today. Won't you, Bob? Bill? Frank? Sue?" Adam turned his pleading eyes on the mules.

Luke shook his head. He'd never met such greenhorns.

When Bill snapped his teeth at Alex she lost her temper and headed for the nearest shrub, to cut herself a switch. Adam followed, still pleading.

"I'll be back in a minute," Luke told Delilah, scratching her ears before heading for the Alexanders' wagon. While Adam pleaded with Alex, Luke calmly harnessed the mules. He was astonished by the runt's reaction when the kid returned, brandishing his crude switch.

Alex gaped, speechless at the way the mules had followed Luke without protest. "You are the most impossible creatures!" The switch whistled through the air as she threw up her hands.

"What are you talking about?" Luke said. "They were as placid as can be."

Alex looked back and forth between the mules and Luke. She flushed. Luke was looking at her like she was a mad person. If only he could see the teeth marks and bruises patchworked on her flesh!

"Adam, maybe you should harness them in the future," Luke suggested dryly, gathering his saddlebags and whistling for Delilah.

Alex turned back to the mules. The four of them were regarding her, their furry ears cocked at jaunty angles. "I know what you're doing," she warned them. "And I won't stand for it, you hear? I demand a little respect."

Bill bared his teeth at her, looking for all the world like he was grinning.

She threw the switch at him.

✦ 19 ✦

"WHERE IS HE going?" Victoria demanded, as they watched Luke kick Delilah into a gallop. "He just got here!"

Alex had a fair idea where he was going, and her blood ran cold. *The hunt ain't over yet.* Those had been his words. She swallowed hard. So, if Luke was here, that meant the Gradys were nearby. She resolved to burn every last bond tonight, even if she had to sit up all night to do it.

But for the moment she had to put the Gradys out of her mind and concentrate on the task at hand. The last vivid streaks of dawn color still hung in the east as Sebastian's "Ha!" rang through the cool morning air. Creaking and rattling, the line of wagons began to move. Alex tightened the reins around her fists and braced herself for the jolt as the wagon lurched forward. Victoria hung on for dear life, still frightened by the precariousness of the high seat and the juddering of the wagon on the rough terrain. They fell in behind the O'Brien wagon, and Alex could hear Mal Crawford applying the whip to his oxen behind them. She was glad to be safely in the middle of the train, but she didn't appreciate the thick dust. She thought Sebastian had the best position, out there in front, in the clear air. After an hour or so, she'd drop back a little and let the space between them and the O'Brien wagon grow, so that she could breathe again.

The days were hellishly monotonous: hour after hour of shuddering along, watching the rear ends of the mules, feeling the reins cut into her hands. After a few hours, her shoulders would be sore from the driving, and her back would ache from the jolting, and her mind would be numb from the boredom. Victoria usually surrendered her seat by mid-morning and crawled into the shade of the wagon, where she stretched out on her quilt and tried to read a book. Then Adam would clamber up beside Alex, where he'd occupy himself talking to the mules.

Today, on edge about the Gradys, Alex decided to distract herself by teaching Adam to drive the wagon. He'd been begging her since they'd left and she figured it would give them both something to do.

"Hold on tight, mind," Alex warned.

Adam was glowing with excitement. He sat ramrod straight and held his arms stiffly out in front of him. Alex couldn't help smiling as she watched him. "You're doing a great job."

"Really?"

"Really truly."

She flexed her fingers and tried to relax a little. Now that she wasn't the wagoner, she noticed Jane O'Brien in the wagon ahead. The girl had her arms resting on the back of their wagon and was watching Alex avidly.

Alex pulled her hat down lower so that the shadow obscured her face. She felt hunted. She wished she could climb into the back with Victoria and hide. Or better still, head off on her own, like Luke.

Luke. Just the thought of him filled her with that unsettling, shivery sensation.

"When do you think he'll be back?" As though reading her thoughts, Victoria leaned in between Adam and Alex. "Don't you think it's odd the way he just lit out like that, without a word?"

Alex grunted.

"Do you think he has a sweetheart?" Victoria mused.

"I think a man like him has too many sweethearts," Alex remarked dryly.

"What makes you say that?"

"He practically has to beat them off with a stick."

Victoria stiffened. "I haven't seen any women around him."

"What about those whores back in town?"

"Oh, whores," Victoria said dismissively. "They're not sweethearts."

"When we bought the wagon, Archie said something about a girl back in Oregon." The words tasted like sawdust in Alex's mouth. *Did* Luke have a sweetheart back home? What was she like? Alex would bet anything that she was a real lady, and beautiful. *She* certainly wouldn't be running around wearing overalls and oversized boots. She probably had long, glossy hair and dainty manners. She wouldn't be the type of girl to argue with mules. Or to let a man seduce her out of her virginity without so much as a by-your-leave.

"Ask him," Victoria said suddenly.

"What?"

"Ask him for me if he has a sweetheart back home."

Alex turned around to examine her sister for signs of heatstroke. But Victoria didn't look even the slightest bit flushed. Her brown eyes were clear and utterly earnest.

"I can't do that!"

"Why not? He thinks you're a boy. Surely men talk about that kind of thing. Besides, you can always say that you're curious because of the O'Brien girl. Maybe you're wondering how to behave with a sweetheart?"

"Are you mad?"

"You're a *boy*, Alex."

"No, *Victoria*, I'm a girl. A girl wearing a hell of a lot of dirt and her brother's clothes."

"Please, Alex. For me?" Victoria widened her eyes and pouted.

Alex turned her back on her sister. She ran a hand over her flattened chest, as though to reassure herself that she really was still a girl underneath the disguise. She had the awful feeling that one of these days she'd wake up and she actually would be a boy. And no one would ever know that she'd once been the prettiest girl at the dances in Dyson's barn.

She heard Victoria sigh softly as she rested her chin on her palm. "What do you think he's doing right now?"

RIGHT NOW, LUKE was watching the Gradys follow the Missouri north. He was guessing they'd follow it to where it met the Platte River, and then they'd turn off to follow the tributary westward to Fort Kearney. Which suited Luke just fine. The wagon train had stopped keeping to the river a day or so ago, and was heading overland to Kearney. They'd be long gone before the Gradys got there. Luke was hoping to avoid a showdown until Fort Laramie. If everything went to plan, they could leave the Gradys in the lockup at Laramie, where they could kick their heels until it was time for their appointment with the hangman.

Satisfied, he and Delilah left them to it.

By the time he caught up with the wagons it was late afternoon and the sunlight was falling low and golden over the scrubby flats. He stopped to chat with each driver as he made his way up the train toward the chuck wagon. He wished the wagon wasn't stuffed to bursting with supplies—what he really wanted was to stretch out and take a nap. But this early in the journey there was no room; even Sebastian was spending his nights under the wagon instead of in it.

"Those mules behaving themselves?" Luke teased the runt as Delilah drew level with the Alexanders' wagon. The kid was alone on the bench. Luke peered into the wagon and saw Victoria and Adam sleeping in the back.

Alex sighed. "Don't take their side. You really should see my rear." She blushed, suddenly aware of what she'd said. "I mean, it's black and blue," she stammered. "Every time I get close they take a bite out of me."

"Maybe you ought to feed them more often."

"Yeah," Alex said disconsolately, refusing to see the humor in the situation.

Luke took in the wilted shoulders and the pinched face. He flicked Delilah's reins over the buckboard and swung himself over to the wagon. "Delilah needs a break," he explained when the kid looked startled, "and so do you."

Alex let him take the reins, too surprised to protest. She was very conscious of the bulk of him beside her on the bench, and the way his solid thigh pressed against hers.

"I shouldn't be tired," she said eventually. "Adam drove for an hour or so this morning."

"Everyone else shares the driving between at least two people. Why don't you hand over to Victoria sometimes and take a break?"

Alex wrinkled her nose. "Victoria? Drive the mules?"

"She'll never do it if you don't let her try."

Alex couldn't argue with the logic of that.

They rode in silence for a while. Alex tingled every time his leg brushed hers. Which it did every time the wagon jolted. "The Gradys are out there, aren't they?" she said softly. "That's where you went, isn't it?"

"Let me worry about the Gradys, runt."

She frowned at him. "They're my problem too. I think I have a right to know."

"I'll take care of it."

"I never said you wouldn't, I just want to know if they're out there." Alex gestured at the surrounding plains. "I mean, *here*."

Luke turned to examine her. "You don't have to be responsible for everything, you know. Let me handle it."

Alex gritted her teeth. Let him handle it. As far as she could see he wasn't handling it particularly well, not if the Gradys were right out there, God knows how close . . .

"You seem pretty sure they'd want to come after you," Luke remarked. "I thought they were looking for your sister."

Alex felt like Cranky Bob had just kicked her in the stomach. How the hell did he know about any sister? She tried to keep her expression blank, aware that he was studying her. "What sister?"

"Victoria told me." His voice was gentle, but Alex felt like he'd slapped her.

"She *told* you?" He *knew* she was a girl? Well, why had he waited so long to say so?

"She told me your sister left you to run east," he said. He sounded disgusted.

"Yes," Alex said numbly, her mind racing. So, he didn't know? She chewed on her lip. Victoria must have told him the story they'd worked out.

"I think it's high time you told me what those Gradys want from you, runt."

"They want their gold back," Alex said miserably. She didn't mention the bonds. She'd burned most of them anyway.

"Your sister stole it?"

Alex nodded, flushing with shame. It sounded awful, laid

bare like that. "But you don't understand. They stole from us first," she said fiercely. "They took everything we had. Because Silas . . . Silas wanted . . ." She trailed off. She could hardly tell him what Silas wanted, could she?

"Is that their gold you've been spending?"

Alex nodded again, unable to meet his eye.

"You reckon they'll leave off if you give it back?"

"We've spent it," Alex said numbly.

"On the horse," he sighed.

"Yes."

"Well, they've got the horse, so I reckon that's a fair deal." He looked depressed at the thought of the Gradys keeping the stallion.

"Gideon won't stop until he's got her too," Alex said, her voice hoarse. *Me. He won't stop until he has me.* "You don't know Gideon."

"Well, she ain't here, is she?"

No, Alex thought, looking down at her soiled overalls. Alexandra Barratt had gone, and in her place was a skinny boy.

"Leave it with me, runt," Luke said calmly. "We'll have those Gradys strung up for horse theft, and then you won't have to worry anymore."

"You said the stallion was theirs by rights," Alex reminded him glumly.

"Maybe so. But Isis wasn't. It's a hanging offense to steal a man's horse, and the moment they laid hands on my horse, they made a date with the rope." He began to whistle and Alex felt a mite better.

They rode along for a piece. Alex gradually relaxed, soothed by the bulk of him beside her. Luke Slater had a comforting way of making her feel safe.

"That O'Brien girl is making eyes at you again," he drawled, when he finished whistling his latest tune.

She thought this might be the ideal time to ask Victoria's question for her. That would sure as hell distract him. The last thing she wanted to talk about was Jane O'Brien. "Do you have a sweetheart?" she blurted, determined to get him off the subject.

"What?" Luke was completely taken aback.

"Well, just speaking of making eyes at people," Alex said

clumsily, blindly staring straight ahead, once again glad the dirt hid her blushes. "*Do* you have a sweetheart?"

He grinned. "Sure, I have a sweetheart." He meant Amelia Harding, but all of a sudden his mind filled with a vision of Beatrice in that green gown, dancing under the lanterns in the town square of Independence.

Alex's stomach twisted. "Really?"

"Really."

She didn't want to hear any more but she couldn't help herself. "What does she look like?"

Golden hair. The slightest hint of a cleft in a stubborn little chin. And eyes the color of a rainstorm . . . Luke cleared his throat. "She's pretty."

Of course she is, Alex thought glumly. Luke could have any girl he wanted.

"She has brown eyes," Luke continued, struggling to call Amelia's eyes to mind. All he could see were gray eyes swirling like smoke.

"Oh." Alex felt sick.

"And dark hair." Beatrice's hair had shone with streaks the color of shiny gold coins. And it curled. Unconsciously, Luke reached into his pocket, and his fingers brushed against the battered petals of a cloth rose. "Dark," he repeated, louder than he intended to. *Ripe, swelling curves, as smooth as silk, pressing against him until his pulse raced, until he was wild . . .* hell. Luke scowled. He couldn't do this to himself. She was out of his life for good. There was no point in torturing himself.

"She's a tiny little thing," he told Alex, banishing Beatrice from his thoughts and trying to force his memory of Amelia to take concrete form. "Slight. Slender. Why, I reckon her waist would fit between my hands."

Alex blanched. And then she burned with shame. What must he have thought of her that night at Dolly's? She was everything his sweetheart wasn't. Alex felt something inside her die as she realized that she must have imagined the admiration in his face and the desire in his eyes. He'd made love to her because she was convenient. Because he was used to having any woman he wanted. Luke Slater thought all he had to do was look at a woman and she'd fall at his feet.

Alex's jaw clenched. Well, not any more. This was one woman Luke Slater would never have.

In the back of the wagon, Victoria had to bite down on her fist to contain her joy. Brown eyes, dark hair, slight and slender. She knew it!

He *did* love her!

✣ 20 ✣

WELL, FORT KEARNEY sure was a disappointment. Alex took in the small, rough settlement by the side of the shining river and tried not to feel too deflated. After all, it wasn't like she was a city girl. Her small square of Mississippi had only been settled for a decade or so; it was far from completely civilized. And yet, at least back home there were plantations, and towns, and trade along the river. The land out here seemed so empty. The fort looked insignificant against the huge spread of land and the indifferent flow of the river. It was like a fleabite on an old hide.

Alex wondered what Oregon would be like. Even emptier, she supposed, suppressing a sigh.

"Let Adam handle the mules," Luke said, trotting over on Delilah and extending his hand to hoist her up behind him. "You're coming into town with me."

They'd made camp just upriver from the smudge of a town and Alex had immediately set to the chores. She was hot and she was tired. If she sat down she'd never get back up again.

"Why?" Alex eyed Luke's proffered hand skeptically, suspecting she was being roped into more work.

"I've a mind to buy us steak for dinner."

"Steak?"

"Well, a cow."

Alex winced. "And you want help butchering it." Lord, she hated butchery. It was hard, messy work.

"Come on." Luke snapped his fingers at her.

"I'm not your slave, you know." Alex glared up at him.

"What's going on here?" Victoria asked, gliding over to smile up at Luke.

"He wants me to go into town with him, but I'm not going."

"I'll go," Victoria volunteered.

"Yeah, take Victoria."

Luke gave Alex a warning look.

"I'll have the coals hot for when you get back with dinner," Alex told him with a facile smile.

"Dinner?" Victoria looked back and forth between them.

"I need Alex to help me butcher a cow."

Victoria pulled a face and stepped away.

Luke snapped his fingers again.

"And you can quit that," Alex told him. "I'm not your horse either."

"Would you get up here, you ornery runt?"

Alex ignored him and set off on foot.

"Alex doesn't like horses," Victoria explained. "Her—I mean, his—father was killed when his horse took a fall." She blushed, hoping Luke hadn't noticed her slip.

"A man can't get far in this world if he's scared of horses," Luke observed, urging Delilah after the runt.

Alex screamed as a strong arm seized her around the middle and hauled her into the saddle. "Let me go!"

Luke ignored her and kicked Delilah into a trot. Alex almost flopped off the saddle, until Luke pulled her upright. She squealed and clutched at the pommel. She hated the jarring gait; she felt like she would plummet to the ground at any minute—and the ground looked like an awfully long way down.

"And you say you're sixteen?" Luke said dubiously.

"Nearly seventeen," she managed to gather her wits enough to remind him. It barely felt like a lie anymore.

"Bet you were in the church choir back home."

She tilted her head to look up at him, but at that precise moment Delilah stepped up the pace and Alex felt a surge of panic; she had to return her full attention to maintaining her seat. "What do you mean by that?" she asked suspiciously when her heart had calmed again. She knew there had to be an insult there somewhere.

"Don't choirs like boy sopranos?"

"I'm a contralto," Alex told him primly.

"You'll be a tenor any day now, I'm sure." She could hear the laughter in his voice.

"I'm aiming for bass," she snapped.

Luke looked down at the top of the battered brown hat. The runt sure was prickly. He was as bad as Luke's brother Matt.

And he sure as hell didn't know how to ride, Luke thought with disgust, watching the way the boy flapped bonelessly in the saddle, colliding with the horse at every step. He'd be black-and-blue by the time he dismounted. "Tomorrow I'll start teaching you how to sit a horse."

"No thanks," Alex said swiftly.

"What on earth were you going to do with that Arab if you weren't going to ride him?"

Alex chose to ignore him. Which proved to be impossible.

WHEN IT CAME time to butcher the animal the wretched man started disrobing again. He was certainly proving to be an exhibitionist. Worse, he seemed to expect Alex to follow suit!

"You'll get blood all over you," Luke warned, as he hung his shirt on a fence post and lifted the skinning knife.

"It'll wash out," Alex said stubbornly.

They were working in a dusty paddock owned by the captain who'd sold them the cow. Alex observed the captain's two daughters taking a stroll along the riverbank, just in time to catch Luke's display. She tried to ignore them as she rolled up her sleeves and helped him with the business at hand. They lapsed into a companionable silence as they worked.

"What happened to your pa?" Luke's question came out of the blue, and blindsided Alex. All the breath was gone from her lungs as the grief hit her again.

"Which one?" she asked softly, feeling the sting of tears. She blinked them away and concentrated on her task. "My real pa, or my foster pa?"

"Victoria said there was an accident with a horse?"

She tensed at the undercurrent of sympathy. "That was my real pa. I was just a kid. We'd come to Mississippi because he had a dream about working the land, but he was killed a couple of months after we arrived."

"I'm sorry."

Alex tried to shrug it off. "He wasn't cut out for it. He was trying to pull up tree stumps when it happened. The horse shied, he fell. I was the one who found him. Ma had sent me out with his lunch pail."

Luke paused, his gaze fixed on Alex. He could see the brittleness in the runt's expression. "And your ma?"

"She was pregnant when he died. Had the baby four months later and got childbed fever. Adam's parents took us in, me and the baby, but the baby died before she was one. We woke up one morning and she was just gone. Lying there all still and peaceful; it was hard to believe she'd ever drawn breath."

"But now you have Adam and Victoria."

Alex looked up, startled. Briefly she met his coal-black gaze. But then he was back at work, tactfully giving her a chance to collect herself. "Yes," she agreed. "They're my family now. They're both orphans, like me."

"Victoria's not Adam's blood either?"

"No. Ma and Pa Spar—um, Alexander, were given to taking in strays." She took a deep breath, feeling it was time to broach an awkward subject, but not sure how to continue. "Luke?"

"Yeah?" He stood and wiped the back of his arm across his brow, mopping away the perspiration. Over his shoulder Alex could see the captain's daughters giggling to one another.

"About Victoria . . ."

"What about her?"

"Be careful of her feelings." Alex looked down at her bloody hands. "I think . . . I think she thinks you're more serious than you are."

"Don't they all," Luke sighed. Alex felt her stomach twist. "Don't worry, runt, I'll treat her like the lady she is. And you"—he gave Alex a wink—"you better treat that O'Brien girl like the lady she should be."

ONCE THE BUTCHERING was done and the mess cleared up, Alex and Luke headed for the water pump. "One of these days you're going to have to take a bath," Luke observed, noticing that Alex was only scrubbing her hands and arms, "or you'll stink to the heavens." He eyed her clothes too. The new blood splatters had merely added to the layers of filth. "I'd be giving your overalls a wash while you're at it."

"Oh, Mr. Slater," the captain's wife called, emerging from the house, "I thought these might come in handy." She offered them a cake of soap and two clean towels. "And we'd be mighty glad if you'd join us for a pot of tea. It's the least we can do after you've so kindly given us dinner for the table tonight. I've made a chocolate cake, if you'd care for a piece."

"You're kind, but it's really not necessary. It was my pleasure, ma'am, after your husband sold us the cow at such a reasonable price."

"Of course it's not necessary," the captain's wife fussed, and Alex could see her daughters peering through the window and giggling, "but we so rarely get visitors. You wouldn't disappoint us, would you?"

"In that case, ma'am, we'd be honored."

"Rarely get visitors," Alex grumbled after the kitchen door had clicked closed behind the captain's wife. "They're on the trail, aren't they? I reckon they get a constant stream of visitors."

Luke laughed.

"We both know we're only getting chocolate cake so those girls can ogle you."

"Nothing wrong with that, runt," Luke said cheerfully, tossing Alex a towel. "We can ogle them right back. They looked like mighty pretty girls from what I saw."

"You saw them watching us? You *are* an exhibitionist."

"And you, runt, are a regular thundercloud. Lighten up a little. The meaning of life can be found in a pretty girl's smile."

Alex scowled at his back as she followed him into the kitchen. "What would your sweetheart think?"

"What she don't know won't hurt her."

Damn it. The runt wasn't just a thundercloud, he was a veritable downpour. Now he was thinking of Beatrice again. Which was ridiculous. Amelia was the woman he'd always planned to marry, and Amelia had never soured his enjoyment of a pretty woman. But now his head was full of Bea-

trice and the captain's daughters just didn't look so pretty
anymore. The younger one had a stingy mouth; it wasn't full
and ripe like other mouths he'd known, and her lips were
pale, not the rich red of summer strawberries. And the older
one's eyes were a faded blue, without the slightest trace of
stormy gray . . .

Hell. Luke tried his best to be charming, but his heart just
wasn't in it. He was glad when they took their leave. He filled
the saddlebags with their packages, and was surprised when
he turned to find the runt just standing there.

"I don't know how to get up," Alex admitted, with no
small measure of chagrin.

"Lesson one," Luke announced. "Put your foot in the stirrup and get on. Not that foot. You'll end up facing her rear
end. That's the one."

Alex gasped when she felt his hands against her buttocks,
giving her a push up. She almost went sailing right over the
horse. Glory, it was a long way down! She didn't like it up
here by herself, not one bit. It was a great relief when Luke
joined her. At least it was until she realized that this time
she'd be riding behind him, and there was no pommel. The
only thing to hold on to was him. Even worse, the snug saddle had her groin pressed hard against his buttocks, and her
thighs hugging his.

She resigned herself to the inevitable and held on for dear
life. And, despite herself, she found she began to enjoy the
experience. She felt safer this time. It was something to do
with the solid bulk of him—like holding on to a mountain—
and the way she could feel his thighs guiding Delilah. After
a while she relaxed against him, and let herself inhale his
masculine scent. Oh, he was warm in her arms. Alex sighed.
This trip to Oregon was going to be pure torture.

Alex didn't miss the jealousy in Victoria's eyes when they
cantered into camp. She left her sister for Luke to handle and
disappeared into the wagon to change out of her bloody
clothes. She'd just have time to wash them in the river before
dinner, she guessed.

She met Lucinda Crawford and Ilse Ulrich by the riverside.
Both had their washboards out and their sleeves rolled up.
"Oh, aren't you a good lad helping Luke," Lucinda clucked,

her red hands beckoning Alex closer. "Here, let me take those for you and wash the blood out."

"I can do them," Alex protested, embarrassed. She was used to looking after herself. Even when Ma and Pa Sparrow were alive, she was the one who took care of things. Ma and Pa were both old, and no match for Alex's vigor. She couldn't help herself. Taking charge came naturally to her.

But Lucinda hushed her and snatched the filthy clothes away. "It's no trouble, I'm already doing some."

Alex had to admit that it was lovely to simply sink down on the dry grass while someone else took charge for a change. Above, the sky was turning on one of those spectacular prairie sunsets. She listened to the women chatter and the river swish by, to the sigh of the wind in the grasses and the soft noises of the livestock enjoying the fresh feed, and let herself succumb to her weariness. Her shoulders throbbed from the afternoon's work and her buttocks ached from the short ride on Delilah.

She must have dozed off, because the next thing she knew Lucinda's rough red hand, redolent with the scent of lye soap, was stroking her hair. "Up you get, boyo. Come and finish your nap by the fire while we cook those steaks."

Her motherly voice filled Alex with a sense of peace. It brought back memories of better times. She struggled to her feet, her muscles protesting, and stretched. The sun was the merest sliver of molten gold on the horizon and the sky above was streaked lavender and pink. Alex yawned as she followed the women back into camp.

It was the nicest night they'd had on the trail so far. The steaks were fat and juicy, and there were potatoes roasted whole in their jackets in the coals, while the Watts brothers had picked up a jug of moonshine and were liberally sharing it around among the menfolk. The conversation flowed, and she got to know her traveling companions better. She didn't even mind waiting up to burn the bonds.

The only thing that gave her pause was the way Victoria clung to Luke. Why couldn't she see what kind of man Luke Slater was? Because no woman could when she was caught by his charm, Alex thought with a grimace, remembering the times she'd met him as Beatrice. She'd been like a fly caught in a spider's web. Helpless to struggle, even when she knew she'd be eaten alive.

Gradually, long after the sickle moon had begun its descent, people began to retire. For the first time the Watts brothers were in bed well before anyone else from too much undiluted moonshine.

"They'll pay for it tomorrow," Sebastian yawned, as he headed for the chuck wagon, cradling his bottle of whiskey.

"You won't be sleeping out here every night, will you, Luke?" Victoria asked with concern when Luke fetched his bedroll.

"If it rains I'll join Sebastian. Otherwise I like it just fine out here. I like having the stars for company."

Alex tilted her head back to examine them. She could see his point. It would be a mighty fine view to fall asleep to. There were more stars than sky.

"Well, good night," Victoria said, lingering. Alex wondered what she was hoping for. A good-night kiss?

"Night." Luke wrapped himself up.

"Come on, Alex."

Alex looked away from the stars, startled. She was planning on burning the bonds once Luke was asleep, but Vicky was giving her a hard stare. Rather than argue, Alex decided to come back to the fire once everyone was safely asleep.

Which took much longer than she'd thought it would. Victoria kept tossing and turning and wanting to pepper her with questions about Luke.

"For heaven's sake, Victoria," Alex snapped eventually, "I don't know any more than you do. Would you leave me be?"

In a huff, Victoria rolled over, taking the quilt with her. Alex hoped she'd go to sleep, but it took almost another hour before she did.

Carefully, praying the mules were nowhere around, Alex crept from the wagon to the fire. She'd had no chance to finish burning the bonds until now. Her heart pounded as she took them from the bag. She suddenly felt as though the Gradys would come looming out of the darkness at any minute.

Gradually, she worked her way through the sheaf of bonds. It felt deeply wicked to be burning such a fortune. How had the Gradys come by such money?

It was as she peeled away the next bond that the answer came to her. The last few sheets of paper weren't bonds at all. Staring out at her from the top page was a very familiar face. It was a crude but recognizable line drawing, accompanied by a typewritten passage: "$300 Reward. Runaway named NOAH, negro male, 25 years. Five feet eleven inches. Very dark in color. On his body are several old marks of the whip."

It was the man she'd helped at the Grady place. Alex would have known the face anywhere, even crudely rendered as it was. So he hadn't been the Gradys' slave. He'd been a runaway.

Behind that page was another, and behind that was a page from a news sheet, with column after column listing runaway slaves. The rewards started at fifty dollars and went up into the hundreds of dollars.

Was this how the Gradys made their money? Hunting down runaways? Alex couldn't bear to look at the lists of names, at the descriptions of whip scars and missing teeth. With trembling hands she fed the news sheets into the flames. She wasn't sure she'd be able to sleep tonight. Every time she closed her eyes she'd be sure to see the huge, dark eyes of those frightened children in the root cellar, and the solid metal collars around their necks.

As she disappeared into the wagon Luke's eyes opened. He stared into the coals. What the hell was that runt up to?

❧ 21 ❧

SHE COULDN'T BELIEVE he was serious about the riding business. Both she and Victoria stared at him, shocked, when he rode up the next morning leading Mal Crawford's chestnut gelding.

"But who will drive the wagon?" Victoria asked in a small voice.

"I can't believe a woman like yourself wouldn't be capable, Victoria." It was the use of her Christian name that did it. Not to mention the intimate tone in which he said it. Alex could just about see Victoria melt.

"Maybe tomorrow," Alex hedged. "She's never done it before. I'd best give her a lesson before we leave her alone with these mules."

"Do you need a lesson, Victoria?"

Damn him. Look at the way he was staring deep into Vicky's eyes, like some kind of hypnotist. Alex knew full well the effect of that burning black gaze; her sister didn't stand a chance.

"I'm sure I'll be fine," Victoria breathed.

"I can help too," Adam volunteered.

"There you go, runt." Luke threw Alex a triumphant grin.

She glared at him. Of all the manipulative . . . She should just refuse to go. But then the barbarian would probably just drag her over his saddle again.

"What does it matter to you if I ride or not?" she grumped as she climbed down from the wagon.

Luke shrugged. "Guess I'm just a Good Samaritan."

"Ha," Alex scoffed. "You sure you're not just trying to make my life miserable?"

"You'll thank me one day, runt. You'll be mighty isolated if you can't ride."

"I'll have a wagon."

Now it was Luke's turn to scoff. "You'll harness all four mules to that big old wagon every time you need to go someplace?"

"I don't see why not," Alex said stubbornly.

He jiggled the reins at her. "Are you going to mount up?"

She hadn't made a move to take them from him. She eyed the gelding warily. He looked enormous.

"Get on, runt," Luke said impatiently.

She sighed and shuffled closer. "The stirrup's as high as my head," she grumbled. Somehow she managed to get her foot in. The horse began to turn as she threw her weight against it and she squealed. Damn, she had to stop doing that. She sounded like a hysterical schoolgirl.

Eventually she was up. Oh, it was awful. The gelding was way bigger than Luke's mare; she felt like she was towering over him. If she fell off this horse she'd break her neck for sure.

"His name's Jack," Luke said, passing over the reins.

Alex looked down at them and gulped. She'd rather just grip the pommel and let the horse go wherever it wanted.

"We'll just take a walk away from the wagons, and I'll take you through the basics."

It was a long morning. While Luke was a patient teacher, he was also a strict one. He wouldn't let her get away with doing anything less than perfectly. He rode beside her as she tried to master the art of trotting—which she wasn't good at; she couldn't seem to relax into the rhythm of the horse—and he called out a constant stream of instructions.

"No. Lift yourself up with your legs. Now. *Now.*"

"I am," Alex snapped at him.

"No, you're not, or I wouldn't hear your butt slapping against the saddle."

After a while Alex felt like throwing her hat at him.

"Keep your back straight," he called.

"Move with the horse," he coaxed.

"Stop sawing at his mouth!" he ordered.

It was enough to make a girl scream. She was astonished

when he complimented her at the end of the lesson. "Pretty good for your first time," he said as they walked the horses back to the wagon train. It was hard to miss their party. There was a cloud of dust rising in the distance, neatly marking their progress.

"You'd do even better if you'd listen to criticism."

Alex spluttered. As far as she was concerned, she had put up with his constant harping with exceedingly good grace.

"You're a lot like my little brother, you know," he said, observing her mute outrage.

"I am not!" Alex protested hotly. Forget the fact that she'd never even met his brother; Alex didn't want to be compared to *anyone's* brother at this point. It was just adding insult to injury. Fine, she had to pretend to be a boy. Did she have to be such a convincing one?

"There you are. That's exactly how Matt would respond. I can't say anything without him saying the opposite."

Maybe she'd like this brother of his. She wondered if he was as handsome as Luke was. "How old is he?" she asked curiously.

"Twenty-one. Though he doesn't act it."

"What do you mean?"

"He's always off with his head in the clouds. He's got this idea for a lumber business, and he'll argue till he's blue in the face that we should be building a lumber mill, but does he actually do anything about it? Instead he lives like a mountain man, wandering about the wilderness trapping and trading. Burning up daylight," Luke said in disgust.

"Maybe he likes the wilderness," Alex remarked absently. She was busy examining Luke and wondering about his age. If his little brother was twenty-one, how old did that make him? He didn't look to be as old as thirty, but maybe he was.

"What do your parents think?" she asked. "About Matt wandering about in the wilderness?"

"Our parents died when we were kids. After we left Texas."

"You're from Texas?"

"Mexico originally. Our father was American, our mother Mexican. We lived in Mexico until I was ten, then we lived in Texas. When I was fifteen we left for California, and after a few years we moved on to Oregon. My father didn't like to stay in one place for too long."

"Maybe that's where your brother gets it from." Mexico, Alex thought with a silent sigh. That explained the earth-brown hair and burning dark eyes.

"You think he would have learned," Luke said quietly. "It didn't bring us any happiness, moving all the time. We left California when my mother died. Father couldn't bear to stay. But the journey to Oregon killed him, and now he's in a lonely grave in the wilderness, instead of resting beside my mother."

The sorrow in his voice tugged at Alex's heart. She knew what it was like to be orphaned.

"These trails take their toll," Luke observed, watching the line of wagons rolling steadily across the plains. "So many people die without reaching their promised land."

"But you keep traveling," Alex said.

"Not anymore. I'll be staying put from now on. Maybe there will be a trip to California now and then to auction a horse or two, but I've got roots in Utopia. There's no lonely grave in my future, runt." He turned to Alex, his black eyes serious. "I'll be buried in the Slater plot on Slater land. Where my kids will be able to find me."

"Your kids?" Alex asked through a tight throat.

"Amelia doesn't know it yet, but I plan to have at least a dozen," Luke said with a wink.

Amelia. Her name was Amelia. The name was still ringing in her ears when she dismounted.

"How about you, Adam?" Luke asked. "You want to have a ride too?"

Adam gave an almighty whoop and launched himself from the wagon.

"I'll take that for a yes," Luke chuckled. "Adam, meet Jack."

"You be careful," Alex warned her brother, but he was too busy struggling to pull himself into the saddle to listen. "Make sure he's careful," she said, turning the warning on Luke.

"Don't be such an old woman. Adam's a born horseman, aren't you, Adam?"

Alex watched as they left, Adam's elbows flapping like a chicken's wings with every step.

"I hope you enjoyed yourself out there with Luke, while I was having my fingers sawn off," Victoria said waspishly, handing the reins over to Alex and waggling her fingers, which bore red welts.

"Don't blame me, I tried to get you out of it." Alex winced as she sat down on the hard seat. Her rear end felt battered and bruised. She couldn't see the appeal of this riding business.

"So?" Victoria demanded, after barely a minute of silence. "What did you talk about?"

"Mostly about how awful I am at riding." Alex couldn't keep her mind on the conversation; she kept hearing Luke's voice in her head: *Amelia doesn't know it yet . . .*

"Did he mention me?"

"No, but he did mention that he wanted a dozen kids," Alex said. A dozen kids. She sighed, imagining twelve little Lukes around a dinner table, little black heads bowed for grace, voices raised exuberantly, passing dishes down the table . . . Oh glory, what was she doing to herself? Those children didn't belong to her; they belonged to dark-haired, brown-eyed, slender Amelia.

Alex had never met the woman, but she wanted to scratch her eyes out.

ALEX WAS NEVER going to be a horsewoman. Luke took her out every morning and she tried her best, really she did, but she never could quite overcome her fear of horses.

"He's responding to you," Luke scolded her, when Jack skittered. "Would you stop being so nervous?"

"It's got nothing to do with me," Alex snapped, pulling hard on the reins and cursing when Jack danced sideways. "I think he's been talking to those damn mules."

Luke gave her an exasperated look.

"It's true! I saw him with them this morning. Those wretched animals have poisoned him against me." Alex knew she sounded ridiculous, but she couldn't seem to button her lip. She was flustered and embarrassed by her failure with the horse. Why didn't animals like her? She gave Jack a poke behind his ear. "What did I ever do to you, you brute?"

"Do you want to swap horses?" Luke offered.

Alex gave Delilah a withering look. "Don't think I haven't noticed the looks she's been giving me."

"It's all in your head." But even Luke had to admit that Alex lacked a certain rapport with horses. The minute Jack saw the runt coming, he tensed up and got jumpy. And the gelding was one of the most placid horses Luke had ever seen.

Still, at least the kid could sit a horse properly now. And he really wasn't bad in the saddle, or wouldn't be if he didn't shriek with fear every time the horse did something he wasn't expecting.

Not like his brother. That Adam was a born horseman. You only had to show him something once and he was doing it like an expert. And he genuinely loved the animals. Luke enjoyed riding out with him; he wished either one of his own brothers had half as much interest in horses.

Alex wondered what he was thinking about. He had surprised her in the last few days. She'd had him pegged as a social animal. She'd figured that a man who flirted with every woman he met must like the company of people. And he seemed to, in moderation. But once they rode out on the plains, and the wagons had receded into the dusty distance, he tended to be quieter, more introverted. Now that she'd learned the basics of riding, he was prone to just light out and leave her to follow.

She thought that that was when he was happiest—when he and Delilah were tearing across the plains, moving as one, leaving a plume of dust in their wake. Sometimes they'd ride a whole morning and he'd barely speak. And, to her relief, Alex found herself beginning to relax around him.

It was easier, of course, like this: when she was a boy. He didn't turn that burning black gaze on her and melt her mind to mush. She watched him do it to the other women in the party: Lucinda Crawford had taken to doing his laundry, Victoria and Ilse Ulrich fought over who would cook his dinner (sometimes he ate from both cook pots, just to keep the peace), and even five-year-old Ellen O'Brien and six-year-old May Crawford competed for his attention around the campfire at night.

Now that she was no longer subject to his charms, Alex

had a chance to examine him as he bewitched the females of the species. It wasn't necessarily that he was a shameless flirt, although Alex hadn't ruled out that explanation entirely; it was simply that he gave a woman his full attention. He looked right into her eyes and nothing distracted him. She became the entire world to him. And what woman could resist that? Coupled with the fact that he looked like some kind of fallen angel.

"Here it is," Luke announced, as he pulled Delilah up beside the river.

"What?" Alex almost sailed over Jack's head as the horse stopped short. She swore he did it deliberately.

"This is where we'll cross this afternoon, and tonight we'll camp at Ash Hollow."

"We're crossing the river?" Alex looked dubiously at the swirling river.

"We have to. The river splits up yonder. If we kept on this south side we'll end up in Colorado."

"You want me to drive the wagon across that?"

"It's only a couple of feet deep. At most." He noticed the runt's disgruntled expression. "Are you going to complain about everything on this trip? 'Cause it's going to get pretty tiresome."

"I'd hate to tire you," Alex snipped, "but I'd think you could have given us a little warning that we'd be fording rivers today."

"*A* river, runt. You'll be fording *a* river. And it ain't much of one if it's only two feet deep."

"But I have to take your word for it that it's only two feet deep."

"Stop being such a girl. Come on, I'll race you back." As always, he didn't wait for her.

She had no chance of catching him, so she didn't bother. She kept to a brisk trot, taking the opportunity to practice her skills. She thought she might be getting better—she could certainly feel the muscles in her legs working.

When she got back it was to find Delilah hitched to the back of their wagon, and Luke asleep on Victoria's quilt. "What's he doing back there?" Alex snapped, peering between Adam and Victoria into the depths of the wagon.

"He was tired, poor thing," Victoria said.

"Where have you been?" Adam demanded. "It's my turn to ride Jack."

"But Luke's asleep."

"He said I could ride alongside the wagon."

"But no further, Adam. Remember?" Victoria warned. "He said Jack would be tired after all Alex put him through."

"All I . . . ?" Alex was offended. "I didn't put him through anything. If anyone suffered it was me."

Jack whickered and Alex gave him a dark look.

"Hi, boy." Adam beamed, offering him a handful of sugar. He was in the saddle the minute Alex had clambered over to the wagon.

And Victoria shoved the reins at her the minute her rear hit the bench. "Did he tell you about the river?" Alex asked crankily.

"What about the river?" Now that she was no longer driving, Victoria swiveled so that she had a clear view of Luke asleep in the back. Alex noticed with no small measure of satisfaction that he'd covered his face with his hat, depriving Victoria of her chance to ogle him.

"We're fording the damn thing this afternoon."

"Watch your language. What do you mean we're fording it?"

"We're crossing it." Alex was satisfied to see the color drain from Victoria's face. "I know," she commiserated, "that's how I feel."

Victoria looked at the spangled surface of the Platte. "Well," she said carefully, "if Luke thinks we should."

"Aw, hell, Victoria."

"Watch your language!" Victoria snapped again. "What would Ma and Pa say? Just because you're dressed like a boy is no reason to act like one."

Alex hissed and jerked her head at Luke's sleeping form. Victoria flushed.

"Well, it isn't!" Victoria muttered.

"Actually," Alex said in a forceful whisper, "I think it's every reason!"

"Not when we're alone, it's not. I don't see why I should have to be subjected to your vulgarity."

"Oh, don't be such a girl," Alex snapped, borrowing Luke's phrase.

Victoria turned her back and refused to speak. She was still as silent as a stone a couple of hours later when it came time to cross the river. By then Luke was in the middle of the river, on Delilah, directing traffic. To Alex's horror, Adam was right beside him, the water lapping at his boots while Jack stood calmly in the current.

"Get off that horse," she ordered when they reached the river and Luke and Adam came to check on them.

"He'll be fine," Luke insisted, "he can stay with me."

"He can't swim."

"He won't need to."

"What if he falls in?"

"He won't. And even if he does, the water'll barely wet his knees." The man was impossible. Alex had to grit her teeth as she watched him take Adam away from her. And now look at them both, out there mid-stream, as though they were invincible. All right, so the river was only a couple of feet deep, but that was hardly the point, was it?

"Now, listen, you lot," Alex said, addressing the mules as their turn came to cross, "no funny business, you hear?" They ignored her and plunged straight in.

After all of Alex's worrying the crossing was accomplished in just a few minutes. It was what came after that she should have been worrying about. After the endless plains, she saw they now faced a sharp incline.

Alex swallowed hard as she watched the wagons in front tackle the steep hill. "Get out of the wagon, Vicky."

"I will not." They were the first words her sister had spoken for hours and they were said in the frostiest tone imaginable.

"If the wagon tips over, I don't want you in it."

Victoria blinked. She looked back and forth between the hill and Alex. She noticed the way Alex's fingers trembled as they held the reins. "But what about you? What happens to you if the wagon tips over?"

"I'll be fine."

"Then so will I."

Alex took in Victoria's firmly set jaw and felt a little less afraid. She hadn't quite realized the distance that had sprung up between them since they'd arrived in Independence. She had to admit that she was glad she wasn't facing the forbidding hill alone.

They heard the hoofbeats as Adam came down the hill toward them. "You get off that animal right now," Alex demanded. "Suppose he falls down the hill? You'd break your neck."

Adam ignored her, and kept well out of her arm's reach, in case she tried to haul him into the wagon. "Luke says to fan out, don't stay behind the O'Brien's. He says to stop when you reach the top and we'll go down one by one." Alex couldn't believe the change in her brother. There was actually a note of authority in his voice.

"Luke wouldn't have us do this if it wasn't safe," Victoria said firmly.

"He isn't God, you know," Alex muttered as she watched the mules strain against the harness as they pulled the wagon up. She made the mistake of turning to look back. Through the canvas-covered hoops of the wagon she could see the sharp, grassy drop. Her stomach lurched and a cold sweat broke out on her forehead. "How on earth are we going to get down the other side?" she asked in alarm.

"Luke will know how."

Alex resisted the urge to pitch her sister down the hill. If Luke was so fantastic why wasn't he right here driving the wagon, instead of sitting safely on the crest of the hill on his wretched horse?

Of course, Luke did know how they were going to get down safely. And wouldn't you know it, Alex grumbled, his solution required Alexandra Barratt to get her hands dirty.

The chuck wagon was the first one down. Sebastian and Luke tied ropes to the wagon and all the men were enlisted to act as human breaks. The Watts brothers took one rope, Mal Crawford and Ned O'Brien another, Reinhard Ulrich and Adam another, and Luke and Alex the fourth.

"Brace yourself with your feet, runt," Luke warned, taking his position behind her and grasping the rope with his gloved hands. "Everyone ready?" he called. When he'd received the affirmatives, he yelled for Sebastian to start down.

The sudden weight of the wagon almost jerked Alex off

her feet. She dug her heels into the soft turf, but still felt herself slide. The ropes creaked as the wagon strained against them, but slowly they eased it down to the valley floor below.

When they were safely down, Alex bent double, trying to catch her breath. The muscles in her arms, back and thighs were screaming.

"Only five more to go," Luke said.

She looked up at him in horror. Five more? She wasn't sure she could do *one* more. Hell, she'd barely managed that one. And she still had to walk back up that devil of a hill!

The women were waiting at the top with flasks of water. The Watts brothers ignored them and dug out their moonshine.

If she thought the chuck wagon was hard work, she found the Crawford's wagon murder. Theirs was a massive broadwheeled monster of a wagon, which needed six oxen to pull it. This time Luke reached his arms around Alex, gripping the rope slightly ahead of her hands, so that she could brace herself against his body. As the wagon pulled them down the hill, leaving deep grooves in the earth, she could feel Luke straining, and could hear his breath come fast and shallow.

When that wagon too was at rest in the valley Alex collapsed on the grass. It was soft and cool. "I'm not getting up again," she huffed, as she watched Luke draw deep, hitching breaths.

"Come on, runt," he coaxed, and she swore there was a teasing gleam in his eye, "you don't want everyone to think you're a girl, do you? What about Jane O'Brien? She's right up there watching you."

"So let her take a rope," Alex suggested waspishly. But she took his hand when he offered to help her up and trudged after him up the hill.

Alex didn't know how she managed it, but somehow she struggled up that hill four more times, and strained against that rope four more times. And eventually they were all down that devil of a slope.

"Welcome to Ash Hollow," Luke announced with a flourish of one tired arm. When Alex recovered enough to look up she thought they may well have entered Paradise.

❖ 22 ❖

IT WAS ONLY when she saw the stands of cottonwoods that Alex realized she hadn't seen a tree for weeks. Spring had burned into summer as they crossed the plains, leaving them sunburned and sweaty and dusty. Ash Hollow was like a memory of spring: shadowy and cool and lush. Luke had them circle the wagons beneath the green shade, enclosed by a verdant riot of wild roses, grapevine and currant bushes. The air was heavy with the mineral tang of fresh water and the heady perfume of flowering jasmine.

"Oh, Luke," Victoria exclaimed, taking his arm and giving it a squeeze, "this is just how I imagine Eden must have looked."

"Ah, well," he laughed, neatly disentangling himself, "this is nothing compared to Oregon." He plucked a full-blown rose of palest pink and offered it to Victoria.

Alex watched, fascinated. Look how he managed to get away from her without hurting her feelings. While Victoria was busy inhaling the perfume of the rose, he simply disappeared into the milling livestock. And poor old Victoria thought she'd been honored. She thought the rose meant something.

Alex remembered the night of the dance, the way Luke had made her feel special, bribing the band to play only slow dances. Given time, she too would have been distracted with a rose while he slipped away to the next girl and the next dance.

Oh, she was such a fool. She felt the familiar sick flush of shame. She'd thrown herself away on him. On a man who already had a sweetheart waiting for him. The poor woman, Alex thought. She had no idea of the life ahead of her: always wondering which woman would catch his fancy next. Because a man like Luke Slater would never be faithful, not when every woman swooned at his feet. And not when he could escape them so easily, without leaving a shred of anger in his wake.

She pushed aside her gloomy thoughts. She was tired of the way her mind ran in circles since she had met Luke, going over the same things time and time again. She left Victoria to prepare dinner—she felt she'd earned a night off after the exertions of the afternoon—and headed for one of the freshwater springs, near where Adam was grooming Luke's horse.

"That man sure is good at getting other people to do his work for him," she muttered as she sank into the pillowy grasses. The spring water was sweet and cold, and Alex couldn't resist removing her boots and submerging her feet. It felt heavenly.

"It ain't your feet that need a wash, runt," an all-too-familiar deep voice said, fracturing her peace. "Have you had a look at your face lately?"

Alex sighed as he set himself up at the same spring with his saddlebag. Why couldn't he let her be? She dropped onto her back, without removing her feet from the water, and scrunched her eyes closed. Maybe if she couldn't see him, she could forget he was there.

"You've gone surly again," Luke observed as he removed his shaving gear. "I thought we were getting along just fine lately."

"We are," she mumbled, not opening her eyes. He was right. They had lapsed into a comfortable relationship . . . so why was she feeling out of sorts with him? She listened to the sound of him soaping his face, and then she heard the dull rasp of his razor.

"It's your sister, isn't it?"

Alex's eyes snapped open. "What about my sister?" She struggled upright and fixed him with a stern look. "You haven't touched her, have you?"

Luke cocked an eyebrow. "And when would I have had a chance to do that? You're never more than an arm's length away." She shot him a dark look. "I just meant . . ." Luke paused, looking like he was trying to choose his words carefully, "I just meant, are you surly with me again because . . ." He cleared his throat. "Because she's set her cap for me?"

"Her cap?" Alex echoed.

"Look, runt, I've known a fair few women and I know when one has serious designs on me."

"You should marry her," Adam chimed from where he was giving Delilah a good brush. The horse whickered, seemingly in agreement. Alex scowled at them both. She had a great sense of satisfaction when she turned back to find that Luke had nicked himself with the razor.

"Now, Adam, don't get me wrong," he said, as he mopped at the blood with his hand, "I like your sister a great deal, but I ain't looking to marry her."

"That's a shame," Adam sighed. "I would have liked living with you and all your horses." He brightened suddenly. "Hey, if you don't want to marry Victoria, you could always marry Al—"

"Adam!" Alex yelped, cutting him off. "Didn't you hear the man? He's not looking to get married!"

Adam visibly wilted. His big eyes filled with tears and he turned back to Delilah and began brushing furiously.

"I'm sorry, Adam," Alex apologized, feeling awful, "but you can't go pestering people like that." She'd have to get him alone later so she could explain herself. And he obviously needed reminding about her situation.

"Don't worry, Adam," Luke called, "I'm not offended." He gave Alex an evaluating look. "A little harsh, don't you think?"

"You're still bleeding," Alex told him tartly. She watched as he staunched the blood and resumed his shaving. She kicked her heels in the water, more than a little peevishly. "So are you going to marry this sweetheart of yours?" she asked, despite herself. It was like prodding a sore tooth; she just couldn't resist doing it, even though it caused her pain. "Adelia, was it?" She knew very well it wasn't.

"Amelia."

"Oh, right. Amelia. Are you going to marry her, then?"

Luke frowned down at his reflection and didn't answer. The truth was he'd asked her. Twice. And both times she'd said no. Luke had never met a woman who could resist him until he met Amelia.

It gave his brothers no end of amusement to watch him pretty himself up every Sunday in a vain attempt to win her favor.

"I hear Josh Masters dined at the Hardings' last night," Tom would say, with a wink at Matt. "I reckon there could be an announcement soon."

"Josh Masters? Why, I heard she favored Dell Pritchard," Matt would say to play along. And they'd both laugh long and hard at his black looks. Well, not anymore. Once he bought that stallion off Victoria, Amelia wouldn't have any reason left to say "no" to him. Victoria seemed amenable to letting him buy the horse and, as the adult in the family, she had the final say over their property, as far as Luke could see. The runt had been rash buying the animal. In fact, if you thought about it, Luke would be doing them a favor, taking the stallion off their hands. And once he had the horse, he'd be established. As established as Amelia's father, who was the richest man in the valley.

Alex felt sick as she watched him. Every time the subject of Amelia came up he retreated deep into himself, and she had no idea what he was thinking. He was probably remembering how beautiful she looked in her Sunday best, or the soft press of her hand against his, or the enchantment of her kisses . . .

Damn it, there she went again. "Sorry," she apologized. "It's none of my business."

Luke cleared his throat and when he looked up he gave Alex a grimace. "I guess it is, runt, if you're worried about your sister. I promised you I'd treat her like a lady, and I will."

"I don't think that's going to help." Luke gave her a quizzical look and she decided to be blunt. "Listen," she explained, "I don't think you can help it, but you lead her on every time you even look at her." She paused, aware of his gathering frown. "Could you try not to . . . well, to act so much like *you* around her?"

"Try not to act like me?" he echoed dubiously.

"I know it sounds stupid," she sighed, "but when you look at women, they do this whole melty thing."

"You want me to not look at her?"

"That would be a start. Just keep your eyes on your boots or something."

"So she won't do the whole melty thing?"

She could hear the amusement in his voice and she scowled. "Fine. Mock me. But you won't be the one having to pick up the pieces after you've gone and married that Adelia woman."

"Amelia."

"I know her name!"

"So if I stop looking at your sister, you'll stop being surly?"

Alex looked up, startled. "Yeah," she admitted, "I guess. Can you not talk to her too?"

"No, runt," he shook his head, exasperated, "I can't stop talking to her. She's a paying customer."

"Well, at least stop giving her roses, then."

"It's a deal." Luke held out his hand for Alex to shake. "Friends?"

Alex looked at his hand. Now was the time, she decided, to stop running in circles. Luke Slater belonged to another woman. And she was welcome to him, shameless flirt that he was. He was willing to treat Victoria honorably, and he genuinely liked Adam. So perhaps they could be friends. Taking a deep breath, and telling herself that she was letting go of her feelings for him, Alex took his hand.

"Friends," she agreed.

It was as though a great weight had been lifted. Alex found she could relax by the spring as he went about his grooming, without being bothered in the slightest when he changed shirts. Well, almost . . . she peeked a little. She was only human, after all.

DINNER THAT NIGHT was a festive affair. The women had prepared a feast and everything was declared communal. Alex was starving after her hard day's work and had three helpings of Ilse's dumplings. She also accepted a mug of Sebastian's precious whiskey, pointedly ignoring Victoria's disapproving glare.

By the time she'd finished the whiskey she was having a fine old time. Sebastian dug out his accordion and she joined in the singing lustily. She was aware of Adam yawning and noticed when Victoria bid Luke good night—glad to see he kept his gaze on the dancing flames of the campfire when he answered her—but she felt no desire to go to bed herself. She was perfectly happy lolling in the warmth of the fire, listening to the low chatter and watching the stars flicker overhead.

It was only when Henry Watts passed out on the opposite side of the fire and began snoring loudly that Alex became aware how late it was. Joseph threw a blanket over his brother, and he and Sebastian wandered into the darkness. Adam had also fallen asleep, curled up into a ball on his side. Alex noticed that Luke had tucked his own bedding around him.

"I guess I'd best get to bed," she sighed.

"A little too much whiskey, runt?"

"I only had one mug."

"Sebastian poured a mighty full mug, and I'm guessing you ain't used to it."

Alex tried to rise and gave a short scream. She couldn't move. Her muscles had frozen solid. She looked around wildly.

Luke started at the sound of the scream.

"I can't move," Alex whimpered, feeling a stab of panic. She tried again; she managed to force her petrified muscles an inch, but it was agony.

"Calm down," Luke soothed, as he got to his feet and made his way over to her. "It's just from those wagons today. Your body isn't used to it."

"Suppose I'm paralyzed," she yelped. "I can't afford to be a cripple. Who'll look after Victoria and Adam?"

"You won't be a cripple," he sighed as he sank down behind her. "Stop being so dramatic. You do give yourself airs. 'Who'll look after Victoria and Adam?' I don't know if you've noticed, runt, but seeing as how you're the youngest, I reckon *they* are supposed to be looking after *you*."

Alex yelped again as Luke's big hands settled on her shoulders. "What are you doing?"

"Just relax." The big hands began to dig into her knotted muscles. "Trust me, this will help."

"It's not helping!" Every movement of his fingers caused her pain.

"It will in a moment. It'll hurt until your muscles loosen up a little."

"Hurt! This isn't hurt, this is torture."

"You know your problem?" he mused, as he kneaded her rock-hard shoulders. "You manage to find the worst in every situation."

"I do not," Alex protested, "I'm always optimistic." She ignored his snort of disbelief. And then suddenly his fingers weren't causing her pain anymore. Suddenly his touch was sending the most glorious sensations swirling through her body. His thumbs rubbed lazy circles and she had to bite back a moan. "You can stop now," she breathed, but she didn't really mean it. "It doesn't hurt anymore."

"I just want to make sure all the knots are out."

There wasn't a single muscle in her back he left untouched. And those muscles were connected to the oddest places—her toes were tingling, shivers raced up and down her arms, and there was an aching throb . . .

His hands drifted back to her neck, his thumbs circling again behind her ears, and Alex was liquefying under their touch. Her head tilted, exposing the long line of her neck, and her eyelids fluttered closed. She'd been mad to think he had no power over her as long as she was a boy. It wasn't only his burning black gaze that could turn a woman to mush . . . his hands were just as dangerous.

Alex was so drugged with sensation that she barely noticed when he dropped his head close to her ear, so close that his lips brushed her earlobe, and his breath swirled hot against her skin.

But then he spoke and, with a shock, she was suddenly stone-cold sober.

"So, now that we've agreed to be friends, do you want to tell me why you're all dressed up like a boy . . . *Alexandra*?"

❋ 23 ❋

Luke had been suspicious for a while. A dozen little things had given her away. There was that voice for a start—although it might be a pleasant pitch for a girl, it was far too high for a sixteen-year-old boy. And then there was her habit of crossing her ankles every time she sat down. Not to mention that ear-splitting scream she was prone to. Luke had never heard a male scream like that.

Even if she *had* managed to give a perfect performance, Victoria and Adam were hopeless. Both of them slipped several times a day. Luke couldn't count the number of times they'd referred to Alex as "she." And then there was this morning in the wagon, when Victoria had said it outright. Even though he'd suspected as much, it was a shock to hear her say it. *Just because you're dressed as a boy is no reason to act like one.*

His mind ran back over his encounters with the runt. No wonder Victoria had torn a strip off Alex that first night, when she'd tended to Luke's bath. Good Lord, if she was his little sister he would have bent her over his knee and tarred the hide right off her for a stunt like that. What was she thinking being alone with a naked man?

Luke's hands tightened now around Alex's neck. Her long, slender neck, without the slightest hint of an Adam's apple. Luke shook his head. How had she ever managed to fool him?

The kid was rigid with horror. She struggled out of his grasp and crouched before him like some kind of wounded animal. Her eyes were huge, gleaming with reflections from the fire.

"The infamous lost sister, I presume?" he drawled. She looked like he'd just kicked her. He wouldn't have been surprised if she'd given a whimper. "Hey, runt," he said gently, "we're friends, remember? Your secret is safe with me." He reached for her and frowned when she flinched. "Wait here," he said soothingly, heading for his saddlebags. When he returned he offered her a flask. "Come on, sweetheart, take a sip. It'll help calm you down."

Alexandra's head was spinning. He knew? She didn't understand. How could he know who she was? And why wasn't he mad that she'd deceived him? She accepted the flask and took a long swallow. The whiskey burned her throat on the way down and she choked.

"Ah, sweetheart, I'm sorry. I shouldn't have sprung it on you like that. I keep forgetting how young you are."

Alex coughed. "How young?" She didn't think almost twenty was that young.

"I know you say you're sixteen but, let's be honest, you can't be more than thirteen at the most. You're a beanpole."

Alex gasped and looked down at Adam's baggy old clothes. A beanpole? Thirteen at the most? Tears sprung to Alex's eyes. He still didn't recognize her. Even knowing that she was a female, he couldn't see who she really was. Had she meant so little to him?

Luke was flabbergasted when she gave a low sob and fled to the wagon. He hadn't handled that too well. He put it down to the fact that he didn't have much experience with young girls. Women, now, women he knew. He sighed. Shame she wasn't a good few years older. He wouldn't be having these troubles if she were.

He'd just have to apologize to her in the morning.

Even though she tried to bury her tears in the flour sack, Alex's sobs were loud enough to wake Victoria. "Alex?" she whispered, confused. "What's wrong? What's happened? Is it Adam? Oh God, what's happened to Adam?"

"Nothing," Alex wailed, crying harder.

Victoria leaned over her sister and rested a hand on her shuddering back. She frowned. It wasn't like Alex to cry. "Please, Alex," she begged, feeling a band of fear close around her, "tell me."

"He knows."

"What? Who? Who knows what?"

"Luke," Alex sniffled, pushing herself up from the flour sack and regarding Victoria with puffy eyes, "Luke knows."

"Knows what?" Victoria asked, completely exasperated.

"He knows I'm a girl."

Victoria jerked back, snatching her hand away. "He knows?" Her heart sank. That was it, then. All her hopes dashed. Once he saw Alex in her dove-gray dress, with her beautiful face free of all that muck, she would have no chance with him. Although . . . he loved *her*, Victoria, didn't he? She'd practically heard him say so, right here in this wagon.

"And he thinks I'm a *child*," Alex cried, dissolving into further tears.

"He . . .?"

"He thinks I'm a child. Twelve or thirteen. And you thought I couldn't make myself flat-chested enough," she sniffed.

Victoria's eyes narrowed as she regarded her weeping sister. "And why," she asked slowly, "does it matter if he thinks you're a child?"

Alex's mouth opened and closed, but no sound came out.

"You didn't mind him thinking you were a boy," Victoria reminded her.

"That's different."

"How?"

Alex had no answer for her. She collapsed miserably face-first into her flour sack. Things just kept going from bad to worse. She didn't want Victoria to suspect that there was anything between her and Luke. There *wasn't* anything between her and Luke, she wailed silently. He thought she was a child!

Victoria crept back to her side of the wagon, feeling sick to her stomach. So, Alex had feelings for Luke, did she? Victoria didn't blame her. But Luke was *hers*. For once in her life she was the pretty sister, the one that men went out of their way to talk to. Victoria reached in the darkness for the pale pink rose, which she lay on top of her Bible. It was only just beginning to wilt, and was still fragrant. He loved her, she knew he did, and she wasn't prepared to surrender him without a fight. First thing in the morning she would talk to him.

"Alex," Victoria said softly, hoping she was still awake. A sniffle was her only reply. "I think it would be best if you *do* let him think you're a child, at least until we reach Oregon. We need to keep your disguise for as long as possible, until the Gradys are caught. You know how men get around you"— Victoria couldn't keep the bitter edge from her voice—"and we need Luke clear-headed until those wretched men are locked up." And hopefully, Victoria thought, by the time they got to Oregon she would be Mrs. Luke Slater, and it wouldn't matter in the slightest how old he thought Alex was.

Alex didn't need to read Victoria's mind to know what she was thinking. Oh, how could she have gone to that dance? She'd known how Victoria felt about Luke. Why couldn't she have let Victoria have her one night of glory? But no, she had to go and get all hot and bothered over that horrid Slater man, and now look at the mess they were in. She could tell by Vicky's voice that her sister was angry. Imagine if she ever found out what had actually happened in Independence!

She mustn't find out. Ever. Luke Slater could never know that Beatrice and Alexandra were one and the same. If he did, she'd lose Victoria forever.

VICTORIA LAY WAKEFUL most of the night, and was up and dressed the moment she heard the birds stirring in the cotton-woods. She dressed carefully in her new yellow calico, and she brushed her hair two dozen strokes, until it shone. Then she left the wagon, expecting to be able to snatch a moment alone with Luke.

No such luck. There were already quite a few people up, sipping freshly brewed coffee. Luke wasn't among them, and he wasn't asleep in his bedroll.

Victoria ran a nervous hand through her hair.

"Good morning, Miss Alexander," Ned O'Brien greeted her eagerly. She gave him an absent nod, but he wasn't put off. He never was, she thought with a sigh. The man sought her out every chance he got. And he was always quoting poetry at her. It was quite off-putting.

"You look beautiful this morning," he told her. "A rose with all its sweetest leaves yet folded."

"Milton again?" Victoria asked dryly.

"No," he stammered, "that was Byron." Ned flushed. He couldn't quite bring himself to tell her that only Byron could capture the wild surging of his blood when he beheld her. It was difficult enough to quote other people's words at her—words of the greatest poets, no less—but he didn't think he would ever have the courage to tell her how he felt in his own words.

Ned had never supposed to feel this way again. He had believed his heart was buried with his wife. The first time he'd met Miss Alexander he'd thought her merely pretty, but the second time, that night at the dance when she'd glowed like a second sun, he'd barely been able to breathe. And when she'd let him dance with her . . . there were no words to describe the sensations. Oh, Ned was no fool, he knew how she felt about Luke. But all women lost their heads around Luke and, as far as he could tell, her feelings weren't reciprocated. Luke certainly didn't look at Victoria the way he'd looked at the woman in green that night at the dance.

Ned could wait. When she got her heart broken by Luke, he would be there to help her pick up the pieces.

"I was looking for Mr. Slater," Victoria said now, having little to no interest in Lord Byron.

"I believe he's tending to his horse. You've heard we'll be starting out late today? Luke said mid-afternoon should be early enough. We'll put in a few miles before we camp again . . ." Ned trailed off. Victoria had left him the minute he'd told her where Luke was. Ned watched the sunny yellow sway of her skirts. She certainly was lovely.

Victoria hastily neatened the folds of her dress as she approached Luke and Adam. Luke was showing her brother how to clean the dirt out from the horse's hooves. Victoria cleared her throat delicately to get their attention.

"I've already eaten breakfast," Adam said defensively.

"I was wondering if I could have a private word with you, Mr. Slater?"

Luke looked up, startled. "Go ahead."

"Privately," Victoria repeated, with a significant glance at Adam. "I thought perhaps we could take a walk?"

Luke straightened reluctantly. "I was hoping to speak to Alex. I'd hate to miss . . . him." There he went too: almost referring to the runt as "she."

"It's Alex I want to speak to you about. I promised him I'd talk to you this morning."

"Oh." Luke paused. "Have you got the hang of this, Adam? Can I trust you with it?"

"Oh yes!" Adam exclaimed, wriggling with pride that Luke would trust him to clean Delilah's shoes.

Luke didn't offer Victoria his arm. She tried not to be disappointed, telling herself that he simply didn't want to get her pretty dress dirty. After all, he'd been working with the horse. They wandered in silence through the lush grove, finally pausing by one of the springs.

"So, what was it you wanted to speak to me about?"

Victoria plucked a cluster of jasmine that was bobbing in the breeze and ran her finger over the pink undersides of the blooms. "Alex says that you know."

Luke didn't ask for clarification, he simply nodded. "Yes, I know."

"For how long?"

"Does it matter?"

Victoria frowned. This wasn't going the way she'd pictured it. He was supposed to be glad for the opportunity to have her on her own. Was he mad at her? Because they'd all deceived him about Alex? That must be it. "I'm sorry," she apologized, laying a hand on his arm, "we didn't mean to lie to you."

"I can see why you did," he remarked, "the way those Gradys were sniffing around for her." He took her hand from his arm, gave it a quick squeeze, and then pulled away to kneel at the spring.

Victoria watched, frustrated, as he took a drink.

"Why do they want her anyway?" He'd heard the answer from Alex, but he was curious to see if Victoria would sing the same song.

Victoria bit her lip. She could hardly tell him that Silas had lusted after her sister since the moment he'd laid eyes on her, not if she wanted Luke to believe that Alex was just a child.

"It's got something to do with all of that gold you were carrying around, doesn't it?" Luke prodded.

Victoria paled. "Alex said they owed us," she stammered.

"It's all right," Luke reassured her, "I won't be turning you into the law."

"You don't understand," she pleaded, "they did the most awful things to us after Ma and Pa died. Silas was always coming around, and they took our food and left us starving because he wanted . . . Silas wanted . . ." Victoria threw up her hands, at a loss to explain.

"You don't need to say it aloud," Luke said, rising. He knew he'd promised the kid he wouldn't lead Victoria on, but he couldn't bear to see a woman in distress. He took her hands, which were trembling. "I can well imagine what he was after. A lovely young lady like yourself, all alone in the world, with a kid brother and sister to support. I'm sure he thought you were easy pickings. He didn't lay a hand on you, did he?"

Victoria thought back to that horrible day, when Silas had closed in on Alex on the porch, crushing her against him. "Just a kiss," she said brokenly. She knew it was a sin to lie, but Luke was looking at her with such tenderness, and his hands were so big and strong around hers. Surely God would understand one little lie?

Luke's expression turned black. They were vile, those Gradys. Hunting that poor kid down like she was an animal, abusing Adam and trying to take advantage of an innocent like Victoria. "I'll get them," he promised her. "They won't bother you that way ever again."

A tear rolled down Victoria's cheek and splattered on the sunny yellow of her calico. Luke did what came naturally, and pulled her close to comfort her.

ALEX HAD SPENT most of the night drowning in her churning thoughts. As a result, she slept later than usual. She knew without having to look that her face was swollen from crying. She rubbed at her eyes half-heartedly, but she had lost any sense of vanity by now.

Why had they let her sleep so late? she wondered. Why weren't they on the move already? They usually left camp just after daybreak.

When she emerged from the wagon, Alex was startled

again by the beauty of Ash Hollow. The dappled light through the leaves of the cottonwoods, the air rich with the perfume of the wild roses. It lifted her spirits just to see it.

"Good morning, sleepyhead," Adam greeted her. He had finished with Delilah and had moved on to grooming the mules. Alex had never seen anyone spend so much time brushing a mule's coat before, but she didn't have the heart to say so to Adam.

"Have you seen Luke?" she asked. She wanted to get this conversation over with as quickly as possible. She would admit to being thirteen—for Victoria's sake—and confess the whole sorry story about the Gradys. Well, obviously not the whole story, not the part about Silas believing himself in love with her, but the rest of it: the gold and the bonds and the escaped slaves. Friends, he said. Well, fine, they'd be friends, and he could help her shoulder this awful burden.

"He went for a walk," Adam told her absently, gesturing in the direction of the springs.

Alex set off through the dew-damp grass with a heavy heart. She was so sick of pretending to be someone she wasn't. For one wild moment last night, when his lips had touched her ear and he'd whispered those marvelous words—*do you want to tell me why you're all dressed up like a boy*—Alex had thought the charade was over. In that breathless moment she'd imagined that she'd turn to see him looking at her the way he had at Dolly's, with that hungry, black gaze that promised so much and seared her to the core.

But when she'd turned he'd been looking at her in the most brotherly way imaginable. And his "sweethearts" were mixed with "runts" and "kids."

So here she was: no longer a boy. Now . . . now she was a child.

She couldn't wait to get to Oregon. She would surrender control to her older brother, Stephen, lace herself into her old dresses and be grateful for the rest of her life that she could simply be plain old Alexandra Barratt.

Alex emerged into the grove and stopped dead. There, in a slant of golden sunshine, was Victoria. In Luke's arms.

That bastard sure didn't waste any time.

"**Y**OU CAN QUIT glaring at me," Luke said dryly. "For one thing, if you don't pay more attention to that horse you're liable to fall off." He eyed the kid with no small measure of exasperation. Alex had refused to speak to him ever since she'd blundered into the glade and misinterpreted things between him and her sister. He suspected she'd only come along for their usual morning ride to keep him well away from Victoria. "I get the feeling you don't exactly trust me, runt."

She gave him an evil look, but still didn't speak.

"I don't see why you're getting hot under the collar," he sighed. "I was only offering her some comfort."

"I could see that," she muttered under her breath.

"Hell, what was I supposed to do? She was in a state about the way that Grady manhandled her."

Alex straightened in the saddle. "What?" One of the Gradys had interfered with Victoria? Why hadn't she told Alex? Alex's blood ran cold at the thought of one of those greasy lowlifes laying a hand on her sister.

"She told me how Silas came sniffing around her. The way he threatened you to get at her. The way he tried to force himself on her."

Alex drew a sharp breath, completely missing the cold anger in Luke's voice. In her mind's eye she could see Victoria standing in the shaft of sunshine, leaning into Luke, staring up at him with big moist eyes. She could well imagine the way Victoria had manipulated the situation, painting herself into the story, in place of Alex. Oh, her sister was headed for such a world of heartache. "You said you'd leave her be," she said sharply, turning the evil glare back on Luke.

"I ain't the type to leave a lady in distress."

"So offer her your handkerchief," Alex snapped, "there's no need to go sweeping her up in your arms like that. Don't you know what that will do to a girl?"

Luke's eyes narrowed as he took in the kid's agitation.

All of a sudden he broke into a grin, the dimple flashing in his cheek. Alex frowned suspiciously. She didn't see what he was smiling about.

It was suddenly clear to Luke. The kid had a crush. He may not know much about young girls, but he remembered well enough what it was like to be thirteen. Hell, he'd about died of love for Rosita, their cook. She'd been a good fifteen years older than him, with deep-gold skin and jet-black hair. He'd dreamed about her every night, and could barely manage to say two words in her presence. Rosita had only to look at another man and he shriveled with jealousy.

Luke remembered the way the kid had wilted under his massage the night before. And the rage in her eyes when she stumbled into the clearing to find Victoria pressed against his chest. It all made perfect sense. The kid was jealous.

Alex didn't like the patronizing way he was grinning at her. "If you hurt my sister," she warned in dire tones, but she could tell he wasn't listening.

"How many times are we going to have this conversation?" he remarked. And then the annoying man actually started whistling.

She could still hear him whistling a couple of hours later, when she was back driving the mules. He and Adam were up in the front with Sebastian, both easy in the saddle, their faces turned happily into the golden sunshine. Alex had to grit her teeth at the sight. Her own rear was rubbed raw, and that golden sunshine was burning her nose. Every time Victoria shifted on the seat beside her Alex wanted to jab her with her elbow. She wouldn't be feeling so wretched if Victoria had kept her damn yellow calico packed away where it belonged.

A sudden gunshot echoed across the plains, resounding like thunder.

Alex and Victoria screamed as Cranky Bob stumbled. He went down hard, dragging Surly Sue with him.

"Get in the wagon," Alex ordered, giving Victoria a shove. Her sister scrambled into the back of the wagon. Much good it would do, Alex thought wildly, as she tumbled from the wagon, looking around for the source of the gunshot; that canvas was no match for a bullet.

"You shot the mule?" Luke said in disbelief, as he and Adam came charging down the line.

"Of course I didn't shoot the mule!" Alex snarled, crouching behind Bob's still body. Her heart was racing like a jackrabbit. There, right in front of her, was a small, deadly hole in Bob's hide. The poor thing hadn't stood a chance; the bullet had gone straight through his brain. "Get down," she hissed at the men.

Beside her, Sue was braying in panic as she tried to get to her feet. She was harnessed closely to Bob and was having trouble standing. Adam dismounted and went to her aid. Alex seized his arm and dragged him down beside her in the dirt. He went rigid as he was confronted with Cranky Bob's corpse. Alex heard his breath catch and her heart ached for him. "Would you get off that damn horse?" she snapped at Luke. Didn't the fool realize what a target he made, sitting up there, silhouetted against the horizon?

Luke wasn't listening. He yanked his spyglass from his saddlebag.

"What are you doing?" Alex's fingers clenched around Adam's arm as she watched Luke scan the plains. "He'll shoot you!"

"Who'll shoot me?" Luke asked calmly, swinging down from Delilah. He tossed Alex the spyglass and moved to disentangle Sue. Alex fumbled and the spyglass rolled away. She slithered on her belly through the dust to retrieve it.

"Gideon," she snapped as she lifted the glass to her eye with trembling fingers. "Gideon will shoot you!" Far in the distance she could see a pale thread of dust rising. It was a rider. Her heart stopped, until she realized that the rider was receding into the hazy distance, and not looming closer.

"What makes you think it was Gideon?" he asked her, as Sue gained her feet with a relieved *heehaw.* "Why wouldn't it be Silas? Isn't he the one who's set on your sister?"

"Silas can't shoot that straight," Alex told him.

Luke dropped to one knee beside the fallen mule. He rested a sympathetic hand on Adam's shoulder. "Well," he remarked, "whoever shot this animal was a crack shot. Unless they weren't aiming for the mule."

Alex dropped the spyglass. Suppose he hadn't been aiming at Bob? Suppose the gun had been pointing at Victoria . . . Would Silas go to such lengths to intimidate her?

Or had it been Gideon? Maybe killing the mule was his way of threatening them. Which one of them was out there? Or were they both out there? She had only seen one rider. "Where are you going?" she asked wildly, as Adam got to his feet. "Would you get down!"

"Relax, runt, whoever it was has gone now," Luke said.

"How do you know? How do you know that rider was the one shooting at us?"

"I don't see anyone else."

"He could be hiding!"

"Where?" Luke gestured at the featureless plain.

"What's happening out there?" Victoria shrilled from the wagon.

"Just stay there for the moment, Miss Alexander!" Luke called.

At that moment Adam came back with a shovel. Without a word, he stopped beside Alex and began digging. She squealed when he dumped a shovelful of dirt on her foot.

Luke cleared his throat. "I'm not sure we have time to stop and bury him, Adam."

Adam stabbed the earth and the explosion of dust had Alex coughing. She staggered to her feet, shaking off the dirt. Another shovelful went flying, striking her in the chest. "Adam!"

"You never liked him!" Her brother scowled.

"I told you I didn't shoot the damn mule! It was the Gradys!"

"He never did anything to you."

"Oh, no? You want to see the teeth marks?" She darted behind Luke as another shovelful of dirt sailed in her direction.

"Alex didn't shoot him, Adam."

"I know. She can't shoot straight either."

Alex and Luke looked at each other helplessly. By now the other members of the wagon train had gathered. "What the hell happened?"

"Who's doing all the shooting?"

"Thank the Lord it was just the mule!"

"Is it Indians? Tell me it's not Indians!"

"Calm down, folks," Luke called, spreading his hands and giving them all a rueful look. "For all we know it was just a hunter's stray bullet."

A hunter's stray bullet? Alex poked him in the ribs, but he ignored her.

"We'll just take a minute to bury this poor animal, and then we'll be back on our way."

"Is it safe?" Ned O'Brien asked nervously.

Luke scooped up his spyglass and passed it to the easterner. "Have a look around. We're alone out here." Alex poked him in the ribs again. He didn't blink an eye. "Our best bet is to press on to Fort Laramie." He captured Alex's hand as she went to jab him again. "Just to be on the safe side, I'll ride scout, and Mal can bring up the rear. And we'll post a lookout at night. It's nothing to worry about."

The sound of Adam's shovel punctuated Luke's words and sent a chill through Alex. What if they didn't make it to Fort Laramie? Unconsciously, her hand tightened around Luke's. He felt it and gave her a squeeze.

"Come with me," he murmured to her, as the group dispersed. "We'll get a couple more shovels, Adam, and be right back."

Luke led her to the chuck wagon, keeping a tight grip on her trembling hand. Once they were inside she was astonished to find herself pulled into his arms. She went rigid.

His large hand was rubbing circles on her back.

"What are you doing?" she asked tightly, trying to pull away. He wouldn't let her. His arms were like iron around her.

"I know you're trying to act tough, kiddo," he said, "but you're still a little girl. I know you're scared."

She clenched her jaw and glared up at him. A little girl?

"Grown men would be frightened in your position," he told her.

Glory, she'd forgotten how dangerous his eyes were. They

were so liquid and warm, black as a moonless summer's night and just as heady.

Gently, Luke set her away from him. He recognized that look in her eyes, and he didn't want to lead the poor kid on. But at least she wasn't frightened anymore. He chucked her under the chin and handed her a shovel.

Alex stared at it witlessly. She had the sudden urge to hit him over the head with it.

❧ 25 ❧

ALL WAS CALM until the night after they passed Court-house Rock. It was the first time Luke hadn't let a group take a detour to look at the rocks. He wouldn't admit it to the Alexanders, but he was mighty nervous about those Gradys. He wouldn't rest easy until those vultures were safe behind bars at Fort Laramie. So, despite entreaties from the Watts brothers and Ned O'Brien, he wouldn't waste time sightseeing. The rocks were several miles away, and he'd known groups to while away a whole day poking about, taking in the views from their pinnacles.

When they made camp the hulking rocks loomed in the distance, turning grayish-blue in the fading light. After the sun had set, a huge yellow moon rose and the wolves started up. They gave Alex the shivers. "Adam," she pleaded, "please sleep in the wagon with us?"

But her brother was still mad at her. He'd tied the mules to the wheels by his bedding and chose to spend his time with them. He was especially attentive to Sue, who nuzzled him gratefully.

Another wolf let loose; the undulating cry echoed, bouncing off the rocks and rolling through the camp. Victoria moaned and grasped for Alex's arm.

"You'll be fine," Luke assured them. "I'll be right out here, and so will Adam. No wolf is going to come into the camp."

Alex gave him a sour look. It wasn't the wolves she was worried about. Not the four-legged kind anyway.

"I'll sleep right by your wagon, if it would make you feel better," he volunteered.

"Oh, it would," Victoria hastened to agree.

Alex couldn't sleep. She didn't feel safe, not even with Luke sleeping at the foot of the wagon. Through the canvas arch she could see the flicker of distant lightning, highlighting the scudding clouds. A brisk breeze was picking up and the hair on the back of her neck began to prickle.

One by one the wolves fell silent. Alex sat up. She had an awfully bad feeling. A sudden crack of thunder made her yelp. For a moment, she thought it was another gunshot.

Within a heartbeat Luke appeared. "What's wrong?"

"Nothing," she stammered, "I just thought . . ."

He gave her a sympathetic smile. "It's just a summer storm."

She nodded, but tears sprang to her eyes. She couldn't banish the image of Adam lowering poor old Bob into his dusty grave.

"You want me to sit up with you for a bit?" Luke whispered. Without waiting for a reply, he climbed up beside her. One long arm settled around her shoulders. Silently they watched the lightning flash. There was an eerie silence for a breathless moment before the thunder rumbled.

They were out there, Alex thought desperately, they were out there and they were coming for her. Somewhere out there Silas was licking his lips as he fantasized about capturing her. And Gideon . . . She shivered. Dear Lord, she thought she'd rather let Silas have her than face Gideon.

Against the horizon Alex could see the haze of a rainstorm, marching closer.

"I'd best get my bedding and move under the wagon with Adam," Luke remarked.

Alex looked up at him. His profile was outlined against the stark night. She didn't want him to go. She felt calmer, safer, when he was by her side. "Couldn't you stay in here?" she asked in a small voice.

He looked down at her, startled. He kept forgetting how young she was. Most of the time she strode around like the boy she pretended to be, confident and ornery, bossing her brother and sister around like she was the eldest. But just now, looking down into those wide, anxious eyes, Luke could see the vulnerable girl she really was. When he'd tried to comfort her after the mule had been shot she'd resisted him. He was surprised to find her asking for comfort now.

"It wouldn't be proper," he told her gently.

"No one knows that I'm a girl," she reminded him.

"I can't, Alex."

A fat tear tumbled down Alex's cheek. She batted it away, irritated with herself.

Luke grimaced. Hell. He should just go. But he'd always been a sucker for a female's tears. "Someone's got to have a talk to you about decent behavior," he grumbled as he slid from the wagon to rescue his things before the storm hit. "I suppose you don't want me anywhere near your sister," he whispered, as he settled himself in her usual spot, leaving Alex between him and Victoria.

No sooner had he lain his head down than they heard the first spatter of raindrops on the canvas. Alex relaxed. Now that Luke was here the wagon seemed cozy, the rain more a comforting lullaby as it beat on the hoop above than a portent of doom.

She sighed and settled back against her flour sack. They didn't speak again. She watched the dance of lightning and listened to the rain and thunder, exquisitely aware of Luke stretched out beside her. She knew the moment he surrendered to sleep. His breathing deepened and his limbs loosened, one hand lolling against her side.

Unable to resist, Alex rolled over to observe him. He was like a statue of an ancient god, she thought. As hard and perfect as marble. Without thinking, she traced her finger over the hand that rested against her. He certainly wasn't cold like marble; his skin was warm and smooth.

How she remembered the feel of that skin against hers.

Propping herself on one elbow, she examined him freely. That straight nose, the hollowed planes of his cheeks, the square jaw, the slight dent where his dimple flashed when he smiled . . . Gingerly, Alex reached out and rested a featherlight fingertip against that dimple. It was rough with day-old stubble.

He shaved every morning. Every other man, including Adam, whose beard was barely more than wispy fluff, didn't bother; by the time they reached Oregon they'd all be as scruffy as mountain men. But not Luke.

He would never disappoint the ladies by hiding behind a beard, Alex thought dryly.

As though he could hear her thoughts he frowned in his sleep and a sigh escaped those full lips. Alex's finger moved to his mouth. Not making contact, she traced the line of his mouth, lingering over the full curve of his lower lip.

His sigh became a faint moan. Alex wondered what he was dreaming about. Or who he was dreaming about.

She was startled when those divine lips pressed against her finger in the barest of kisses. She felt as though the lightning had entered her and was coursing through her veins. Her own lips tingled with the memory of his kisses, and that wild pulse began to beat deep inside.

The rain was lashing in earnest against the canvas roof of the wagon, drowning out the rasp of her labored breath. She couldn't control herself, she bent forward and lowered her lips to his. She could feel the warmth of his breath, and the heat radiating from his skin. Her eyelids fluttered closed as she tasted him, and felt the slippery satin texture of him.

She almost gasped when his mouth slanted against hers, his lips parting, allowing her access to the deeper heat of him. Tentatively, she slid her tongue into him, feeling a thrill as his tongue met hers.

Beatrice. Luke was having the most incredible dream. At the first taste he was wild with desire, hard and hurting with the force of it. Oh, she tasted even better than he remembered. He reached for her, finding the familiar curve of her neck and the firm, muscular length of her back as she bent over him. He took her tongue into his mouth, before plunging into hers, tasting the secret corners of her slick heat. No woman had ever driven him so close to madness. His beautiful Beatrice.

A scream tore him from his fantasy. A high-pitched scream of pain. Immediately, the kiss was over; the dream was over. Luke sat bolt upright and struggled to get his bearings. He was in the Alexanders' wagon. Beside him Alex sat bolt-upright, wild-eyed and frozen by the inhuman screaming. And behind her he could see Victoria, rigid with terror.

Luke scrabbled for his gun and flew out into the storm.

"Luke!" Alex gasped, tearing after him without thinking. He couldn't face whatever was out there alone!

The storm had turned their camp into a quagmire, and Alex struggled to keep her feet as she scurried after Luke. She could barely see him through the sheets of rain. She screeched as her boots slid out from under her, and before she knew it she was flat on her back in the mud, with the stinging rain pelting her full in the face. Every time she tried to stand she slid, until she was coated with the vile stuff.

By the time she'd crawled to the nearest wagon and hauled herself to her feet there was no sign of Luke.

"Alex?" Ned O'Brien said, bewildered, peering through the opening of their wagon. Alex saw that he was nervously brandishing a spanking new six-shooter.

"Who was that screaming?" Jane whispered, peering around her father, her face white and terrified.

"I don't know," Alex huffed, trying to regain her breath. Before they could ask her another question she was off, slopping through the mud. Where had Luke gone? Two shapes loomed out of the rain and her heart stopped. The Gradys!

"Alex?"

It was only the Watts brothers, both armed and anxious. "What the hell is going on?"

"I don't know!" Alex snapped, squealing as she slipped again. She grabbed Henry's arm. She almost took him over with her, and he grabbed for Joseph. When Luke found them they were in a heap, splattered and slimy and snarling at each other as they tried to extricate their tangled limbs.

"Watch your rifle doesn't go off," he told Henry tersely as he grabbed the man by the arm and hauled him up. Alex was the last one up, and she didn't appreciate the faint amusement in Luke's eyes.

"Who was screaming?" she demanded. His amusement died and she felt a chill. "Who?" she whispered, not sure she wanted to know.

"Get back to your wagon, runt," he said gently.

"Why?"

"Just go back, and stay there until we get the mess cleared up."

"The mess?" With a heavy heart, Alex pushed him out of the way.

"Don't," he warned, reaching for her, but she evaded him.

Dear Lord. Oh dear, dear Lord. Alex's knees gave out. Luke caught her easily, one arm looping around her waist and holding her up.

It was Jack. Poor old Jack, Mal Crawford's chestnut gelding. The horse she'd been riding every day at Luke's side. Or at least what was left of him . . .

She was going to be sick. Luke held her head as she vomited, one hand firm against her forehead. "I told you not to look," he sighed.

"Aw, hell," she heard Henry rasp. And then she heard him vomit too.

"It was Gideon," Alex said desperately, her hands clawing at Luke. "It was Gideon."

"Hush," Luke soothed, sweeping her up and starting back to her wagon. The kid was wild with terror; he could see the whites of her eyes as they rolled, and feel the shudders wracking her body.

"It was because we rode him. He must have seen Adam. He thought Jack was our horse." Alex felt icy. Black spots swarmed before her eyes. "Imagine what he'll do to me . . ."

"Hush," Luke said grimly.

When they got to the wagon they found Adam peering out from under it, and Victoria cowering behind the buckboard. The sight of Alex, limp and colorless in Luke's arms, didn't reassure them. "What happened?" Victoria wailed, at the same time as Adam slithered out from under the wagon and hurled himself at Alex, unmindful of the rain and mud.

"I'm sorry," he cried, panicked. "I didn't mean to be mad at you—I know you didn't shoot Bob. I know you liked him. Deep down you did."

"She's not hurt," Luke said in his calmest voice.

"You mean *he's* not hurt," Adam corrected, clambering up into the wagon after Luke and Alex.

"It's all right, Adam, he knows I'm a girl."

"Really?" Adam brightened. "Now that you know, are you going to marry her?"

"What?" all three of them gasped, looking askance at Adam's enthusiastic grin.

"If you marry her then I can come and live with you and your horses."

"She's a little young, buddy," Luke told him.

"How old do you have to be to get married?"

"Old," Alex said quickly. Her color was flooding back.

"Oh." Adam visibly wilted. "So I guess you can't marry Vicky either."

"And why not?" Victoria asked sharply.

"Well, you're even—"

"Enough," Alex interrupted shrilly. "Why are we talking about marriage when the Gradys are out there?"

"The Gradys?" Victoria gasped.

Alex noticed the way she leaned in to Luke for comfort, unmindful of his sodden clothes. She also couldn't help but notice that his natural impulse was to place a protective arm around her.

"All of them?" Victoria asked, her distress evident.

"I promised I wouldn't let him hurt you again," Luke reminded her.

Alex was mighty sick of watching her sister melt into a puddle at his feet.

"I don't think Silas was here," he told Victoria. "Alex tells me it looks like Gideon's handiwork."

"Gideon?" Victoria's gaze flew to where Alex sat huddled, dripping all over her flour sack. Their eyes met, and each could see the terror in the other.

"Slater?" The Watts brothers appeared at the end of the wagon, flanked by the other men. Each and every one of them was armed to the teeth. "What in hell is going on? What kind of maniac goes around shooting mules and slaughtering horses? Tell us straight, was it Indians?"

Luke sighed. He guessed the time had come for plain talking. "It ain't Indians," he said.

"Horses?" Adam and Victoria chorused, distressed.

Luke held a hand up to silence them. He turned back to the men. "We can discuss it in the morning. There's no need for you to stand out there in the rain through a bunch of long-winded explanations. This is something personal—the rest of you aren't in any danger."

"The hell we aren't," Mal snapped. "That was my horse that was just butchered."

"Jack?" Adam said, dismayed. "What happened to Jack?"

"There's a bunch of brothers, low types, who are set on plaguing the Alexanders," Luke admitted. "They thought the horse belonged to them."

"The ones who stole that Arab back in Independence?"

"The same."

"Why are they plaguing them?" Joseph demanded. Each and every eye was evaluating Alex and her siblings.

"And what's to say they'll refrain from hurting us?" Mal grumbled.

"One of them is set on Miss Alexander here," Luke said, knowing the men had a soft spot for Victoria, "and he don't seem to want to take no for an answer."

"Is that true?" Ned O'Brien asked Victoria. He was bristling like a porcupine at the thought. Victoria flushed miserably. "What are we going to do?" The easterner asked Luke sternly.

"We?" One of Luke's eyebrows rose. "*You* are all going to stay here in camp while I go see what those vultures are up to."

"By yourself?" Alex gasped.

"By myself." He gave Alex a warning look. "I'd suggest everyone gather together in a couple of the wagons, post lookouts and keep your weapons handy. I'll be back as soon as I can."

There was a heavy silence, broken only by the slowing patter of the rain on the canvas roof of the wagon.

"Hell," Sebastian said in disgust, "it's a poor plan, but I'll be damned if I can think of a better one."

Mal snorted. "I say we get a posse together and hunt the bastards down."

"I'm with Crawford," Joseph agreed.

"Did you see what was left of that horse?" Henry protested, still looking a little green. "We ain't dealing with a sane man here."

"I'll go alone," Luke said, in a tone that brooked no argument. "We've got women and children in camp, and our first responsibility is to them. How are they going to fare if their menfolk get cut down in a gunfight?"

Alex saw, by the way Mal Crawford glanced back toward his wagon where his young family was huddled anxiously around their lantern, that Luke had won.

But she'd be damned if she'd let him go alone.

❧ 26 ❧

THE KID WAS going to be the death of him.

Luke approached Delilah warily, amazed to see the runt had managed to saddle her. He couldn't believe that she'd dealt with the horse on her own. And she was up there in the saddle already, giving him an impatient look.

"What took you so long?" she asked him archly. "Saying good-bye to Victoria?"

He refused to take the bait. "Down you get," he ordered.

"I don't have a horse, now that Jack . . ." She trailed off and swallowed hard. "We'll have to ride together."

Luke gave her a hard look.

She gave him one right back.

He sighed. Shaking his head, he approached. "You're not going anywhere, love."

She got in one short scream before he had her gagged and bound and deposited on the floor of her wagon. "See that the runt stays that way till I get back," he commanded. The Watts brothers were in charge of guarding the Alexanders for the night. Neither of them blinked an eye at Luke's instruction.

Alex turned her outraged glare on Victoria and Adam.

"It's for her—" There he went forgetting again. He was as bad as they were. Luke darted a glance at the Watts brothers, to see if they'd noticed. They hadn't. "It's for *his* own good," Luke amended, turning a stern look on Victoria. "If you let him free he'll only come charging after me, and I'll be lucky if I bring him back in one piece."

Alex couldn't believe that they would leave her tied up like this. But then again, Victoria would jump off a cliff if

Luke Slater asked her to. She bucked and strained against her bonds.

"You'll only rub your skin off," Luke warned her. "Relax, love," he said, lowering his voice so that only she could hear. "I'll be back before you know it. There's no need to worry about me."

Worry about him! Alex growled. Why, that bigheaded . . . In his tiny little mind he'd come to the conclusion that the skinny little beanpole girl had a crush on him. And he thought it was funny. Just wait until she got out of these ropes. She'd give him something to laugh about . . .

It didn't take Luke long to find the Gradys' camp. By the time he got there the rain had stopped and the only sound was the keening of the wind through the low scrub. He could see their campfire from a mile away—they didn't seem too worried about being found. Luke left Delilah tethered a way out and crept in low to the ground. He could see the magnificent Arab (he still couldn't bring himself to call him Blackie Junior) by the light of the flickering fire. Thankfully, the animal looked healthy enough. Luke turned his attention back to the Gradys.

It looked like he'd walked in on an argument.

"I don't recall anyone putting you in charge," Silas was saying, poking the weaselly one in the chest with his finger.

Gideon shrugged him off. "I don't recall asking for your opinion."

"Let's just end it," one of the bigger ones complained from where he sat on his sodden bedding. Their camp was a mud puddle after the storm. Bert and Travis looked miserable as they regarded their waterlogged belongings.

"We can't just end it, genius. Not until we get our money back."

"And killing animals is going to get our money back?" Silas asked in disbelief. He eyed his brother distastefully. They all knew about Gideon's proclivities. Ever since he was a boy, animals had been turning up with broken limbs and burned hides. Or, more often than not, dead. Then there were those slaves he kept down in the root cellar. Silas didn't want to know what went on down there. He tried not to think about why Gideon was never in too much of a hurry to hand them over to their owners, despite the reward money. If it weren't for the money Silas doubted he'd hand them over at all; he guessed there'd be a lot more holes in the ground out by the swamp.

Gideon gave a short bark of laughter. "You'd rather snivel around her skirts like a beggar."

"That's enough," Silas snapped.

"You really think she's going to wake up one day and realize she loves you? That's what you want, ain't it? A declaration of love?" Gideon snorted. "You should have just taken the bitch and got her out of your system."

It took every bit of Luke's willpower to stay where he was. He couldn't believe anyone could talk that way about mild, ladylike Victoria. He was glad when Silas lunged at his brother in an attempt to defend her honor. "That's my *wife* you're talking about!" Silas bellowed as he charged.

But Gideon was quicker, and meaner. In the blink of an eye he had a knife to his brother's throat. Luke didn't miss the way Gideon was breathing quickly, his face flushed and his eyes glittering. The bastard was actually excited by the thought of slitting his own brother's throat. And Silas knew it.

Which was why Silas held up his hands in silent surrender. And why Travis and Bert stayed frozen, afraid to intervene.

"Let me handle it," Gideon warned, lowering the knife as the glitter faded from his eyes. "When I'm finished with her the bitch won't only return the money . . ." Gideon grinned wolfishly and Luke felt his skin break out in gooseflesh. "When I'm done with her she'll be begging to be your whore," he told Silas. "It's my gift to you. Brother."

Hell! Luke stole away, back to Delilah, his mind racing. There was no way to shake the Gradys—four men traveling light could keep up with the fastest wagon train. He wished he could pick them off, one by one. He was a good shot, but even so, he'd probably only get two of them before they came for him. He didn't like those odds. Although, if he made sure Gideon was the first one down . . . Luke grimaced. It would sure solve a lot of problems, but it was too close to cold-blooded murder for his liking. They'd just have to get to

Laramie as fast as was humanly possible, and be vigilant in the meantime. Maybe he could send someone ahead to sound a warning. But who would he send? He'd go himself, but he couldn't leave the Alexanders unprotected. And no one else knew the way, except Sebastian. And then who would he get to drive the chuck wagon? Hell and double hell.

ALEX DIDN'T SLEEP a wink. And that lousy bastard didn't come to untie her, even though she heard him ride in well before dawn. Everyone was asleep, except for Joseph Watts, who was perched on the edge of the wagon with his shotgun clenched in his lap. He chewed on his tobacco and sang bawdy songs to himself under his breath and generally irritated the daylights out of Alex. She saw Joseph straighten when Luke came back, and saw him lean so far out of the wagon he almost fell out as he tried to see where Luke was headed.

Alex lay rigid as she waited. But he didn't come. She heard the clink of Delilah's bridle as Luke unsaddled her and settled her. She heard the creak of his saddlebags as he hefted them; she heard his spurs jingle as he strode across the camp. That bastard. Didn't he realize that her hands were going numb? Not to mention her dignity, which was just about rubbed raw.

She lay there stewing until daybreak. It was only when the sky was lightening to a pearly gray that Luke appeared. He couldn't help grinning. The mud had dried, leaving Alex looking like she was wearing a clay mask, and her clothes had stiffened, so they looked like they were made of cardboard. She even creaked when she moved. "See," he remarked cheerfully, "I made it back just fine."

She gave a muffled growl through the bandanna and fixed him with a murderous stare.

The sound of his voice woke Victoria. She blinked and looked around. When she spotted Luke she gasped and bolted upright, her hand flying to her hair, which was tumbling from its pins. "You're back."

"I am. I thought Alex might want to dig free of all that mud. I'll give him an escort to the river, if he promises not to cause me bodily harm when I untie him."

Alex would promise no such thing.

"*You'll* take her to bathe?" Victoria echoed dubiously.

"I'll be at a perfectly discreet distance. But she can't go alone, it's not safe."

There was no way Victoria was going to let that happen. Suppose he happened to catch a glimpse of Alex out of her disguise? She looked at Alex now, unrecognizable beneath the filth. She preferred things exactly as they were. "I don't think Alex wants a bath," Victoria said slowly. She was glad to see Alex shaking her head in vigorous agreement.

"You can't be serious. She looks like a statue made by a bad potter. She'll have a bath even if I have to throw her in the river myself."

The sisters exchanged alarmed looks.

"Fine," Victoria sighed, "but I'll have to come along as chaperone." She brightened. Actually, this might be the perfect way to spend some time alone with Luke.

She just hadn't bargained on how angry her sister really was.

"SHE BIT ME!"

"I'll do more than bite you if you touch me again, you bandy-legged braggart!"

"Bandy-legged?" Luke laughed. "I've been called many things, brat, but never that."

She couldn't believe he was laughing. She should have bit him harder. "Don't you come near me," she warned when he bent over her.

"You want to stay bound?"

"Victoria can untie me."

"If you say so." Luke stepped from the wagon and waited, whistling softly to himself.

"Why do you have to be so ornery?" Victoria complained, as she struggled with the knots.

"The man tied me up, Victoria!"

"For your own protection."

"I'm not a child!"

Victoria blinked.

"Just because *he* thinks I am," Alex grumbled.

"I can't do it," Victoria sighed.

"What?"

"I can't get these knots undone."

Alex scowled. She'd be damned if she'd give him the satisfaction. "Adam!" She kicked her brother, none too gently, to wake him up. "Adam, untie me."

"No," he moaned, rolling over and pulling the blanket over his head. "I promised Luke."

"Luke *wants* me untied!" she snapped.

Her only reply was a snore. She looked around for the Watts brothers, but found they'd taken their leave now that Luke was standing guard.

"You're being ridiculous," Victoria complained.

Alex wanted to scream. Instead she had to swallow her pride. "Fine," she snapped, "he can come back and untie me." Alex fixed her gaze firmly on a knothole in the wagon bed and seethed as Victoria called Luke back.

At least the oaf didn't speak this time. He made short work of the knots and Alex immediately tried to crawl away. But she hadn't counted on the fact that her legs had gone to sleep. They immediately collapsed beneath her and her face slapped against the floor. She clenched her teeth, bracing for the smart remarks.

But he was silent. It wasn't until they were close to the river, and Alex was hobbling along on feet shooting with pins and needles, that she heard him say quietly to Victoria, "She's sure got a temper on her, doesn't she?" Victoria giggled.

Did no one see? The man had *tied her up.* And yet they thought *she* was being unreasonable!

"Be careful," Luke warned her when they reached the banks. The rain had swollen the river and the current was swift. "Stay close to the edge. And don't stray out of earshot. I'll be over here. Victoria, you keep an eye on her."

"Alex likes her privacy," Victoria protested. "I'd best stay with you."

Luke looked dubious.

"She'll scream if she sees anything, won't you?" Victoria nudged Alex with her elbow.

"Why don't we just forget the whole idea?" Alex suggested. She wasn't sure how she was going to explain dirtying her face straight after bathing anyway. Although, the water looked so inviting, she thought wistfully. Dawn was breaking and the dreamy pink sky was reflected in the rippling surface.

Luke rubbed his face. He was too tired to argue. "I'll be over there," he told the ladies. "I don't care whether you bathe or not."

They watched as he settled himself with his back against a rock, his face tilted to take in the pastel sky. "Stop being so difficult," Victoria hissed at Alex. "At least give me half an hour with him." She turned with a snap of her skirts and advanced on her prey.

Exhaustion hit Alex like a wave. The last twenty-four hours had been so draining. What she needed was to clean herself up, eat a hot meal and sleep for the entire day. She didn't suppose she'd be allowed to sleep, not with the Gradys out there; she'd have to drive that wretched wagon all day. Maybe she could coax Victoria into taking the mules for a couple of hours . . .

Alex shook herself. She was practically dozing on her feet. Oh well. Maybe she wouldn't get a nap, but at least she could scrub herself off. She headed for a small twist in the river, which was screened by a low wall of shrubs. She pulled her boots off and waded in. She had every intention of bathing fully clothed—she wasn't about to risk Luke finding out who she really was, especially after that stunt with the ropes—but as soon as the water rushed over her bare feet she changed her mind.

It was deliciously crisp and cold. She peered back toward Luke. There was no way he could see her through the screen of shrubs. Besides, Victoria was with him, and there was no way she'd let Luke out of her sight. With a naughty thrill, Alex tore off her stiff clay-coated clothes and dropped them on the shore.

The feel of the strong current against her naked body was wonderful. She could feel every particle of dirt being swept away. She scrubbed her face and hair and then drifted happily to the shore and dealt with her clothes in the shallows.

She was enjoying herself so much that she didn't even realize she had company.

It was only when he cleared his throat nervously that she looked up.

Silas. Her eyes flew wide and she opened her mouth to scream. Silas shook his head and held a finger to his lips. He looked as terrified as she felt.

"Hush," he whispered frantically, "you have to listen to me. Gideon doesn't know I'm here."

"You leave me alone," Alex hissed, ducking under the shallow water and wrapping her arms across her chest. How long had he been there? What was he going to do to her? She looked back toward Luke. All she had to do was scream and he'd come running.

"Don't," Silas pleaded, reading her thoughts. "I'm trying to help you."

"Help me?" Alex said in disbelief.

"You need to give me the money—the gold and the bonds. If you give me the money Gideon will head back home and leave you in peace, I swear."

"And what about you?" Alex demanded. "Will you leave me in peace?"

"He won't stop at killing animals," Silas warned, avoiding her question. "Once all your mules are dead, what do you think he'll do then? Who do you think he'll take a knife to next?"

"I've got a gun," Alex retorted, her bravado undermined by the tremor in her voice.

"You'll never see him coming," Silas said darkly. "One morning you'll wake up and that feeb will be spread across your camp, just like the horse."

"Don't call him that!" Alex's voice broke. She kept backing away from him, until she was deep in the river.

"And after him Gideon will come for your sister. And he won't just cut her."

"Stop it!" Alex was close to the far bank. As soon as she reached solid ground, most importantly solid ground on the opposite side of the river to Silas Grady, she was going to scream. And then she'd smile as she watched Luke shoot him down like the dog he was.

"Just give him the bonds. Give them back and it will all be over."

"I don't have them." Alex hurled the words at him like daggers. "I burned them. You go back and tell your maniac brother that! I burned them. Every last one!"

The blood drained from Silas's face. He looked like a man staring down the barrel of a gun. "Come with me," he cried desperately, lunging into the river for her. "Come with me! We'll head south to Mexico. We need to get you where he'll never find you!"

Alex panicked as he surged through the river, reaching for her. She shrieked and threw herself up the riverbank.

"Alex!" Silas cried.

"Luke!" Alex screamed.

She dove at the bushes, tearing her skin to ribbons and landing face-first in the mud. She struggled to rise, looking behind her in panic. Silas wasn't there. He was standing limp in the current, watching her mad flight with enormous, haunted eyes. She met his gaze and was frozen to the spot.

"Run," he said. "Run for your life."

And then he was gone.

"Alex!" Luke came flying, the cold iron of his gun flashing in the morning sun. He stopped dead at the sight of her muddy face rising out of the bushes.

"Silas," she stammered, shaken. She pointed in the direction Silas had fled, and Luke was off.

"What happened?" Victoria squeaked as she skidded to a stop. She registered Alex's nudity and gave a choked squeal. "Did he . . .?" She fumbled for Alex's sodden clothes.

Alex shook her head, she couldn't speak. She sank down into the mud, her heart hammering in her ears. Dear Lord, what had she done? She was a dead woman.

"Quick, get dressed." Victoria nudged her with the wet clothes. "Before Luke comes back."

COME WITH ME," Luke demanded when he returned. By then she was dressed in the heavy wet clothes, shivering from the chill as well as the shock of seeing Silas. Luke took Alex's hand and led her toward the chuck wagon.

"Did you find Silas?" she asked numbly, unable to dislodge the memory of his haunted eyes. He'd been terrified. Her shivering turned to shaking. She'd just seen her own death reflected in Silas Grady's gaze.

When Alex had refused to move from behind the bushes, Victoria had dressed her in the sopping clothes and led her back to the wagon. But Victoria couldn't get a word out of her. She toweled Alex dry, careful to leave the mud on her face, and dressed her in a pair of Adam's clean overalls. Then she fretted as Alex sat like a bump on a log, staring blindly ahead and not uttering a sound.

"What did he *do* to her?" she whispered to Luke when he came back. Victoria felt like the world had been turned upside down. Alex was the strong one. She needed Alex to be the strong one.

Luke reassured Victoria, and then he took Alex to the chuck wagon. He didn't answer her question. He simply handed her up onto the bench and climbed up beside her. He gathered the reins, flicked the whip at the oxen and they were off.

Alex blinked. "What are you doing?" She finally began surfacing from her daze.

"Driving."

"I can see that," she said tersely. "But why are *you* driving? Where's Sebastian?"

"I sent him on ahead to Laramie," Luke said. "They'll have plenty of warning to prepare a nice little cell for our friends the Gradys."

"If we get to Fort Laramie," Alex told him faintly. *Run for your life.* Silas's words echoed in her head.

"I think we need to talk, runt."

"I told you not to call me that," Alex said absently, out of habit. Then she looked around, straightening in her seat. "Why am I here?"

"That's just what we need to talk about. You said you stole his gold. Just how much gold was it?"

"No, I mean, why am I in the chuck wagon?" She leaned around the side of the wagon to see the vehicles behind. "I need to be with Victoria and Adam."

Luke yanked her back, worried she'd fall and be crushed under the wheels. "Victoria and Adam are fine."

"No, they're not. Not while Gideon's out there."

"I thought he was after *you*? For his money."

"He is. But he won't come for me, not yet. It's not his way. First, he'll kill everyone I love, and then . . . then it will be my turn."

Luke couldn't believe the change in the kid. All of the fire was gone, replaced by a cold expression and a toneless voice. She was giving him the creeps.

"Let me down," Alex ordered. "I have to ride with them."

"I told you they're fine," Luke snapped. "Victoria's riding with the O'Briens and Joseph's riding shotgun with Adam. I wanted to put Adam with the Crawfords, but he wouldn't leave those mules. They're as safe as we can make them."

Alex's stomach twisted. They would never be safe. Not until Gideon was dead. And it was her fault.

Luke took her chin in his fingers and turned her to face him. "I need to know what's going on." He bent his head until he captured her gaze.

Alex felt herself being sucked into those familiar black waters. There was such concern there, and such strength.

"Trust me," he said gently, his voice husky. It was more than Alex could bear. Her eyes swam with tears. His fingers loosened on her jaw and reached up to stroke her cheek. "Trust me, love."

Oh, how she wanted to. "He's going to kill me," she said helplessly.

"Not while I'm here."

The tears tumbled down Alex's cheeks, dampening the dried mud. Dear Lord, what if Gideon killed Luke too? What would she do then?

"I've had my share of men try to kill me," Luke told her, reading her thoughts, "and none of them have managed it yet. I'll be damned if I'll let the honor go to that little weasel."

Oddly, it was the twinkle in his eye that calmed her. "I bet it'll be one of your women that kills you in the end," Alex sniffed.

Luke laughed. "You're probably right," he agreed. He dropped his arm around her shoulders and hauled her up against him, giving her a brotherly pat in the process. "It may even be you, brat."

"Maybe. If you ever tie me up again."

"If I apologize, will you tell me why that madman is after you?"

"If it's a good apology."

"I'm sorry."

"Very sorry."

"Very sorry," he agreed.

"And you'll never do it again."

"Never ever."

"Are you crossing your fingers?" she asked suspiciously, leaning around him to check. He gave her a sour look. She settled back into the jolting seat, grateful for the weight of his arm around her shoulders. Somehow, she wasn't quite sure how, he had managed to drive her fears into the background, and she felt a little more like her usual self.

It was a relief in the end to tell him about the bonds, and the slaves, to let the truth replace the lies. Well, most of the lies. As far as Luke was concerned, Silas Grady was obsessed with her sister, Victoria, and not some runt of a beanpole with a muddy face.

"So he came to warn you?"

"I think so," Alex said, still bewildered. "You should have seen him. He looked terrified. I think . . ." Alex paused for a moment, grappling with an unbelievable thought. "I think he must really love . . . her."

"That's my impression," Luke agreed, going on to tell her what he'd seen at the Grady camp.

"Poor Silas," Alex sighed, feeling a pang of sympathy.

"Poor Silas? The man's an animal."

"But what chance did he have, with a family like that?" Alex thought back to the times Silas had shown up at the dances in Dyson's barn, with his shiny-kneed suit and freshly combed hair. She'd never considered that his feelings for her might be genuine. She'd thought it was lust. And maybe the desire to own the prettiest girl in the county. But today . . . the way he'd tried to save her from his brother . . .

"That's no excuse," Luke snapped. "A man chooses whether or not to be an animal. The way he's treated your sister is inexcusable. When you grow up, runt, don't you ever let a man treat you like that."

"At least he's loyal," Alex said tartly. "He's never paid the slightest attention to another woman. Unlike some others I could mention."

Luke rolled his eyes. "You're too young to understand."

Alex snorted. She was silent for a minute, regarding him from the corner of her eye. And then she couldn't resist prodding him. "How *should* a man treat me? When I grow up, I mean."

Luke gave her a sideways grin. "You got any man in particular in mind?"

"Well," she said slyly, feeling a wicked impulse to torture him, "not really. Although Jane's father is awfully attractive, don't you think?"

"Ned?" Luke couldn't keep the disbelief out of his voice.

"He's mighty smart."

"A little old for you, ain't he?" Luke said dryly.

"Well, maybe not him exactly. But a man like him." She sat back and enjoyed the disgruntled expression on Luke's handsome face. "You haven't answered my question. How should a man treat me?"

"I don't think you need to worry, not if that's the kind of man you're aiming for."

"Oh. Well, what if it was a man like you? Just for an example."

"A man like me?"

"Yeah. How do you treat Adelia? Just for an example."

"Amelia."

"Isn't that what I said?" she asked innocently.

He gave her a sharp look, and she looked away. "How do I treat Amelia?" Luke echoed thoughtfully, making a great show of pursing his lips and considering. "Well," he said, "I sit with her at the service Sundays, and afterward I'm invited to sit awhile on the porch. And if I'm lucky her folks will ask me to stay for dinner."

"Do they like you? Her folks?" Alex's curiosity was genuine. She had a vivid picture of Luke sitting on the porch of a neat little whitewashed house, next to a very pretty girl. In her mind's eye they were on a swing, their thighs brushing; they were surrounded by roses and jasmine, and the smell of fresh-baked blueberry pie wafted out the kitchen window.

Sighing blissfully, the pretty girl leaned her head against Luke's shoulder as her soft white hand was enveloped by Luke's large brown one.

Alex looked down at her own filthy hand, callused from driving the mules, and grimaced.

"Harding's the mayor of Utopia—officially he likes everyone," Luke told her, interrupting her thoughts.

"What about unofficially?" Alex perked up.

"He sure didn't say no when I asked for her hand."

Alex's mouth popped open. "Her what?"

"Her hand."

Alex couldn't speak.

Luke took one look at her shocked face and felt a stab of pity. "When you grow up, brat, I'm sure there'll be men lining up to ask for your hand too. Especially if you wash all that muck off. Why, I bet you'll look just as pretty as your sister."

"We're not blood related, remember," Alex told him numbly. He was getting married. Married! And yet that deceitful, disloyal wretch had flirted shamelessly with Beatrice in Independence! Had seduced her, even! Alex had to bite down on her tongue to keep from blistering him with it. "I suppose congratulations are in order," she forced herself to say.

"They are?"

"For you and Arnelle."

"Amelia."

"Yes," Alex said coldly, "the fortunate Miss Hardway."

"Harding."

"Indeed. Congratulations are in order for you and the fortunate Miss Hardly." Alex was clenching her teeth so hard it was a wonder they didn't snap.

"Well, they would be, only I haven't asked her yet," Luke lied. He wasn't about to advertise the fact that she kept turning him down. Even his brothers didn't know.

Amelia Harding was going to be his wife. She just hadn't realized yet that women didn't say "no" to Luke Slater.

"You haven't asked her?" Alex tried not to think about why that news should fill her with joy. Relief for poor Ariella Hardwig, she rationalized. Perhaps she would learn what a philanderer he was before she had to suffer marriage to him, while Alex was simply experiencing the common bond between women in the face of a man's perfidy.

"Haven't found the right time," he said, not meeting her eye.

"Glory," Alex said, "I hope she's not married to someone else by the time you get back."

Luke scowled.

Alex was so busy picturing Aurelia Hardnose walking down the aisle toward a bridegroom who wasn't Luke Slater that she forgot about Gideon Grady.

At least for a while.

❧ 27 ❧

ALEX HAD THOUGHT she'd known what fear was. But that was before she woke up to find herself staring at Gideon's knife.

It was embedded in the wooden floor of the wagon, barely an inch from her nose. And pinned beneath it was a scrap of sunshine-yellow calico. There was a note, consisting of five childishly scrawled words. *Come alone or she dies.*

Alex sat bolt upright, wildly searching the wagon, her heart pounding. She was surrounded by a sea of sleeping Crawfords.

How had he gotten in without waking a single person? How had he stabbed the knife through the boards without alerting them? He was like some kind of demon, Alex thought with a shiver.

And Victoria! Alex stifled a moan as she thought of her sister. Luke had said she'd be safe spending the night with the O'Briens. And she'd believed him!

Wrenching the knife from the boards, Alex reached for her gun and slithered through the tangle of bodies toward the tail of the wagon.

"Alex?" Lucinda asked sleepily.

Alex froze. "I need to go to the hole." Luke had told them to keep her in sight at all times. But Lucinda was still half-asleep and she merely muttered and rolled over. Within a moment her breathing was deep and even again.

It was still deep night, Alex realized as she dropped from the wagon. She could hear the Watts brothers talking softly. They were supposed to be keeping watch on opposite sides of the camp, but had obviously taken the opportunity for a nip of moonshine and a chat. Alex felt a blaze of rage. Some watchmen. While they gossiped like a pair of old women her sister had been taken by the devil.

Alex crept from the circle of wagons, pausing as she passed beyond the faint light cast by the fire. A sliver of moon cast a pale glow, illuminating the vast plain. Where was she supposed to go?

A sharp whistle made her jump. She turned to see a horseman silhouetted against the night sky. He was too far away for her to make him out. It could have been any of the Gradys. Her hands clenched around the butt of her gun. She was glad she'd loaded it before she went to bed.

The horseman jerked his head, indicating she should approach. As she took a step he turned the horse. He wanted her to follow him. All of a sudden Alex felt deadly calm. Her knees stopped trembling as she strode out after the slow moving horseman.

This was the moment. She had no doubt that tonight she would come face-to-face with Gideon Grady. And one of them would die.

THE SCREAM WOKE Luke.

He was out of his bedroll, gun in hand, before he registered that it was a scream of rage. He scratched his head and watched as Victoria snatched a length of calico off the saltbrush by her wagon.

"Adam!" she shrieked. "What did you do to my dress?" She stalked over and kicked at Adam's feet, which protruded from beneath the wagon. "I'm out of the wagon for *one* night, and look what you do!" She shook the yellow fabric, and Luke could see that the bodice had been torn.

Adam's head emerged. "Vicky?" He blinked sleepily. "What happened to your pretty dress?"

"That's what I want to know!"

"Good morning," Henry Watts said nervously, as he slithered out from behind Adam. "You're looking lovely this morning, Miss Alexander."

She blushed, suddenly aware of how shrewish she looked.

"That's a shame about your dress," Adam said ruefully, as he too clambered out from under the wagon, "you looked real nice in it."

Luke shook his head and set a pot of coffee on the fire.

"You didn't do this?" Victoria asked Adam.

"No," Adam said, offended. "I liked that dress. It's as pretty as a daffodil."

"But who would do such a thing?" She held her lovely dress out before her. Tears welled in her eyes as she regarded the damage. There was no way she could repair it; it would need a whole new bodice.

"Don't cry," Adam said, alarmed. He didn't like it when his sisters cried. They made him feel so lost and helpless. He looked to Luke, who sighed.

He didn't see why crying women had to be his lot in life. "Now, there," he soothed patiently, offering Victoria a mug of coffee, but not getting close enough for her to collapse against him. "I'm sure you can whip yourself up another just as pretty when we get you to your brother in Amory. And maybe while you're at it you can get that wildcat sister of yours to dress like a lady too."

Alex! Victoria's eyes narrowed. She remembered the envy on Alex's face at the dance in Independence. Not to mention the fact that her beautiful sister was obviously developing feelings for Luke. Imagine how she felt knowing that Luke wanted Victoria! Mad enough to shred a yellow dress, Victoria guessed. Her lips thinned, and without another word she stalked away, leaving Luke holding the coffee mug.

"Alex doesn't wear dresses anymore," Adam reminded him in a conspiratorial whisper.

"So I've noticed." Luke didn't pay much attention to Victoria as he fixed himself and Adam breakfast.

"What's the name of that red horse?" Adam asked dreamily.

"What red horse?" Luke said, vaguely distracted by the voices from the Crawfords' wagon.

"Your red horse. That one you said I could buy."

"You've got a memory like an elephant." He passed the boy a plate of sausage and a hunk of stale bread. "He doesn't have a name."

"Why not?"

"I guess I just haven't got around to it. I've got an awful lot of horses."

"So I can name him?"

"As long as you don't call him Blackie the Third." Luke rose to his feet, concerned. Victoria's voice had gone shrill. He frowned. He wasn't in the mood to break up a catfight between the sisters.

The next thing he knew Victoria was flying across the camp, the yellow calico streaming behind her like a sail. "She's gone!"

"Who's gone?" Luke grunted as Victoria slammed into him.

"Alex!" She burst into hysterical tears, unable to say more.

Luke thrust her into Adam's arms and headed for the Crawfords' wagon. Mal and Lucinda met him halfway. "Oh, Luke, we feel just awful," Lucinda moaned, wringing her hands. Luke felt his stomach drop.

"Lucinda heard him get up," Mal told him, pulling his wife close.

"He told me he was going to walk to the hole."

"No one went with him?"

They blanched. "I was asleep," Mal said.

"It's all my fault," Lucinda admitted, her face crumpling. "I should have gone. But I was so tired, I barely woke up enough to ask him where he was going."

"What time was this?"

"I don't know." Tears rolled down her cheeks. "Late. It was pitch black."

"Henry!" Luke roared.

Back at the campfire Henry Watts choked on his mouthful of sausage as he watched the taller man approach. Luke's expression was black, his eyes flat and cold.

"Something wrong, Slater?" Henry asked nervously.

"You were on watch last night."

"Sure was."

"You didn't doze off?"

Henry bristled. "Hell no. I didn't so much as close my eyes until Ulrich relieved me at dawn."

"And you didn't see anything?"

"No."

"Not even Alex heading to the hole?"

Henry swallowed hard. The hole was right beyond where he should have been standing lookout. "Well, now," he said, clearing his throat anxiously, "there was a moment when I might have joined my brother. Just for a nip to keep myself awake, you understand."

Luke swore.

"Has something happened to the kid?"

But Luke didn't hear him; he was running to the Crawfords' wagon. "Nobody move!" he ordered. "Not an inch, not until I tell you to."

Everyone froze, turning to look at Luke with wide-eyed confusion.

He didn't want her tracks getting any more obscured than they already had been. But hell, all the Crawfords had left their wagon already and at its base was a mess of prints in the dirt. There was no chance of making Alex's out.

She'd told Lucinda she was heading to the hole, so suppose she had been and was snatched while she was gone . . . Luke followed the path she would have taken, his gaze trained on the ground.

It looked like every person in camp had been to the hole this morning, but eventually he found a small boot print he thought might be Alex's. The tracks led away from the circled wagons. He frowned. There was just the one set of prints. Where the hell had she been going?

If he'd kept following the trail he would have found the hoof prints, but before he could get that far he heard the click of someone pulling back the hammer of a gun, and then he felt the kiss of cold iron against the base of his skull.

❧ 28 ❧

ALEX FELT LIKE she must have walked halfway to Oregon. The horseman hadn't stopped for a moment. Now and then he seemed to turn in the saddle to check that Alex was still trailing him, but he never slowed his pace and she was no closer to finding out which Grady she was following.

By daybreak she was pretty sure she knew his plan. He was taking her on some kind of wild-goose chase, making sure that by the time he led her into their camp she would be too exhausted to fight.

It was working.

Every muscle in Alex's legs was screaming for mercy, and her mouth was as dry as a boll of cotton. After a few hours the sun peeked over the horizon and a burning angry orange sky flared in the east. If Alex thought she was suffering already, it was nothing compared to the discomfort the sun caused her now as it rose into a cloudless sky. She hadn't brought a hat and as the sun beat down on her she felt her skin begin to burn. She didn't remember ever feeling so hot in her life, and all she could think about was water: the shining stretches in the swamp back home, the gush from the pump, the mineral tang of water from the depths of the well and the cold flow of the river against her naked skin. She pictured thrusting her face into its icy depths and drinking it in, but the fantasy only caused her stomach to cramp with longing.

She was almost insensible as the day drew on; she barely registered the gigantic spear of rock rising before her. They'd been seeing it in the distance for days: Chimney Rock, Luke called it, the eighth wonder of the world.

Alex didn't feel wonder looking at it now. All she could

think about was the thin blue shadow stretching from its base across the scrubby plain. She didn't care about that stupid horseman anymore. She didn't care if Gideon had Victoria. All she cared about was that beckoning shadow, with its promise of relief and rest. It would be cool, she thought, as she veered from the horseman's path toward the rock. In her fevered state she half imagined she would find an oasis at the point where the shadow joined the rock; a pure and unpolluted pool, cold as melting snow. She would collapse beside it in the cool blue depths of the shadow and drink until she too was as cold as melting snow.

She was almost there before the horseman realized that she was no longer following him.

She heard quickening hoofbeats as she stumbled into the narrow shadow. She slumped to the ground in bitter disappointment. It wasn't blue and cool. It was just as orange and scrubby and horrible as the plains. There was no pool. There was nothing but rock and scratchy grass and dust. Alex could have wept.

She rolled over on her back as the staccato hoofbeats came to an abrupt halt. Staring up at the gargantuan pointing finger of rock, she could hear the creak of saddle leather as the horseman dismounted.

"Aw, hell," she heard a rough voice say.

Then there was the press of a canteen against her lips and the welcome rush of water against her tongue. "Don't drink too much," the voice warned, "or you'll be sick."

As the canteen was taken away, Alex stared up into a horribly familiar face. "I'm sorry, darlin'," he said, "I didn't realize you were feeling poorly."

He made Alex so mad she could spit.

A WIRY ARM reached around Luke and removed his gun from its holster. "My brothers have the girl, Slater," a sly voice said against his ear. "Any funny business and they'll shoot her."

It took all of Luke's self-restraint to keep from belting the weasel.

"Turn around," Gideon ordered. "Walk slowly back to

your cook fire. And remember, no funny business or"—he paused, grinning, obviously enjoying himself—"*boom*."

Luke's jaw clenched at the thought of Alex in the hands of this weasel. God only knew what he'd done with her. Obediently, he walked back to the camp, his mind racing as he tried to figure out how to take control of the situation.

He found the camp much as he'd expected: the campers were huddled around the fire, subdued in the face of the Grady brothers' shotguns. One squeeze of the trigger and the lot of them would be peppered with buckshot. Victoria was trapped by Bert's meaty arm. He'd hauled her close against him and had his hand wrapped around her throat. Luke could see her trembling.

If there was one thing he couldn't abide it was a man who mistreated women. He flexed his fingers. Just wait until he got his hands on the bastard.

"Watch yourself, Slater," Gideon reminded him. He slid around in front of Luke, keeping his weapon trained on the bigger man. "You lot"—Gideon gestured at the campers—"get yourselves in that wagon." He pointed them toward the Crawfords' massive wagon. "Slowly and carefully. Travis, you keep guard."

He was smart, this weasel, Luke thought. If the campers were in the confines of the wagon Travis could not only watch them, he could hit them all with a single shot of buckshot. Luke watched as they climbed into the wagon. The brutish Travis stood at the opening, peering along the barrel of his raised shotgun.

Victoria squealed and Luke turned his attention back to Gideon, only to find that he'd snatched Victoria away from his brother. Now Bert's shotgun was aimed directly at Luke.

Victoria was breathing shallowly, panicked, as Gideon held her in front of him and rested the barrel of his gun against her cheek. "She's lovely, isn't she?" Gideon taunted, rubbing the weapon over her soft flesh. "I've noticed you spend a lot of time with her, Slater. You like the ladies, don't you?" Gideon leaned into Victoria until his lips were brushing her ear. She shuddered. "He tell you about how he likes whores, sweetheart? And they sure do like him in return."

The weasel's eyes flicked up and met Luke's. They were narrow and mean. "That night of the fire," he hissed into Victoria's ear. "I heard 'em through the wall. You never heard such moaning from a woman."

Luke's blood boiled and he started forward. He couldn't bear this animal talking that way about Beatrice. He stopped dead when Gideon slid the tip of his gun into Victoria's mouth. Her eyes were huge with terror.

"You see how he loves his whores, sweetheart? You see how he wants to defend their honor?" Gideon laughed softly.

"What do you want, Grady?" Luke asked tersely, unable to tear his eyes away from where the gun disappeared between Victoria's lips.

"What I've always wanted, Slater," Gideon hissed. "The Barratt bitch."

Luke frowned, confused. What did he mean? He'd taken Alex in the night. Hadn't he?

"Don't play dumb with me, Slater."

My brothers have the girl. He'd meant Victoria. Suddenly a thought dawned on Luke. "Where's your brother Silas?"

Gideon laughed. "He had a little accident."

The memory of the knife at Silas's throat flared in Luke's mind. Hell. If the man had no compunction about killing his brother, then what would he do here and now?

Victoria whimpered as the gun slid deeper into her mouth.

In that moment Luke wanted to kill him. Slowly.

"Hand her over, Slater."

What would the maniac do if he discovered Alex wasn't here? How twitchy was his trigger finger?

"Give me the bitch, Slater, and you can have your sweetheart back."

"Why do you want the girl so much?" Luke stalled.

Through a gap in the canvas, Ned O'Brien watched the tense confrontation. He couldn't hear their words, but he could see clear as day the gun violating Victoria's sweet rosebud mouth. His heart galloped in his chest. He'd never considered himself a brave man, but there came a time when a man had to act: *The truly brave, when they behold the brave oppressed with odds, are touched with a desire to shield and save.* Byron again. Ever since he'd met Victoria he had been full of Byron, full of the same wildness and passion as the romantic poet. And now here he was, facing down a shotgun, and a man twice his size, about to do the craziest thing he'd ever done.

Slowly, his hand only barely shaking, Ned withdrew his brand new gun from the inside pocket of his coat. He'd never got around to getting a holster, and the brutes hadn't bothered to check their victims' pockets. Speed was the key, he thought, as he drew a shaky breath. On the count of three . . . *one . . . two . . .* He'd emptied the barrel before the brute knew what was happening.

Travis went down.

Shocked, Bert and Gideon turned to see what had happened. Luke launched himself forward, knocking Victoria and the weasel to the ground. Gideon's gun went flying and Victoria screamed. Luke registered blood, but didn't pause. His hands wrapped around Gideon's scrawny throat.

"Travis?" Bert called anxiously. "Gideon?"

As Gideon clawed at Luke's hands, his face turning red, Luke stole a glance at Bert. He was jiggling on his feet, on edge, his gaze flicking back and forth between his brothers, his finger spasming against the trigger. He looked like he'd pull it at any moment.

"You shoot me, you'll hit your brother," Luke warned him, struggling to keep his voice flat and calm. Gideon was bucking under him, trying to get his knee up toward Luke's crotch. Luke tightened his grip around the weasel's throat, glad the man was so weedy. He wasn't sure he would have been able to subdue Travis or Bert so easily.

Gideon's eyes rolled over in his head and suddenly he was still.

Luke released him. He'd only passed out from lack of oxygen. Luke would have to hurry up and get Bert under control so he could bind Gideon before he came to.

Ned's ears were ringing from the gunfire, but he wasn't about to lose his advantage. "Stay here," he bellowed at his children, as he scrambled to the tail of the wagon. His heart stopped in his chest when he reached the tailgate and Travis loomed before him. He'd fired six bullets at the man. He'd gone down like a sack of potatoes.

Not because he'd been hit, Ned knew with a sense of sickened horror. The brute didn't have a scratch on him. The only reason he'd dropped to the dust was out of an animalistic sense of self-preservation. And now here he was again, his shotgun practically touching the tip of Ned's nose. The world slowed down. Ned could see the man's finger curling around the trigger, he could see it begin to squeeze.

For the first time in his life, Ned O'Brien did something without thinking. He threw himself forward a mere heartbeat before the gun discharged, knocking Travis backward. The buckshot scattered through the saltbrush, snapping twigs and sending up puffs of red dust as it hit the ground.

Ned didn't have time to reload his weapon. Instead, still acting on instinct, he smashed the gun into Travis's jaw. And this time the man really did go down. Hard.

Before Luke could get to him, Bert had grabbed Victoria. Her hands were clenched to her mouth and blood dribbled through her fingers. "Stay back!" Bert called, his voice revealing his panic.

"Give yourself up, Grady," Luke said, slowly rising. Behind Bert he could see the men dropping down from the wagon and stepping over Travis's prone body. "You're outnumbered."

"You won't do anything to me while I've got the girl."

Luke could see Ned fumbling to slide fresh bullets into the barrel of his gun. Hurry up, O'Brien, he thought impatiently. Luke met Victoria's glazed brown eyes and silently tried to reassure her. "What are you going to do?" he asked Bert calmly. "Both of your brothers are down."

Bert's eyes were beginning to roll. Luke had to keep him calm. The last thing he wanted was for him to get trigger-happy. "If you let her go, we'll let you walk out of here."

Bert snorted.

"I swear," Luke assured him. "You have my word." Bert was sweating. Luke could see the sun glinting off the moisture above his lip. "I'm not armed." Luke held his hands up. "Just let her go and you can walk out of here unscathed."

Bert grunted and clenched Victoria even more tightly. "I don't think so, Slater. The girl's coming with me."

"Over my dead body," Ned rasped, as he stuck his gun behind Bert's jaw.

Hell. Luke half expected the shotgun to go off, half expected to see Victoria fall. But Bert's nerves were stronger than he'd thought. The man simply froze. And it was with a measure of relief, Luke thought, that he dropped his weapon and surrendered.

Victoria sank to the ground, sobbing.

"Fetch me as much rope as you can find," Luke called to the Watts brothers. He could hear the women and children weeping. He wanted to get this nightmare over as fast as possible.

As soon as Luke grabbed Bert by the scruff of the neck, the gun fell from Ned's suddenly trembling fingers. All vestiges of calm left him. He'd shot at a man; he'd pistol-whipped a man; he'd threatened a man with cold-blooded murder. Him! Ned O'Brien!

Victoria's sobs pulled him to his senses. Hastily he removed his jacket and wrapped it around her, pulling her into a close embrace. "Hush," he soothed, rocking her as he did his youngest daughter when she woke from a nightmare.

It was only when Luke had the Gradys gagged and bound, watched over by the armed Watts brothers, that he remembered Alex. The brat was still out there somewhere, in who knew what kind of trouble.

❧ 29 ❧

"WHERE'S MY SISTER?" Alex demanded, glaring up at Silas. "And what the hell happened to your face?"

One of Silas's hands self-consciously rose to brush the ugly raw slashes across his face. "Gideon happened," he said grimly.

Alex gaped. "He did that to you? His own brother?"

Silas gave her a hard look. "He said it would remind me."

"Of what?" Alex asked cautiously, struggling to get to her feet. Silas Grady was almost the last person on earth she wanted to be alone with, second only to his crazy brother.

Silas gave a sharp bark of laughter. "Have a look more closely. What do you see?"

Nervously, Alex examined his cuts, which were only just beginning to scab over. Her eyes widened in horror and the hair on the nape of her neck stood on end. The slashes formed a crude letter A.

"He said you owned me, so I might as well bear the mark of a slave."

Alex flushed.

"He followed me that day at the river," Silas said bitterly, "he heard every word."

"I'm sorry," Alex breathed.

Silas shook his head. "Don't you see? If you'd come with me he would have killed us both."

"Where's my sister, Silas?" Alex was alarmed by his talk of murder.

Silas looked confused.

"Victoria," Alex pleaded, "please tell me she's all right, please tell me he hasn't killed her."

His expression cleared and an odd smile played around

the corners of his disfigured mouth. "Haven't you figured it out yet? No one has your sister."

"But the note, her yellow dress . . ."

"I had to get you away," Silas told her, sounding proud of himself. "He was coming for you. He would have killed you. After he . . ." He trailed off significantly, a black scowl darkening his face. "You're mine, Alex. I'll kill any man who touches you."

"You bastard," Alex gasped. "What do you think he'll do to them when he finds me gone?"

Silas shrugged.

Alex grabbed a rock and hurled it at him. It smashed him in the mouth and he gave a yell, which echoed across the valley and off the low hills nearby. "And to think I actually felt sympathy for you," she spat.

"I don't want your pity," he shouted, outraged.

"You won't even get that!" Alex shouted right back at him. "You have nothing but my contempt."

He came after her. She tried to run, but he was too quick for her. He tackled her to the hard ground, his knee forcing her legs apart and his hot breath hitting her in the face.

He looked down into her furious gray eyes, feeling her writhing beneath him, and he lost control. Ignoring the pain in his ruined lips, his mouth assaulted hers. Alex screamed into his kiss and tried to claw at him, but he'd caught her wrists.

Alex's rage dissolved into blind terror as his knee rammed into her. Oh hell, she was alone out here in the wilderness with this savage. She began to panic when he clasped both of her of wrists in one hand, freeing his other to tear at her clothing. The bib of her overalls tore. The buttons popped free of her shirt, and then his hand was ripping at the bandages binding her. When she felt his hand close around her bare breast she snapped, and bit down hard on his tongue.

He screamed, blood pouring down his chin, but he didn't loosen his grip. He'd dreamed of this moment for too long to relinquish it.

Alex fought like a wildcat but, despite her best efforts, she was soon half-naked and in danger of losing the battle. And then she heard a whistle. Silas went rigid and screamed even louder than he had when she'd bitten him.

There was another whistle. Silas scrambled off her and as he fled Alex saw two arrows sticking out him, one in each buttock. As he ran there was another whistle and, with a meaty thud, a wicked-looking arrow, bristling with stiff white feathers, lodged in his shoulder. He went down, shrieking.

In shock, Alex turned to see a dark silhouette looming above them near the base of the jutting rock. As she watched, it slunk down the steep rock, silent and graceful. It was an Indian man. Alex felt a stab of fear. She'd never been so close to an Indian before in her life. And this one was terrifying.

He was broad across the shoulders and chest, a fact emphasized by the fringing on his long buckskin shirt. His jet-black hair fell well past his shoulders and was decorated with a single black-tipped feather. His face was angular and cruel. But it was his eyes that really struck fear into Alex. They were so pale they were almost colorless, and were piercing like the eyes of a wolf. They seemed devoid of human emotion.

But then, as he stared down at her, she thought she saw a twinkle.

"I have been watching you all morning," he said in perfect, unaccented English. "I thought you were a boy." His gaze dropped to the lush curves of her breasts, which she was struggling to hide with her hands. "I was wrong."

She scowled at him, not appreciating his dry humor.

In one smooth movement, the Indian pulled his buckskin shirt over his head. He dropped it across Alex's lap. "I don't think yours will do you much good anymore."

If she had never seen Luke Slater she would have thought that this man was perfect. His body was all long muscle, burnished by the sun. She tore her gaze away and struggled into his shirt. She was surprised at the suppleness of the leather; it felt like velvet against her bare skin. On her the shirt fell to her shins, becoming more of a dress. Thank heavens it fell straight, and didn't cling to her curves. The last thing she needed was everyone in camp seeing she was a girl. Or Luke realizing that she wasn't a child.

As she dressed, the Indian strode to where Silas lay whimpering in the dust. He gave a high whistle and after a moment a horse and pony came trotting around from behind the base of Chimney Rock. Alex watched as the Indian trussed Silas up and tossed him over the back of the pony. Then he tied Silas's roan to the pony's harness.

"Where are you taking him?" Alex asked warily.

"That depends," the Indian replied.

"On what?"

"On where I am taking you."

"You don't have to take me anywhere," Alex said nervously, "I mean, thank you, it's a very kind offer, but I'll be just fine walking back by myself."

One elegant black eyebrow rose as he regarded her dubiously.

"And thank you so much for the shirt," she blathered on, beginning to back away. "I'd really best be off now, everybody must be dreadfully worried about me." And, truth be told, she was dreadfully worried about them. What if Gideon had shown up while she was gone?

With a polite smile, she bid the Indian farewell, trying not to think about what he'd do to Silas, and headed back the way she'd come. Only . . . she couldn't exactly remember which way that was. The sun had come up on her left. Hadn't it? Or had it been directly in front of her? Oh glory, she'd been too distracted to pay attention.

She heard hoofbeats and the jangle of a bit. The shadow of the Indian fell across her. "You came from that direction," he told her calmly, gesturing.

"Thank you." Alex set off. She'd forgotten how sore her muscles were. And now she had the extra discomfort of the bruises she'd received when Silas had tackled her to the ground. She was aware of the Indian riding slowly at her side. She was also aware of Silas glaring at her from where he hung upside down over the pony.

"I would be more than happy to take you where you're going," the Indian said.

"I couldn't put you out," she insisted firmly. There was no way she was getting up in the saddle with such an intimidating man. He might be as much of a maniac as Gideon was, for all she knew.

"You're very stubborn," he observed. And then he scooped her up and deposited her in the saddle in front of him, as though she weighed no more than a feather. She grabbed for the pommel. She was getting mighty sick of the way these men kept hauling her about like a bale of hay.

"I don't even know your name," Alex said tightly.

"Is that what's bothering you?" She thought she could detect a note of amusement in that cool voice. "That we haven't been formally introduced?"

Formally introduced. It was the last thing she expected an Indian to say. Where had he learned his English?

"My name is Rides with Death," he introduced himself. "And may I say it's been a pleasure, Miss . . . ?"

"Barratt," Alex said, too shocked to lie about her name. *Rides with Death?* Oh Lord, he *was* some kind of maniac.

"But let's not stand on ceremony. Please feel free to call me Nathaniel."

Now she was sure she heard amusement. "Nathaniel?" she giggled, relaxing. So that Rides-with-Death thing had been a joke?

"My friends call me Nate."

"Nice to meet you, Nate," Alex said graciously. "You can call me Alex."

"Ah no, you are too lovely to be an Alex."

"How can you tell when I'm wearing all this dirt?" she scolded, tilting her head to look up at him.

His gaze dropped significantly to her chest, now covered by his buckskin shirt, and she blushed. "A little dirt cannot hide such loveliness."

"My full name's Alexandra," she said shyly, looking away.

"Now, that is a lovely name for a lovely woman."

Silas grunted and they both turned to look at him. He visibly wilted under the Indian's cold stare.

"What kind of Indian are you?" Alex asked conversationally as they crossed the plain. "If you don't mind me asking?"

"Arapaho. Mostly. And such a beautiful woman can ask me anything."

She blushed again. The man was almost as much of a flirt as Luke. Luke. She wondered if he was worried about her. She wondered what he'd think when she rode into camp in front of an Indian. Would he be shocked? Would he draw his gun on the poor man? "Maybe you should leave me just outside the camp," Alex said nervously as the wagons came into view. The Indian ignored her, threading his way between the wagons and straight into the center of the camp.

Alex almost fell off the horse. There, trussed up like turkeys, were the other Grady brothers.

"Well, I'll be damned," Luke's voice drawled, snatching her attention away from the Gradys. He was lounging against her wagon, looking for all the world like her tormentors weren't disarmed and helpless right in front of him. And there beside him, munching happily on a bucketful of oats while Adam fussed over him, was Blackie Junior, looking none the worse for wear for his little adventure. And next to Blackie was Luke's missing mare, Isis. "It's been a long time, Deathrider," Luke greeted the Indian.

This time Alex did fall off the horse. Well, it wasn't so much a fall as a tumble, as she scrambled down as fast as she could. "I thought you said your name was Nathaniel!" she accused the Indian.

Luke laughed. "That's one of his names."

"How many do you have?"

"Aside from Nate?" The Indian slid gracefully from the horse. "I told you I was also called Rides with Death."

"And don't forget Angel of Death," Luke drawled. "And Plague of the West."

"That last one was made up for the dime novel," the Indian said in disgust. "That Archer fool keeps writing stories about me. Let's just say her grip on reality isn't great. Causes me no end of misery."

"I see we should add Varmint Catcher to the list," Luke said appreciatively, approaching Silas. He gave the man a cheerful slap on the cheek. "What happened to your face, Grady?"

Alex blanched, hoping he wouldn't notice the A carved into Silas's flesh. No such luck. He leaned in for a closer look, his brow furrowing. "Gideon tried to carve a V on him," she blurted. "For Victoria. He said Silas was owned by Victoria and ought to show the mark of a slave. Because he tried to help us." She was mighty glad Silas was gagged, because he was giving her a strange look. So was the Indian. She gave him a pleading glance.

"It doesn't look like a V," Luke remarked.

"Gideon slipped," Alex invented swiftly. "See there," she crossed to join Luke, and jabbed at the slashes. "It's an almost perfect V, and then he slipped and joined it together."

"Like an A."

"Is it?" Alex said blithely. "I hadn't noticed. He must have been doing it upside down." She knew she sounded witless and cast about for a means of distracting him. "What on earth happened here?"

"Nothing you need worry about, brat. Why are you wearing Deathrider's shirt?" He looked back and forth between them, his brows drawing together again.

"Would you stop calling him that!" Alex snapped.

"It's his name."

"No," Alex corrected firmly, "his name is Nathaniel."

"Well, maybe Nathaniel can tell me why you're wearing his shirt?"

"Hers was torn." Deathrider spoke in a low voice, so no one but Luke and Alex could hear.

Luke's eyes narrowed. "Torn?"

Alex threw the Indian another pleading look.

"In the fight."

She glared at him.

"What fight?" Luke demanded.

"That one attacked her."

If looks could have killed, the Indian would have been dead on the spot.

"Her? You know she's a girl?" Luke's voice dropped to a fierce whisper.

"It was kind of hard to miss once her shirt was gone," Deathrider said dryly.

Luke turned a speculative gaze on Alex. Unconsciously, she crossed her arms over her chest. "Aren't you going to tie Silas up with the rest of them?" she asked Luke imperiously. The minute his back was turned she kicked the Indian in the shins. He didn't so much as flinch.

"Why do you kick me?" he asked in a voice too low for Luke to hear. "Slater already knew you were female."

"He thinks I'm a child," she hissed.

Once again the Indian's gaze dropped to her chest. She couldn't resist kicking him again.

"I wouldn't do that if I were you, brat," Luke warned, turning in time to catch the latest kick. "There's a reason he's called Rides with Death."

"He should be called Irritates to Death," she muttered as Luke carried Silas over to his brothers. She could have sworn the Indian smiled faintly.

"I can't see how Slater can believe you're a child."

"I work hard at it," she snapped, "and I don't appreciate you coming along and ruining it." Now she was sure he was smiling. "What's so funny?" she growled.

"The fact that Slater doesn't know."

"I don't see why that should be so amusing."

"Don't you? A beautiful woman right under his nose?"

"He has enough women in his life," she sniped. "He doesn't need any more."

"You too?"

"Me too what?"

The Indian turned his pale gaze on Luke. "The man seems to have some kind of power over women."

"I know," Alex sighed.

This time the Indian laughed. "Ah, Alexandra, if he could see you the way I did, I'm sure you would find that you have some kind of power over him too."

Alex grimaced. He *had* seen her that way. But her power hadn't lasted beyond the stroke of midnight. Wasn't that the way of fairy tales? The magic always had a limit.

❖ 30 ❖

IT WAS A merry crew that delivered the Gradys to the lockup at Fort Laramie. The journey there had been somewhat tense, as the Gradys sat glowering among them in the camp every night. During the day they were tied to the back of the Watts brothers' wagon and expected to walk. Luke rode behind them, weapon drawn and ready. He had ample opportunity to listen to Gideon's low and awful threats as he taunted his brother Silas.

"I should have killed you," the younger Grady sneered. "I should have known that you'd go sniffing after that bitch." Silas never responded, but Luke noticed that he had a tendency to stumble whenever Gideon started in on him. He must have been mighty glad that Bert and Travis were sandwiched between them. Even chained, Gideon Grady was frightening. "You woulda been wise to head home to Mama, Spineless. What I've got planned for you ain't pleasant."

"We all woulda been wise to head home to Mama," Bert muttered.

Gideon's foot shot out and tripped him. Bert dragged along the rocky ground for a fair piece before he could regain his feet. "I hope it was worth it," Gideon continued, unfazed by Bert's ordeal. "I hope you got a taste of her at least. Was she sweet, Spineless? Did she wrap those lovely legs around you?" Gideon sniggered. "Of course she didn't. Even that stupid bitch knows she's too good for the likes of you."

Luke frowned. Silas hadn't been anywhere near Victoria.

"That bitch needs a real man, Spineless. After I take her she won't remember your name." Gideon's voice was low and venomous. "After I've finished with her she won't even be able to walk."

Needled to breaking point, Silas exploded. He charged sideways, knocking all of his brothers to the ground, like a row of skittles. "I'll kill you," he howled.

Gideon's mad laughter screeched through the afternoon. The hair rose on Luke's arms. The man was insane. "Stop the wagon," Luke shouted.

"Oh, Alexandra," Gideon was calling in a high, fluting voice. "Oh, Alexandra! Come and kiss your lover better— he's gone and skinned his knee."

UP AHEAD, ALEX and Victoria exchanged horrified looks. Alex felt like her heart was being squeezed between two merciless hands.

"He'll know we lied," Victoria breathed, as the wagons pulled to a halt. Her hand rose to shield her mouth as she spoke; she was painfully conscious of her split lip and broken tooth.

Alex vaulted through to the back of the wagon and leaned over the tailgate to get a look at the commotion. Victoria was close behind her. They watched as Luke dragged Gideon along the ground, up toward the chuck wagon. As they passed the string of wagons Gideon caught sight of Victoria and Alex. He began to laugh again, wild loonish laughter that made Alex shiver.

"Why, Miss Barratt, I had no idea," he called as he took in her male disguise. He sounded gleeful but his eyes were murderous. "No wonder I couldn't find you!"

Alex blanched.

"Shut up, Grady," Luke snapped, yanking on the rope. He harnessed the madman to the back of the chuck wagon, and left Deathrider to keep a close watch on him. Then he rode back to Alex and Victoria. Neither of them would meet his eye. "Something you'd care to tell me?" he asked eventually.

"Oh, Luke, I'm so sorry," Victoria said miserably, speaking into her cupped hand. "But we just couldn't tell you the truth."

"Which is?"

Alex couldn't look at him. Her heart was hammering in her ears. Oh glory, what did he think of her? Now that he

knew that Silas had been after *her,* not Victoria, he would
know that she wasn't a child. And then . . . would he finally
look at her and *see*? She was too scared to find out.

"It was Alex," Victoria admitted. "Silas always wanted
Alex."

Alex risked a peek, only to see Luke's distaste. Her heart
sank.

"What did he do to you?" he asked blackly.

"Nothing," she stammered. Was he worried about her? Or
was he jealous? "I mean, he tried . . ."

"Deathrider had to give you his shirt," Luke snarled.

Alex flinched, feeling again the force of Silas's knee against
her and the taste of his blood between her teeth. "Nothing happened," she insisted. "Nathaniel came and saved me."

"*Nothing* happened," Luke echoed. "But you needed
Deathrider to save you." He wheeled Delilah around and galloped back toward the Wattses' wagon.

"What's he doing?" Alex gasped. They watched in disbelief as he reappeared, dragging Silas behind him. He led the
man out onto the plain. Her blood ran cold when she saw
Luke slide from Delilah and throw Silas's rope to the ground.
The crazy man was untying him!

Oh glory, now he was tossing his pistol aside. What the *hell*
was he doing? She gave a startled yelp when she saw Luke's fist
slam into Silas's gut. Alex scrambled over the tailgate of the
wagon and pelted toward them. As she ran she could hear the
smack of flesh against flesh, and by the time she reached them
Silas had collapsed into a bloody heap at Luke's feet.

"What are you doing?" Alex shrieked.

Luke gave her a hard look and grabbed Silas's shirt, pulling him to his feet. Silas swayed, insensible. "If there's anything I hate more than a man who abuses women," Luke
growled, "it's a man who abuses children." His fist flew,
cracking against Silas's jaw. The eldest Grady fell, out cold.

Alex slid to a stop, breathing hard. *Children?* She felt like
someone had thrown a bucket of cold water over her.

Luke was breathing hard too. He approached her and
took her jaw in his strong fingers. "You should have told me,
brat," he said, his voice full of compassion.

She searched his warm dark eyes, her mouth open. She was speechless. So speechless that she didn't even notice Victoria skidding to a halt beside her.

"She made me promise not to tell," Victoria lied breathlessly.

Luke stared at them both, shaking his head. He couldn't believe what these poor girls had been through. "No more lies," he said softly.

"No," Victoria promised. Her gaze drifted to the unconscious Grady at their feet. "There's no need anymore."

"So, your name isn't Alexander," Luke prodded.

"No."

Alex's head was spinning as she listened to them.

"Are you all Barratts?"

"No, Adam and I took Ma and Pa's name."

"Which is?"

"Sparrow."

"It's nice to finally meet you, Miss Sparrow."

Victoria blushed. Alex noticed that she was wringing her hands again. She kept looking back and forth between Alex and Luke.

Luke gathered Silas up and threw him over Delilah's saddle and together they began walking back to the wagons. "I can understand why you dressed the kid up as a boy," Luke sighed, "with a pervert like Grady after her."

The kid, Alex thought sickly as she saw the hope reignite in Victoria's eyes.

"So, how old are you really, runt?"

"She's fourteen," Victoria blurted.

Alex felt like screaming. It was never going to end. She was going to be stuck in these horrid old clothes for the rest of her life.

"I still say you don't look a day over twelve."

The man was an idiot.

So THE MERRIMENT was understandable when they could finally hand the Gradys over to the American Fur Trading Company at Laramie.

"We're a third of the way there," Luke told his group as

they settled down to camp in the shadow of the adobe buildings. The Watts brothers set up a mighty whooping.

"We'll rest up here for a couple of days, so you can regroup. We've still got a long piece of traveling ahead of us." Luke paused and grinned at them. "Let's hope it won't prove to be as eventful as the miles we've already done."

There was applause and laughter, everyone's relief evident.

"How about tonight we celebrate?" he suggested. "I'll supply the liquor, if the ladies don't mind putting on a spread."

Alex stood at the back of the group, feeling out of sorts.

"I thought *you* more than anyone would be pleased," a cool voice said at her elbow.

Alex jumped a mile. She scowled up at the Indian. "Must you sneak up on people? It's not natural, being so quiet."

"I would starve if I was not. A hunter must be silent."

She rolled her eyes, too irritable to deal with his logic.

"Alex," Luke was calling, beckoning her.

She ignored him, turning back to Nate as though they were engrossed in conversation. "Will you be moving on now?" she asked pointedly.

"I haven't decided." He looked between her and Luke. "For now I will be staying at the camp across the river." She followed his gaze to where a cluster of tepees nestled by the Laramie River.

"Are they your people?"

"No, they are Cheyenne. But I know them."

"Alex." Luke grabbed her elbow and turned her toward him. Victoria was with him. Her eyes narrowed as she noticed that Luke had her sister by the hand.

"Yes?" she asked archly.

"Didn't you hear me calling?"

"Why, no. Were you calling?"

The Indian gave a quiet snort. Alex trod on his foot.

"I have something for you."

"Oh?"

"Both of you wait here," he ordered, "and close your eyes."

Victoria did as she was bid. But, Nate noticed with amusement, Alex stubbornly refused, her gaze following Luke as he headed for the chuck wagon. He had to suppress a smile as those expressive gray eyes widened at the sight of Luke's gift.

"You didn't close your eyes," Slater scolded when he returned.

"What is *that*?" There was venom in her tone.

Luke was startled. The brat was as changeable as a summer storm; he never knew what temper he'd find her in. "I thought you'd appreciate it, now that the Gradys are locked up." He handed it over, bewildered to see her scowl down at it.

"Can I open my eyes yet?" Victoria asked.

"In a minute. Hold out your hands."

Victoria held them out.

"Now you can look," Luke said, grinning as he laid the bolt of daffodil yellow satin across her arms.

"Oh, Luke!" Victoria was overjoyed. Her brown eyes shone as she stroked the slippery fabric. "Wherever did you get it?"

"Here in Laramie. I thought you could make yourself another dress. You looked mighty pretty in yellow."

Alex grew blacker at the sight of Victoria's pleasure. Who did he think he was, going around making her sister happy and stupid? "Where the hell is she going to be able to wear satin?"

"Watch your language," Luke and Victoria said simultaneously, making Alex mad enough to spit. She was damn sick of being treated like a child.

"I think *you* will look magnificent in this color," the Indian whispered near Alex's ear, as his hand reached over her shoulder to stroke the bolt of rose-colored cotton she held stiffly in front of her.

"In *pink*?" Alex snarled, unable to let go of her anger.

"You, Alexandra, would look magnificent in just about anything," he continued, still speaking too low for the others to hear, "and even more magnificent in nothing at all."

She flushed. At least *someone* treated her like a woman. If only it wasn't the wrong man.

"I'm only sorry you won't be able to wear new gowns tonight," Luke said, "but make yourselves as pretty as you can. Tonight we celebrate your freedom."

What freedom? Alex grumped as she threw her gift into the wagon. She watched as Victoria glowed over her yellow satin. She felt like kicking something. Or someone.

❧ 31 ❧

"I ALREADY HAVE a drink," Luke protested, as the Watts brothers pressed a tin mug into his hand.

"Two drinks are better than one," Henry laughed, raising his own glass in salute. As Luke took a mouthful he could hear Joseph guffawing. He grimaced. Whatever they'd given him tasted like kerosene.

He noticed Ned O'Brien standing nearby. The easterner was pretending to watch his daughters dance to Sebastian's appallingly off-key harmonica, but any fool could see that he was really watching Victoria Sparrow. A number of people from Laramie and the surrounding camps had wandered over, and were also twirling about to the god-awful racket. A constant stream of young men approached Victoria and asked her to dance, but each time she gave them a closed-lipped smile and shook her head.

"Why don't you ask her?" Luke suggested.

Ned shook his head. "She would only say no."

"Surely not to the man who saved her life," Luke insisted, giving Ned a gentle nudge. "You need more confidence, O'Brien."

"Oh, that's not it," Ned said, sounding surprised. "She'll say no because of her tooth."

"Her what?"

"The tooth Grady's gun chipped. She's self-conscious about it. Haven't you noticed how she always holds her hand over her mouth when she speaks? Or how she hardly smiles anymore?"

Luke hadn't.

"Actually," Ned said, clearing his throat, "I was thinking that maybe *you* could go over and ask her to dance. She would never refuse you. And maybe while you're dancing you could mention how becoming you think her smile is. Just say something to make her realize that no broken tooth could ever dim her loveliness."

Luke looked down into Ned's eager face and grimaced. He'd never seen a man so witless over a woman. "I really think it would be better if you did it, Doc. I didn't even notice that she *had* a broken tooth."

"Exactly." Ned gave Luke a tentative push in Victoria's direction.

Luke drained his mug full of kerosene and gave Ned a sour look. Hell. One of these days he'd have to learn how to turn his back on wounded women. He tried to turn his grimace into a smile as he headed toward the wounded woman in question.

Her eyes lit up when he asked her to dance and she nodded, still smiling with her lips pressed close together. Somehow they managed to dance to Sebastian's squawking harmonica, although as the Watts brothers' moonshine hit Luke's system the noise grew increasingly painful to his ears.

"Who taught you to dance so well?" he asked, trying to think of a way to raise the subject of her tooth.

Victoria pulled her hand from Luke's shoulder and surreptitiously covered her mouth, trying to look as though she was simply dabbing at her upper lip. "My brother Stephen." He caught her hand and they came to a standstill. Victoria looked up and found herself mesmerized by his liquid dark eyes. "You don't need to do that," he told her in a husky voice.

He decided that he couldn't put it any better than Ned had, and quoted him verbatim. "No broken tooth could ever dim your loveliness." Ah hell. Why were her eyes swimming with tears? Had that been the wrong thing to say?

Victoria melted against him, burying her face in his shirt. He patted her back awkwardly and they began to shuffle to the music. To his great relief someone soon dragged out a fiddle and Sebastian's honking harmonica was drowned out by a lively reel.

ALEX DIDN'T DANCE a single dance. She barely touched the feast. By midnight she was thoroughly sick of pasting a smile on her face. And then she saw Victoria spinning in Luke's arms, a wide smile on her lips as he flung her about.

Alex headed for the river.

"Still a boy, I see," a horridly familiar, cool voice remarked, interrupting her gloom.

"Still here, are you, Rides Like a Dolt?"

"Your temper ruins your charm," the Indian remarked lazily, reclining against a large boulder, his long legs stretched out before him.

"No, Dimrider, I think you'll find that it's this muck on my face that ruins my charm," she said petulantly.

"So wash it off."

Alex rolled her eyes. "It's not that simple."

"No? The Gradys are behind bars, aren't they?"

"Yes," she muttered, kicking at the sagebrush like a cranky child.

"I'm missing something."

"I can't wash it off," she snapped at him, "because of Victoria."

"I'm still missing something."

"If you haven't noticed, she has feelings for him."

"For him?"

"Luke!" Alex growled.

"I think she is not the only one."

Alex gave him a sour look.

"Ho'nehe?" A velvety voice slid out of the darkness. In its wake glided an elegant woman, clad in a long dress of supple leather decorated with quills and beads. Her hair fell in a shining midnight wave over her shoulder. Alex felt a pang of envy. Once her hair had been long and pretty too.

"I will be there shortly," Deathrider told her, still speaking in his clipped, unaccented English.

"I will not wait all night," she replied, her own English lilting.

"You will not have to."

Her lips curved and her eyes grew moist with promises, and then she melted back into the darkness from which she'd come.

"Why hide yourself from Slater?" the stubborn Indian inquired the moment his bedmate was gone. "He's a decent man. You seem to have a certain . . ." He paused. ". . . *fondness* for him."

"I told you, my sister has feelings for him."

"But he has none for her."

Despite herself, Alex could feel her heart leap. "How can you tell?" The Indian shrugged. Her heart fell again. "It doesn't really matter how he feels," she said, with no small measure of disappointment.

"So this is a question of loyalty?"

"Yes," she insisted.

"You're not curious about how he would react to you if he saw you as you really are?"

"I know—" Alex bit her tongue, but it was too late. His dark eyebrows shot up in surprise.

He was equally surprised to see the tears welling in her eyes. He had seen this woman fight like a cougar, and yet now she was weeping over Slater? "Everyone is occupied," he said slowly. In the distance they could hear the sound of the fiddle. "Why not take the opportunity to wash the dirt away?"

Alex gave a cynical laugh. "You want me to go for a swim, with you sitting right there?"

"The river is shielded by the sage."

"What would be the point?" she demanded. "Everyone keeps telling me to bathe, but what's the damn point if I just have to muddy myself right up again afterward?"

"The point," the velvety female voice curled from the darkness, "is that you are eating yourself up inside. You would do well to remember who you are."

"Yellow Bird," Deathrider sighed. "You do not need to spy on me, I told you I would come."

"Your promises are as faithful as the wind, White Wolf."

"White Wolf?" Alex echoed, exasperated. "How many names do you have?"

"He has many names, and he has none." Yellow Bird again made herself visible, ignoring Deathrider's flinty stare.

"And you do not have enough names," he said tersely. "You should also be known as Flapping Ears."

"You should do as White Wolf says," Yellow Bird told

Alex, ignoring him. "I will stand watch with him. You will come to no harm."

Alex capitulated, but mostly because she wanted to be left alone.

"You just wanted her gone," Deathrider accused Yellow Bird as they watched her walk down to the riverbank.

Yellow Bird sank down beside him and slid her warm hand between his shirt and his skin. "Yes, I did," she admitted. "I do not like you talking to other women."

"You have no say in it."

Her fingers traced circles on his flesh. "I have say enough." She nuzzled his neck and had just felt him begin to relax when there was a crashing in the sagebrush and the sound of a man swearing.

"Slater?" Deathrider asked, disbelief coloring his usually flat voice. The man was barely able to stand.

"Those damn Watts brothers," Luke complained, stumbling through the bushes toward them. He was bleary-eyed and swaying on his feet. "That moonshine is evil stuff."

A sly glint came into Deathrider's pale eyes. "Wash your face in the river," he suggested, "it will help." Yellow Bird made a small noise of protest, but Deathrider gave her a warning look.

"Just what I was thinking," Luke mumbled, staggering off down the riverbank.

"What are you up to?" Yellow Bird asked suspiciously.

"Is that what you want to do?" he replied. "Talk?"

The moment his hot mouth claimed hers she forgot all about the crazy Americans.

DOWN AT THE river Alex dove beneath the black waters. The current was gentle, teasing her with its pull. She could feel herself growing lighter as the dirt dissolved and she realized that Yellow Bird had been right: it felt marvelous to be herself again.

It was a hot night and the water was pure pleasure as it slipped against her naked skin. With a surge of energy she stroked upriver against the current, reveling in the sensation. She swam until she was exhausted, and then she rolled over on her back, turning her face blissfully toward the multitudes of glittering stars, and let the current carry her back downstream.

The night was mild and perfumed with sage, and the heavens above were breathtaking. It was enough to make her forget Luke Slater completely. Well, almost.

LUKE COLLAPSED BY the river, feeling hot and sweaty and more than a little disturbed by the way his heart kept skittering and skipping. He felt like liquid fire was tearing through his veins. Just wait until he got his hands on those Watts brothers.

He groaned and splashed his face. The cool water helped a little.

He had to revise his opinion when he sat up and his vision swam. He held his breath and submerged his head beneath the dark water. When he came up he opened his eyes cautiously. That seemed to help.

For a moment.

When he tried to stand the world spun and he crouched, worried he'd fall. His thoughts were muddy and slow. And he was just so damn hot. Perspiration streamed down his back. He was going to burn alive, he thought dimly. He had to put out the fire.

Clumsily, he undressed, struggling into the water, grateful for its cool bite. He sank beneath the surface, rubbing his hands over his face and through his hair, and when he rose he felt cooler. But damn if his vision wasn't worse—everything was blurred around the edges. If he went blind he'd string those Watts brothers up by their heels and leave them for the vultures.

Luke stood midstream, suddenly distracted by the moon's reflection in the rippling surface of the river: it was a heavy pearl, round and creamy. Like her skin, he thought vaguely, besieged by memories of ivory curves and smoky-gray eyes.

As he stood, lost in thought, something slammed into him, borne by the current directly into his arms. Instinctively he caught it. And, looking down, lots his wits completely.

Alex gasped. Oh glory, it was him. She'd just been thinking about him. Or rather, trying not to think about him. And now here he was, right before her, holding her up, and, oh glory, he was naked. Her eyes grew wide. She could feel him hard against her, like a slick wall of rock.

His eyes were fixed on hers and she was sinking into their midnight waters. She could feel his hand pressing just above the swell of her buttocks and his legs tangling with hers beneath the surface of the water. The river didn't seem so cool anymore. Alex could feel a slow burn spreading from her core.

And then his gaze dropped to her mouth. She couldn't breathe. She'd wanted this moment for so long, had stared at his lips every day and wished for another taste. Her heart thundered in her ears as she waited for his kiss. When he didn't so much as move a muscle she couldn't wait any longer. With a soft moan, she surrendered to her desire, lunging forward and kissing him.

It was more than he remembered. *She* was more than he remembered. He had forgotten the faint cleft in her chin, and the perfect straightness of her nose; he had forgotten how lush and soft her body was, and the way his blood raced when she was near. He was hallucinating, he knew, but he didn't care. He gave in to the vision, not feeling quite so murderous toward the Watts brothers anymore.

Oh God, the sweet taste of her. The hallucination was so vivid. And the way her breasts pressed against his chest, her nipples like hard pebbles. He groaned into her kiss as his hands traced the full curve of her buttocks, pulling her against his straining desire. He wanted her in a way he hadn't wanted a woman since he was fifteen. Impatiently, overzealously. His tongue assaulted hers.

He was completely unrestrained, his hands everywhere at once, his mouth driving her wild with its burning promises. Alex couldn't think. She was all sensation, all need. When he lifted her against him, wrapping her legs around him, she was ready. This time there was no pain. There was just a pleasure so exquisite she could have screamed.

He couldn't control himself. His hot mouth played with her neck as he drove into her, moaning with frustration as he struggled to gain purchase on the shifting floor of the riverbed.

She barely noticed when he moved them to the river's edge. Falling onto his back he kept tight hold of her hips, pulling her upright, astride him. She completely lost control, riding her pleasure, chasing something so elusive . . .

The sight of her slick wet flesh, the heavy, perfect thrust of her breasts, nipples dark and pouting, the generous curve of her hips moving on him in an ancient rhythm was more than he could bear. When she cried out, her back arching as she exploded into shivers of ecstasy, filling his vision with those perfect, perfect breasts, he rolled her over, reclaiming her mouth and plunging his tongue into her hot depths as he joined her in ecstasy with one final, brutal thrust.

And then he was sucked into rising blackness.

❋ 32 ❋

WHEN HE OPENED his eyes he found himself staring at a pair of dusty moccasins. Luke groaned and covered his eyes with his arm. The sunlight was piercing. His mouth was dry, his tongue swollen and his head was ringing with pain.

He felt something nudge his hand and he opened his eyes a crack to see a small wooden cup. "Drink it," Deathrider's cool voice said. "Yellow Bird prepared it for you. It will help the pain."

Luke struggled to sit up and was surprised to find himself buck naked. What the hell had he been doing?

Deathrider pressed the cup into his limp hand and he downed the bitter brew in one swallow. He felt a sudden wave of nausea and bent over. When the sensation passed he opened his eyes to find the Indian still squatting before him, watching him intently. "What?" Luke growled.

"Who is Beatrice?" Deathrider asked curiously. He didn't miss Luke's look of shock.

His dream came flooding back. The feel of her slick wet body, the taste of her mouth, the sight of her arching above him, silvered by moonlight. He felt himself begin to harden and hastened to pull his pants on.

"You called her name," Deathrider told him, sitting back on his heels, his gaze still keen.

Luke kept dressing and didn't respond. He felt an awful sinking in his stomach. Why did he have to wake up? He wished he could will himself back into the dream, or better yet, will Beatrice here. Right here, right now.

"I thought your girl's name was Amelia," the Indian continued relentlessly.

"It is," Luke snapped.

"Then who is this Beatrice you call for?"

"She's nobody," Luke said, "just a girl I met in Independence. A girl I'll never see again." He yanked on his boots and strode off through the sagebrush, one hand still shielding his tender eyes from the sun.

Deathrider rarely smiled, and when he did it usually struck terror into the hearts of those who saw it. But now, watching poor Slater's slumped shoulders, he smiled . . . a genuine smile that warmed his pale eyes to crystal blue and transformed his features from handsome to breathtaking.

He had intended to head out today, but now he thought it might prove amusing to ride along with Slater for a while. If he wasn't mistaken, it would prove to be a mighty entertaining journey.

ALEX WOKE UP smiling. And she kept smiling for days. Who knew there was such magic in the world? Her body tingled at the memory, and whenever she caught sight of Luke she burned. At night she dreamed about him. Dreams like she had never had before, and when she woke it was hard to suppress the urge to go to him. She supposed she should have been upset that he remembered none of it; that the Watts brothers' moonshine had rendered him insensible. But the words he'd whispered as he'd passed out kept her smiling. *Don't leave me again,* he'd breathed into her ear as he collapsed beneath her. And then he was unconscious. She'd lingered for a while, allowing herself to rest her cheek against his warm chest, the sprinkling of dark hair tickling her cheek as she listened to his heartbeat.

How Victoria would hate her if she knew.

But Victoria would never know. That moment in the river had been a beautiful interlude, a suspended time of enchantment. It had nothing to do with real life. Sometimes, when she sat opposite Luke at breakfast, or rode out beside him on Blackie Junior, she felt a stinging sadness that he couldn't be hers. She wondered how different things would have been if there had been no Gradys. How different things would have been if she could have met Luke before Victoria had set her cap for him. Would Luke have liked Alex enough to court her? Would he have forsaken all other women for her? If only the Gradys had never existed . . .

But then, if there had been no Gradys she never would have met Luke. She would still be safely home in Mississippi, completely unaware that such a magnificent, charming, stubborn, irritating, marvelous man existed. She had never thought to see the day when she'd be grateful to the Gradys for something.

"Why are you still dressing in that getup?" he asked her, exasperated, as they rode scout one morning. They were following the Sweetwater River, which was wending its way to Devil's Gate, a narrow chasm of rock that they would have to detour around.

Alex had been expecting the question. She didn't want to lie to him, but neither did she want to admit the truth. She'd decided that evasion was the easiest way to respond. "After Silas . . ." she said, trailing off significantly and dropping her gaze, as though reliving horrid memories. And, in truth, the mere mention of Silas's name did bring back the revolting sensation of his body on hers and his tongue in her mouth.

Luke blanched. Of course. It made perfect sense that the kid was wary of attracting male attention. And what better way to avoid it than dressing the way she did? "You can't escape your gender," he told her gently. "One of these days you'll grow up, and fill out, and no amount of dirt will be able to hide you then."

She had to keep her gaze fixed on the pommel of Blackie's saddle to avoid rolling her eyes. The man had no idea. "I suppose when we meet Stephen in Amory I'll have to go back to normal," she said huskily, feeling a pang at the thought of leaving Luke.

Luke frowned. He was actually going to miss the kid when they parted ways. Alex was soothing company. She didn't chatter away at him while they rode; she seemed to understand that he liked the peace of his own thoughts. She'd even taken a liking to riding, now that she was riding Blackie. The stallion seemed to have a soft spot for her, and responded to her every shift in the saddle, which was fortunate, as Alex had no natural aptitude at all. When Luke did feel like talking, Alex was an interesting conversationalist.

Now and then, they chatted as they rode amiably side by side, and sometimes they sat up long into the night, discussing their families, and Luke's plans for the future.

"You really want a dozen children?" she asked him once, as she rested her head on her interlinked fingers and looked up at the spray of stars above.

"At least," he said.

"Your wife will be plumb wore out," she teased.

"Well, maybe we could adopt some of them. Like your Ma and Pa Sparrow."

"Are there many orphans in Oregon?"

"Enough. A lot of people die on the journey out west."

"Really?" She sounded dubious.

"Don't judge all groups by ours, brat. This is a dream run—we've had good weather and no disease."

"Just a few stray maniacs out to torture us."

He laughed. "Well, there is that." They lapsed into a moment of silence. "What about you, brat? When you finally find a man like Ned to settle down with, how many kids do you want?"

Alex shrugged. She could hardly tell him that his dozen sounded perfect to her, especially if they all looked as darkly beautiful as him. "I don't think I have much say in it, do I?" she said instead. "Babies come when they come." She thought of Dolly's little packet, which she'd tossed into the river some days back, unopened and unused.

"Sure you do," Luke chuckled. "You can always kick your husband out of bed."

A vision of Luke in her bed swam before her eyes, and she indulged in a pleasant little daydream about what she'd do to him. Kicking him out wasn't high on the list.

BY THE END of summer Deathrider gave up in disgust. The man was blind. How could he not see the way her hips swung when she walked? Or the way the cloth of her pants clung to her plump behind when she bent over the fire? How could he not see the desire for him in those dark-fringed smoky-gray eyes?

Deathrider had seen enough. He'd drop by the Slater

place in the next year to see how things turned out, but he
didn't have the patience to watch Slater play the fool. Hell,
think of all the nights the man was wasting, sleeping alone
in his bedroll when lush Alexandra (or should he say Beatrice?) was only feet away, burning for him.

The Indian didn't bother saying good-bye; he simply
slipped away in the dead of night.

"Where would he have gone?" Alex asked when she discovered his absence. She looked around, bewildered. She
couldn't imagine anything more frightening than being alone
in the wilderness.

The land was mountainous now, thick with stands of pine
and larch, maple and cypress. The leaves of the deciduous
trees were beginning to turn, speckling the treeline with red
and gold, and the nights were crisp and cold. Alex shivered,
imagining spending a solitary night out there.

Luke shrugged. "Who knows where he goes."

"Doesn't he live somewhere in particular?"

Again, Luke shrugged. "I have no idea. Whenever I see
him he's always on the move. Jim Bridger reckons he's some
kind of ghost, haunting the trails."

They'd met Jim Bridger back at Fort Bridger. He was a
rough-edged mountain man, set on making his fortune in the
fur trade. Fort Bridger itself was under construction: a raw
little patch of land in the forest where a few crude log cabins
were being erected. "I think Bridger keeps trying to convince Deathrider to do some trapping for him," Luke continued, "but I can't imagine him working for anyone."

"Are all Indians so lonesome?"

Luke laughed. "No, brat, they're not. But then, Deathrider ain't your regular Indian. Hell, I'm not even sure how
much of an Indian he really is—I've never met one with eyes
like that before."

Alex was astonished. "He's not a real Indian?"

"Don't get me wrong, brat. To all intents and purposes
he's Arapaho, if a solitary one. Two Bears formally adopted
him, I hear. But no one really knows who he is. According
to that dime novel he simply appeared out of nowhere. Riding out of a winter fog, the book says, pulling a travois."

Luke lowered his voice. "According to the book the travois was carrying his family. Each and every one of them stone-cold dead."

Alex stared at him, wide-eyed, feeling the hair rise on the nape of her neck.

"But then," Luke said, breaking the mood with a chuckle, "everyone knows that those dime novels are full of rubbish."

Alex wondered if she could get her hands on that book. She kind of missed the cold-eyed Indian. There was something reassuring about having him with them.

"I DON'T SUPPOSE you know how to fish, runt?" Luke asked that afternoon, as he rode alongside their wagon, sharing lunch.

"I love fishing," she told him, smiling at old memories. "Once, I caught the mightiest catfish in Mississippi."

"You caught the mightiest hiding in Mississippi," Victoria interrupted, eager to join the conversation. Despite her best efforts, she'd spent very little time with Luke since the Gradys had been captured. The night she'd danced with him at Laramie had been the last time he'd so much as touched her.

Alex grinned. "Didn't I just? Ma Sparrow was furious with me."

"For going fishing?" Luke asked.

"For going in her Sunday dress," Victoria corrected. "Her *white* Sunday dress. Ma made her scrub it and scrub it, but it was never white again. That river mud is black as tar."

"She didn't even let me eat any of my catfish," Alex said ruefully.

Luke laughed. He could just picture her in a sopping, muddy Sunday dress, her face as filthy as it was right this minute.

"Stephen was in worse trouble than me," Alex admitted. "He was kept to bread and water for a whole week as punishment. She said he should have known better, that he should have sent me back the minute he saw me instead of giving me a line and tying worms to my hook."

"She sounds pretty strict, your ma."

"She was. I think that was one reason Stephen headed out to Oregon."

"It just about broke her heart," Victoria said sadly. "He was her only natural child."

"I guess she'd be horrified to see you now, brat," Luke remarked.

Alex grimaced. He had no idea how right he was.

"I was going to try a little fishing this afternoon while everyone makes camp," Luke said, "if you'd care to join me. I thought fresh fish would be a welcome change from salt pork."

"Oh," Victoria exclaimed quickly, "do you think I could come too?"

In the end, to Victoria's bitter disappointment, it was a veritable party that gathered on the riverbank as the sun was falling thin and gold through the stands of pine. And she wasn't even anywhere near Luke Slater. She stood morosely, limply holding her line, watching Luke laugh at something her sister said to him. Look at that, Victoria thought grumpily. Even looking like a scarecrow Alex managed to capture the attention of men.

Why didn't Luke approach *her*? He'd been so tender that night at Laramie and she carried his words around with her constantly: *No broken tooth could ever dim your loveliness.* He thought she was lovely. And then there was that time he was talking to Alex about his sweetheart, when he'd described *her*, Victoria Sparrow: dark hair, dark eyes, slender frame and all. And what about that time in Independence, when she'd swooned and he'd carried her up the stairs at Ralph Taylor's boarding house, and laid her on the bed? They way he'd looked at her . . . she shivered now just thinking of it. Surely a man didn't look at a woman like that unless she meant something to him?

A sharp tug on her line brought her out of her thoughts with a gasp.

"You have a fish," Ned O'Brien exclaimed.

The line tugged again, cutting into her fingers. "Help me," Victoria squealed, "what do I do?"

Ned passed his own line to his eldest daughter, Jane, and his warm hand closed around Victoria's, guiding her. With his help she brought in a magnificent trout, its belly streaked red from mouth to tail. Thrilled, Victoria beamed up at him.

Then, with a shock, she remembered her monstrous tooth and clamped her mouth shut.

Ned's own smile faded as he saw the way she prodded the broken edge of her tooth with her tongue. He felt a surge of tenderness toward her and the strength of it drove all poetry from him. Even Byron was not enough. "You are the most beautiful woman I have ever seen," he said simply, his earnestness obvious. He was gazing at her in wonder.

Victoria flushed. No one had ever looked at her that way before.

"That's some fine fish," Luke exclaimed, as he came for a look, breaking the spell between the couple. Flustered, they couldn't meet his eye.

❧ 33 ❧

Fort Laramie

BRIAN CLEARY WAS having a bad day. Worse than bad. Catastrophic. The Gradys were his responsibility. And now, on his watch, they'd escaped. Every last one of them.

And it was that woman's fault.

She was still in the cell where they'd locked her, and Cleary had no intention of letting her out. He was fighting the urge to take a horsewhip to her.

"What the hell happened?" his boss demanded, bursting through the door. Cleary jumped a mile. Unable to summon any defense for himself, he simply pointed in the direction of the cell.

It wasn't really a cell, just a windowless room in the low adobe building. But it was as secure as any cell, and those Gradys should have been kicking their heels until the marshals came for them. Cleary's boss threw the door to the cell open and groaned.

There before him was a ravishing redhead, sitting quite calmly on a rough-hewn wooden bench.

"Hell and damnation, Ava!" Hewitson roared.

The redhead rose, straightening her short, leather waistcoat and gathering her hat. "Must you be so crude?" she sighed, not in the slightest bit ruffled by his barely contained rage.

"Let me guess," Hewitson blasted her, "you came sniffing around for more news of that damn Indian!"

"Well, I did hear tell that he helped to apprehend them." She pulled a notebook from the pocket of her suede riding skirt. "Is that correct?" She licked the tip of her pencil.

"If you want a story," Hewitson snarled, grabbing her elbow and pulling her from the cell, "I'll give you one: Damn Fool Female Releases Cold-blooded Killers."

"They killed someone? The way I heard it the only casualties were the livestock. But of course it will be far more exciting if someone was actually killed. Imagine, the ice-eyed Plague of the West facing down the Gruesome Grady Gang."

"The Gruesome Grady Gang?"

"My publisher likes alliteration. This time I think I might call him White Wolf. I hear that's one of his names."

"You, Miss Archer, are a menace to civilized society."

The redhead gave a musical laugh and peered through the doorway at dusty old Laramie. "This is not civilization, Mr. Hewitson. People would hardly want to read about it if it *was* civilized."

"One of these days, Miss Archer, I hope you come face-to-face with your Plague of the West," Hewitson said direly, giving her a shove out the door. "Then you'd really have something to write about in your dime novels."

Ava sighed, nibbling on the end of her pencil. If only she *would* come face-to-face with the Deathrider. She was fast running out of ideas for her books. She set her hat on her head and pondered which avenue to pursue now. The Grady angle hadn't quite worked out as she'd planned. She supposed she was fortunate that they were too set on escape to assault her. She had to admit that she'd felt a thrill of fear looking into Gideon Grady's mad eyes. She wondered if the Deathrider's eyes looked like that. She doubted it. In her novel she'd described him as dark and handsome, mostly because that was what the readers wanted, but also because she'd met a fair few people who described him that way.

"Except for the eyes," one young lady had added, giving a nervous shiver. "His eyes are strange."

"Strange?" Ava had prodded, her pencil at the ready.

"Like they've got no color," the girl said. "Pale, you know, like ice."

So in her book he'd been an ice-eyed killer. Now, staring at the treeless plains around Laramie, her pencil tapping thoughtfully against her notebook, Ava wondered how she was going to finish her next book. She was already well past deadline and her publisher was screaming for it. Well, she thought with a shrug, if the Gradys had flown, without leaving her any the wiser about what had transpired, she only had one option left. She'd make it up.

"Why the hell did you leave her alone with them?" Hewitson snapped at Cleary, as they watched her through the window; neither could resist lingering on the alluring sway of her hips.

"She was only going to talk to them through the door," Cleary said miserably, remembering the way his thoughts had flown from his head like butterflies when she'd fixed him with those beautiful dark eyes.

Hewitson resisted yelling at the lad again. Hell, he too had fallen victim to her in the past. It was the deceptive openness of her expression that did it every time. She looked like butter wouldn't melt in her mouth.

"Send word with a rider," he ordered Cleary, "we need to warn the forts along the trail . . . as far as Oregon City, you hear. I'd hate to have those varmints attack Slater unawares. Get Jed Hacker. He's fast."

"At least Slater's got a long head start," Cleary said hopefully. "His group will be all the way to Oregon before the Gradys reach South Pass."

"Let's hope so," Hewitson said grimly. "And let's hope Jed's fast enough to catch them before the Gradys do."

But they hadn't bargained on the fact that Jed Hacker had been shot clean through the temple.

It looked like Ava Archer had her cold-blooded killers after all.

❧ 34 ❧

THEY WERE ALL going to die.

Alex was numb with fear as she regarded the churning Snake River. "You want us to cross *that*?" she demanded.

"It's the quickest route," Luke said, eyeing the thunderheads massing on the horizon. The wind was blowing in their favor and would hopefully keep the storm at bay, but he didn't want to risk it. If the Snake flooded they would have no chance of crossing it safely.

"And you've done this before?" she asked dubiously.

"Many times." What Luke didn't say was that he'd seen men die here, had seen entire wagons swept downstream, and mules drown as they were dragged down by their harnesses.

Below them the Snake was at its widest, splitting into four streams around three islands. The water boiled and frothed, its current wicked and swift. "We'll swim the livestock across first," Luke told his gathered campers. "We'll use two of the islands as stepping stones to get them to the far shore. Then we'll pull the wagons across with ropes." He tried to sound as reassuring as possible, aware of their pinched white faces. "The womenfolk and children will be best off in the wagons. But keep to the front, close to the buckboards; if anything happens, you're to jump free and make a swim for it."

"Miss Sparrow?" Ned approached Victoria anxiously. "I know you must be apprehensive, but I was hoping I could ask you to ride with my girls."

Victoria looked over at the O'Brien wagon, where the three girls were huddled together. Her heart twisted at the sight of their frightened faces. She too had once been motherless. "Of course," Victoria said bravely, trying to quash her own fears.

"What about me?" Alex squeaked when her sister informed her.

"You're a grown woman," Victoria said, "and they're just children. They need me."

"*Now* you decide I'm not a child," Alex muttered. Oh hell, she'd be alone in the wagon. Luke had already decided to take Adam with him when they swam the livestock. "He'll be the first one over. He can watch over the animals and keep out of trouble," Luke had told the sisters in a low voice. "He'll be safe."

"As long as he doesn't drown on the swim over," Alex said darkly.

"He'll be on the Arab," Luke had soothed her, "and that horse is as strong as ten men."

Alex was surprised now when Victoria swept her into a hard embrace. "Good luck," her sister whispered, giving her a swift kiss. And then Alex was alone, clenching the side of the wagon with white knuckles as she watched the mounted men plunge into the churning river. Mules were braying and oxen lowing as they hit the river, and then they fell silent as they struggled to keep their heads above water. Luke and Adam were way out in front, and Mal Crawford brought up the rear, riding Delilah.

Alex wasn't aware that she was holding her breath until white spots swarmed before her eyes. She drew a shuddering breath just as Blackie and Isis pulled themselves from the current, their flanks straining with the effort. Adam and Luke had made it to the first island. Her nerves could barely stand it as she watched them cross two more raging streams. Worse, she had to watch Luke come all the way back again, bearing the ropes. The river pulled at him, frothing around his hips.

"We'll take the wagons with children first," Luke yelled over the rushing of the river.

One by one the wagons were floated across, buffeted by the surging waters, twisting alarmingly in the current. Alex was so proud of her sister; Victoria protected those three girls like a she-wolf, her white face deathly calm. Faintly, over the noise of the current, Alex could hear her voice as she soothed the girls.

Alex's wagon was last. By the time it was her turn to cross the daylight was starting to fade and the men were gray with fatigue. "Hold on tight," Luke called to her from the first island, his voice hoarse.

She'd thought, stupidly, that she'd have an easier time of it because their wagon was small and light, but the minute it hit the water she realized how wrong she was. The wagon was as fragile as a leaf, its lack of heft meaning that it was more susceptible to the power of the river.

She managed to white-knuckle her way across to the first island, but as they rolled the wagon back into the water she heard the threatening sound of thunder. Looking up, she noticed the thunderheads were churning as violently as the river beneath. A brisk wind whipped the surface of the river into frothy, white-tipped wavelets.

Midway in the second stream of the Snake, Alex felt the first heavy drops of rain. When the wagon shuddered to a halt on the last island Luke rode over to her. As he did the heavens opened and they were pelted with torrential rain.

"I'm going to head over to the shore," he tried to yell above the pounding rain. Alex followed his gaze. The far shore was invisible; they could only see shifting sheets of steel-gray rain. "Mal and Sebastian will hold the ropes from here, and the rest of us will pull from the bank."

Alex nodded, too scared to speak.

"You hold on tight," he bellowed. "Forget what I said before. Don't try swimming. Not in this. The ropes will keep the wagon afloat and we'll keep pulling no matter what. Just hold on and keep your head above water."

Clenching her teeth against the terror, Alex nodded again.

By the time Luke reached the shore and gave a tug on the rope, telling them to proceed, the Snake was beginning to swell and flood. As soon as the wagon hit the water, Alex felt the strengthening current snatch at it. It yawed, straining against the ropes, and instinctively Alex knew she wasn't going to make it. Rain and river obscured the island and the shore.

She was alone.

* * *

LUKE FELT THE rope go slack. It had snapped, unable to bear the force of the current and the weight of the wagon. "Alex!" he howled into the gale.

Without thinking, he grabbed for the other rope and dove into the surging river. It was madness, but he couldn't leave her. He was whipped downstream, the rope sliding through his fingers, burning his skin, while he tumbled violently through the churning maelstrom. He struggled to keep his head above water, choking on mud and debris.

He prayed the wagon hadn't tipped, that she could hang on and remain buoyant. He slammed into a boulder and the breath exploded from his lungs. He grabbed for the slippery rock, scrabbling against its slick side. Muscles straining, he hauled his body above the waterline, trying to breathe normally.

The rain began to ease, and he found he could see again. Gradually the shore loomed through the slackening rain and Luke's heart leaped as he caught sight of the wagon fetched up against a jagged line of rocks. It was in the process of being smashed to pieces. Luke could hear the timbers rending with a sound like an animal screaming.

"Alex!" he bellowed, the minute he had breath. "Alex!" Cautiously, he pushed away from the boulder, trying to angle himself so that the current would carry him to the wagon. He flew into its disintegrating belly, sucked beneath the water momentarily, until he grabbed a naked hoop, its canvas long since shredded, and pulled himself up.

Straining, he hauled himself around the wagon, to the rear. There was no sign of the kid. "Alex!" he howled again.

"Luke!"

He felt a relief so acute it was almost painful. He looked for her. The rain had become the lightest of drizzles and he could see her bobbing in the water, holding desperately to the broken tailgate, swirling in whichever direction the current took her. He tore the splintering buckboard away from the wagon and followed her example, launching back into the river, hoping the timber would keep him afloat.

Alex was half-drowned, choking on the muddy water, her arms tiring as she struggled to hang on to the splintered wood. The current kept trying to snatch the timber away from her. She couldn't hang on much longer.

She went limp when she felt Luke's strong arm grab her, and the tailgate flew from her grip, lost in the flood.

He hauled her from the river, his arms like iron bands around her. She spluttered, tasting mud and rain. It was only as she collapsed, heaving, on the sodden bank, spitting up sediment, that the full horror of her situation hit her.

She struggled to pull free of his grasp, aware of how the overalls had been ripped and how Adam's old shirt clung, transparent, to her bandaged breasts.

"Alex," he gasped, his tone rough with concern.

"Let me go!" A note of panic crept into her voice as she tried to roll away from him. The river had washed the grime from her face and the grease from her hair. She couldn't let him see her like this!

But he wouldn't let her go. His hands pressed her down on the riverbank.

And then he went very still.

The world seemed to follow suit. The sound of the rushing waters receded. Alex clearly heard the terrible thundering of her own heart.

His eyes were as black as shadows.

Now that the grime was gone, now that the battered brown hat had been swept away, the delicate face, with its faintly cleft chin, was only too visible. Her wet clothes were plastered to her lush curves, outlining the swell of her hips and the line of her full breasts through the saturated bandages.

"You," he said.

She did the only sane thing she could. She fainted.

✦ 35 ✦

IT WAS A shame Eden was cursed. Alex took in the dense forests of Amory, her brother's home. The thick, green woods were sprinkled with yellow-leafed maples and orange sequoias, but she saw emptiness.

"Well, here we are," Stephen said proudly, stopping his wagon in front of a rough log cabin. "Home sweet home." He flushed as he took in his siblings' morose expressions. Victoria was staring glumly at her hands, which she was compulsively twisting in her lap; Adam's eyes were fixed in the direction of Oregon City, which they'd left far behind; and Alex looked like someone had shot her pet cat.

"I know it's not much," Stephen admitted, clearing his throat. "It's a bit rough . . ." He supposed now wasn't the time to tell them that the chimney smoked and the roof leaked.

"It's lovely," Alex said numbly, trying to shake herself from her stupor. But of course it wasn't lovely. Nothing had been lovely since that awful day she'd almost drowned in the Snake. She hurried from the wagon, trying to escape the memory. The thought of it still made her burn with shame. The way he'd looked at her . . .

She squealed when her skirt caught on a wheel, catching her mid-descent with a painful jerk. Damn it. She couldn't get used to wearing skirts again. They were always dragging in the dirt, or swinging too close to the fire, or catching on things. She never thought the day would come that she actually missed her overalls, but she thought longingly of how she'd been able to walk with a free stride and clamber in and out of wagons. Back when Luke Slater would still look her in the eye.

She sighed and unhooked her skirt from the wheel. It was

best not to think about it. Luke was out of their lives for good, and it was for the best. Although Vicky sure didn't think so. Alex stole a glance at her whey-faced sister. Victoria hadn't said two words since they'd parted ways with the wagon train in Oregon City.

Neither had Adam for that matter. But that was no surprise, Alex admitted, sighing again. Adam would probably never forgive her for selling Blackie Junior.

"Victoria and Mr. Slater say they had a deal," Alex had told him firmly, ignoring the fact that she'd never had any intention of honoring their wretched deal. All she knew was that she couldn't bear to look at the magnificent Arab; in the long, lonely days ahead he would only remind her of Luke: of him teaching her to ride, of the long months spent on the trail, of their rambling talks and serene silences . . . The memories made her lungs seize up so she couldn't breathe and her heart hurt fit to burst. No, she couldn't be dying of hurt every time she looked at the stupid horse. Luke was best forgotten.

"Why do you keep calling him Mr. Slater?" Adam demanded.

"Because that's his name," Alex had snapped, closing the subject. She'd started calling him Mr. Slater about the time he'd started calling her Miss Barratt. She winced, remembering the way his voice had dripped with sarcasm. The man hated her.

And now Adam hated her too.

She noticed Stephen standing awkwardly, regarding his log cabin with a depressed eye. "It really is lovely," she assured him, straightening her shoulders. She was sick to death of dragging about, feeling oppressed. She was young and strong, wasn't she? Her family was here with her, safe and sound, and the Gradys were locked up. What on earth did she have to complain about?

She pushed her memories of the last few horrid weeks aside and sized up her new home, not missing the irregular shingles or the smoky windowpanes. And not to mention the gaps around the frames. Glory, the place must be drafty. Stephen always had been more of a bookworm than a tradesmàn. Alex rolled up her sleeves and headed into the house, aware of her brother following anxiously.

"But it's only one room," Victoria complained as she stepped over the threshold.

"I didn't know you would be living here," Stephen said defensively. "I thought it was just for me."

Alex ignored them and began poking around the sparsely furnished cabin. It looked like Stephen had lain in enough supplies to get them all through winter. And there was a new brass bed set up by the fireplace, which she guessed she and Victoria would be sharing. She wrinkled her nose as she noticed the soot stains on the sheets.

"But what about when you get married?" Victoria demanded.

Stephen scratched his head. "Who would I marry?"

Victoria blinked, startled. "There must be some eligible girls in your congregation?"

"Not really." Stephen was blushing again. "There's just me and the Amorys."

"What? What do you mean just you and the Amorys?"

"Well," Stephen sputtered, "and now you three, obviously."

"But I thought there was a town!"

Alex saw the color drain from Victoria's face and hurried to reassure her. "I'm sure more people will come soon."

"They don't seem to be," Stephen said glumly. "They seem to be settling further down the valley."

Victoria's eyes were huge. "We're alone out here?"

"No," Stephen objected, "the Amorys are here too."

"But they don't have any daughters for you to marry," Victoria reminded him snappily. "Do they have any sons?"

"Well, no, it's just the two of them. Ted and Wallis."

"Ted and Wallis? They're both men? How old are they?"

"I've never asked them."

"Guess," Victoria growled.

Stephen looked sheepish. "I'd guess Ted's about fifty, and, well, Wallis is his father."

"His father!"

Alex tried to lead Victoria to a chair, worried that she might swoon—she certainly looked peaky—but Vicky batted her away angrily. "Are you telling me that there is no one around except for us and a couple of octogenarians?"

"There's nothing octogenarian about them," Stephen protested. "They're fur trappers."

"Victoria!" Alex gasped, when her sister grabbed for the frypan and brandished it like a weapon.

"I have been looking forward to civilization for months," Victoria shouted, swinging the frypan to punctuate every word, "and now you're telling me there isn't any!"

"But look at it," Stephen cried, neatly putting the table between him and his crazed sister, and gesturing at the forest outside. "Isn't it beautiful?"

"No! I'll tell you what's beautiful: whitewash and lace curtains; a cooking range and water pump; a general store! Hairpins are beautiful, and scented soap, and Saturday dances, and church on Sunday attended by more than just a couple of mad old trappers. Yellow calico dresses are beautiful. And best of all is satin, bright yellow shining satin!" Victoria burst into tears.

Stephen looked helplessly at Alex, who sighed. "She's just overwrought," she told him, as she tried to give Victoria a hug.

"No, I'm not," Victoria hiccupped, shrugging Alex off. "I just want to live like a regular person."

"But this is God's own country," Stephen said, bewildered.

"Isn't Oregon City God's own country too?" Victoria wailed, burying her face in her hands and crying as though her heart would break.

Things didn't get much better from there. They settled in for the night as the darkness crept around the little cabin. Alex agreed with Victoria. She didn't like the isolation either. After poking at dinner, which nobody really ate, they retired to their beds. Almost immediately Alex had to get up and open the window; she felt like she would suffocate on the wood smoke that came rolling from the fireplace in big white clouds.

She jumped every time a branch scraped against the wall of the cabin, or when she heard the low cry of an owl hunting. And in the long reaches of the lonely night she couldn't help her thoughts from turning to Luke. She could see with crystal clarity the look on his face on that last day in Oregon City.

The wagons had rolled into town in the late afternoon, each person struck dumb at their first sight of genuine civilization in months. Oregon City didn't seem like a frontier town: there were churches and stores; mills and smithies; a street full of neat, whitewashed buildings. There was even a local newspaper.

Alex had barely considered what awaited them at the end of the trail. Oregon had merely been a way to escape the Gradys, but now she realized that this would be home. This was where she would spend her life. She couldn't help her gaze drifting to Luke. He was working his way down the line of wagons, bidding everyone farewell before he headed home. She wondered if he lived close by.

"I guess this is it," he said shortly, once he'd pried himself loose from Adam and Victoria. Both had tears welling. Adam wanted to go with Luke; he'd been begging for days. "Blackie Junior needs me," he kept insisting.

"You can't leave your sisters," Luke said gently, refusing to look in their direction.

"They could come."

Alex blanched at the way Luke's expression blackened at the suggestion.

"Adam," Victoria interrupted, "don't harass him."

Alex clenched her teeth as she watched Victoria turn doe eyes on Luke. She knew that deep down Victoria still harbored the hope that Luke wouldn't let her go, that he would sweep her into his arms and beg her to marry him.

But Luke, of course, did no such thing. Instead he offered Victoria his hand, ignoring the tears flooding her brown eyes. "Try not to break the heart of every man in Amory."

All Victoria could do was sniffle.

Luke released her hand and, with a visible effort of will, he turned to Alex. "I guess this is it," he said shortly.

"Yes." Her chin lifted as she tried to keep her composure. He was so cold. For the first time since that day by the river he looked her in the eye, and those dark eyes, usually so liquid and warm, were as flat and hard as jet.

They'd been that way ever since she'd woken from her swoon. Now, lying in the dark in Stephen's smoky cabin, Alex screwed her eyes shut, trying to block out the memory. It was too awful. He'd made her feel as though she'd taken a knife and cut his heart out.

Which was ridiculous, she thought, turning over irritably and staring into the red coals of the fire. The man didn't care a fig for her. All he cared about was the fact that he'd been deceived. He'd never trusted women anyway; he thought they were duplicitous. And now she'd confirmed his opinions, Alex thought grumpily.

"I've organized a room for you at Mrs. Guthry's," Luke had told her gruffly in Oregon City. "Officially she's got a full intake of boarders, but she's agreed to take you as a personal favor." Alex had blinked, surprised at his thoughtfulness. "Her son will hunt down your brother for you. You'll be comfortable there until he comes."

Alex had felt a lump grow in her throat. He was really going to leave her. "Luke!" She couldn't help herself calling after him. Did she imagine the sudden heat in his eyes? It flared and died before she could be sure.

"What?"

Alex hadn't been sure what she wanted to say to him. So she shrugged weakly. "Just . . . good-bye."

He scowled and she thought she would die.

Before she knew it, he was heading down the main street, away from her, Delilah and Blackie Junior trotting after him.

Oh, *why* couldn't she stop thinking about that wretched man? She pulled the pillow over her head and stayed that way until she heard the birds twittering in the trees outside the open window. She didn't feel like she'd slept at all. She dragged herself from the bed and busied herself with breakfast, still battling against images of Luke Slater. Luke Slater riding Delilah, his face open and happy; Luke Slater watching the lightning flicker, his profile outlined against the stormy night sky; Luke Slater naked in the lamplight at Dolly's, his hard body all hers . . .

Alex pounded the dough until her fists were sore from hitting the table beneath. She was so wrapped up in her thoughts that she didn't notice anything out of the ordinary.

And neither did anyone else. It wasn't until they were sitting at the table, in front of steaming hot biscuits and crispy bacon that they noticed something was wrong.

Adam was missing.

And when they found the mules gone, along with their harnesses and all of Adam's meager possessions, they panicked.

"Where would he go?" Stephen demanded, wild with worry.

Alex knew exactly where he was going. And she couldn't deny the surge of joy that ran alongside her fear. Adam was heading for Blackie Junior.

And Blackie Junior was with Luke.

Her heart raced at the thought.

✦ 36 ✦

SHE WAS A liar. A cold-hearted, two-faced liar. So why couldn't he stop thinking about her? Luke hadn't been able to think straight for weeks, not since he'd found himself stranded on the muddy banks of the Snake, the woman of his dreams unconscious in his arms. The woman of his dreams, he thought with a snort. The woman of his dreams didn't exist. And neither did the runty little beanpole he'd come to call his friend. In their place was a perfect stranger.

The minute his shock began to fade he'd felt the first stab of anger. As he lifted her from the mud, he could feel her ripe curves press against him. How had he ever thought her a beanpole? How had he not noticed the swirling smoke of her eyes? How could he have been such an idiot?

Was he the only one she'd fooled? Suddenly Luke remembered Deathrider's words: *It was kind of hard to miss once her shirt was gone.* That damn Indian had seen her naked. He'd known exactly who she was. The memory of the sly, knowing expression on Deathrider's face the morning Luke had woken up by the Laramie River leaped into his mind. *Who is Beatrice?* That bastard had known exactly who Beatrice was. In fact, Luke remembered, almost dropping Alex's unconscious form in shock, it had been Deathrider who suggested he head down to the river that night. *Wash your face in the river, it will help.* Luke flushed, humiliated. Everyone had been playing him for a fool. He could well imagine the amusement the damn Indian must have felt as he watched stupid Luke Slater stumble down to the river.

Luke stopped dead.

It hadn't been a dream, he realized numbly. He looked

down at her, limp in his arms. She'd been there, in the river. Images assailed him: of her silvered by moonlight, glistening wet, arching, moaning.

He felt himself tighten and clenched his teeth. When he'd stumbled into camp the very next morning the kid had been waiting, he remembered, ready with a sympathetic smile and a mug of coffee. Hell, the woman had no shame. She'd left him naked on the riverbank. Unconscious and naked on the riverbank. How she must have been laughing when she pressed that damn coffee on him.

And what about back in Independence, he thought with a snarl. He'd gone back into the blazing whorehouse, risking his life to find her, when she'd been safely outside in the street. And what about earlier that night? She'd let him think she was a whore!

My cousin Beatrice . . . Dolly's voice rang in his ears. Luke felt like someone had thrown a bucket of icy water over him. Dolly had been laughing at him too. Had all the girls known? Had they all been laughing at him? He could picture them, each and every one of them sniggering at dumb old Luke Slater, who'd lost his head over a curvy, gray-eyed blonde.

Luke Slater, who never lost his head over any woman.

He was black with rage by the time he stalked his way upstream to the wagons. He thrust the unconscious witch into Adam's arms and, ignoring the worried babble of the campers, mounted Isis and rode off. He couldn't bear to look at any of them. How many of them had guessed? And what about Adam and Victoria—did they know what an idiot he'd been? Never again, he vowed, as he rode out. Never again would he lose his head over a woman.

He thought he had himself well under control by the time he returned. He'd gone back to the Sparrows' smashed-up wagon to retrieve what he could. There wasn't much left, just one trunk that had lodged itself in the mud of the riverbank, heavy enough to resist the current. He flipped it open. Dresses. He fought to keep his rage under control as he grabbed what he could carry. He wasn't about to drag the entire trunk back through the mud. At the bottom of the trunk he found the bolt of rose-colored cotton he'd bought her. With a snarl he threw it into the river, not bothering to watch as it was borne away by the current.

The sight of her sitting by the fire, wrapped in blankets, made him consider how tenuous his control was. When he saw the denim cuffs of her overalls peeking from beneath the blankets he wanted to throttle her, and when she looked up at him it took all his willpower to stay in the saddle. His hands clenched.

She was perfect. Look at that creamy skin, no longer hidden by a mask of mud; those clear gray eyes; that ripe strawberry mouth. And look at the way the Watts brothers flanked her, their hungry eyes fixed on the faint swell of cleavage revealed by the gap in the blankets. Luke glared at her. She knew precisely what effect she had on men. He remembered the way she'd turned to him, that night at Dolly's, as though she'd been expecting him, her breasts rising indecently above the low neckline of the green gown. A virgin, he thought angrily, his scowl deepening. She hadn't been too protective of her virtue, had she?

Kiss me, she'd said, standing unashamedly naked before him, tilting her head to allow him access to that ripe mouth. She sure hadn't kissed like a virgin. He wondered how many men she'd kissed before him.

"Make yourself decent," he snarled, throwing the armful of dresses at her and turning away before he could see the shock and dismay on her delicate features.

He couldn't have borne seeing her dressed as a boy, not once he knew. He would have been tortured by the faint line of her legs through the fabric, or the hint of her curves as she walked, not to mention the thought of the Watts brothers noticing those same curves. But the sight of her in a dress was torture too.

She was just so beautiful.

He hated the way he reacted to her. She disgusted him. She was a shameless, wanton, lying witch. But he couldn't seem to stop noticing her. He was intensely aware of her. He knew where she was at any given moment; he couldn't seem to help it. He was attuned to the sound of her voice. She owned three dresses, and he could recognize each and every one of them from the corner of his eye.

Luke had always been able to control himself around women. But now, he found himself unable to control his own body. His blood raced when she was near. And when he looked at her he was flooded with memories—the way the naked swell of her breasts felt against his chest, the sweet taste of her mouth, the way those gray eyes looked when they were hazy with desire.

He was glad when they reached Oregon City and he could be rid of her. Once he'd left her behind he'd be free. The leave-taking was awful, of course, as he'd known it would be. His heart beat at his ribcage like it was trying to break free when she called his name.

"Just . . . good-bye," she'd said, and he'd felt an almost irresistible urge to haul her against him, to make her heart beat the way his did, to make her as stupid with desire as he was.

It was bliss to be free of her, he assured himself, as he headed south to Utopia. He could finally resume his life. And the first order of business was to get himself hitched to Amelia Harding as soon as possible.

❧ 37 ❧

THEY WERE BARELY a mile from the cabin when they spied a wagon headed their way. "It's Ned," Victoria gasped. Both Stephen and Alex were too distracted with worry to notice the way she blushed and immediately began fussing with her bonnet.

Sure enough, it was the O'Brien wagon.

"You haven't seen Adam, have you?" Alex demanded the moment they were in earshot.

Ned blinked nervously. He still wasn't used to Alex in a dress. Behind him, Jane hid a little deeper in the wagon. More than anyone, she had been horrified to learn that Alex was a female.

"No," he stammered. His gaze went immediately to Victoria, and she flushed with pleasure at the way his eyes lingered on the lines of her body. After thinking herself destined to spend the rest of her life stuck in the wilderness, living out her days as a spinster, it was a joy to find herself faced with an appreciative male again. And no man had ever appreciated her as much as Ned O'Brien did.

"I thought you were going to settle in Utopia, with Luke," Victoria exclaimed, her dark eyes shining with joy.

"We can't stop to talk," Stephen interrupted, "Adam's missing."

"He's not missing. He's gone to Luke," Alex insisted.

"You *think*."

"I *know*."

"He doesn't know the way."

"He'll find out," Alex said stubbornly. She and Stephen had been arguing ever since they'd discovered Adam was missing. Stephen wanted to head for Oregon City; Alex was all for bypassing it and heading directly to Utopia.

"I don't know where Utopia is!" Stephen had shouted. So she'd agreed to head for Oregon City, but only to get directions.

"Wait," Ned said, alarmed, as Stephen flicked the reins. "I came to see you."

Victoria gave him an encouraging smile. Had he come to court her? To ask Stephen for her hand? She began planning speeches in her head; *Oh Ned, if only my heart didn't already belong to another. Can you ever forgive me? One day you'll find a good woman . . .* She scowled suddenly at the thought. She didn't want Ned to find a good woman. She wanted him to stay in love with *her.* He was the only man who'd ever fallen in love with her. Not like Alex, who broke hearts wherever she went. Except for Luke's, she thought smugly, remembering the way he'd completely ignored her beautiful sister. He didn't so much as look at her. Neither did Ned, Victoria thought with a dreamy smile. Maybe Alex was losing her touch.

"It's the Gradys!" Ned called after them, struggling to turn his wagon on the narrow track. His oxen lowed irritably.

Alex's heart stopped. She grabbed the reins from Stephen and yanked. "What?" They waited for Ned to pull up beside Stephen's wagon.

"They sent a rider from Laramie. I said I'd bring word to you. The Gradys have escaped."

"How?" Alex asked numbly.

"I don't know, but it was weeks and weeks ago."

Weeks ago? Alex felt faint. Gideon would come for her. She knew he would. She remembered the insane rage in his eyes and his loonish laughter. And what about Silas? She'd just about bitten his tongue off when he assaulted her, and then he'd been peppered with Deathrider's arrows and beaten senseless by Luke. He would have reason enough to come for her too. Oh hell, and Adam was out there alone. Suppose he ran into them? What would they do to him?

"There's more," Ned said gently, watching the blood drain from their faces. "They found one of them outside Fort

Hall. Dead." He refrained from saying more. He could hardly tell the ladies that the man had been gutted, pinned out and disemboweled like an animal. By his own brothers.

He didn't need to say it; the look on his face told them enough.

"Another one was picked up heading back toward Independence. Apparently he was cut up pretty bad."

Gideon, Alex thought sickly, remembering the jagged A carved into Silas's face. If he could maim and kill his brothers, what would he do to her?

"We have to hurry," she said, an edge of hysteria in her voice, "we have to find Adam."

"If you think he's heading for Luke, I can take you," Ned volunteered. "Our land is right by the Slater place."

"Your land?" Victoria said numbly, still white with shock.

"Six hundred and forty acres," he said proudly. "We'll be staying with Luke until the house is built."

"Oh." Victoria was barely listening. All she could think of was the feel of Gideon's gun between her lips and against her tongue.

"Miss Sparrow can ride with us," Ned suggested. "It can't be too comfortable in the back of that wagon."

Stephen's wagon was just a light farm vehicle and Victoria was rattling around in the back tray. She let Ned help her across and sat gratefully beside him. It was comforting to have him close. She remembered that it was he who had defeated the Gradys last time. She inched a little closer.

Alex and Stephen fell in behind the covered wagon. Consumed with fear, they didn't speak.

"LUKE'S GOING COURTING again," Tom chuckled, when Luke emerged from his room, freshly shaven and dressed in his Sunday best.

Luke ignored him. "Why aren't you dressed for church?" he snapped at Matt, who was still lounging at the kitchen table.

"What church?"

Utopia didn't have a church to speak of yet. Church services were held in Harding's barn when there was a crowd, and in his parlor when only a smattering of people showed up. Luke was hoping they'd be in the parlor today. Then he might be able to sit next to Amelia on the love seat.

"You're not wearing that," Luke objected when Matt rose and jammed his mangy old coonskin cap on his head. Matt ignored him and headed outside.

"Do you have to?" Tom sighed. "You've only been back a week."

"It ain't decent." Luke settled his own hat on his newly cropped hair and headed out too.

Tom rolled his eyes. Things were always tense when Luke and Matt were under the same roof. Tom figured that in another few days Matt would decide that he'd had a gutful and he'd disappear into the wilds for a bit. He had to laugh when he got outside to find Matt saddling Fernando, the old gray donkey.

"What the hell are you doing?" Luke was growling. "There's a whole corral full of horses right there."

Matt didn't respond. He didn't need to. The horses were Luke's, except for Tom's two paints.

"I'm not having you ride in on a damn donkey," Luke snapped.

Ignoring his older brother completely, Matt mounted the donkey and set off in the direction of the Harding place, his feet just about dragging on the ground.

"I don't see what you find so funny," Luke said, turning on Tom.

"I must say," Tom observed, following him into the barn, "you've been in a fine temper since you returned. Something you'd care to tell us? I thought you'd be full of sunshine after getting that Arab you were after. Speaking of which, why the hell aren't you riding him?"

Luke scowled as he saddled Isis instead. He wasn't about to tell Tom that he could barely stand to look at the Arab. He wished he hadn't bought him; when he looked at him he thought about Alex and the feel of her palm when he'd handed her the money. He'd barely even touched her, just the merest brush of his fingertips against her hand. Yet his fingers tingled at the memory.

"It's Amelia, isn't it?" Tom said sympathetically. "I know you went to see her the other day . . ." He trailed off. Luke thought it was some kind of secret that Amelia kept refusing him, but just about everyone knew. Tom couldn't understand his brother's fascination with that empty-headed little twit. Unless it was the fact that Amelia was the only woman who'd ever offered Luke a challenge. Mostly they melted at his feet.

Luke *had* gone to see Amelia. Had sat in the parlor with her, on that plush little love seat by the window, sipping her mother's overly sweet tea and nibbling at those dainty little cakes they had that seemed to fall apart in his big hands. He'd listened to Amelia chatter, filling him in on the local gossip, and he'd meant to ask her again, he really had. But for some reason he couldn't bring himself to do it.

She'd seemed like a complete stranger.

He'd looked at her as though he'd never seen her before. He'd never noticed how fine and straight her dark hair was, without even the slightest hint of a curl, or how close together her brown eyes were, or how narrow her upper lip was. He'd never noticed how high and clear her voice was, without even a hint of huskiness. And she was so little. All fine-boned and delicate. Instinctively he knew that if he pulled her hard against him he would feel the jut of her hipbones. Amelia was small and sweet, and breakable.

He left feeling very mixed-up. He rode the familiar trails of the lower Cascades until both he and Isis were exhausted, and returned home feeling empty and strange.

As he and Tom rode up to the Harding place for the Sunday service he felt the same mixed-up feeling rising behind his breastbone.

"Luke!" Pam Cressley yipped when she caught sight of him. Beside her, Johanna Sprat and Mary Tonkin waved enthusiastically.

Tom noticed that every one of the local women, the married ones as well as the maids, had dressed in their best today. Word had obviously got around that Luke was back.

"More people than usual today," Tom drawled as he joined Matt by the porch. Matt was slouching and looking surly. His unkempt beard reached halfway down his chest and looked like it could comfortably accommodate half a dozen birds' nests. Matt looked like the roughest of mountain men, but Tom knew it was mostly for Luke's benefit.

Matt would paint his face green and dance naked on Courthouse Rock if he thought it would annoy Luke.

They watched as a flock formed around their brother. Matt snorted. "Look at him. Happy as a pig in mud."

"No, I don't think so," Tom said thoughtfully. "Haven't you noticed how ornery he's been since he got back?"

"Luke's always ornery."

"Only around you, little brother," Tom laughed. "Seriously, look. When have you ever noticed him be ornery around a flock of women?"

Matt looked. Luke's smile was thin and tight. In fact, he seemed to be trying to get away. "Maybe it's because Curt Loughlin proposed to Amelia," he said with a dismissive shrug. He didn't really care why Luke did the things he did.

"He did?" Tom said, surprised. "I wonder why."

"She's the prettiest girl around, Tom," Matt told him with a measure of exasperation. Tom didn't seem to notice girls at all. Matt didn't understand it; the girls seemed to think Tom was good-looking—he came a close second to Luke, anyway—and he was a happy, genial sort. But women lost interest the minute they saw that he didn't really care for them. Tom's whole world was his damn ranching. All he was interested in was driving his herds down to California.

Tom's gaze searched Amelia out curiously. "I guess she's pretty enough."

"Well, who would you say is prettier?"

Tom was able to answer that question a couple of hours later when he and Matt returned home, leaving Luke to have dinner with the Hardings. There, waiting on their front porch, was the prettiest girl he'd ever seen in his life.

She wasn't just pretty, she was breathtaking. So beautiful he would have sold every last head of cattle he owned just to know her name.

ALEX'S HEART PLUMMETED when she saw that it wasn't Luke. From a distance she'd thought it was him and her heart had lodged in her throat. "Are you sure this is the right place?" she asked nervously as she watched the two men approach. One was as big and dark as Luke, riding a hardy-looking brown-and-white speckled horse. The other looked as wild and frightening as Jim Bridger, and seemed about to break the back of a tired old donkey.

"According to Luke's directions," Ned assured her.

Alex had her doubts. The house was so pretty. It was a large two-storied house with a long porch. It even had a porch swing and lace curtains at the windows. There was wild honeysuckle growing up the posts, and a few hardy sweetbriar roses were still flowering by the stairs. Not too far in the distance Alex could see the Cascade Range rising above wooded slopes of pine and fir, maple, mountain ash, hemlock and a dozen other kinds of tree she couldn't name. Every window of the house would have a perfect view of this bountiful Eden. Had he built this place for Arnelle Hardnose?

The two strange men came to a halt directly in front of her and Alex fixed a smile on her face. They were staring at her like they'd never seen a woman before. She fiddled nervously with her skirts and wished she'd changed into her best pink-flowered dress. She'd just about worn this gray to death and she was painfully aware of its stained hem and frayed cuffs.

"Good afternoon," she said politely, wincing under their stares. Now that she could see them properly she knew very well who they were. There was no mistaking their resemblance to Luke. What had he told them about her? They were looking at her like she had two heads. "I hope you don't mind us intruding," she blathered on, blushing as they remained silent. "It's just that my brother has run away, and we assumed that he would come here, because of Blackie."

"Blackie?" the scruffy mountain man rumbled, his bushy eyebrows drawing together.

"The horse," she stammered, blushing more than ever. Oh God, he'd told them everything; she just knew he'd told them everything. "The Arab."

"The Arab?" The one who looked the most like Luke fixed her with his intense eyes. Eyes that were green, she noticed with surprise, and not like Luke's at all.

"Who *are* you?" he asked.

"Alexandra," she said through numb lips. "Alexandra

Barratt." She could tell by their faces that they had no idea who she was. Alex wanted to sink through the floorboards of the porch. This was worse than if he'd told them everything. Luke hadn't mentioned her at all. She'd ceased to exist for him.

"Alex!" Stephen's voice rang across the yard. "I found him!"

Forgetting about the Slater brothers, Alex tore down the steps and across the yard. Her bonnet flew from her head and they watched her gold-streaked curls bounce as she ran.

"Who *is* she?" Matt asked admiringly.

"I saw her first!" Tom was off the paint in a second.

"Hell, you did!" Matt was close on his heels.

When they burst into the barn they found her wrapped around a large youth. A large youth who was wrapped around Luke's Arab. Next to them stood a thin, ascetic-looking man, who was pulling nervously on a narrow mustache.

"Don't you ever do that again!" the beauty was shouting, as she rained kisses on the squirming youth.

"Go away!" the youth bellowed. "I'm staying here with Luke. I'm going to help him with his horses."

"You know Luke?" Tom blurted, his heart sinking. Hell. There went his chances with her.

But the beauty was too busy shouting to notice him. "Luke said no," she was yelling.

"I'm dreadfully sorry," the nervous man apologized, approaching the Slater brothers. They eyed him. He couldn't be her husband, surely? "I'm afraid she was very upset when Adam disappeared."

"And you are?" Tom asked.

"Stephen Sparrow," he said, extending his hand. "I'm a pastor. From Amory."

"Amory? Never heard of it." Sparrow. She'd said her name was Barratt. So he wasn't her husband. Tom brightened and shook his hand enthusiastically.

"It's just up the valley, north of Oregon City." The pastor wilted a little. "I'm afraid it hasn't turned out quite as I expected. I only have a congregation of two, sometimes not even that if they decide to go trapping." He sighed. "I'm afraid my sisters were awfully disappointed. They seem to have their hearts set on somewhere a little more civilized."

Sisters! So there was another one somewhere. Tom's green eyes gleamed as he imagined finding a way to foist the sister on Matt so he could have the beauty all to himself. "You know," he said thoughtfully, "we don't have a real preacher around here. Our mayor does a reading on Sundays. That's where we've come from. You'd be a mighty welcome addition to Utopia."

While Tom was busy with the preacher, Matt took the opportunity to approach Alexandra. "I'm staying!" Adam was still bellowing as Alex tried to pry him away from the Arab.

"You can't."

"I will!"

"You won't!"

"You know," Matt interrupted them, "that horse ain't had his oats yet. I reckon your shouting might be making him hungry."

Alex jumped, embarrassed, and turned to find herself staring into a pair of golden-brown eyes. She was astonished that such an unattractive man could have such beautiful eyes.

"Why don't you let the boy feed him, and we can go in the house and talk this over?" Matt's voice was warm and friendly. "We'd be mighty pleased to have you join us for Sunday dinner."

"Oh, we couldn't," Alex protested.

"Sure you could," the man with the beautiful eyes insisted.

"No, really. There are too many of us."

"Three extra mouths won't be any trouble."

"Eight," Alex mumbled.

"Pardon?"

"There are five more in the covered wagon by your porch," she said sheepishly.

"The more the merrier."

"Right," Tom announced, clapping his hands and approaching them. "I've settled it with Pastor Sparrow here. You'll stay with us until you get some land of your own."

"What?" Alex gasped, appalled.

"We need a pastor, and he tells me that you and your

lovely sister were unhappy in the wilderness. Utopia isn't quite Oregon City, but we're growing fast. We have a store and a mill, and our own telegraph office. We have a congregation even, although we have no minister."

Alex was speechless. She turned huge eyes on her brother, but Stephen looked almost as bewildered as she felt. He wasn't quite sure what had happened, but somehow in the course of the conversation he'd been employed as the town minister. He'd even shaken hands on it.

"I'm afraid we don't have a hotel," Tom was plowing on, "or even a boarding house, but we'd be thrilled to have you stay with us. Wouldn't we, Matt?"

"Thrilled," Matt agreed, his eyes twinkling at the thought of spending the winter under the same roof as Miss Barratt.

"We won't be able to start building you your own place until the snows melt next spring," Tom said apologetically, "but as you can see it's a big house, so we should manage here just fine for the winter."

"Our brother plans to fill it with kids," Matt added. "He built six bedrooms."

"If Matt and I move up to the attic we should all fit quite comfortably. And respectably," he qualified, "as your brothers can chaperone you."

Alex stared into the beaming faces of Luke's brothers and felt her stomach twist. Oh heavens . . . "We can't," she blurted, at the exact moment that Adam yelled, "We'd love to!"

"There you go," Tom said, clapping his hands again. "It's settled. How about we welcome our new pastor with a nice Sunday roast? I put the joint on before we left this morning and there should be enough."

Alex let herself be herded up the stairs, her head spinning. What had just happened?

❧ 38 ❧

LUKE SAT THROUGH the service sitting on the love seat by Amelia's side. He sat awhile on the porch with her afterward, sipping her mother's too-sweet lemonade. He sat opposite her at her parents' lace-covered dining table. And he took her on a brief stroll around the garden before he left.

He had every opportunity in the world to ask her to marry him. But he didn't. There were times when the moment was right, when she seemed to pause as though expecting it, but he stayed silent. And when he left he didn't even try to kiss her. He simply tipped his hat, mounted Isis and left. He tried not to think about why this was.

By the time he arrived home, the sun had dropped behind the ranges to the west and the valley was blue and shadowed. The leaves were in color, glowing like orange and gold coals in the twilight, and the air had a chill. Soon it would snow and he would be facing another long winter, alone in his cold bed. He needed a wife.

Next Sunday, he decided, he would ask her next Sunday.

He took his time with Isis, giving her a thorough grooming, not looking forward to going inside and facing Tom's teasing. He noticed regretfully that his brothers had already fed the horses. He wished he could have had the excuse to linger outside a little longer. On his way out of the barn he noticed the oxen and mules. He frowned.

When he emerged he saw the O'Brien wagon, parked beneath the big old beech tree. He felt a wave of relief. Thank God, Ned was here . . . that should keep his brothers from needling him about Amelia.

As he approached the house he noticed Matt at the woodpile, gathering an armful of wood for the stove. Luke stopped

dead, his mouth open in shock. "What happened to you?"
Luke didn't remember the last time he'd seen Matt without
his beard. Actually, he had a funny feeling that Matt had
never shaved; from the minute his whiskers grew he just let
them keep on growing. Staring at the smooth planes of his
little brother's clean-shaven face, Luke was astonished. He'd
had no idea Matt was so handsome. He looked like their
father—the same long straight nose, the same hollow cheeks,
the same cupid's-bow mouth. Now that he'd shaved, even his
longish hair didn't look so bad. Partly because it was clean,
Luke thought, with another shock. So clean it shone in the
lamplight falling through the windows.

"What do you mean?" Matt replied with studied nonchalance.

Luke approached him, unable to tear his eyes away. "I
mean, what the hell happened?"

"I shaved," Matt snapped, flushing.

"Why?"

"Felt like it."

The sound of laughter drifted through the partly open
kitchen door and Luke remembered Ned. "You've been taking care of the O'Briens?"

"They had dinner with us," Matt said, grinning.

Luke blinked. He didn't remember the last time his little
brother had grinned at him either. His teeth were straight
and white. Luke felt disoriented. What on earth had happened around here in the last few hours?

Luke pushed the door open.

And felt time stop.

His kitchen was crammed with people, but he only saw
one clearly. She was sitting by the stove, her face flushed
from the heat, her eyes sparkling. Her still-short hair curled
around her face and shone with golden lights. She was wearing that dress, the gray one, the one that made her skin look
like fresh cream and her eyes glow, the one that clung to the
curves of her breasts and hugged her small waist. She was
laughing. He'd never seen her laugh. Not like this. He'd seen
the boy-Alex laugh, but he'd never seen this woman laugh.
The sound was low and husky and sent shivers down his
spine.

His gaze charged the air between them like a lightning storm, and she lifted her eyes. Luke felt his stomach drop, like he was falling from a great height. Her eyes were like rain, like thunderclouds, like floodwater, like smoke. They were every shade of gray in creation.

One by one they fell silent as they noticed Luke in the doorway. "Luke," Tom greeted him jovially, "some friends of yours dropped by."

"So I see."

Alex winced and looked away. She felt sick to her stomach. He didn't look happy to see her. She'd known he wouldn't be, but some fool part of her had hoped . . . Dear Lord, how would he react when he found out she was going to be *living* with him? He might well kill her, she thought nervously.

"How did it go with Amelia?" Tom's voice cut through her thoughts like a knife through butter. Her gaze flew back to Luke. Had he finally asked Aurelia Hardwig to marry him? Had she said yes?

"Excuse me," she muttered, rising from the table, pretending she needed the conveniences. She couldn't sit here and listen to him talk about Arnelle. She was grateful for the cold air on her burning skin as she stepped outside. She took a deep breath.

For the sake of appearances, she made for the outhouse that was hidden among a small cluster of juniper bushes. She walked around in circles for a while, not wanting to go back inside. The daylight had faded and the blue twilight was becoming purple night. Squares of yellow light fell through the windows onto the porch. It was such a beautiful house. Homely. Welcoming. Built for another woman. Alex sighed. She supposed she couldn't stay out here forever.

She heard the click of a door and jumped. Someone was coming. She darted around to the front of the house, thinking to enter through the parlor door, in order to avoid whoever it was. She had a horrible feeling it might be Luke coming to wring her neck.

She flew up the stairs. And straight into a dreadfully familiar wall of muscle.

Luke had left through the front door. He was too furious

to speak and didn't want to run into the witch on her way back from the outhouse. He had every intention of saddling Isis and making for the saloon in town.

But the minute he opened the door he was hit by an armful of soft, trembling female. Once again, he made the mistake of looking into her eyes. He thought he'd learned not to do that on the torturous trip from Three Island Crossing to Oregon City. The minute he met her swirling gray eyes he was witless. When she'd careened into him his natural impulse had been to grab hold of her, and now he found his hands cupped around her shoulders, his thumbs mere inches from the swell of her breasts. He could feel her legs and thighs brush against him as she jerked sharply backward. His hands tightened on her shoulders. He could smell soap, something light and floral, and, underneath, a scent that was uniquely hers.

He might have had the strength to push her away if she hadn't parted her lips and given a small gasp. The action caused his gaze to drop to that ripe strawberry mouth; that slick ripe strawberry mouth that haunted his dreams.

With a hopeless, helpless groan, Luke crushed her to him. His mouth descended to plunder hers, rough and demanding, full of the longing and confusion that had plagued him for all these months. One hand moved to grasp the back of her head, and the other dropped to the hollow of her back, pressing her to the hard length of him. It was a punishing, bruising kiss; a hungry kiss, meant to devour her.

It was only when she surrendered, threading her fingers through his shortened hair, that he came to his senses.

He shoved her away. Would he *never* learn? Look at the way she swayed toward him, lips parted. She was practically begging him to kiss her. He'd never met such a calculating, manipulative woman in his life. Luke was glad it was too dark for her to see the color rise in his face. Once again, he'd been made a fool, grabbing for her like a callow youth. "Stay away from me," he snarled, stamping off toward the barn.

Alex stared after him in shock. She struggled to regain her composure. Eventually, when she thought her heartbeat had quieted, she slid into the parlor. Where Matt Slater was standing in the dark, an enigmatic smile playing around his sharply bowed lips. Alex stopped dead in horror. Had he seen? She knew by the look in his eyes that he had. She was mortified. What must he think of her? And how much worse would it be when Luke told him the whole story?

Maybe he already had, Alex thought with a stab of fear. Maybe he'd told them while she was outside in the cold, as they sat there at the table in that lovely, homey kitchen. Maybe he'd told them about the night in the whorehouse, about the night in the river . . . maybe they all knew how shameless she really was. And how little he cared for her.

"Hey," Matt protested when he saw her beautiful eyes flood with tears. Instinctively he pulled her into his arms. In that way at least he was like his brother. Alex closed her eyes and couldn't stop herself from pretending that they were Luke's arms around her, that it was his hand rubbing comforting circles on her back. But she knew the difference all too well.

Matt watched through the window as Luke appeared on Isis and galloped off for town. He couldn't help but grin. This could prove to be a lot of fun, he thought, resting his cheek on the soft gold curls and narrowing his eyes speculatively. As long as Tom didn't go and get serious about the girl. He'd never seen Tom taken with a woman before and wasn't sure how smitten he was. Hopefully it wouldn't take him long to discover that the girl was besotted with Luke. Hell, weren't they all?

But, Matt thought, still grinning, he'd never seen Luke besotted in return before. Oh, he kept chasing about after that stuck-up Amelia Harding, but Matt would bet that he never lost control with her, not the way he just had with this beauty. And who could blame him, Matt thought with a sigh as he felt the lush curves pressing against him.

So why was his brother out there in the cold, and not in here enjoying these curves? What had happened out there on the trail? Something to make his brother stupid where Alexandra Barratt was concerned, that was certain. He wondered how long it would take for Luke to come to his senses. And how much fun he could have with him before that happened.

"Would you like me to show you to your room?" he asked gently, pulling away before the curves drove him crazy.

Alex wiped at her face and looked at him, confused. "We're still staying?"

"Why wouldn't you be?"

"But Luke . . . Didn't Luke . . . ?" She drew a hitching breath.

"Luke didn't say much of anything," Matt said truthfully. "Tom pretty much presented him with a *fait accompli*. Come on," Matt said soothingly, "you've had a long day. I'll show you to your room."

She followed him up the stairs, to a neat corner room. It had brand new mahogany furniture, the walls were creamy white and simple curtains hung at the window. It was a comforting room.

"Sorry it's so simple," Matt apologized. "Luke kept all of these rooms pretty blank. I think he plans to turn them blue or pink depending on whether he has boys or girls." He rolled his eyes.

"He planned the house?" Alex asked, watching as Matt drew the curtains for her.

"Down to where every nail would go," Matt said dryly. "And built it with his own two hands. He's always had a very specific idea about this place, and about who would live here, and *how* they should live here."

Alex heard the faint bitterness in his tone and remembered Luke's stories about his brother. She also remembered how demanding Luke had been when he was teaching her to ride. "He can be domineering, can't he?"

Matt gave a short laugh. "To put it kindly."

"I guess I can too," she sighed, sinking onto the bed. "It's not always easy being the responsible one." She thought of the Gradys, out there in dark, and shivered.

"Who is he responsible for?" Matt snapped. "I'm a grown man."

"But you weren't always." Alex couldn't believe that she was defending Luke, not after the way he'd treated her tonight.

"I'm not a boy." Matt yanked her to her feet and gave her a short, hard kiss. "I'm as much a man as he is." He slammed the door behind him.

Alex felt a swift piercing rage. Oh, these horrid Slater

men with their unpredictable tempers and their habit of man-handling her. She threw the pillow at the door, completely unsatisfied with the soft sound it made as it flopped to the floor. She wished she had something to throw that would smash. Loudly.

❋ 39 ❋

SHE WAS DRIVING him out of his mind. Everywhere he went, she was there. When he went down to breakfast she was there—more often than not standing at the stove, with an apron tied around that neat little waist. When he went into the barn, she was there—usually trying to coax Adam to eat something. The boy was so obsessed with the horses that he barely remembered to breathe, let alone eat. Even at night, when Luke locked himself in his room, she was there. Some hideous quirk of fate meant that she'd been given the bedroom next to his, and he could hear every move that she made—her bare feet on the floorboards, the sound of the window opening, the bed creaking beneath her weight as she turned in her sleep.

And when he closed his eyes things were even worse. She came to him in dreams: wet, naked, the river rushing over her as she rode him. Waking, swollen and aching for her, it took every ounce of willpower he had not to burst into her room and take her then and there.

She'd only been there for seven days, but it felt like a lifetime.

He lay in bed, dreading going down to face her. Mealtimes were appalling. He had to watch his idiot brothers falling over themselves for her attention. Hell, every time she smiled at Tom he just about swooned. And today was Sunday, he thought darkly. Sunday meant church. This meant she'd be coming along to the Hardings'—where every man in the area would fall in a heap at her feet.

He scowled at the ceiling just thinking about it.

"Give me your coat, Stephen," he heard her husky voice calling up the stairs, "and I'll give it a brush for you."

He pulled his pillow over his face, unable to resist a quick fantasy. They were leaving. She'd come up the stairs to see where he was. *Luke? You'll miss the service.* She'd turn to call back down to the others. *Go on without me; I'll wake him up.* They'd hear the door close. They'd be alone in the house. *Luke?* she'd call softly as she entered his room. He would be asleep. She'd come over to the bed. Her hand would give the sheet a gentle tug. He'd be naked beneath. She would reach out . . .

Such fantasies caused him physical pain.

He was the last one down to breakfast, so by the time he got there all the food was gone. The O'Brien girls were doing the dishes, while everyone else fussed about, getting ready to leave for church. Luke poured himself a coffee, although all that was left at the bottom of the pot was a thick sludge. Disgruntled, he sat at the table and stirred sugar into his sludge.

"Don't forget your speech, Stephen," he heard Alex call from somewhere deep in the house. The hair rose on the back of his neck and he scowled. Why couldn't he simply ignore her?

"He'll forget it," she was sighing as she entered the kitchen. At least he had his back to her. Although he could still see the flick of her skirts from the corner of his eye. Today she was wearing the muslin sprigged with little pink roses. Not his favorite. It was too sweet for his taste, and too virginal for her, he thought dryly.

"Where's Adam?" she asked, as she hung Stephen's freshly brushed jacket on the back of a chair.

"I think he's out with the horses," Victoria said shyly, stepping into the kitchen.

"Oh, Victoria," Alex breathed, and Luke turned to look. Victoria was resplendent in a brand new dress of primrose yellow. She'd never looked prettier. Blushing, she pirouetted to show off her handiwork.

"What have we here?" Tom remarked appreciatively, as he came into the room behind her. "There's a wildflower sprung up in the kitchen."

"You look mighty fine," Matt agreed, elbowing Tom aside. "Ned sure knew which color would suit you."

A few days before Ned O'Brien had come back from town laden with bolts of cloth, each and every one of them yellow:

sunshine yellow, lemon yellow, sherbet yellow; cotton the yellow of buttercups, muslin sprigged with yellow daisies, lawn striped with sunflower yellow; pale gold satin, and a silk the color of ripe wheat. A veritable wealth of yellow.

"Oh, Ned," Victoria had exclaimed, her eyes growing wide at the sight.

"You looked so beautiful in that yellow dress," he told her nervously. "I hated to think of it lost in the Snake like that. Not when . . . I mean"—he gathered his courage and let the words flow from him in an anxious flood—"that night in Independence, when we danced, you glowed like a second sun."

"Byron?" Victoria guessed.

"No." He turned bright red. "That was just me."

He was blushing again now as he watched her pirouette happily in the kitchen. Luke couldn't help noticing the faint envy in Alex's eyes as she plucked at the worn skirt of her pink-flowered dress.

"You look beautiful," she told Victoria sincerely, obviously mastering her envy, before gathering her bonnet and heading out to collect Adam.

A few minutes later they heard an ear-splitting scream.

Luke was out the door and bursting into the barn before anyone had quite registered what they'd heard. "What happened?" he demanded, his heart pounding. He half expected to find Gideon Grady's knife at her throat. His knees went weak with relief when he saw that she was unmolested.

"We'll make glue of you!" she was shouting at one of the mules. She was holding her rear, and he noticed her skirt was torn.

"He bit you?"

"Of course he bit me! The beast hates me!"

Luke started to laugh. She looked so earnest, her feelings genuinely wounded by the mule.

"It's not funny," she snapped, as Tom and Matt burst in behind Luke, brandishing their rifles.

"You frightened me to death!" Victoria scolded when she realized it was only a mule bite.

"Well, it hurt," Alex sulked.

"Oh, your dress!"

Alex finally noticed the large tear in the back of her best dress. Her dismay was obvious.

"I'll make you a new one," Victoria said quickly, noticing the telltale shine of tears in her sister's eyes.

"But what will I wear *today*?" Alex moaned. "My gray is dirty and the other one isn't fit to wear out."

"You'll wear one of mine," Victoria said firmly, shepherding her from the barn.

Alex couldn't believe it. She'd washed and pressed her dress especially, and now this. She eyed Victoria's dresses glumly. "We're not the same size," she reminded her sister.

"I know. But we could try my navy skirt with a blouse. What else can you do? You don't want to stay home and miss Stephen's first service."

There was that. Although mainly she didn't want to stay home and miss seeing what this Adelia Hardup looked like. She dutifully crammed herself into Victoria's clothing. The skirt was fine, if a little snug around the upper swell of her hips, but the blouse was obscene. It didn't button all the way up—the last button they could fasten left a scandalous cleavage on display.

"Oh my," Victoria sighed, tugging helplessly at the sides of the blouse.

What was she going to do? Why couldn't Adam own a nice white shirt? Alex's eyes widened as she was seized with inspiration. How hard would it be to find a white shirt in a house full of men? Stephen was wearing his only clean one, but Luke had lots.

She felt a thrill as she slid into Luke's bedroom. She paused to look around, curious. It was another simple, welcoming room, full of the same mahogany furniture as hers. Only in here the curtains were dark blue, and it smelled of leather, soap and horse. A smell she associated with Luke. Feeling unbelievably wicked, Alex crept to the wardrobe, and sure enough there was a row of crisp white shirts. Hastily, she pulled off Victoria's blouse and tossed it on the bed. The collar of Luke's shirt was far too big, so she left the top two buttons undone. She had to roll the sleeves up to her elbows, as they were too long, but once she'd tucked it in and cinched Vicky's belt she didn't think she looked half bad.

It was certainly better than wearing a torn dress, she thought happily, snatching up the blouse. As she pulled it from the bed she knocked his pillow to the floor. When she went to replace it she noticed something small and crumpled lying on the sheet. It was a cream-colored cloth rose. Alex picked it up, her heart skipping a beat. It was the rose she'd worn in her hair that night in Independence. The one Dolly had pinned in her curls to disguise her short hair.

What was it doing here, under his pillow? Alex felt the blood rush to her cheeks. He'd kept it? All this time?

Her fingers stroked the petals as she struggled with this new knowledge. Gently she placed it back on the sheet and rested the pillow on top of it. When she joined everyone downstairs, she was still flushed and flustered.

"Is that my shirt?"

"We're late," Alex said abruptly, cutting Luke off. She gave Stephen a shove toward the door and dove for the wagon before Luke could protest.

She rode beside Stephen in the wagon, unable to tear her gaze from Luke's strong back. He rode ahead on Delilah, flanked by Tom on his paint and Adam on Blackie. Bringing up the rear, his heels dragging in the dust, was Matt, jolting along uncomfortably on Fernando's bony back.

Faintly, Alex could hear a slow and lovely two-step, and feel the phantom press of Luke's arms as he danced her around the square beneath the swaying colored lanterns.

LUKE WASN'T SURE who caused more of a stir: Alex or Matt. He'd expected the swarm of men who gathered around Alex, but he hadn't expected the ladies to flock to his brother.

"If only he'd shaved years ago," Tom said dryly, "you would have had a quieter time of it."

Luke grunted, too busy keeping a close eye on Alex to listen properly. Tom rolled his eyes. It hadn't taken him long to work out that Alexandra Barratt was the reason his brother had come home ornery. The man was obviously head over heels. Tom couldn't for the life of him work out why he didn't make a move. She was just as obviously in love with him.

He shrugged. What did he care if his brother acted the idiot? It gave the rest of them a chance to woo her. And who knew, maybe they'd succeed in turning her head. The men of Utopia were certainly giving it a serious try. Even Dell Pritchard and Josh Masters, who'd long ago declared their undying love for Amelia, were fluttering about Alex like suicidal moths.

"Well," Tom declared heartily, slapping his brother on the back, "at least the competition for Amelia seems to be thinning." Grinning at the sight of Luke's scowl, he headed off to join the moths.

"I wish they wouldn't make such fools of themselves," Amelia Harding sighed, catching sight of the usual knot of women through the delicate lace curtains of the parlor window. She always made a late entrance on Sunday. Otherwise she found herself buttonholed by one particular beau, which upset the others terribly. Why, it had taken her all week to sweeten Curt Loughlin after Luke had monopolized her last Sunday.

"Surely they know by now that Luke isn't interested?" she continued, checking her reflection in the mirror above the mantel. Her hair, as usual, was sleek and flawless. She pinched her cheeks briskly to make them bloom.

"It's not Luke they're interested in," Moira Duthy said slyly. She was plastered to the window, unable to tear her eyes from Matt Slater. Who could have guessed that he was hiding such looks under that hair?

"Who is it? One of the new people? Didn't you say one of them was in at the store this week, buying cloth? What does he look like? He can't be more handsome than Luke, surely?" Amelia elbowed Moira out of the way.

Her mouth popped open. "It can't be . . ." Amelia's dark eyes narrowed as she took in the chattering women surrounding Matt Slater.

Moira recognized the look. Amelia wasn't about to have a desirable man taking after any woman but her. Moira giggled. Just wait until she went outside and saw the new girl. The one in the daring white shirt, who was surrounded by all of Amelia's beaus. She hastened to fix her bonnet so she could follow Amelia into the garden. She wouldn't miss this for the world.

"Why, Matthew Slater," Amelia sang, too focused on Matt to notice the throng by the barn. "I barely recognized you!"

"Really?" Matt said in a bored tone. "I can't imagine why." He didn't know how Luke put up with these women. Their chatter was making his ears ring.

"You've lost your beard, silly," Amelia giggled, none-too-gently pushing Cathy Loughlin and Johanna Sprat out of the way.

"Time for the service, folks," Harding bellowed from the mouth of the barn.

"Oh, wonderful," Amelia said, threading a proprietary arm through Matt's. "Won't it be lovely to hear a real preacher again?"

Matt grimaced as he realized he was expected to escort her into the barn. How had that happened? Meanwhile, across the yard he could see Tom taking Alex's arm. Lucky bastard.

Luke couldn't believe it. Not only did he have to watch Tom pawing Alex, but now Matt had gone and sweet-talked Amelia. Well, he'd be damned if he'd let them see him standing alone at the back of the barn. "Miss Sparrow?" He turned to Victoria, pasting a warm smile on his face. But Victoria was oblivious to him, her arm already neatly entwined with Ned's. Luke clenched his jaw. Fine. Who needed women anyway? They were nothing but a mess of trouble.

He followed the group into the barn, where everyone gathered in a semicircle around a nervous Stephen Sparrow.

"This here's our new preacher, everyone," Harding was announcing, "and I hope you'll all go out of your way to make him welcome. He comes to us from Mississippi, and with him are his brother and sisters. Perhaps they'd care to step forward so we can all get to know them?" Blushing, Alex and Victoria stepped forward, followed by a very shy Adam, who kept his gaze fixed firmly on the floor. "This is Miss Alexandra, Miss Victoria and Adam. You can find them at the Slater place this winter, until they get a house built."

Every male head swiveled to look at Luke. He struggled to keep his expression neutral. "Do she and Tom have an understanding yet?" Dell Pritchard whispered, keeping a close watch on how Tom hovered over the beautiful blonde.

Luke scowled. "Not as far as I know."

"You mind if I come around sometime?"

He had to resist the urge to belt the man. "I thought you had an understanding with Amelia," he said instead.

Dell snorted. "We all know she'll marry you eventually. Although, it looks like your brother might be giving you some stiff competition."

The man had no idea how close he was to a broken nose.

"Just before I pass the floor over to the pastor," Harding said, "I want to announce that we've set a date for the winter dance. We'll be holding it on the first weekend of December. Rich and Bea have kindly offered their general store for the venue and my lovely daughter, Amelia, will be heading up the decoration and refreshment committee. If anyone is interested in helping out, you can speak to her after today's service." Amelia gave a giggle and a wave.

So that was Adele Hardnose, Alex thought numbly. She really was very pretty. And nothing at all like Alex. She had a pointy little chin, a snub nose and glossy dark hair. She was as slight as Victoria, with the coy girlishness of many petite women. And she was so stylish. Her gown was made of rustling blue-and-green-plaid taffeta, with round little puff sleeves and ruffles around the hem. Alex fiddled self-consciously with the buttons on Luke's shirt. She wished the damn mule hadn't torn her pink dress.

Luke pulled at his collar. It was so stuffy in here, he could hardly breathe he was so hot. His eyes were riveted to Alex's fingers. Any minute he expected one of those flimsy buttons to pop right off, the way she was tugging and pulling at them. Hell. Wasn't it torture enough that she was wearing his damn shirt? Was she *trying* to put him in an early grave?

Luke heard Dell Pritchard's breath catch and turned to see the man's eyes similarly riveted on Alex's fingers. And next to him, Clay Sprat was openmouthed, mesmerized by the way her hand had settled at the button directly between her breasts. Luke cleared his throat and when they looked up at him he glared at them. They both flushed and turned their attention back to the preacher.

He'd be damned if he'd let her leave the house in that shirt again.

"You'll join the committee, won't you, Matt?" Amelia demanded once the last hymn had been sung. She was refusing to release his arm, even though he was trying to pull away. "We need a big strong man to cut boughs for us."

"How about Tom?" Matt said a little desperately, grabbing his brother as he walked past.

"How about me for what?" Tom gave Matt a sly grin as he tugged Alex's arm a little more firmly through his own.

"The decoration committee, silly," Amelia said with an overly breathless laugh. She was busy sizing up the new girl, Matt saw. He guessed it didn't take her more than a second to realize that Alex put her in the shade. Matt could feel her talons digging into him. "And of course we'd love you to join us, Miss Sparrow, was it?" Amelia's voice dripped with syrup.

"Barratt," Alex corrected, equally sweetly, "and that's very kind of you, Miss Hardway."

"Harding," Amelia said through a tight smile, "but please, do call me Amelia." She feigned a slight frown. "Barratt, did you say? So, we should be calling you Mrs. Barratt, then?"

"Miss," Alex assured her.

"But, I thought . . . We were led to believe that the pastor was your brother?"

"Stephen's parents took me in."

"How kind. But aren't you concerned what people will say—living with a man who isn't a blood relation?"

"I believe she's living with several men who aren't blood relations," Matt said dryly, "but fortunately for the reputations of all concerned, there are other females about too."

"Your house must be bursting at the seams," Amelia remarked.

"It's a big house," Matt said sharply. She colored. It was common knowledge that Luke had built it for her.

"Where *is* your brother?" Amelia asked suddenly. She hadn't seen him all day. "He usually joins us for dinner after the service."

"Not today," Tom observed, nodding toward the gate, where Luke was kicking Delilah into a trot as he fell in behind a departing wagon. "Looks like Maggie McCauley collared him today."

"And who is Maggie McCauley?" Alex asked waspishly, when they finally broke free from Amelia.

Tom sighed. He really didn't stand a chance. He turned

Alex toward him. "Maggie McCauley is no one you need to worry about, darling. She's all of four-foot nothing and as round as a prize pig, but she's a very sweet girl. Her parents run the store, so he's probably gone to buy some goods."

Alex blinked. Tom was giving her a knowing smile.

"You may not have noticed, but Luke hasn't so much as looked at another woman since you arrived."

Alex turned crimson.

"And if you want my opinion, you'd be a fool to wait for him to come to his senses. He's a stubborn man, it might take years. If I were you, I'd do the wooing myself."

She was mortified. Was she so obvious? Did everyone know how she felt about him?

"And, Alex," Tom said softly, "if he's more of an idiot than I suspect, and he never comes to his senses, just remember that there are plenty of us who would treat you like a princess." He dropped a kiss on her forehead and left her to her whirling thoughts.

She was turned upside down inside. The cloth rose under his pillow . . . Tom telling her to woo him . . . She would be glad to lock herself away in her peaceful corner room, where she could privately sift through her thoughts.

But when she got home and opened the door to her room she found anything but peace of mind. Piled on her bed were two stacks of cloth. There was bolt after bolt in dozens of colors and patterns: lawn, muslin, linen and cotton; taffeta, silk and finely woven wool. There was even a neat little pile of lace and a bundle of satin ribbons.

"There's no yellow," a low voice said softly behind her.

She turned to find herself captured by Luke's intense black gaze.

"The McCauleys were sold out," he said. He moved closer and she could feel the heat radiating from him. His liquid eyes were serious and unreadable. "I bought everything else they had," he said softly, his fingers resting lightly against the button between her breasts—she could feel his touch burn through the cloth, right through to her skin.

"Why?" she asked witlessly.

"Because," he growled, releasing her button, "I don't want you wearing my shirt anymore."

❧ 40 ❧

IT WAS PERFECT. Alex examined herself in the mirror and couldn't resist laughing, already relishing her triumph. The man would have to be dead to resist her tonight.

Luke had been studiously avoiding her for almost three weeks. He didn't even seem to notice her new clothes. She'd had such high hopes the morning she'd worn the first dress, which she'd stayed up all night sewing. It was the exact same green as the dress she'd worn to the dance in Independence. She'd primped in front of the mirror for almost an hour before she went down to breakfast, carefully pinning up each wayward curl, and pinching her cheeks until they glowed. But he didn't so much as bat an eye. He growled his usual "good morning" and headed out to his wretched horses.

But not tonight, she thought giddily, swiveling to examine the back of her beautiful new gown. Tonight was the winter dance, and she'd been working on this dress for more than a week. It was made of deep cranberry-colored satin—a color that brought out the vivid hue of her lips, and made her eyes shine. She'd deliberately cut the neckline daringly low, almost as low as the dress Dolly had laced her into, and her breasts swelled above the ripe-red satin, pale and full, rising and falling with every breath she took. Just see if he could ignore that.

She heard a breathy laugh and peeked between the curtains. Below, she could see Ned handing Victoria up into his wagon. Her wheat-colored silk skirts peeked beneath her new wool coat. The girls, all in white organza, were huddled beneath the canvas hoop, blankets and furs piled high around them. Even from here Alex could see the way her sister's face glowed with joy.

There, Alex thought with a stab of excitement, went her last argument for staying away from Luke Slater. The morning after Luke had given Alex the bolts of material, Vicky had crept into her room. "What's all this?" her sister had gasped, tripping over a stack of sprigged muslin.

Alex had swallowed, worried about how Victoria would react. "Luke gave them to me."

"I guess he didn't like you stealing his shirt," Victoria remarked, sitting on the bed beside Alex.

"I guess not."

Victoria reached over and took her hand. "There's something I need to tell you," she announced, almost wriggling in her excitement.

"What?"

"Ned means to ask Stephen for my hand."

Alex wasn't surprised.

"And I mean to say yes!"

Now she was. "But I thought . . . I thought you had feelings for Luke."

"Oh, that," Victoria said with a sigh. "I thought I did. But every woman has feelings for Luke, don't you think? Just look at all of those ninnies at the service yesterday."

"They seemed more interested in Matt than Luke," Alex observed.

"Not for long. You should have heard them talking afterward. You'd think he was some kind of *god* the way they go on about him."

Alex scowled. "Why? What were they saying?"

"It doesn't matter," Vicky insisted. "What matters is that I was wrong. I thought he felt the same way about me, but it's plain that he doesn't."

"Oh."

"I'm not sure Luke feels that way about any woman."

Alex was scowling again.

"I'm sorry," Victoria said sympathetically, giving her hand a squeeze, "I know you had feelings for him too. But I don't want to see you hurt."

"I don't want to see you hurt either," Alex replied. "Are you really sure you want to marry Ned?"

"Oh, yes," Victoria exclaimed, throwing herself back on

the bed with a sigh. "Have you seen the way he looks at me? He says I glow like a second sun."

Alex giggled. "More Milton?"

"No, not even Byron. It's all his own idea," Victoria said, marveling that anyone could think such a thing about *her*—plain old Victoria Sparrow.

"I'm happy for you," Alex assured her, giving her a hard hug.

"I'm going to have a June wedding," Victoria said dreamily. "And I'm going to wear French lace—"

"Will it be yellow?" Alex interrupted with a laugh.

"No, of course not. Although I might carry yellow flowers," she admitted, her eyes sparkling. "And maybe the girls can wear yellow. And you, of course. What shade do you think you'll suit?"

"Me?" Alex said, flooding with warmth at the thought.

"Of course you, you ninny. You're my sister."

"Victoria?" Alex called after her when she was leaving. "Hmm?"

Alex's stomach was a ball of knots. "If you don't have feelings for Luke anymore . . ." She plucked at the quilt, unable to look her sister in the eye. "You wouldn't mind if I . . . ?"

"No, Alex," Victoria said in a compassionate voice, "I wouldn't mind at all. But be careful. Don't go getting your heart broken."

Now, on the night of the dance, as the first winter snow began falling in glittering swirls, Victoria looked up at Alex's window. Ned flicked the reins and the wagon jolted forward. She raised her hand in a good-luck wave.

Alex waved back.

When she stepped away from the window her heart was pounding. Dell Pritchard was due to pick her up at any minute. She grinned as she imagined the look on Luke's face when she descended the stairs. Should she wait until Dell arrived before she went down? Maybe if she went down earlier, Luke would be overcome enough to take her into his arms . . .

No, that wouldn't do. They might never make it to the dance, and she did so want to get there. After all, she'd

worked hard this morning to help decorate the McCauleys'
store. They'd hung wreaths and boughs, cut snowflakes out
of crisp white paper and dangled them from the ceiling on
wisps of string and scattered the room with candles. She
knew it would be beautiful by candlelight.

She smiled dreamily, imagining how the night would
play out. In her mind it was so like the dance in Independence: Luke would spend every moment with her; he would
bribe the band to play slow songs; he would stare down into
her eyes as though she were the only woman in the world.

And it would be made sweeter by the fact that Aurelia
Hardwig would be there watching.

She knew it was mean-spirited, but she couldn't seem to
help herself. In every version of the fantasy, Arnelle was
standing in the corner, alone (sometimes looking lank-haired
and pimply even), and Luke didn't even notice she was there.

Maybe that was too harsh . . . She adjusted the fantasy so
Aurelia could dance with Matt. Or Dell. Ah hell, Alex
thought, feeling suddenly magnanimous, she could dance
with any man she liked, so long as it wasn't Luke.

"We're leaving now, Alex," Matt bellowed up the stairs.
"We'll see you there!"

Her heart lodged in her throat. What did he mean they
were *leaving*? Luke couldn't leave yet—he hadn't seen her!

As she flew from her room she heard the click of the front
door. She was halfway down the stairs before she noticed
him.

Luke stopped dead, frozen with his fingers at the button
of his stiff collar. Hell and damnation. The woman was practically naked. Look at the way she came spilling out of that
dress with every breath.

It worked, Alex thought breathlessly, noticing the heat in
his black eyes as they explored every last inch of her. She felt
that wonderfully familiar pulse begin to beat deep inside.

"You're not leaving the house in that," he said through
gritted teeth.

She frowned.

"Get right back up there and change into something respectable. That green one you wore the other day will do just
fine."

She drew an indignant breath. This wasn't going the way she'd imagined.

"And stop breathing," he bellowed, alarmed by the way she swelled over the low neckline of the gown.

"I beg your pardon," she said stiffly, her excitement turning to ashes, "but this dress is perfectly respectable." Well, maybe not perfectly, she amended silently, but it was respectable enough. "Now, if you'll excuse me, I'll just get my coat. My escort should be here any minute." If the gown didn't work, maybe the threat of competition would.

He'd be damned if he'd let Dell Pritchard see her in that.

Alex watched in astonishment as he spun on his heel and left. She stomped her foot. What was wrong with the idiot man? Didn't he realize that he was supposed to be enchanted? Besotted? Or, at the very least, appreciative? Maybe he wasn't attracted to her anymore, she thought sickly. She heard footsteps and looked up. Her eyes flew wide and she gasped. "You wouldn't dare!"

He was coming for her, a stubborn gleam in his dark eyes. In his hands he held two coiled ropes. "You are *not* going out in that. Either you change, or you stay."

She screamed and bolted for her room. She'd barely scaled the stairs before she felt his iron grip. She struggled like a woman possessed.

Grimly, Luke hoisted her over his shoulder. He could feel her fists pounding his back, and her flailing feet were coming dangerously close to his groin. He kicked open the door to her room and tossed her down on the bed. "Last chance, sweetheart," he warned.

"There is *nothing* wrong with this dress," she shouted at him, completely infuriated. He was supposed to *like* the damn thing!

With every word her breasts heaved against the cranberry satin and Luke's glare grew blacker. "Have it your way," he snapped, pinning her beneath him as he grabbed her wrists. She bit and bucked and kicked and screamed, but nothing deterred him, and before long she was tied firmly to the bed. Luke stood back and regarded her with satisfaction, unmindful of the bruises he'd sustained.

"Dell will hear me scream," she shrieked at him.

He grabbed a length of satin from the pile of off-cuts by her sewing basket. "You can't stop me wearing this dress," she managed to bellow before he gagged her. "I'll wear it every day for the rest of my damned life if I want to!"

She noticed with satisfaction his sudden look of impotent rage at her words. Then her eyes widened in horror. Triumphantly, Luke withdrew the long-bladed silver scissors from her basket. He snipped the scissors in the air a couple of times. He wouldn't!

He would.

She didn't care if she was gagged, she shouted every vile word she could think of at him. He ignored her muffled ranting and approached her, a dark gleam in his eyes. With a look of satisfaction he took the scissors to her beautiful satin dress. The rasp of the blades rang in Alex's ears. She could feel the cold hard press of the metal against her as he cut the dress away from her body. He was merciless. He didn't stop until the gown lay in ribbons around her.

It was only when there was nothing left to cut that the red rage began to recede and Luke saw what he'd done. She was deathly still. Her face was as white as the sheet. Only her eyes were alive, and they burned with wrath. Luke was in no doubt that if looks could kill he would have keeled over right then and there.

A staccato knocking at the front door startled them both.

"I suppose that will be Dell," he said sardonically. "Excuse me for a moment, won't you, sweetheart." The scissors clattered to the dresser and she heard his footsteps as he descended the stairs. There was the sound of the front door opening.

"Dell," she heard him say faintly, a note of regret hanging heavy in his voice, "I hate to be the bearer of bad tidings, but I'm afraid Miss Barratt has taken unexpectedly to her bed."

The unbelievable bastard. Alex bit down hard on the satin and imagined that she was biting through his jugular.

"Is there anything I can do?" Dell was asking.

"No, it's nothing a night of peace and quiet won't cure."

She'd give him peace and quiet, she thought, her eyes fixed on the shining blades of the scissors. The minute he untied her she'd plunge those blades through his cold dead heart.

LUKE WATCHED A very disappointed Dell Pritchard climb back into his wagon and head into town alone. Once the sound of the wagon had receded he sank to the porch steps, feeling suddenly shaky. What on earth had come over him? He'd acted like an animal.

Luke rubbed his face, taking big gulps of the cold air. The snow was falling steadily now, and he was glad of its chill kiss on the bare skin of his hands and face. Lord, but she'd been beautiful, coming down those stairs. He could still see the way the lamplight clung lovingly to her lush curves, casting shadows in the deep hollow between her breasts. And that face. Like some kind of wood sprite, out to tempt and tease.

Luke groaned, hearing the phantom rasp of the scissors. He was going mad. Every day the torture got worse, not better. Every morning she showed up in some new dress, prettier and prettier until he thought he'd never sleep again for the dreams she inflicted on him.

He was lost, he thought, lowering his hands and staring into the swirling snow. Completely and utterly lost. He had been ever since he'd seen her at Dolly's, sprawled out in Delia's bed, all sleepy and warm. She'd spoiled any other woman for him. He hadn't touched another woman since their first night together, he thought in shock. He compared every woman he saw to her, and they came up wanting. Even Amelia Harding. Especially Amelia Harding, he thought with a sigh. What had he ever seen in her? She was so shallow, so vain.

He couldn't imagine Amelia lopping off her shiny hair and dressing in Adam's old clothes. He couldn't imagine her helping him to butcher a cow, or to lower a wagon down a hill. Or screaming at mules, he thought with a grin.

He looked up at the light burning in Alex's window. She was never going to forgive him for this.

With his tail between his legs, Luke climbed the stairs. Sure enough, she still looked mad enough to kill. He paused in the doorway. It probably wouldn't be a good idea to untie her until she'd cooled off a little. He'd be liable to find himself hit over the head with a chair.

Cautiously, he sat beside her on the bed. She was completely, ominously silent, and her gray eyes were fixed on him, as though willing him to drop dead on the spot. He sighed and tore his gaze away from hers.

Which was a dangerous thing to do, he found, suddenly aware of how skimpy her underclothes were. He'd managed to shred her petticoats along with the gown and she was completely naked except for her corset and a gossamer-fine chemise. He noticed the evil-looking bruise curving around her hip.

"That mule really got you, didn't he?" Instinctively he reached out and brushed his fingertips over the teeth marks. She flinched. As she did her hips lifted off the bed and he swore. Her rear end was covered with a massive yellowing bruise. No wonder she'd screamed. And it had happened three weeks ago—imagine how bad it must have looked then.

Without thinking, he bent and pressed the lightest of kisses against the bruise. He heard her draw a sharp breath and he looked up, without lifting his lips from her hip. He could see the confusion mixed in with her wrath. Experimentally, he kissed her hip again, still holding her gaze. The confusion dissipated, replaced with something smoky— something he hoped might be desire.

"I'm going to touch you," he said softly. "And kiss you. You let me know if you want me to stop." Not wanting to anger her further, he proceeded slowly. He trailed a series of butterfly-light kisses along the edge of the bruise, not breaking eye contact. When she stayed still, stretched as taut as piano wire, not making a sound of protest, he flicked his tongue against her skin.

Another sharp hiss of breath through her teeth, and he felt her muscles leap. But she didn't yell, or try to pull away. Encouraged, he traced the very tip of his tongue along her hipbone. She tasted warm and salty and he felt himself swell with desire. When he reached the dip of her stomach he paused. His hands began to stroke the backs of her thighs, following the firm curve of muscle up to her buttocks, and down again to the hollows behind her knees. He felt her tremble beneath his touch.

He looked up again to find that her eyelids had fluttered closed, her eyelashes forming dark fans on her flushed cheeks. He sat up and her eyes snapped open. He knew disappointment when he saw it. He felt an unexpected hope slowly uncurl in his chest. Could he make her forget her rage?

He stretched out beside her on the bed and propped himself on one elbow, so he could look down at her. He traced the curve of her jaw with one lazy finger and she snapped at him like a turtle. He laughed, but quelled it when he saw the ire flare again in her smoky eyes. He lowered himself to place the barest whisper of a kiss by her ear.

"I'm sorry, sweetheart," he sighed, noticing how she shivered when his hot breath swirled against her skin. "It was the thought of every man in town being able to see you like that. Dell Pritchard," he breathed in disgust, grazing his teeth against her earlobe. "I'd want to kill him if he saw you like that." He took her earlobe in his mouth and heard her sigh. As he nipped it gently between his teeth his finger began a torturously slow descent down the long arch of her neck, resting briefly where her pulse leaped, before continuing down to where her breasts rose above the corset. So light that the touch was almost imaginary, his fingertip brushed across the luscious swell. He gave her earlobe one last long suck and then released it. "You're so beautiful," he breathed, watching as gooseflesh rippled her skin. Her eyes had fluttered closed again.

His finger dipped into the shadowed hollow of her cleavage and she moaned. He could see her nipples thrusting at the fine lawn of her chemise, and couldn't resist brushing over them on his way to the hooks on the front of her corset. She arched and moaned again.

One by one he unhooked the metal eyes of her corset, pushing it open slowly, knowing that the cool air would rush against her skin in a sinuous, sensual wave. Now the full ripeness of her breasts was revealed, pushing against the flimsy chemise. He lowered his mouth and kissed her though the thin material. She almost came off the bed in shock. He smiled against her and circled her pleading nipple with his tongue. The moistened lawn stuck to her skin, teasing him. He placed his open mouth over her and sucked, while his hand cupped her other breast. He rubbed his palm over her until she was arching hard against it.

When he pulled his hand away, she sighed with disappointment. His hand followed the firm contours of her stomach, tracing the dip above her hipbones, and then it went lower. As his fingers explored her, he pulled the gag from her mouth with his other hand and kissed her before she could make a sound. His tongue mimicked the thrusting of his fingers and he felt her becoming molten beneath his touch.

His desire was so acute it was painful, but he made no move to undress. All he cared about tonight was giving her pleasure.

When she was mindless with wanting him he released her mouth. She groaned and strained against the ropes. When his tongue replaced his fingers she thought she would die of pleasure. His hands slid over her body as he sucked and caressed her; when they settled on her breasts and he took her nipples between his fingers she began to cry out. She couldn't bear it.

Her hips were rocking against him. He settled into a slow rhythm, his tongue sliding across her again and again until she was screaming with the joy of it. She was a white-hot ball of sensation; the fury of it kept building and building, the heat surging until she thought she would be burned alive.

He quickened his pace as he felt her begin to shudder.

She was screaming his name, pulling against the ropes and arching into the insistent thrust of his tongue until suddenly, with a burst of unbelievable pleasure, the world seemed to implode around her.

❧ 41 ❧

H E WAS GONE when she woke. And so were the ropes.
       She might have thought she'd dreamed the entire
night if it hadn't been for the tangle of ruined satin next to
the bed. Shaken, she slid from between the sheets, wincing
as the cold air hit her naked body. She pulled on the first
thing to hand, which happened to be her old gray dress,
which she'd worn the day before while she was out cutting
branches for the decorations. Her fingers trembled on the
buttons as she fastened them. Had that only been yesterday?
   Oh, she'd had such high hopes.
   She kicked at the mangled cranberry-colored gown, feeling confused. She clung gratefully to the remnants of her
anger. Anger was easy. She understood anger.
   She yanked the curtains open to find a white world,
barely lit by the pearly predawn glow. Nothing moved; the
snow had ceased to fall and there wasn't a breath of wind.
Everyone was still asleep. She wondered if they'd enjoyed
the dance and felt a renewed blaze of rage.
   If Luke Slater had been standing in front of her right then
she would have kicked him. Where the hell was he anyway?
What kind of man left a woman alone after he . . . after
he . . . Alex spluttered, unable to decide what exactly he had
done. The night came back at her in random flashes: the
ropes, the rage, his hot black eyes, the swirl of his breath
against her ear, the expert stroke of his hands, the way his
tongue . . .
   She pressed her cold hands against her hot cheeks. Oh
glory. What kind of woman let a man do that to her after he'd
tied her up like some kind of criminal?
   He'd tied her up! She still couldn't quite believe it. How

could he have done it to her *again*? How could she have let him! She eyed the scissors. She had a mind to hunt him down right this minute. She set her jaw and resolved to do just that, snatching up the scissors on her way out.

She knocked softly at his door, and then arrested herself mid-knock, appalled. Why should she knock? He was the one who should be knocking at *her* door! He should be groveling on his knees, she thought with a snarl.

She pushed the door open.

His room was empty. The bed was neatly made and the curtains were wide open. She scowled. Had he risen early, or had he not gone to bed? How late had he stayed in her room? She had a vision of him lingering, watching her sleep, and her anger flared even hotter.

She knew very well where he'd be. With his damn horses. They were about the only thing he cared about. Alex was too piqued to stop for a coat; she strode outside toward the barn with only her fury for warmth.

At the door to the barn she stumbled and almost fell, her heart stopping in her chest. There was blood in the snow. Vivid, scarlet, fresh blood.

"Luke?" she called, her voice cracking. The interior of the barn was pitch black compared to the pearly white world outside, and she couldn't see a thing. She broke out in a cold sweat.

She heard a faint moan.

"Luke?" she called again, hearing the panic in her own voice.

"Alex."

She flew into the blackness of the barn, horrified by the weak rattle of his voice. Before her eyes could adjust to the darkness rough hands seized her.

She knew who it was before he spoke. She should do, he'd manhandled her often enough. "You need to come with me," Silas wheezed. She struggled against him.

"Luke!"

The shattered rasp of Silas's bitter laughter was horrific. "He can't help you now. We have to go."

"Luke!" she screamed as Silas dragged her from the barn. She screamed even louder when they emerged into the breaking daylight. Silas was a monster. He was barely recognizable; his face had been pummeled into a gut-wrenching mess of raw meat. He was missing his ears, Alex noticed sickly. She tried to jump free, but he held on to her with all the strength left in his broken body. He was barely alive, Alex observed. He was operating on basic instinct, and his basic instinct had been to come for her.

Panicked, Alex stabbed at him with the scissors, but Silas barely seemed to register the pain. She stabbed again as he tried to throw her over his horse. The scissors lodged in the meat of his arm and she couldn't pull them out again. She gagged, revolted by the feel of the scissors moving in his flesh. "What have you done to Luke?" she yelled as he mounted the horse. He didn't answer her.

He applied his spurs without mercy and they plowed into the lower ranges of the Cascades. "Let me go," she begged, somehow knowing that he could barely hear her. Silas was locked in a world of pain.

She kept hearing the rattle in Luke's voice. "What did you do to him?" she pleaded. Was he dying back there in the barn, all alone?

Silas didn't speak. She looked up and saw to her horror that his eyes were full of blood. He was dying. Dear Lord, he was dying. And he was taking her deep into the mountains as he died. How would she ever get back? She didn't know the way, and it was freezing cold and she didn't even have a coat. She wasn't even wearing stockings! Or any underwear for that matter! All that stood between her and the frigid mountain air was her frayed old gray dress. She would freeze before the day was out.

She couldn't let that happen. Not when Luke was back there, possibly bleeding to death. She only hoped her screams had woken everyone in the house, that they'd come running out and find Luke, that they'd hurry for the doctor. Oh hell, she couldn't even remember if Utopia *had* a doctor.

She stayed deathly still for a while, hoping to lull Silas into a sense of complacency. But his iron grip didn't loosen even a little. She wondered if he was dead already. Maybe she was trapped in the arms of a stiffening dead man. But no, there was the tortured wheeze of his breath.

She heard the staccato crunch of hooves on snow before he did. Someone was coming fast behind them. Alex bent sharply to peer around Silas's ruined body. He yanked her back, but not before she'd caught sight of a familiar dark head.

He was alive!

"Luke!" she shrieked, her voice echoing through the mountains, despite the snow. The granite rock faces sent her cry ricocheting back and forth above their heads.

Silas urged his horse between a narrow pass and onto a ledge above a steep chasm. He dismounted, pulling her from the horse, and aiming his gun at the opening in the rock.

"Let her go." Luke's voice seemed to come from every direction at once, bouncing from rock to rock and mountain to mountain.

"I can't," Silas rasped desperately, pulling Alex closer, "he'll kill her."

"*I'll* kill you if you don't." There was the sound of a hammer being pulled back. It made an ominous *click*.

Silas began to laugh. It was a hopeless sound. "Go ahead, Slater. You can't kill a dead man."

"Just watch me." The single shot was deafening. Alex felt Silas jerk. And then he was slumped at her feet, a rivulet of blood running from him and pooling in a depression in the rock.

A silhouette appeared between the narrow pass. Alex ran toward him as he slid from Blackie Junior. The Arab whickered. Alex threw herself at Luke, gasping as he wilted against her. Her relief evaporated. "Luke?" she breathed, alarmed.

"It's just a little knife wound," he said through dry lips, "nothing to worry about."

She *was* worried. He was gray and clammy, and he was having trouble keeping his feet. There was a vivid scarlet blossom staining his shirt.

He saw her dismay. "Don't fret, sweetheart, it's just a nick." He swayed. Alarmed, she lowered him onto a nearby rock. And that's when she heard the mad laughter. Alex spun, feeling raw hysteria claw at her. Gideon! Where was he? The wild giggles were echoing, seeming to come from every dark shadow and secret hollow.

"It looks like I have to thank you, Slater," Gideon's disembodied voice crowed, "for taking care of my last bothersome brother."

Luke lifted his weapon, but a sudden *crack* echoed through the mountains and the gun went flying from his grasp. Alex screamed.

And Gideon laughed. "Keep screaming, darling. I love it when you scream."

"What do you want?" Luke called.

"What do you think?"

"If you lay so much as a hand on her . . ."

"I don't plan to do any such thing," Gideon sang, his insane voice bouncing from rock to rock. "She'll do my dirty work for me."

Alex and Luke exchanged bewildered looks.

"Now, bitch Barratt," Gideon called, "I want you to listen to me well. If you don't do exactly as I say I'm going to shoot your precious lover."

"Don't listen to him," Luke hissed.

There was another *crack* and Luke gave a shout. There was a spray of blood and Luke gave a terrifying yell. "Get away from him, or I'll shoot again," Gideon hooted.

Panicked, Alex scuttled back, unable to tear her gaze away from Luke's blood.

"Walk to the edge of the cliff," Gideon ordered.

"No!" Luke bellowed. Another *crack* and a spray of blood rose from Luke's forearm.

Alex screamed and ran for the edge of the cliff. She began to sob. There was so much blood. She remembered Sheriff Deveraux, his belly blown open.

Luke struggled to sit up, trying to catch her wild gaze. His face was bloodless, making his eyes appear as black as night.

"Now," Gideon ordered, his voice ringing with triumph, "jump, you thieving bitch!"

"Don't do it, Alex!"

She stood frozen on the lip of the chasm.

Crack.

Blood.

"Don't," Luke rasped, his voice barely audible.

"Jump!" Gideon whooped, his disembodied voice filling the entire world.

If she didn't jump, Luke would die.

"Don't," he begged, stretching a hand toward her.

Crack.

All she could see was scarlet. "I love you," she said hopelessly. She stumbled, and went tumbling over the edge of the cliff. Her hands instinctively scrabbled for purchase as she went over the lip; they clawed into a fissure and her arms were almost jerked out of her sockets as her fall was arrested.

"Alex!" She heard Luke's agony. "Alex!" She tried to draw breath to call out to him. She heard him dragging across the rock, and then his face appeared above her. His tortured expression, and the acute relief in his black eyes, made her start to cry. He reached for her. The blood ran down his arms and dripped on her face.

"I can't hold on," she cried desperately, feeling her sweaty fingers begin to slip. Just as they slid from the fissure Luke grabbed her by the wrists.

She could see the tendons straining in his neck. How could he lift her? The blood was flowing faster and faster down his arms. His skin looked like the skin of a corpse, a frightening bluish gray. Saving her would cost him his life, she realized.

"Let me go," she begged. She couldn't bear it if he were to die.

"No," he growled through gritted teeth.

But they could both feel her weight pulling him slowly over the lip of the precipice.

"How touching," Gideon drawled, suddenly looming over them in the flesh, his rifle dangling from his hand. He leaned over to consider the drop. He gave a low whistle. "Sure is a long way down, ain't it?"

Slowly he pulled the hammer back on the rifle. And then lazily, nonchalantly, he rested the barrel against the back of Luke's head. "Let go of her, Slater," he said conversationally, "or I'll shoot you. Then she'll go over anyway."

"Listen to him," Alex whispered, feeling his grip begin to slip and seeing the desperation in his eyes. "Let me go." She knew he was fighting pain and a threatening black wave of unconsciousness.

"I love you," he gritted, tightening his grip on her wrists. It was his way of saying *Never.*

Tears flooded from her. She'd never known how much she wanted to hear those words fall from his lips, but not like this, she thought with a sob. Not like *this.* "I love you too," she said, knowing what she had to do.

She drank in her fill of his face, counting down silently until the moment she would wrench her arms out of his grasp. Her death would buy his life, and it was a price she was willing to pay. *Three . . . two . . .*

Before she got to *one* there was a gunshot. She screamed, thinking he'd shot Luke.

But she was still hanging above the steep drop. And Luke was still holding on to her. "Silas, you dumb bastard," Gideon sighed, lifting the rifle away from Luke's head, "why won't you ever stay dead?"

"Back off, Gideon," she heard Silas rattle.

Gideon hooted. "Or what? You'll shoot me? We both know you can't shoot straight."

"Hold on," Luke hissed at her. His left hand released her wrist, shooting out to grab hold of Gideon's ankle. "Go to hell, Grady." With the last of his strength he yanked Gideon's feet out from under him.

Crack. Silas fired simultaneously.

Alex saw Gideon's eyes widen in astonishment. Luke's shove, coupled with the force of Silas's shot, threw him backward. His arms flailed as he went over. And then he was plummeting past her, his body making an eerie whistling noise as it fell. As long as she lived she would never forget the sound his body made as it landed in the forest below.

Silas collapsed beside Luke. He was weeping blood now. Alex didn't know how he could still be alive. He reached down and gripped her arms, just above Luke's hands. With a bone-shuddering cry, he helped Luke haul her up, and between them the two wounded men managed to pull her back up onto the ledge.

Alex rolled over and kissed Luke. She tasted blood. His

gaze was glassy. "Hold on," she whispered through her tears. "I'll get help. Don't you die on me."

"Alex?" A tortured rattle pulled her attention away from Luke.

"Silas?" she said gently, wincing as she took in the monstrous mutilation of his face.

"I'm sorry," he rattled. "I'm sorry. I didn't mean for this . . . for any of this."

"I know." Alex felt a pity so acute it hurt. "You saved me, Silas."

"Us," Luke rasped. "You saved *us*."

Silas turned his head to look at Luke. "Look after her," he wheezed, as his last breath eased through his broken body, "you lucky bastard." And then he died, broken and brotherless, but with the woman he loved alive and whole before him.

Alex swallowed and carefully closed his vacant eyes. Luke began to cough and she scuttled to his side, alarmed. "Don't you die on me," she ordered again.

"I wouldn't dare," he sighed, as he succumbed to the insistent blackness.

❧ 42 ❧

LUKE DRIFTED IN and out of consciousness. His hands stayed clenched around the sheets. He had to hold on. He couldn't let go or she'd fall.

But then her face swam over him, her gold-streaked curls tumbling over her furrowed brow as her rainstorm-colored eyes stared deep into his. "I love you," he mumbled, "I won't let you fall." And then the rainstorm broke into swirling smoke.

When he finally came to, he was as sore as hell. Every muscle ached and there were burning points of agony: one in his arm, one in his shoulder, one in his leg. He groaned.

Alex leaped up from the chair beside his bed and the dime novel she was reading tumbled to the floor. "You're awake!"

"I wish I wasn't," he moaned.

"Tom! Matt!" she shouted, rushing to the door. He winced. There was a clatter of boots on the stairs and then his brothers appeared in the doorway. They broke into smiles when they saw he was awake.

"What happened to your face?" he grumped at Matt, noticing that a beard was bristling again.

"I got sick of shaving."

"He means he got sick of the attention," Tom hooted.

"Quiet down," Alex said primly, "this is a sick room, not a dance hall."

"Who was bellowing down the stairs a minute ago?" Tom reminded her.

"Never mind that. I called you in here for a reason."

"We can see. Luke's awake."

"Not that."

"No?"

"Well, yes that," she amended, "but not just that." They stared at her in puzzlement and she began to blush. She cleared her throat nervously. "It may have come to your attention that your brother is in love with me."

Luke looked at her in astonishment.

Tom and Matt rolled their eyes. "You mean, because of the way he's been shouting it at the top of his voice every few hours?"

Luke scowled. He'd done no such thing. Had he?

"That's enough, Matthew," Alex said sternly. "Your brother has been very ill."

"Lovesick," Matt agreed.

Alex glared at him, but he didn't look in the slightest bit chagrined.

"Hurry up, Alex," Tom sighed, "I'm due to head out."

"That's why I wanted to talk to you."

"So, hurry up and talk to me."

"You're completely ruining the moment," she complained.

"Would you all hurry up," Luke sighed, "you're giving me a headache."

Alex gave him a sympathetic look and leaned over to feel his forehead. He couldn't help but appreciate the weight of her breasts against his chest.

"You're hardly going to be able to *feel* his headache," Matt said, exasperated.

"I really do have to go," Tom complained.

"Oh, you two are impossible," Alex exclaimed, stamping her foot.

"I told you, didn't I?" Luke said smugly.

She planted her hands on her hips. "You shush too. I can't ask them if you keep interrupting."

"Ask them what?"

"Thomas, Matthew," she began formally, "I'd like to ask you for your brother's hand in marriage."

There was a round of choking noises as they struggled not to laugh. Alex glared at them. "Well, I don't know," Matt said dryly, "you don't seem to be too good for his health."

"Shut up, Matt," Tom sighed. "You're welcome to him, Alex."

"Thank you." She moved to the doorway. "Stephen!" she bellowed.

The Slater brothers blinked as Stephen Sparrow appeared as if by magic. He'd obviously been waiting just outside the door. Adam skipped in behind him, followed by Victoria, who was bearing two handfuls of what looked like weeping spruce, which she'd tied together with satin ribbons. "You *would* get married in winter," she said apologetically, passing a bunch of spruce to Alex before taking up her post as Maid of Honor, her own spruce held solemnly in front of her.

Luke blinked and looked at his brothers. They seemed as bewildered as he felt.

"Now, he's very tired," Alexandra told her brother, "so we don't need a long service. Just the basics will do."

And before Luke knew what was happening Stephen was asking him if he'd take Alexandra Antoinette Barratt to be his lawful wedded wife.

"I didn't know your middle name was Antoinette," he said.

"There's a lot you don't know about me," she observed. "Now answer the question."

"I guess I do," he said, vaguely astonished.

And the next thing he knew Stephen was declaring them man and wife and asking him to kiss the bride. Which his suddenly bossy bride didn't let him do; she took matters in her own hands and kissed him first.

Then she took it upon herself to send everyone packing. "He's still ill," she kept saying, as she pushed them bodily from the room.

"I'll see you when I get back from California, Luke," he heard Tom call as she closed the door.

He watched, amused, as Alex fussed about the room, avoiding his gaze. "Come here, wife," he ordered.

She blushed. "I guess you think that was high-handed," she said, taking the offensive, "but if I'd waited for you to come to your senses I might have died an old maid."

He grabbed her by the wrist and hauled her down on the bed beside him, wincing at the pain in his shoulder. But who was he to let a little pain spoil his wedding night?

"Don't think that my marrying you means I've forgiven

you for tying me up," she warned him, before she could melt under the heat of his dark eyes.

"I'll never do it again," he swore, as he pulled her toward him, his gaze dropping to her ripe mouth.

"I've heard that before."

"Would you feel better if I let you tie *me* up?" he murmured against her mouth, as he began to kiss her.

Alex's eyebrows shot up. She had a sudden vision of Luke Slater at her mercy. Naked.

Oh glory.

Turn the page for a sneak peek of

BOUND FOR SIN

Coming soon from Jove

✤ 1 ✤

A respectable widow of means seeks resourceful frontiersman for the purpose of matrimony. The lady seeks passage west to land owned in Mokelumne Hill, California. The advertiser presumes her manner and appearance will recommend her and expects applications from responsible parties only. Interviews are scheduled for the 6th of next month, beginning at nine o'clock in the morning, in the front parlor of the Grand Hotel. Please be prompt.

Independence, Missouri, 1849

Now *THAT* WAS how a man should look. Suffocating in the stuffy hotel parlor, Georgiana Bee Blunt looked longingly out the window, where she could see a backwoodsman tethering his animal to the hitching rail outside Cavil's Mercantile. The fellow was a *brute*. He had a wild head of bristling black hair and a stiff beard, and his arms were the size of smokehouse hams. And if that wasn't enough to make him look like a character from one of her dime novels, he was also clad head to toe in buckskin. And the *size* of him! My, but he looked like he could rip an oak from the earth barehanded. That was exactly the kind of man she needed, and exactly the kind of man she had advertised for.

It was also exactly the kind of man who had *not* answered her advertisement. Georgiana sighed and looked over at the candidate sitting opposite her. He was a dapper, charming,

handsome man, with very white teeth and very shiny hair.
His fingernails were perfect ovals. And his shoes . . . They
were spit polished until they gleamed. How did he do it? She
couldn't set foot outside without the bottom inch of her dress
getting covered in dust. Had he shined them in the foyer before he'd come in for his interview?

She couldn't imagine the brute outside doing that, she
thought, stealing another glance. He was reaching over to
unbuckle his saddlebags, and the buckskin stretched tight
over the broadest back Georgiana had ever seen. She sighed
again. It was probably too much to hope that he'd come to
answer her advertisement.

"So, as you can see, Mrs. Smith, I have a pedigree that
would please even the most discerning mother." Mr. Dugard
beamed at her with his white teeth.

Oh no. He wouldn't do at all.

"Thank you so much for your time, Mr. Dugard." Georgiana tried to smile back. "But as you can see, I still have so
many people to interview, and the hour is growing late . . ."
She stood and, because he was a gentleman, he stood too.

"If I could ask you to leave your details, I'll be in touch
as soon as my decision is made," she assured him.

"As luck would have it, I'm staying right here in the hotel," he said.

Of course he was. Most of them were. She resolved not to
use the dining room tonight; she had no intention of talking
to any of them again, let alone marrying one of them. They
were all so sociable and polite and courteous and *civilized*.
It was enough to make a woman scream. Her ad had clearly
specified *frontiersman*. She didn't want a well-bred man, or
a good-looking man, or a charming man, or a clever man.
She'd had quite enough of that with her first husband (God
rest his sordid soul). All she was looking for was a simple,
hardworking and reliable *brute*. Like the one outside.

The one who was *not* walking toward the hotel to answer
her ad. She watched glumly as he headed in the exact opposite direction. He'd been joined by another rough-looking
man and was heading for the saloon.

Perhaps she should have scheduled her interviews for the

saloon, she thought with a sigh. The men there were probably far more likely candidates than the ones she was meeting here.

"May I say, Mrs. Smith," Mr. Dugard was saying in his low, suave voice, "I hadn't expected to find you so young, or so beautiful."

She flinched. God save her from men with silver tongues. She wouldn't be in this situation if it hadn't been for Leonard and his pretty words. She had no interest in listening to any more pretty words in her lifetime.

Mr. Dugard took her gloved hand and raised it to his lips. His dark eyes were moist with admiration. It took all of Georgiana's willpower not to yank her hand away. She suffered through the press of his lips on the back of her glove.

There was a disapproving cough from the doorway. The hotelier, Mrs. Bulfinch, was glowering at them. "I hate to break up your tête-à-tête," she said in her clanging voice, "but there are still *men* in my foyer." She said it like they were an infestation of mice. "You promised me, Mrs. Smith, that this affair would be done by mid-afternoon. It's now almost five." She gave a sniff and drew herself up to her full height of four foot nothing. "I've dismissed them all and told them to come back tomorrow. This is a respectable hotel and I shan't have men clogging up my foyer at all hours."

Oh, thank heavens for ghastly old Mrs. Bulfinch! Now Georgiana wouldn't have to interview another pale, clean, nice man! At least not until tomorrow . . .

And maybe before then, she could hunt the brute down, and she wouldn't need to face tomorrow at all, she thought hopefully. She stole a glance at the saloon. It was a shame ladies weren't allowed in there, or she would have headed straight over the road and through the doors.

"May I escort you into supper?" Mr. Dugard asked hopefully.

Lord, no!

"I'm sorry," Georgiana said, skipping out of his reach before he could take her arm, "but I really must collect the children."

If she could get through the knot of hopefuls on the

porch, that was. They were milling about, just waiting for a chance to speak to her; each and every one of them was holding his hat politely in his plump, clean hand and giving her an earnest smile. They were a horrific sight.

She'd never moved so fast in her life. She grabbed her bonnet and dilly bag and was out the front door and off the porch before anyone could so much as make a move in her direction.

She took a deep, grateful breath of dusty air as she plunged down the street. She'd been cooped up in that parlor all day, with its smell of desiccated rose petals and burned coffee. Mrs. Bulfinch didn't hold with open windows: too much dust. After today, Georgiana was sure she would forever associate the smell of mummified roses with the smell of disappointment.

She'd met at least two dozen men today, and not a single one of them was suitable. They'd be eaten alive out west! Just imagine if they met Kid Cupid or the Plague of the West on the trail! They'd probably faint dead away. No, she needed someone who could get her safely to her son . . .

The thought of Leo took any trace of sunshine out of the day. Her son, her eldest . . . all alone out there with those horrible men . . .

Don't think about it. You can't afford to think about it. You have to keep moving.

He was safe so long as they needed her signature on that deed. And she was on her way. *Soon*, she thought desperately. *Soon I'll be there.* She felt the two thousand miles between them like a searing pain. Goddamn Leonard for taking the boy with him. And double damn him for dying and leaving her baby stranded on the other side of the country, twelve years old and all alone, held hostage . . .

Don't. Don't think about it.

Georgiana was sweating but felt icy cold, even though she caught the full flood of afternoon sun as she headed to Mrs. Tilly's to get the other children. Leo was tough, she reminded herself. Of all the children, he was the most resilient; he'd had to be, he'd been the man of the house since he was knee high. His father would swan in and out of their lives for years at a time, telling Leo to look after his mother, and it was something the boy had taken to heart. He wasn't one to cry or feel sorry for himself. She used to watch the way he kept his head high and his expression brave every time his father left, and the way he'd comfort her and the younger children, and her heart would break for him. Her eyes welled with tears. Her poor boy.

It was just one more disaster in Leonard's long line of disasters, and he wasn't even here for her to rage at. This was precisely why she would be choosing her next husband with her head rather than her heart. Her next husband would protect her children and not abandon them (or kidnap them and take them two thousand miles away from her); he would be frugal and sensible and not sell the rug out from under her; he would be predictable and reliable and not flit from place to place with no thought of building a home for his family. If she had to give up hopes of marrying a man she was attracted to, she would. After all, what real use was attraction? And she was certainly happy to give up any idea of a love match. Love had caused her nothing but pain.

"DID YOU FIND your Prince Charming, then?" Mrs. Tilly asked her hopefully, when Georgiana stepped through the front door of the Tea Rooms. "I saw that nice Mr. Dugard heading over to the hotel. He's a handsome-looking man."

"Yes, he is." Georgiana pulled a face as she let Mrs. Tilly usher her to a table by the window and pour them cups of tea. The older woman also put out a plate of strawberry tarts and immediately popped one in her mouth.

"And he's a capable man," she said as she brushed crumbs from her lip. "He used to run a furniture store in St. Louis."

"He might be capable enough for St. Louis, Mrs. Tilly," Georgiana sighed, "but he didn't look anywhere near capable enough for the *wilds*. I can't imagine him fording a river or shoeing a horse."

Georgiana flushed as Mrs. Tilly looked pointedly at Georgiana's silk skirts and heeled slippers.

"It's a wonder you want to go at all, if it's so fearsome." Mrs. Tilly clucked as she sipped her tea. "You'd be better off keeping the little 'uns here. We have a school and lots of nice men."

Ugh. *Nice* wasn't what she was looking for.

"I'm committed to going to California, Mrs. Tilly," Georgiana said firmly. "That's where our land is. Leonard built us a house in the lovely little town of Mokelumne Hill." Or so he'd said. "It has a wraparound porch and enough bedrooms for the children to each have one." She'd believe it when she saw it. But that's certainly what he'd written in his letters. "And my son is there." Oh no, there went the tears again. Georgiana fumbled for her handkerchief. She hated crying in front of people, but these days the tears just erupted. She could be perfectly serene and then, bang, she'd be crying. She had to stop thinking about Leo. She couldn't afford to be crying all the time; there'd be time for crying once he was safe.

"Oh, you darling love." Mrs. Tilly was welling up in sympathy. "How insensitive of me! I'm sure your people are looking after the lad, but I know how a mother feels."

Georgiana just wanted the whole moment to end. She didn't want comfort or fuss—it didn't do any good. She just wanted to get on with the whole ordeal: get the husband, pack the wagon and get on the trail. The sooner she got on the trail, the sooner she could get to her son. Crying solved nothing at all.

"How were the children today?" she asked, desperately trying to change the subject as she blotted her eyes.

"Energetic." Mrs. Tilly didn't quite meet Georgiana's gaze.

Georgiana stood. "I should get them out of your way, it's getting late."

"Oh no!" Mrs. Tilly looked a touch panicked. "Finish your tea first. And have one of the tarts, the children helped make them. They're with Becky, they're fine, no need to worry."

"I really should feed them."

"They had some tarts less than an hour ago." When Georgiana didn't sit, Mrs. Tilly got to her feet too. She was looking a trifle anxious, Georgiana thought. Her stomach sank. Oh dear. What had the children done *now*?

There was a clanging sound from the back of the house. Georgiana saw Mrs. Tilly flinch.

"Now don't be too mad at them!" Mrs. Tilly cautioned. There was the sound of something breaking, and Georgiana turned on her heel and made for the kitchen. "They're high-spirited boys!"

The devils looked up with wide-eyed innocence as she threw open the door to the kitchen. Their faces were white with flour. Even her daughter Susannah, the sensible one, was covered in powder from head to foot.

"Mama!" two-year-old Wilby shouted, holding out his pudgy hand. Pasty, white sludge oozed between his fingers. "Glue!"

"Oh my."

The stuff was everywhere: dripping from the wall sconces, blobbed on the bench tops, splattered across the windows.

"Well," Georgiana said, aiming for calmness, "aren't you all very clever, discovering the recipe for glue."

"Glue!" Wilby shouted again, before shoving his hand in his mouth.

"William Bee! Don't eat that!" Georgiana pulled his hand from his mouth and got glue and slobber all over her glove. She eyed it distastefully. Mothering really was a messy business. This was only her second month without a nanny, and, she had to admit, she was struggling.

"He can eat it," one of the twins (Phineas?) said impatiently. "It's just flour and water."

Georgiana cleared her throat.

"It's really Becky's fault," Mrs. Tilly said quickly in defense of the children.

"My fault!" The girl was outraged. She popped up from in front of the stove, which she'd clearly been scrubbing vigorously. She was a mix of soot and glue. "How is this *my* fault?"

"I told you to watch them," Mrs. Tilly scolded. "You know what they're like."

Georgiana blanched. If she'd been a better mother, this never would have happened. *You know what they're like.* Wild. And running wilder every day. They certainly hadn't been like this when Mrs. Wyndham, the nanny, was still around.

Georgiana bit her lip. What would Mrs. Wyndham do in this situation?

"How was I to know they'd make *glue* while my back was turned?" Becky complained.

This never would have *happened* if Mrs. Wyndham had been here. That was the whole problem.

"Well, your back shouldn't have been turned. Don't think I don't know where you were. I saw Fancy Pat's horse tethered up outside. And I don't know how many times I have to tell you that you're throwing good after bad, consorting with the likes of him."

"His name's *Pierre*," Becky said, sounding more outraged by the minute. "It's *French*."

"Now, now," Georgiana interrupted, still striving for calmness as she surreptitiously looked around for something to wipe her slobbery glove on. "It's hardly Becky's fault." She turned a stern look on her children. Only Susannah had the good grace to look shamefaced.

"They promised me they'd clean it up before you came in, Mrs. Smith," Mrs. Tilly said hurriedly. "And really there's no harm done."

"See," the other twin said (was it Philip? Surely a good mother would be able to tell them apart), "she doesn't mind."

Georgiana shot him a black look. "My dear Mrs. Tilly . . . and Becky . . ." It was proving difficult to keep her voice even. "The children and I would like to take you to supper to make this up to you. Please. If you'd like to go and freshen up . . ." She cleared her throat dubiously as she took in Becky's filthy face. "The children and I will get your kitchen in order. And then we'll all go out for a nice meal." Georgiana peeled off her slobbery glove.

"Oh no!" Mrs. Tilly sounded scandalized. "I can't let a lady like you scrub my kitchen."

"Oh, don't worry," Georgiana said grimly. "*I* won't be the one doing the scrubbing."

"You don't need to, Becky can—"

"Becky can get scrubbed up for tea in no time," Becky said quickly, cutting Mrs. Tilly off midsentence. She wriggled out of her apron and hung it on the back of the kitchen door on her way out.

"Please, Mrs. Tilly." Georgiana tried to smile at her. "It would be our pleasure."

Mrs. Tilly looked dubious but nodded and retreated. She paused at the door. "They were perfect angels for most of the day," she said weakly.

"Were you?" Georgiana asked once the door swung closed.

"We're perfect angels *now*," Phin said, rolling his eyes. "We're only *not* angels if you don't like glue."

"Indeed." Georgiana felt ill as she looked at the paste smeared in lumps all over the kitchen. "How does one clean glue?"

"Vinegar," came a muffled voice from behind the kitchen door.

"Thank you, Mrs. Tilly! We'll see you in an hour for supper!"

There was a pause and then they heard footsteps retreating down the hall.

"We could let Wilby lick it all up," Philip suggested.

To Georgiana's dismay, Wilby didn't look entirely unhappy at the prospect.

"Listen," she said, thinking fast, "if you can get this place clean by the time she comes downstairs for supper, I'll buy you rock candy from Cavil's Mercantile in the morning."

"How much rock candy?"

"More than you deserve. And if you *don't* get it clean, I'll tell Mrs. Bulfinch that you'll help her wash her unmentionables tomorrow. It's laundry day at the hotel."

"You wouldn't!"

Of course she wouldn't. And of course Mrs. Bulfinch wouldn't either. But the twins didn't need to know that. "Just test me."

Maybe parenting wasn't so hard. She watched as they hurried to grab mops and buckets. They were the only good things Leonard had ever done in his life, she thought fondly, as she watched their curly dark heads bent over the concoction of vinegar and water they were brewing in the sink. They were working the water pump madly. With any luck, they could clean up the mess without destroying Mrs. Tilly's kitchen. Georgiana tugged off her other glove and set to work helping them. She didn't have much experience scrubbing kitchens, or . . . well, anything. But now that her trust fund was exhausted and they had no more money for servants, she guessed she'd just have to learn.

❧ 2 ❧

"**W**HAT ARE YOU doing here?" Matt snapped when Deathrider joined him outside of Cavil's Mercantile. "I told you I'd bring the doctor to you."

Deathrider looked like his name personified. He was greyish white and waxy and his eyes had the unfocused stare of someone who was using up all his energy just to stay conscious.

"No beds," he grunted.

"What do you mean, no beds?"

"The man at the saloon said there are no beds."

Matt felt like punching something. This last month had been the most hellish month of his life. He'd been holding on to the idea that things would get easier once they got to Independence, but so far that just wasn't the case.

"Is this because you're an Indian?"

Deathrider shrugged. His usually proud frame was hunched over, curved around the gunshot wound.

"Because Sam should damn well know better." Matt unbuckled his saddlebags. His old gray donkey Fernando gave a cranky hee-haw. Matt pulled his ears absently and then hefted the saddlebags over his shoulder. He was bone-tired from being on the trail and the last thing he needed was trouble finding a bed. "C'mon," he growled, "let's get you somewhere comfortable while I rustle up the doctor."

"Sam!" he bellowed as he pushed into the dark saloon. "What's this I hear about you not having a bed for me?"

"Well, look who it is," the bartender said. He spat tobacco juice into a spittoon so full it made a wet sloshing sound as the stream hit. "You're late. You said you'd be here by the end of March."

Matt always stayed at The Lucky Star when he was in town. Mostly because it was the only place that didn't run whores. Matt didn't like whores. They made him uncomfortable. And he didn't want to stay in a bunkhouse; he wanted his own room, away from other people. Matt didn't care much for people.

He nudged Deathrider into a chair.

"I had a room for you at the end of March," Sam told him.

"We got held up."

Matt saw the way Sam's eyes slid over Deathrider.

"We?" There was another slosh as Sam spat his juice.

"This is my friend." Matt emphasized the word friend. Hell, after the winter they'd just been through together, Matt was tempted to call him "brother."

"He said you don't have rooms for us."

Sam shrugged. "I don't. I ain't in the business of keeping rooms empty when there's money to be made. I don't know if you've heard, but there's a gold rush on."

Matt grunted. He'd more than heard; he'd had a busy few months at the end of last year finding the fools lost on the Siskiyou Trail from Oregon down to California.

"They're piled four deep up there," Sam told him, jerking his head at his rooms upstairs. "And you'll find it's the same everywhere. Town's bursting at the seams. On the upside, you should do a roaring trade putting together your train this year."

This would be the fifth year in a row Matt was taking a train on the trail. As always, he was dreading it. He didn't know why he did it to himself, except he was good at it and he couldn't think of much else he would rather be doing. It paid well, but Matt didn't really need or want the money. He'd sort of just fallen into it when his brother Luke had given it up; it was either stay home and be a third wheel in the house with his brother and his new wife, or find something else to do. He'd tried running cattle with his brother Tom for a while, but he found he hated cows even more than he hated people, if such a thing was possible. At least with the wagon trains he got to ride out by himself a lot. People tended to stay in a neat clump and did not have to be herded the way cows did. But they complained a lot more than cows.

"Are you telling me there ain't a single bed in town?" Matt felt more than ever like punching something. He didn't fancy another night sleeping rough.

"'Fraid so. I can sell you a drink, though."

"I bet you could," Matt said sourly. But there wasn't much daylight left and Deathrider needed seeing to.

"Forget the room, we're taking you straight to the doctor," he said, hooking his arm under Deathrider's armpit and yanking him to his feet. He didn't miss the way his friend was soaked through with cold sweat.

"Doc's moved since you were here last," Sam called. "He went and got married. He lives next to The Grand Hotel now."

Matt grunted his thanks and half dragged his friend out into the street. Deathrider's Indian dog was waiting outside for them, his ears swiveling madly. He wasn't happy. "Don't worry, Dog, we'll get him some help."

"I hate to upset your dignity," Matt told his friend as they stumbled back toward the horses, the dog trotting ahead, stopping to check on them every few paces, "but I reckon you're gonna need a boost into the saddle."

It was a marker of how far gone Deathrider was that he didn't protest when Matt boosted him up. It was more of a lift than a boost. Deathrider seemed to have gone boneless. Matt put him on his own horse, as Deathrider's was a skittish animal at the best of times and probably would have bolted at Deathrider's clumsy slumping in the saddle. Pablo, on the other hand, was a stolid workhorse, who needed a heavy boot to the ribs to even get moving. Deathrider could barely even hold Pablo's reins; Matt had to give the horse a slap on the flanks and pull on the reins to get him walking. He decided to walk beside them, with one hand on Deathrider's leg. Just in case. Dog clearly had the same idea, keeping pace on the other side, giving the occasional reassuring bark.

The other animals, well trained after months on the trail, fell in behind.

"Don't you die on me," Matt told his friend as they wound through the busy streets.

Deathrider made a noise that might have been a laugh. Or a death rattle. It was hard to tell.

Ready to find
your next great read?

Let us help.

Visit prh.com/nextread

Penguin
Random
House